An  r
e

Jeffrey DeShell

Starcherone Books / Buffalo, NY

Peter
An (A)Historical Romance

Jeffrey DeShell

Starcherone Books
PO Box 303
Buffalo, NY 14201
www.starcherone.com

Cover photograph: "Profane Waste," 2002, Digital C. Print, Dana Hoey. Courtesy of Friedrich Petzel Gallery.

Cover Design: Geoffrey Gatza

Proofreading: Florine Melnyk, Ed Taylor

Thanks to Brandon Stosuy

Library of Congress Cataloging-in-Publication Data

DeShell, Jeffrey.
  Peter : an (a) historical romance / Jeffrey DeShell.
    p. cm.
  ISBN 0-9703165-2-6 (alk. paper)
  1. Americans--Middle East--Fiction. 2. Sisters--Fiction. 3. Women, Palestinian Arab--Fiction. 4. Middle East--Fiction. I. Title.
  PS3554.E8358P47 2006
  813'.54--dc22
                              2005033528

"Love will surely not weary of image forming.
Happy is this folk to revere its God so."

Aaron, from *Moses and Aaron*,
Arnold Schoenberg

"God is an American."

David Bowie

BEL AIR
SPRING 1999

BOOK I

CHAPTER ONE

I deserve a break today, so get up and get away (McDonald's, circa 1987). With these words, the first words to come into his consciousness, sung mentally to himself in a remarkably accurate representation of the melody, Peter sprang out of bed and wandered down the hall into his bathroom to pee. He had a full day planned. He looked at the Leningrad Cowboy Wall Swatch ($149.95, Sharper Image in Fashion Island): it was already nine thirty. Time to boot up.

He finished peeing, flushed, and looked at himself in the mirror above the sink. Not bad, but the goat might have to go. He'd get Wanda to do it; she enjoyed doing things like that, would probably wear something swish (that expensive see-through beaded thing [Kritzia $4700], or that Bill Blass silk gown [$900]) as she scraped his face with the Gillette, singing Puccini or some such crap — no, it wasn't crap — careful not to get any menthol Edge on that pistachio moiré. She'd probably want to vid it, or maybe even do it at Club Stick, make a phenomenon (her word) out of it. He'd try to get her to shave him nude, in her bathroom, her nips brushing against his shoulder, like an r-rated version of that Schick commercial, the one where that girl somehow gets a streak of shaving cream on her belly . . . or that movie, what was it, with Travolta? Phenomena, of course (some coincidence) . . . that wasn't the one where he was an angel, was it? No, that was something else. Anyway, she'd circle him slowly, then stand behind him, his head against her stomach, her bush rubbing against his shoulder, as she gently and carefully removed his (admittedly thin) beard. And after she shaved him, maybe he'd shave her, that would be only fair (maybe they could vid that).

He was holding his dick, little Pete (littler Pete) in his hand and was getting hard. Pete and Repeat. He had no time for a quick wank now (when was Wanda getting back?). He had to get some work (a report on acid jazz) done before meeting Kay for lunch. Since prep school (when they both were in town), he and Kay would lunch at Marinetti's (owned by Tony Curtis, father of cow Jamie [although she was semi-hot in Trading Places]) every Tuesday and Thursday at precisely one pm, at a table near the back (not near the kitchen, certainly); and over pasta (primavera [$17.95] or alfredo [$14.95]) and a single glass of wine (Pauillac Pichon Lalande [$12.95] or St. Julien Gloria [$16.95]) for Kay, and duck ravioli ($22.95) or angel hair with pesto ($18.95) and one or two Sierra Nevada Pale Ales ($4.95) for Peter discuss their lives (real estate deals [hers] and school, then work projects and recently ever so vague engagement [marriage] arrangements [his]) and plan their twice or thrice yearly travels (he had released little Pete sometime ago which had quickly contracted to normal size). There were two subjects never mentioned: his parents and her boyfriends (all of whom Peter loathed [one or two who were within five years of Peter's age]). Kay always paid. If you live through this hmm hmm hmm I will die for you (Hole, Mother May I Music, BMI 1994). It was time to get going—take a shower (Zest and Paul Mitchell $8.99 [wasn't Gabrielle Reece hot {or did she play for Nike?}]), brush teeth (Rembrandt 6 oz $7.99), dress, check email (shaving could wait) and see what the (virtual) world was up to. With any luck he could remain at home until lunch and not hit the street or the office until two thirty or so although he could use some cino venti right now and there was a Bucks on the way to work.

    After completing his ablutions he returned to his bedroom to Fall into the Gap green cotton briefs ($8.95), long slate gray jean shorts from Big Dawg ($42.95 on sale), black leather belt from Hard-On Leather ($49.95), black Ministry t-shirt (Jesus built my hot rod [maybe a gift from somebody {Freddie?} or some promo shit from the office]) no socks and black and white Puma Trainspotters ($59.95 [Eh mate 'airs me fickin 'eroin Shute yer fickin gob]). As he tied his laces he absent-mindedly stared into a pile of dirty clothes (Tina [$14 per hour] was on vacation [he'd have to go out or make his own cino]) and day-dreamed about buying a new computer. His big tower (Mac G3 300 mhz 64 meg SDRAM 512 backside cache 24x cd-rom 4.4 hdd [$2099] upgraded to 8 [$389] with internal Jaz drive [$299], Sony 17sfII Display [$799 retail], Cambridge Soundworks MicroWorks 3-way computer speakers [$349], an HP DeskWriter 870Cse printer [$499] with a brand new Global Village Fax/Modem 56 bps [on loan from the office retailing for about $400 from MacMall he guessed] was already three years old, and he was strongly considering trying to fit in with the rest of the world and make the move to a Windows based machine (possibly the Sony PCV 205 [although he was a bit sick of Sony] with a 600 MHz Intel Pentium III processor and 128 MB of fast SDRAM and a DVD player [a steal at $1,699.99], or a Compaq Presario 4880 500 mhz 192 Syncdram with DVD IV [$2299], or even one of those overpriced Dells [he wouldn't touch Gateway with that hick ass cow box] like the Dimension XPS R500 with 500 Mhz Pentium III and 128 mhz burst cache with 11.5 hdd, DVD IV and a Zip [$2299 but since he already had a monitor {although a new flat panel (17' $1000) would be sweet} maybe they'd cut him a deal]). He would keep his Powerbook (G3 250 mhz, 64 mb RAM, 20 x cd, 13.3` active matrix screen and 56 flex modem [$3199] ), but the big Mac would have to go. He suddenly noticed a regular geometric shape amidst the soft chaos of dirty laundry — the remote control to his box (Sony CVC3000, birthday present from Wanda or more precisely Wanda`s stepfather [probably around $599 cost]). He`d been searching for it for days — dude! An omen, perhaps, of a truly awesome day. He picked it up and pointed it at the box in the corner. What does the fm have to offer this a.m.?

KROQ sucks! Listen to us anyway. He smiled (he loved that commercial) and repeated it out loud: KROQ sucks! Listen to us anyway. He thought about going to his own (out of milk) or Kay`s kitchen (the kitchen of the main house [$900,000 in 1980, probably 3.5 million now {he occupied the guest cottage in back}]) for some cappuccino or even regular Joe, but thought better of it, afraid that he might run into (who was it this week?) Pavo, lounging around the jacuzz, working early on his George Hamilton and Kay`s Bombay Sapphire (Hi Pavo `sup? What? How ya doing? Fine . . . uncomfortable pause You? Fine . . . another uncomfortable pause You wanna drink? who needs that shit; I`m a loser baby, so why don`t you kill me [motherfucking Beck]). As long as he could avoid a splitter he could skip the java, get some on his way to lunch or something — or if he had to go to the office, pick up a venti at Bucks. He remoted the radio off and went to the big room (the studio) where he kept his toys: his six year-old Yamaha PSR 320 keyboard ($499), his 32 inch (he should have gotten the 35 damn) Sony XBR tv ($1499 cost [thank you Wanda`s stepfather]), Sony SVHS 528A ($599 cost) and Mitsubishi 3568 ($499) video tape decks with a Panasonic 14A video mixer ($400), a Nintendo 64 ($199 on sale) with assorted cartridges (FIFA Football, Super Super Mario Brothers, Sim City 4000 Deluxe, Dennis Rodman Scores! and Total Recall, all around $59.99), his Yamaha (R-V901 $399) and JBL Home Theater System (SCS120 $1299), a Sony 8 mm camcorder with color LCD monitor (CCD-TRV22 $700), his seldom used Powerbook (which was actually gathering dust while Tina was absent), and his big Mac, plus assorted software (Microsoft Word 99 [$179 upgrade], Adobe Photoshop 6.0 [$600] with Pagemaker 7.5 [$180], Virtual PC with Windows 98 that never really worked [$100], Norton Utilities and AntiVirus [$75] Britannica 98 [$75], Death Lord [$49], Civilization II [$39] and SimCity [$39] for Mac, as well as CyberKill [$29], The Simpsons [$29], Riven [$49], John Madden 99 [$55] and other games for Windows). Ok Scully, time to boot up, because the truth is out there.

Peter loved, absolutely loved, switching on his gear: the subsonic hum of the electronics (perhaps imagined), a few seconds of the X-Files theme music, do de do de de do (substituted for the simple beep, indigo or droplet alert sound [although he was beginning to tire of the show: the recent plots seemed unnecessarily intricate and hard to follow, while at the same time they had begun to repeat themselves]), the high pitched whine of the hard drive followed by the whoosh and cackle of the monitor screen and shazzam: the threshold of a brave new world! He sat down and logged in, thinking vaguely of the almost translucent facial paleness (that was one white woman) and incorruptible (unbelievable) skepticism of Gillian Anderson (Dana Scully). Downloading Messages from Server Erasing Messages Off Server You Have New Mail of course I have new mail, don't you know who I am? I'm Peter the Great arbitrator of hip, master of cool, infrared connection between back alley and boardroom, cellular pimp between the baggies and the suits, between Century City and Woody boulevard, between those who sell and those who (want [need] to) buy (and everyone sells and everyone needs to buy). I'm the Q rating behind the Q rating, the calculation behind the pose, the data behind the face. I give you the freedom to choose what you want (to be [sold]). Sweet dreams are made of this (the Marilyn Manson version, whatever happened to that andry Lennox anyway). Sweet dreams are made of me.

What do we have here? Seven new messages:

From: efphelps17@ubos.stud.edu
To:ptrgreat@fortunatoresearch.com
Re: Message from Wan...
cc:

Who is efphelps17, you boss stud you. Oh, from Wanda. Great.

dear peter
i'm fine. having fun but missing you. we went to a bookstore yesterday and i bought a book on lingerie for you and david bowie for me. tried to remember the name of that author who slept with her dad but couldn't and didn't want to go up to the melvin at the counter his glasses had bulletproof lenses i swear hey what's that book about that girl who hosed her old man is that on sale i think not he was checking elise and me out as it was. gotta go we're going to comme des garcons. anyway moms wants to stay another week so I won't be back tomorrow another week of flying solo you'll make it up to me when i get home. or else. keep it stashed, love & lust, wanda

Christ! Another week; seven days and nights, no eight counting tonight, eight nights at least without the furry. What was he gonna do? Maybe a little substitute action, but who? Everybody he knew knew Wanda too. Denise, his old girlfriend, might oblige . . . no, he wasn't that desperate yet. There was always rough trade but he didn't want to pull a Hugh Grant. How much did hos cost, anyway? And how did one set up a commercial boot knock? He didn't want to cruise around and pick up some infected roach motel, he wanted something clean, regulated, inspected: US Government Grade A furry, prime cut. Maybe Tino would know. He'd just have to wait. Goddamn Wanda, why couldn't she stay home, sick grandmother his ass, she just creams for shopping, although Comme des Garçons does have men's clothes and she'd surprised him before (gray cashmere jacket [$750], black Pima cotton shirt with turquoise buttons [$250]). Hmmm. Still, he was pissed (blue-ball rage), and decided not to reply until the evening, maybe. Next message.

From: suarez@film.ucsantabarbara.edu
To:ptrgreat@fortunatoresearch.com
Re: Lakers
cc:
Hey dude, how about the Lakers tonight? They're only playing the Nuggets but my dad gave me his tix. Let me know by 2 this afternoon, okay? Later, Suarez.

Could be, could be: maybe a little Shaq attack was just the thing. Unless he was supposed to do something, let's see.

From:Karla@fortunatoresearch.com
To:ptrgreat@fortunatoresearch.com

Re: Islamic Art
cc: bryan@fortunatoresearch.com,yashikamori@fortu-
natoresearch.com
Peter,
I need you to go to an Islamic art opening and reception
tonight, at the Drake Center, eight o'clock. Bryan will
vid and Yashika will chat, I just need you to keep an eye
on things and mix. Two single-spaced pages tomorrow
at noon will be appreciated. Sportcoat ok, tie optional.
Have fun, Karla.

Wonderful. Instead of hoop, towel-head pictures of camels and shit — sand, turbans, veils, rocket
launchers, a real chuckle. Maybe Karla (Latin, leggy,
married [to Hector the owner]) would go with. Then
after the sandfest a little horizontal rumba. Yeah right,
twiddle the owner's wife (as if she'd have anything to
do with him, the bossy, frigid bitch [still, if legs could
kill. . .]): smooth move x-lax, that'd look great on a
resumé (and Hector'd probably cut his nuts off with a
butter knife before canning him). Why couldn't she
send Lazy Susan; that was more up her alley? She was
in Frisco covering some gay thing. Ok fine, he'd have a
few beers and scope on some Arabian furry (moustach-
es and Huggy Bear gold bracelets and rings), let Bryan
and Shika (how old was she, twelve?) do the work,
write some bullshit up in the a.m., no big deal. Suarez's
dad had nosebleeds anyway.

From: KJohns@Powerealty.com
To:ptrgreat@fortunatoresearch.com
Re: Lunch
cc:
Don't forget dear, Marietti's at one. Until then, Kay.

Yeah, had he ever forgotten? No. Next message.

From:bryan@fortunatoresearch.com
To:ptrgreat@fortunatoresearch.com
Re: Islamic Art
cc:
Pete,
Can I bumb a ride? I'll be at the offfice, its almost on the
wya. Lemme know if you cant', ok? Also, what time.
Latre, Bryan.

No problem, mooch. Learn to write, you illiterate
fuck.

From:Karla@fortunatoresearch.com
To:ptrgreat@fortunatoresearch.com
Re: Acid Jazz
cc:
Dear Peter,
Don't forget your piece on acid jazz is due Friday AT
THE LATEST! I know it will be magnificent. Karla.

Reply

Do you want to include original message in reply?

Yes

>Dear Peter,
>Don't forget your piece on acid jazz is due Friday AT
>THE LATEST! I know it will be magnificent. Karla.
Dear Karla.
I don't have Alzheimer's, and I'VE NEVER MISSED A
DEADLINE YET. So get off my fucking back. Peter.

Close.

Do you really want to close without sending?

Yes. Next message.

From: PhilipeDyou@waltdisney.pub.com
To: ptrgreat@fortunatoresearch.com
Re: Jim Carrey
cc:
Dear Peter,
We're hosting a party to promote Jim Carrey's latest film, Dumb, Dumber, Really Stupid, April 18, at the Waldorf Hilton downtown. If you're interested, I'll send an invitation to the office. Let me know before Friday. Best, Philipe.

Finally, something he might like (he loved Jim Carrey [even The Cable Guy], though The Truman Show sucked [confusing and disappointing]), although Disney wasn't exactly famous for their shindigs (Dalmatians was bad wine and cheese and Family Circus completely dry). Plus Philipe was such a high-pressure prick (used to work for Nike, 'nuff said). Still, he and Wanda liked dressing up, and no telling who'd be there (Alicia Silverstone? Buffy [Sarah Michelle Gellar]? Jennifer Aniston? [Schwimmer was such a schmuck], or that Tyler chick, Liv [Love in an elevator, livin it up while I'm going dow-wown]); so it might be fun. He clicked on his calendar to make sure he was clear, then wrote Philipe back to provisionally accept. He checked his wealth (Peter liked to see what he was worth [he had tried daytrading once and had lost two grand in three hours]: Cisco 171 1/2, Sprint 110 even, Storage Tech 79 1/4), Netscaped the hoop scores on espnet.com (Lakers by ten over the Blazers), then logged out, put on some Jhelisa and worked on his acid jazz piece before dressing (blue jeans from Dolce and

Gabbana [$299], the Hard-On belt, black silk tee from Buster LA [$115], scuffed black lowcut sabots from Doc Marten [£75 at the London Doc Marten Store] and a black linen jacket from BOSS Hugo Boss [most recent birthday present from Kay, probably around $600]) for lunch (Marinetti's was one of the few places south of Carmel that still maintained [imported] a dress code). Before leaving he made sure to grab his AT&T PocketNet ($299 + $49.99 per month data and voice connection) cell phone and sunglasses (vintage Cutler & Gross frame from American Rag [$300] with custom [not prescription {Peter had 20/20} but specially ground UV blocking scratch resisting anti-glare really dark motherfucking lenses {$250}]) with faux zebra-skin case (Sulka, gift from Wanda), his Ghurka leather wallet ($99) and his Betty Boop Swatch Irony ($99) with the real croc band ($200). He added a splash of Christian Dior Ion Pour Homme ($47 3.4 oz eau de toilette). He didn't shave.

Kay was Peter's aunt: his deceased mother's (Julie) younger (by seven years) sister. She (Peter's mother and two uncles [Michael and David]) came from wealthy parents (Isabelle [born Stone, now seventy-six] and Franklin [Frankie, died 1987 of prostate cancer {liver gave out?} at the age of sixty-nine] Connor); had a wealthy ex-husband (Robert Johns, now of San Diego [Kay had kept the Johns]), and had made several killings in real estate (both as a broker and an investor). In addition to the house in Bel Air, she maintained a comfortable apartment in London (she owned a tony block of flats in Knightsbridge [£14 million], one-fifth of a strip mall in Costa Mesa [$10 million], and two or three other income properties in Orange and Los Angeles counties). She drove either a dullish silver (Burnished Sterling) 1987 Mercedes Benz SLK 230 convertible ($45,000) or a new very dark green (Nottingham Forest) Range Rover ($68,000). Peter, though engendered and partially raised (until the age of seven years and three months) by members of the lower middle (although professional) economic bracket (a vaguely disappointed associate professor [his father, Paul Nicholas] of music history [nineteenth and twentieth century opera and lieder, at the University of California Riverside] and a graduate student harpsichordist [the aforementioned Julie]), did okay, thank you, on income from a trust set up by his grandfather (approximately $50,000 per annum), and gifts (including housing, clothing, food, travel, tuition [five years at the University of Southern California, let's say $140,000]   and his blackish purple [Royal Aubergine] with dark red [Claret] interior 1996 Saab 9000S turbo convertible coupe [$37,000]) from his aunt. All this was in addition to his $38,000 job at Fortunato Market Research, as well as an $800,000 stock portfolio (mostly Microsoft, Compatible Systems and Storage Tech, the wise old coot) inherited at his grandfather's death. In short, Peter now wanted, and in the foreseeable future would want, for nothing. Still, it wasn't *that* much money.

And then there was the house. Kay had made hints to Peter (nothing definite) that her wedding (and perhaps final) contribution might be a smallish (but stylish) recently obtained (ex-executive courtesy rental [rumor had it recently inhabited by one of the Lloyd twins]) two bedroom two bath Tudor ($750,000 — $1 million?) near Wilshire Boulevard in Santa Monica. She had taken him there a couple of times after lunch, to see how the new floors look, and while his eye for detail didn't extend to the French polished baseboards, (faux) art deco (the house was only thirty years old) ironwork or Ralph Lauren Heather Mist wallpaper, he did appreciate the skylit master bedroom, the ultra modern eurokitchen (he liked the various gadgets, like the Tappan Microwave XW 4700 [$750], the polished glass and chrome of the Subzero LS refrigerator [$5000], the English Sage Aga Stove [$3200]), as well as the four-sided transparent glaze (with etched daffodils [it reminded Peter of a clear Perrier-Jouet bottle]) of the shower (on his only visit after he became aware of Kay's possible intentions, he imagined a slow 360 pan of Wanda's soaped and slick body through the cut glass and steam). All in all, he thought the place comfortable and somewhat hip (he enjoyed the idea of actually owning property) and would bring Wanda when his aunt's largess became more definite.

Peter, however, was in no hurry to obtain either a house or a wife (although he was definitely interested in both, this acquisition and merger [the first dependent on the second] would be best realized sometime in the nebulous future). Like many (most?) American men of twenty-six years, he found his present circumstances of few worries (he was in excellent physical shape, had sex on a regular basis [between six and eight times a week on average] with a beautiful, intelligent [BA in Art History from Stanford] and wealthy [Wanda's stepfather was a VP of Sony America] artist, had a lot of friends, a cool job [interesting but not too difficult, and because of Kay's investment in the firm he'd be almost impossible to fire {he was vested}]), few responsibilities (no children, no aging parents [no parents at all]), no financial concerns (no mortgage [he didn't even pay rent], no student loans, no saving for retirement [stock portfolio], no car payments, fuck, it was pure black) agreeable indeed, and could see no pressing reason why he should endeavor to introduce change into his situation. Why rock the boat when the sailing was so smooth? Why go looking for trouble when it would find you, sooner or later (in his case, sooner). Peter didn't think consciously about it that much, but when he did, he figured that since the world (God, They) had taken his parents from him when he was seven and a half years old, then it was only fair that he should live a materially comfortable life. After all, most of his friends and many of his acquaintances enjoyed the same economic and social privileges as he did (at least), and they all possessed one, and sometimes four or five parents. Everyone he knew was fortunate (rather than genuinely smart or talented); he had just been a little less lucky than most. It wasn't that he felt he was owed, exactly; it was just that through Kay's generosity the universe was reestablishing its own basic and absolute equilibrium — the Lord taketh away, and the Lord giveth — and who was he to question the methods or the amount by which his account was balanced?

This view (this ideology, although Peter would never use the word) wasn't developed in any detail; in fact, it was less articulated than felt. To be honest, and whether this is to his credit or detriment we cannot yet know, Peter was not a terribly philosophical young man—his consciousness was largely unburdened by abstract questions of why, and not once did it occur to him to rail against the gods, bitterly decrying his fate. The facts were there, they couldn't be changed: Peter's father and mother were killed in a small plane accident in central Turkey, near Ankara, when he was seven and a half years old. He was an orphan. A tragedy, yes, but Peter was never tragic.

This is not to say he wasn't deeply hurt, or saddened by the loss of his parents. He supposed he loved them (what does a seven-year-old know of love?), and for a while missed them very much (one of his earliest, most vivid and fondest memories was playing with his Lincoln Logs™ on the red carpet [bokhara {$3500 (it was rolled up somewhere, too big for his present bedroom)}] near his mother's bench as she practiced [he had no memory of either the music {Bach, Schubert, or simply scales} or the instrument {harpsichord or piano} she was playing] above). But after about six months of vague listlessness and vacant torpor (what might be called, in other situations, moping about) his aunt's solicitousness and hospitality (there were few actual gifts: Kay just made sure that everything he might need was easily within reach) began to thaw his heart, and he began, if not to enjoy (that would require another six months), then at least appreciate his new situation. The anguish he first felt at his parents' demise was slowly replaced by an almost clinical, but insatiable, curiosity about the mundane details of their (especially his father's, of whom he [by the age of twenty] had only the most nebulous recollections) existence. He wanted to know everything.

Kay, however, for reasons never quite fathomed (jealousy? fatigue? or other?) was less than forthcoming with either information concerning or artifacts belonging to her dead sister and brother-in-law. In the beginning, Peter's questions were answered, albeit reluctantly, and their objects rationed to him, although meanly. However, with few exceptions (a videotape of his father lecturing [Schumman's Kriestlieder], his mother's engagement [not wedding] ring [which, according to Kay, had once belonged to Isabelle's mother, Olivia], and a copy of The Compact Oxford English Dictionary with his mother's name printed on the inside front covers of both volumes), these mementos (mori) were all extremely impersonal — they included the bokhara rug, a rather nice cornflower blue and white Log Cabin Amish quilt (folded up in his closet) and a set of four medium cream-colored pasta bowls with enameled red tomatoes with the words "Made in Italy" on the bottom (also in his closet) — they could have belonged to anyone! When pressed, Kay would, at first, often respond with some personal token: a pair of cufflinks from the Vegas Thunderbird Hotel (presumably his father's), an empty cardboard music portfolio (mother's?), a pair of brand new gray men's socks, still on their little plastic hanger (father's).

Then, on Christmas Eve, two years and two months after the accident, Peter received a large foot-locker (Louis Vuitton Venice $850) filled with the photo albums (and photographs) of his parents, as well as five or six videotapes, mostly of himself in various stages of development (infancy through age seven). After letting him rummage through them for a couple of hours, Kay had whisked him off to bed, informing him that the photographs were the last he would see of his parents' effects for a while, as she didn't have the time to run to the storage locker every other week, nor did she have the heart to see reminders of her poor sister (she didn't mention his father) staring her in the face in her own home. It would be better for both of them if they could begin to forget the past and start to move on. She wouldn't throw anything away, she promised him that, and he could have it all when he moved out, but from that day forward, she would not give him anything more that belonged to her (them), nor would she answer any more questions about her life (their lives). She would not prevent him from seeking answers from other quarters, but she would ask that he refrain from speaking about them (she used the plural for the first time) in her presence. This was the only important thing she would ever ask of him; just as it was the only reasonable desire she would ever refuse him. She realized she was expecting a great deal, but he must understand that her sister's death (again, no mention of his father) was extremely difficult and painful for her, and in order that she not be totally crushed by sorrow, she would have to bury the memories away as best she could. It was difficult enough, she reminded him, seeing her sister in his face, his gestures, especially his mouth, but that was okay, because ultimately he reminded her of her sister while she was alive, while her belongings reminded her (Kay) that she (Julie) was dead, and she (Kay) would never see her (Julie) again. She loved him very much, but it was just the two of them now, and their duty was now first and foremost to each other: he could look at the pictures as much as he wanted, whenever he wanted, but was not to ask her any more questions, nor demand from her any more things that had once belonged to them (plural).

After she had made him shake on it, and kissed him on both cheeks, she had turned out the lights and left him in bed, with his eyes wide open, staring at the ceiling. He was fascinated by the photos, yet frightened by his aunt's interdictions: she had never spoken to him so forcefully before (nor would she soon again). He was sensitive enough (he was always perspicacious when it came to his own welfare) to understand and to take seriously the threat behind her requests: failure to comply would provoke at least a stern and silent disapproval and could even bring about expulsion from the warm bed and expensive and abundant toys to which he was beginning to grow accustomed (Kay would never put him out on the street, but a damp, stiff English boarding school, or remote, sadistic military academy might be possibilities. Peter had neither the imagination nor the literary background to imagine [and thus to fear] such contingencies. He did consider the chance that he might have to go live with one of his uncles, two people he knew even less well than his parents. His father had had no family that he knew of). Yet he still wanted to know: what were they like? The photographs he had quickly perused that night (a wedding album, full of glossy, sharp, professional prints [his mother in white, lightly veiled, his father in a black tuxedo, thin, gray {was it the light?} and impeccable; his mother smiling and hugging Aunt Kay, his father in the background looking lost, out of place, as if he'd somehow stumbled into the wrong wedding; the entire family, lined up like royalty, his father looking straight into the camera, smiling bravely, his mother with her head turned toward his father, Kay with her eyes closed, his uncles and grandfather with almost identical grim, pursed, disappointed expressions, with only his grandmother looking appropriately joyous for the occasion], posed and self-conscious [can there be anything more artificial than wedding photos {artifice of artifice}?]), far from satisfying his desire for knowledge, only served to whet his appetite for more information. But he knew enough not to challenge his aunt's prohibitions. He would have to find other sources.

It was strange, too, his aunt's refusal to mention his father. He thought back to the time (two or three years of his memoire voluntaire) before the accident, to see if he could remember any manifestation of tension or hostility between the two — an overheard snatch of conversation, a quickly suppressed grimace, entreaties by his mother to be pleasant, stiff formality or exaggerated courtesy — but no, he could recall nothing that might suggest some animosity (deep or otherwise) between his father and his aunt. As far as he could remember, his father never resisted visiting or entertaining his wife's family (Peter remembered one

big get-together [Easter 1981] at his grandparents'
house [$250,000 in 1970, La Jolla], when his father had
seemed extremely happy and animated, even teaching
the hora to his mother, aunt, uncles and grandmother).

There was the another possibility of course: the
possibility that his aunt might have been in love with
his father, but that was too uncomfortable and confus-
ing for Peter to consider seriously, although the
thought continued to cross his mind from time to
time, always to be dismissed as soon as possible. It
made him feel queasy and slightly dizzy. Perhaps Kay
was even his real mother (he didn't really believe this
[and would find a photograph of an obviously pregnant Julie a couple of weeks later]). That would
explain why she took him in (mother love), why she
was so insistent on trying to erase her sister's memory
(guilt), and why she never mentioned his father (jealousy, rage and guilt). Peter closed his eyes and fought
back tears. No parents, no siblings, no cousins (David
unmarried, Michael and [wife] Dee childless): he didn't
know where he came from or where he was going. He
knew nothing about anything — he was oh so very
alone in the world (empirically, rather than existential-
ly, speaking). He wanted, needed, indeed had the right
to, information about his parents, and yet to pursue
such knowledge would be certain to alienate (piss) his
guardian (Kay never officially adopted Peter), making
his situation precarious.

If only he had someone to confide in: an older
brother or sister to talk to, to share secrets, to reconstruct their (his) past (Do you remember when Dad
put so much lighter fluid on the charcoal that it flared
up and scorched his eyebrows? Yeah that was great).
An older (younger would remember even less and a
twin was too much to even fantasize about) sister

(someone pretty and sympathetic [a brother might be too rough and competitive]) would be best, he decided, with long dark straight hair (his was short, blond and curly), pale skin (he was nicely tanned) like his mother, and blue or green eyes (Peter's were brown). They would have bedrooms side by side, and late at night he would sneak into her room (sweet, mysterious girlsmells, a few stuffed animals [nothing too frilly] and amphoras and vials of fragrances, lotions and cremes), sit on the bed and look at the photographs, and she would tell him stories filled with detail (the name of his mother's favorite perfume; his father's preferred breakfast) about their (his) mother and father; stories which might even begin with I remember the day you were born and go on to narrate his trip home from the hospital, his father frantic with pride (I have a son!) almost sideswiping an ambulance, and his mother (holding him in the backseat) quiet, warm and loving. A sister (the one thing he wanted that Kay couldn't possibly provide) would be wonderful.

"Hello Kay."

Marinetti's was fucking crowded (was that Chris Penn in the black and white camo jacket [Pal Zileri {$1200}], matching cargo pants [$350], a white wrinkled cotton shirt [Façonnable {$83}], a cheap [and ugly] yellow checked tie [Old Navy {$20}] and gray Birkenstock Tatami Trekking sandals [$110]?). Plus he was ten minutes late (traffic) and Kay had already started on her salad. "Sorry I'm late." His aunt usually looked good (like a forty-five dark brunette [sometimes trimmed and highlighted by Corey] version of Elaine on Seinfeld [he loved the one where Kramer joined that cult: Jeeeeerrrrry!] although with a broader face, a smaller mouth and darker, deeper set eyes

32

[her eyes often looked in the need of sleep]. She had tied her hair (lighter this week) back loosely with a tortoise shell barrette [Scarafino's $135]. Kay hadn't, as far as Peter knew, yet had any work [other than dental {wisdom teeth removed two years ago}] done), and today she looked fantastic (a plain gray wool Versace [poor fuck] jacket and thigh-length skirt [$1900] with a Prada scarlet silk blouse [$400], mui mui flats [$575], her small Tiffany pear singles [Very Good, D, IF, 1.76 each $44,000], her burgundy Franck Müller with crocodile strap [gift from her ex, about $12,000 retail]. Her gray Suarez Lizard clutch [$350] was on her lap. Peter wondered if anyone at the restaurant thought them lovers [he flashed on the image of Pavo lounging by the pool, his biceps glowing in the sun]). He bent over to kiss her offered cheek (Chanel Philosophy of Right, $125 per .4 oz), then sat back in a chair recently, discreetly and perfectly placed beneath him.

She stopped her forkful of greens (purslane, mâche and mesclun) in midair and looked at him. "And how is Wendy?" She smiled, then brought the salad to her mouth and began to chew. He looked at her (she wore very little make-up, but this was California and she didn't need much anyway): he wasn't sure how he should react to her question. Kay was aware that Wanda hated the name Wendy (she had changed it [unofficially] during her senior year of high school, when her mother remarried. When they started going out she had said, Christ, can you imagine, Peter and Wendy, what a couple — we'll end up in fucking never-never land. What's wrong with fucking never-never land? Grow up.) and he was having a hard time determining whether Kay's teasing was spiteful or good-natured.

"You look terrific." He opened his menu. He wasn't sure how he should play this: part of him felt like he should stand up for Wendy, er Wanda, but if he was misreading his aunt, and she was merely being playful, then any sort of serious defense would generate irritation and impatience, and lunch would be unpleasant. On the other hand, if she was genuinely making fun of Wanda (he knew Kay wanted them to marry [because of Wanda's family or because she wanted the house to herself] but he was never sure what his aunt really thought about his fiancé) because she was in a bad mood (annoyed at his tardiness?), disliked the girl or merely wanted to vex him, then any spirited retort would only add to her spleen, and Kay's arrows would become more poisonous and carefully aimed. He could feel her gaze through the menu. She was waiting for an answer. A waiter appeared ("Our specials today are mesquite smoked boneless quail with a roasted garlic ancho chili glaze crust for an appetizer, romaine hearts with asparagus, shaved red onions in a rosemary orange yogurt dressing for a salad, fresh clam chowder with roasted corn and a hint of roasted anaheim chilies, and our entrée is an ahi tuna sushi roll, with seaweed, Spanish rice, and a mango roasted jalapeno vinaigrette dipping sauce") and he ordered his pasta and beer. His menu was removed.

"Peter, I asked you a question. How is Wendy?" He could tease her back, but about what? Her boyfriends were strictly off limits (while she had never explicitly excluded her love life as a topic for conversation [as she had done with questions about his parents], Peter nevertheless understood that such inquiry or commentary would certainly transgress some sort of unspoken stipulation, and would be punished accordingly) and his knowledge of her business dealings was much too muddled (he often got lost trying to follow her intricate explanations and narrations of buying, selling, leasing, brokering, points and the like: he did

know she was loaded) to provide any pertinent ammunition. Her outfit was, as usual, beyond reproach.
Fuck it — he would just let it go, his minute betrayal
would never be discovered anyway.

"Wanda's fine. You know she's in Boston, visiting her sick grandmother." His ale appeared, half
poured into a pilsner glass.

"What a lovely story. The young are so idealistic."

Peter smiled. Why was she giving him so much
shit (ragtime or what)? He took a sip of his ale: the
day had gone downhill since he found his remote. And
he still had that goddam camel-jockey art thing to go
to. He sighed and leaned back in his chair, "So, Kay,
how are you?"

She looked at him thoughtfully, chewing some
salad. She placed her fork sideways on her plate, and
pushed it away, her brow creased. Peter thought for a
moment that she was going to tell him something really important, something that would change his life forever, but she simply brought her wine glass to her
mouth, unfurrowed her brow, and, after taking a
drink, said "Busy, dear, extremely busy. Sometimes I
get so bored with this whole thing, and I just want to
chuck it, you know, retire or something. But I can't do
that, at least not yet. Besides, if I think my life is dull
with work, just think how tedious I'd find it without it.
Anyway, I often amuse myself by trying to be clever at
another's expense, and since you're handy, and so
damn cute when you're flustered, it was difficult to
resist the indulgence. Anyway, let's start again, shall
we? Look, here's your salad, and my pasta. I'm sorry
I'm in such a rush, but I have to leave by two thirty at
the latest."

So that was it, verse two hundred and seventeen of the I'm tired of working but what else can I do

song, with a couple of choruses of let's make Peter feel like a deadbeat thrown in for good measure. If you want to relax, stop buying your gigolos (Just a gigolo, everywhere I go, da da da,da da da [where was David Lee Roth now?])Movados (what did Pavo need a $5000 watch for, so he'd know when to turn over and toast his back?), but don't spread your guilt around. He could always move out, find his own place; or he and Wanda could even shack up (that would disappoint his grandmother, and definitely p.o. Wanda's stepfather [that Jap saving face crap]); they didn't need the house in Santa Monica and he didn't need the coach house in Bel Air. There were other places in LA to live. And where was the pepper girl? He was hungry and wanted some fresh ground for his salad.

"You look troubled Peter. Everything okay? You're not upset are you? I was only teasing."

He found the pepper girl and signaled her with his left hand. "I'm fine, I'm just hungry."

"Would you like some fresh ground pepper on your pasta?"

"Yes I would."

"I have Afghan White, Santa Fe, Beijing, and Madagascar Black, Mediterranean Red, and a special house blend."

"I'll try the Beijing, please."

"Very good. Tell me when."

"Thank you."

"And you sir, for your salad?"

"I'll try the house blend."

"Very good."

"That's enough."

"Thank you."

The greens were excellent, fresh and crisp, and because of the pepper, slightly hot. Peter continued to sing the gigolo song in his head. He was angry with

Kay for hanging out with such (good-looking and young) moochers — why couldn't she find someone appropriate (older or at least her own age) and settle down, then maybe he could get on with his life. He realized he was beginning to worry about her, and the reversal was both frightening and annoying: after all, he was the orphan.

Kay set her fork down and took another sip of wine. "You've always had a very expressive face, my dear, and I can see that something's troubling you besides famine. Is everything all right with Wanda?"

He looked up. Way off again, Kay, way off again (why did she call her Wanda?). "Everything's all right with Wanda. Everything's all right with everything."

"But you look like such a sad little Romeo, fretting for his Juliet. Do you miss her that much? Isn't she returning today?"

"I don't look like a sad little Romeo, I wasn't even thinking about her. And to answer your question, she sent a message saying she's not coming back until next week. But I'll live."

"You know, I" (where was Pavo?) "just saw the new version of that the other night, with Leonardo DiCaprio and Claire Danes. Have you seen it?" Yeah right. Peter shook his head. "I adore Shakespeare. Anyway, you're right, you're no Romeo, because Wanda is certainly no Capulet. In fact, she's more Montague than we are, my dear boy." Peter (involuntarily) shrugged, and chewed on some romaine. He wasn't exactly sure who the Capulets and Montagues were. He had read Shakespeare in college, but that was a while ago. He couldn't see how it mattered much, anyway. "You make a perfect couple, Peter, a perfect couple. Let's toast. To Wanda!"

"To Wanda." They clinked glasses. What the

hell was Kay doing? Maybe she did really like Wanda after all. He had the feeling, however, that something else was going on (a feeling he had often). Why couldn't everything be simple, easy, smooth (he had this feeling often as well)? Screw it — he wouldn't worry about it, he'd deal with it when he had to. Here was his pasta.

CHAPTER TWO

Peter's mood worsened the closer he (a beautiful gold green sharkskin suit [$199 at Daffy's Boston
{thank you Wanda} with the Prix Goncourt {?} label],
a tightish pale turquoise cotton tee [Marc Ribot $45],
these rad silver tipped lowcut calfskin cholo-kickers
[he bought them at this baggies store in Pico Rivera
off Whittier for $150] and his silver [gold was cheesy]
Raymond Weil Celestial Calendar Chronograph [gift
from Kay probably around $8000], plus a little YSL
Poetry Language Thought [4 oz. spray cologne
$45.00]), Yashika (silver with pink windowpane
striped big flare jeans from Paul Smith [$240], match-
ing black Bali panties and bra [$40], Venetian blue
Henri Bendel cashmere pullover [$300], raised black
platform Oxfords from Aldo [$69], metallic silver socks
from Gapkids [$12], a black vintage leather swagger
coat from Polkadots and Moonbeams LA, circa 1960
[$475, she added the hood], Clarins Le Rouge Midnight
Stain [$45], Henri Bendel's Awake Mascara [$15.95], T.
LeClerc Pure Black nail polish [$37] and Bulgari Art and
Scholasticism Pour Femme Spray Cologne [$35 per 2
oz.]), Bryan (Nike Kelly Nylon Team Pants [$35], vin-
tage Jockey black cotton tee with Meat is Murder in
white print [$25], Jockey briefs [$19 for three pair] visible above the Nike Teams, black and white Nike
Air'Ogants [$99], Royal Knight black polyester and
cotton socks [$1 a pair at The Dollar Store near the
Grand Central Market], a black and silver Raiders
nylon windbreaker [$89.99]) and Bryan's equipment
(Canon DL1 Digital Camcorder [$4,999] with
Panasonic Mini DVC60 tape 4 pack [$325], 3 BP 950

Battery Packs [$200 each], SUR Md-50 external mic [$175] and Smith Victor Compact Quartz attached 600 Watt Lamp [$80]) approached the Drake Center. For one thing, he was early to the office, and so had to hang around for almost an hour an a half, shooting the shit and watching Bryan (who didn't have to drive, the parasite) guzzle Sam Adams ($6.99 a six, Peter had one) and lecture them (Peter, Yashika and some stoned Black Rain friend [long black calfskin coat {Rei Kawatanaba about ¥150,000}, silver tipped motorcycle boots {modified Harley Davidson Eagles $425}, black wool and spandex flat-front pants from DKNY {$250}, long sleeved black and purple rayon striped shirt from Perry Ellis {$95} and a Kenneth Cole black leather belt {$65}] of Yashika's [who quickly put his head down and slept]) about the dangers (physical and spiritual) of all animal products to the human ecosystem, dangers apparently not limited to the human digestive organs (" don't even wear wool, or leather shoes, man [he had removed the leather swoosh from his Nikes and had mailed them back to the company]). Peter hadn't planned on getting there so quickly, but didn't have that much to do after lunch (he had returned home [Marinetti's was only twenty minutes from his house] and had tried to revise his acid jazz report, but hadn't been able to concentrate. He wrote emails to Suarez and Bryan [but not to Wanda], then listlessly played Quake III Apocalypse Now for an hour or so, but couldn't get past the fourth level. He thought about working out, but the logistics would be difficult [his gym {at the club} was in Brentwood, the office near the downtown bus station [on Wilde Street] and the Drake Center in Pasadena — by the time he got there, did the machines and freeweights, showered and dressed it'd be too late to zip downtown [thanks Bryan] then up to Pasadena [thanks Karla]). So he took a swim (thirty-

five laps [Pavo's return {what time is it, Pavo?} causing an early exit]), then a too short nap (even Bel Air
was not spared the noise of [police?] helicopters), and
an after-nap chubby. He was wired. And grumpy. He
paced around in his shorts for awhile listening to tunes
(KROQ sucks [Pearl Jam Alive, Helmet Pure, Wendy's
{Hey Dave luv your chicken sandwich}, Delouisa Ford
{Our deals are hot hot HOT! But our cars are cool},
Sprint {Talk is cheap. Now its cheaper on Sprint}, Fiona
Apple Cuz he's all I ever knew of love {he wouldn't
mind taking a bath with her, when was Wanda returning, maybe he had time for a shower wank (he put his
hand in his shorts his blue balls were beginning to ache
[furry cold turkey])}, No Doubt Just a Girl {he
stretched on his bed and began to stroke himself why
wait for a shower} and Jewel Who Will Save Your Soul
{talk about a mood killer (gap toothed hillbilly): he
pulled up his shorts found the remote and killed the
radio (KROQ sucks)}]), then sat back on his bed and
leaned his head against the wall. He was even too
bored to chicken choke (goddam Wanda he could surf
some cybersluts but why bother).

    He had been home too long and the walls were
closing in. He could use some reef but he was out and
besides he had to drive all over fuck anyway. He probably should do some googling on that camel-art but it
was enough that he was going (and if he didn't have to
play rickshaw for Yashika and Bryan he might bag it
but then what would he do he already cancelled plans
with Suarez and Wanda was wandering in Boston). He
could get dressed but he really needed a shower now
(smelled like chlorine [he definitely should have gone
to the gym and worked out the water and short
snooze had only jazzed him]) but it was still too early
and he wasn't sure what he would wear because he
hadn't yet decided how he was going to play it tonight

(an icily indifferent Tim Dalton formality [he could wear his vintage {Kay thought late 50's Wanda early 60's} Hackett Tuxedo {double breasted, shawl lapel} with his newish Jack Taylor Beverly Hills Marcella dinner shirt {$185}]; a lizard {never hire a ferret to do a weasle's job}-like sleaze à la Chazz Palminteri [the sharkskin ensemble]; Hollywood spoiled spawn [fuck you my father's a producer — the James Spader/Bridget Fonda we will own everything sneer {dirty hair (his was cleaned by the pool but at least he wouldn't have to shower), torn black Levis, his cholo kickers and an Heidi Fliess tee shirt with his black emanual ungaro (8 oz) silk and wool ($595) blazer}]; or a tired and crazed Gary Oldman Eurojunky [Armani dark brown wool zipper cardigan {$750} and reddish orange, maybe tomato lightweight Ermenegildo Zegna cashmere turtleneck{$400}, brown wide wale Brioni corduroys {$620} with those overpriced {$595} Ken Cole dirt-colored half-boots]).

He got up, wandered into his kitchen and opened his refrigerator: three pieces of week-old shrimp scampi and red pepper za ($15.99 from Guiseppi's of Beverly), a six of dark Heinie ($6.99), two cartons of plain Dannon's (79¢) and a small bottle of Ocean Spray ($1.79 [Wanda's yeastie boys]), a half-empty bottle of Schwepp's diet tonic water ($1.29), and a couple of liters of Alpine Mist Still Mineral Water ($2.09). He decided against a beer, took a couple of swigs of the Alpine Mist (Pure, Natural and Fresh — from Nature's Source), and closed the door: the tonic water reminded him of Pavo, who reminded him of Kay, who reminded him that her (46th? 47th?) birthday was coming up in a few days, and he hadn't yet begun to look for a present. He enjoyed buying presents (he never considered shopping a chore), and he and Wanda usually made a day out of buying Kay's birthday gift (Beverly Hills or Fashions Island, and last year Spago's for a late lunch). What did he get her last year? oh yeah, that Tom Ford crystal bottle with sterling stopper (Gucci without the G's, $800). He'd wait until Wanda returned to shop for Kay, but maybe he could kill an hour at that Malo store: it wasn't too far out of his way (the opposite direction off Santa Monica Boulevard in Santa Monica) and maybe he could buy a shirt (he loved those long-sleeved pique cotton golf shirts [$90]) or something (for himself) and surprise Wanda when he picked her up (he probably should try to find something for her as well [wasn't there a Tower Records {We Have Your Music} close by?]). Suddenly energized by his plan, Peter showered, dressed quickly (he didn't want to get stuck in traffic and have to listen to Bryan bitchin and moanin) and was out the door in no time.

Malo's was shut (no explanation just a sign, SHUT), which put him off Tower Records as well (the parking lot was full and he almost clipped a skateboarder [Watch it asshole!] as he circled [he'd find something for Wanda later like maybe at the airport]). He spotted a Bucks ("Lift up the receiver I'll make you a believer" [Depeche Mode, Personal Jesus from Violator 1990] on the Blaupunkt Reno [$229.95] connected to a CDC AO65 6 disc changer [$329], with four Blaupunkt PCx542 [two in the dash two in the front door @ $79.95 a pair] and two Blaupunkt PCx693's [$109 in the rear sides]), but he didn't feel like java now, he didn't feel like anything, he didn't know what he felt like although he knew he didn't feel like going to the sand eater art thing (although they did make nice rugs [like his bokhara]). Now what? He could return home, but it was way out of his way and with the traffic etc. etc. Fuck it, he might as well go to the office, maybe they had a new toy or something (Lapp

[and Hector] was always collecting swag from everywhere, expensive shit too like those LED VR glasses
from Visionquest [$1789], or that PDA from 3Com
[Palm IV $399]), or, if they didn't, he could shoot the
shit with Lapp and Tino (Tino would think his shoes
were nude), and maybe pick up some comps from
Hector (and scope out Karla's wheels). Besides, he had
just changed the cd's in his trunk unit (Violator
[$10.99], Björk, Homogenic [Columbia House $16.95 +
$2.50 shipping], Filter Short Bus [Hey man nice shot,
$8.85 used], Nirvana Unplugged [free from Columbia
House], Cypress Hill Black Sunday [$12.95], disc 2 of
MJ's HIStory [$19.95 on sale], Ethyl Meatplow Happy
Days, Sweetheart [friends of Wanda], MTV Danceparty
#4 [comp from the office], Jane's Addiction Nothing
Shocking [$12.95] and Kaspar Mute [Wanda's]) and so
cruising down Wilshire, while not exactly jollytime,
might still be tolerable. Anyway, it was better than
going home.

Wilshire Boulevard was extraordinarily, unbe-
lievably, awesomely deserted: it was like that town in
The Andromeda Strain or the Hammer (with Vanilla
Ice) comeback (2 Legit to Ever Quit) tour (for kicks he
and Wanda had actually gone to the Hollywood Bowl
to relive that Can't Touch This groove [comps courtesy
of Hector] and were joined by fewer than eight hundred fellow Angeleno Hammerheads). Other than a
city bus he had to follow (cough cough) for a couple of
miles or so (an accident had closed one lane) and some
spic-holes (yo quiero Taco Bell) in an aquamarine
lowriding tchaivy (who decided to test his commitment
to racial harmony by bottlenecking his ass behind the
bus [they hollered some shit out the window but their
seven thousand watt subwoofer, his Blaupunkt {Come,
as you are, as you say}, AC on high and closed windows
prevented comprehension. He kept his mouth shut {no

Selene Sucks!} and eyes straight ahead on the back of the bus {Gump & Company: Forrest Gump 2 Coming Soon! Visit Our Website @ http://www.boxa-choclats.com}, trying to avoid getting Reginald Dennied by the pachucos]. He thought about turning off near the Art Museum, but that wasn't the best hood and they might follow [they quickly got bored and turned off on La Brea]), he saw almost no one, either Mercedesed or on foot. And, like a dream, he hit every single light from Western all the way to Alverado (what a fucking treat!). He sped through the hazy city, blessed by good fortune, and arrived at the office about seventy before he had planned, only to find Bryan drinking beer and calibrating some equipment while Yashika and her friend ate something smelly in the meeting room (Tino and Lapp had just left, Hector was sick in bed and Karla was working at home and presumably nursing [not the right word she was flat el Mohave man no tetas to speak of] Hector).

Now what? He could join Yashika and her friend in the meeting room and watch them eat, or he could stare at the back of Bryan's head (while he verbally recounted every single dribble, move and shot of his recent ball game [I knew this dude, black dude, was left handed, because I ran with him a couple of weeks ago, we ruled the court, man, won something like seven games in a row till we just dropped. Anyway, this dude comes down, dribbling past half court, and they can win it, you know, with a hoop, so I know this guy's going to go to my right, which is his left, 'cuz he's left handed, so he gets to the top of the key, and I know he's getting ready to spin to my right, his left, for some reason I know he won't take the j, I know he's going to drive and either jam it or dish it . . .]) and watch him do whatever he was doing to his stuff: he should have stayed by the pool and rapped with Pavo.

Well, if the meat world was a drag, there was always the silicon jungle. He wandered over to Lazy Susan's cubicle (she was in Frisco), sat down in her swivel chair, and booted up her Dell Dimension XPS D333 400 MHz Pentium II MMX with 64 megs RAM, a 6.4 GB hard drive, a 19 inch Triniton and an Iomega Zip etc. ($2499). Or rather he tried to boot it up: there was some sort of gatekeeping program (fucking PC's) that wouldn't even let him past the log-in. "When did they install this firewall bullshit?" he yelled in Bryan's direction, "I just want to check my email." Peter didn't have a computer in the office: he would either bring his Powerbook or (clumsily) use Karla's or Hector's machine if he had to print or anything there (he could never do any actual writing at work).

"Hector put that into everyone's machine a couple of weeks ago, after someone came in and sent a whole bunch of nasty spam to Lara Croft from Karla's address." He glanced over at Yashika and company, "People wander in here, day and night. We got some hate mail from their lawyers next day, special d. Hector had to pucker up mighty tight and long for that one. Didn't he email you?"

"Lara Croft or Angela Jolie?"

"Lara Croft."

"Lara Croft's not even a real person, how does she have lawyers?"

"Maybe it was you."

"Yeah right, like I'd waste my time on a cartoon. Can I use your machine for a sec, I just wanna check my mail?"

"Not now, maybe in a couple of minutes: I'm running this defragging program. She's not a cartoon, she's a virtual character. Besides, she's built man, really built."

"You wouldn't happen to know Lazy Susan's

password, would ya?"

"Nope. And even if I did, I wouldn't tell you. Hector told us to keep everything secret. If I told you, and you fucked up, then I'd get in trouble."

"Whatever. I don't know why I talk to you."

"What?"

"I said 'whatever.'"

Peter sighed and switched the Dell off. Fuck it, he'd keep his Mac, let Bill rot. Did every single thinking, feeling human being in western, screw western, human civilization have at least one Dilbert cartoon tacked up on a wall somewhere?   Talk about your international market coverage — Dogbert must have Q rating of over a thousand: Perrobert, or Lobobert, Chienbert, he was sure there was some Chinesebert (Ricebert? he'd have to ask Yashika, although she was a Japa, not a China), and there was probably even some goddam Gookbert on the wall of some rice paddy hooch in the mountains of 'Nam (Bryan reminded him of that Dennis Hopper character in Apocalypse Now) — that guy (what was his name, Addams?) must be raking in the dough. Speaking of rice, the smell (garlic and hot pepper, and something else) seeping from the meeting room was beginning to make him hungry: he hadn't chowed since lunch, and no telling what sort of camelslop they were going to serve at this gathering of the tents. Ironically, there was a kebab stand down the block where he often went for lunch, but he didn't feel like theme eating (nor driving somewhere else); although he should fuel up on something, and no telling when he'd get the chance. What were they eating? Was it from someplace nearby? When Yashika answered twice cooked pork to his first inquiry, Bryan (who had silently followed Peter into the meeting room) had launched into his screed with a Do you know how smart pigs are, man? Do you know how they're killed? He never got to ask the second question, and so never ate anything (he did have a beer). No wonder he was in a bad mood.

They were a little early; the parking lot was less than half full. He did not want to do this, he was tired, lonely, grumpy, hungry, irritated and bored, and so he kept the three of them sitting silently in the car (Jane says, she's done with Sergio) while he weighed the pros and cons of platforms in his head (Apples are expensive, no support, but making a comeback. PC's are everywhere, well supported, tons of software, cheaper. Macs are easy to use and good-looking, he'd have to learn Windows). He looked out the window at three or four Benzos (s and i class mostly [$40 to $90 grand), a couple of Beemers ($45-60), one of those new Lexus 4x4's ($50,00), a Hummer (H1 $67K) and a couple of those inescapable Rav 4's ($18-$24). Maybe there'd be some celebrities, Richard Gere or Basinger or something (no, no, that was Tibet). There was a white stretch at the door, underneath a canvas banner that read New Islamic Art: A Journey From the Ages, with Arabic calligraphy underneath, flanked by a Sponsored by PepsiCo on one side and a Brought to You by Citicorp on the other. There was a web address underneath the calligraphy, www.newislamart. org. Peter's stomach growled. "Ok, everyone knows what to do, right? I'll be wandering around, so if you have any questions or run into any trouble, just stay cool and we'll find each other. Don't piss anyone off, if someone doesn't want to rap or be caught on tape, just smile and move on. Here's a stack of cards to give out if people are interested: it never hurts to drum up business where we can, although I really don't have a clue as to who's going to show tonight. Make sure your nametags are visible — you know the routine. I'm starving, so I'm going to bee-line for the buffet: I hope they have something more than chardonnay and brie (God they had

better). Bryan, you have back-up batteries, right?"
"Copper-top." "Any questions? Okay, let's just do it."

Although it was early, a quarter after eight by
the (electric) sundial in the lobby, there seemed to be
more people (no one he recognized [but who would he
recognize, that slob with the tablecloth on his head
that was always on tv?]) in the joint than the number
of cars parked in the lot would suggest. Perhaps it was
his low blood sugar, but he felt slightly disoriented as
he walked into the gallery. The paintings and textiles
on the walls were full of deep, dark reds, and some sort
of high pitched string thing played too loud for background ambiance. A cloud of incense, patchouli,
Chanel Logical Investigations and (oddly enough [this
was California]) tobacco smoke hung thickly in the
air, and the costuming seemed a bit off, as if the players were trying too hard to create an effect, but as to
what effect, he wasn't sure. It was a mixed crowd with
outfits ranging from those long white robe things on
four or five men (Rock the Casbah, Rock the Casbah,"
[weren't we bombing them or something?]) to nice,
tight black Helmut Lang suits (7 1/2 weight wool
$2200) with white Marc Jacobs cashmere v-necks
($1000) and brown suede Bruno Magli's (ugly-ass
shoes [guilty guilty guilty] $240); from a sort of easy
(and cheap) L.A. look with A&F black denim jeans
($65), Hilfiger primary red and blue sport shirts ($75,
dark, Middle Eastern men should not wear Hilfiger)
covered by a Maurice Malone leather bombers ($675)
and J.P. Tod loafers ($350) to ubiquitous bottle green
Armanis ($1600), jade Robert Talbot ties ($125) with
ankle high Santoni monk-straps ($475), and classic
navy Brooks Bros' suits ($2800) with yellow power
stripe Hermés ($90) and testoni wing-tips ($450);
from identical black cloaks covering four smallish figure (wives?) from head to the floor, to a garish, if still

stunning Lacroix teal chiffon dress ($5200) with what appeared to be a sea green ostrich feather pillbox hat (Thierry Mugler $300) with matching Manolos ($675, the highest heels he had ever seen [this ensemble graced the awe-inspiring tanned, buxom {2 @ $15,000}, at least six and a half feet {in heels} frame of a honey-blonde Aryan Amazon, escorted by a squat {almost square} dangerous looking older {45-55} dude in military garb straight from Midnight Express]), not to mention a number of requisite little black dresses (this year Karl Lagerfeld for Chanel $775), DKNY silk hose ($45 a pair) and either Manolo wannabee stilettos (Prada [$329] or Gucci [$499]), gold platforms (Candies $130), Sergio Rossi sandals ($199) or Justin cowboy boots ($475). There was tons of make-up: lipsticks like Chanel's Cherry Jubilee ($7.99), Estée Lauder's Amazing Greys ($12.99), MAC Lipglass ($9), Erno Lazslo Beaujolais ($10), Bobbi Brown LipShimmer Champagne ($17.50) and Dior Ultrashine (Sulky $45); Chanel, Vincent Longo, Lancôme, Guerlain, Shiseido, Alchemy, Erno Laszlo, Thomas Roth, Adrien Arpel, Kiehl New York, Ilcsi, La Prarie, Crème de la Mer and Clinique concealers, repairs, moisturizers and powders ($15.99-$499.99 oz.); Solution Skincare and Rejuvenation Botox treatments ($300-$7,000); Face Stockholm (Honey Peach $12.99), Tova (Coral Sands $30), Clinique (Winter Cinnamon $17), Nars (Copacabana $15), Chanel Vitalumière Satin ($82) and Prescriptive Vibrant ($30) foundations; Too Faced ($17.50), Max Factor 2000 ($7.49), she uemera ($9), Lâncome Aquacils ($14), Dior Diorshow ($48) and Bobbi Brown Professional ($20) mascaras; Hard Candy (Soul $7 compact), Lâncome (Midnight $17), Fekkai (Pearl $14), Shiseido (Petit Shadow $16), Stila (Rumba $10), Nars (Black Orchid $18) and Napoleon Perdis (Essential $40) eye shadows; and Givenchy (Orange Taffetas $7.99), Chinoiserie

(Twilight and Betty $16), Clarin (Rose Fuchsia $9.99) Essie (Strawberry Sorbet $13), Ink (Respect and Kashmir $20) and Urban Decay (Absinthe, Cult and Uzi $10) nail polish; and perfumes such as Valentino Being and Nothingness ($125 .4 oz), DKNY The Order of Things, ($75 3.4 oz), Phaedo by Davidoff ($100 2 oz), Genealogy of Morals by YSL ($260 1.7 oz), Critique of Practical Reason by Byblos ($790 2 oz), and Phenomenology of Spirit by Philosophi di Alberta Ferriti ($275 3 oz). There was lots of bling bling bling: everything from the most delicate nose hoops ($10) and earrings ($75-$12,250) to lavish Cleopatra carcanets ($16,500) and finger-thick necklaces ($7200); from anklets ($50-$1700) to watches ($125-$225,000), from bangles ($25-$1200) to hair pins ($100-$400), from pendants ($100-$10000) to pinkie rings ($125-$2000). There weren't that many rocks, but he did see one of at least 3 carats (Very Good, DIF), that if real (and it probably was), was worth at least $2 million. Actually, it was kind of cool: the nose rings and dark hair made him think of harem delights (a pierced nose might signify a pierced navel [or other, more sophisti- cated labrets] and he schwinged for belly rings), and he noticed that every woman there wore at least five or six pieces (how would a helmet buff feel with those long nails and thumb rings — my God, that would hurt so good) of jewelry. Maybe this wouldn't be such a bad gig after all (probably no one here [besides Bryan and Yashika] knew him or Wanda [Wanda who?]). But first, he had to find some food.

There was nothing in the main gallery, although he did notice that people were walking around with those clear plastic glasses (some with a clear liquid and ice [water or white wine?], some with red wine and some empty). Yashika and Bryan had already cornered one of the Armanis near a table he had overlooked near the entrance: he could ask the woman there to direct him to the refreshments, but didn't want to crowd the interview, nor did he want to appear hungry and greedy in front of B and Y (he remembered with some embarrassment his growling stomach in the car). Besides, he hated asking directions, and how difficult could it be to search a couple of rooms for a table full of food?

The gallery was in the shape of a large T, with the entrance at the bottom and two smaller rooms forming the cross at the top: these two smaller rooms often led to further galleries and exhibition spaces beyond. He walked slowly (he wasn't going to run to the groceries, no matter how hungry he was) through the middle of the large rectangle, looking both to his left and right, but without stopping or noticing the fabrics and paintings on either side (his view was often blocked by the backs and heads of those who were looking [when in a museum or gallery, he usually focused more on his fellow patrons than whatever was on the walls anyway]). He chuckled (to himself) when he saw one of the (completely) covered women (what'd she have on under that thing? a merry widow with garters? spandex chaps, a leather vest and pasties?) sporting a pair of lime green cat-eyes on the outside of her black veil: Cousin It (da da da dunt click click, da da da dunt click click)!

When he reached the intersection, he turned first to the right (more carpets and fabrics) and then to the left (calligraphy), but found no hint of anything resembling sustenance. Fuck, what kind of party was this? Well he wasn't going to retrace his steps, and so he needed to make a decision: red rugs or weird writing? He noticed Lacroix and the general (was that a Patek Philippe Pagoda [$40,000]?) looking at one of the rugs and the general looked like he'd know where the food was. There were more people to the right as well, so maybe he should follow the crowd. He didn't want to be here in the first place, and here he was, lost in space with a grub jones, wandering around like fucking Cheech Marin (was he the tall or the short one?). All right, to the left then, see what happens. Someone tapped on his shoulder. He turned.

"Do you need assistance?" He turned toward the thickish brit inflected accent, to long black (midnight shadow) hair, pretty green (IV Dynasty Jade) eyes through black Lisa Loeb (LenseCrafter $99) cat-eyes, white (eggshell mist) skin, a rather crooked (Madchen Amick [Twin Peaks was weird]) smile exposing small, sharp little teeth, overred lips (neon fire engine [Lancôme Juicy Tubes {Fraise} $23]) and a biggish beak (Mini Driver): not bad for a hostess or whatever.

"Uh, no, I'm looking for someone," the lie out of his mouth before he could think of a possible reason for it. The smile and the eyes dropped.

"Oh. I thought you seemed lost. I am sorry." She (nice ass, in black Guess? jeans [$39], faded black Jockey tee [$7] with a black leather vest [Serdar Leather $99], and black boots [Timberland Arctic $149] turned back (too easily discouraged to support the notion that she was some sort of guide [this was L.A. after all, and the service {servant} class, while consistently insouciant, was still highly developed in its strategies of pertinacity]) toward one of the walls on his left, and stood in front of a medium sized (6' x 9') black on (bone) white calligraphic picture. His hunger was making him hasty: at worst, she might help him find the buffet, and at best, she'd give him something to look at besides these unreadable weird letters and endless repetitive geometric designs (and at very best, allow him to extract some morsel [although exactly how big a morsel he as yet couldn't say] of revenge on Wanda for leaving him to his own devices). He knew better than to return her shoulder tap (his flirtations tended toward the Bauhaus rather than the baroque: he was no lout), so he ambled up (real nonchalant like) next to her and looked at the picture.

"This is interesting — I like the lines very much. Do you know what it says?" (smooth, very smooth). She turned to look at him, then back at the picture.

"Yes, of course I know what it says. This is mine."

He was aware of a tiny but definite keen of desire, like the ringing of a cell phone in an adjacent room. Still, while he was famished (for food) and nearly dizzy (perhaps that could partially explain his [possibly genuine] interest), it was important to be polite (Anything less would be uncivilized [Charles Barkley]), and so he had to think of a way to convince her to direct and/or accompany him as quickly as possible, but not too quickly, to bodily nourishment. But how? He was usually quite adept at thinking on his feet, but his head felt hollow and his tongue thick. "This is very nice, very interesting, very beautiful. Are all of these yours?" He motioned with his head and shoulders to the seven or eight similar (at first glance identical but with significant differences visible to [the least bit] attentive observation) rectangles hanging on the three surrounding walls.

"Yes. Can't you see that they are mine?"

He wasn't sure that he heard her correctly, but if they were all hers (if that's what she meant), it would be rude to leave before looking at each of them, and he'd probably faint right around the fourth or fifth scrawl. Maybe it was time to forget about this (but there was something intriguing about her) and excuse himself — but to where? He could tell her the truth, that he was starving and had to find food, but then he'd look like a mooch or some sort of art bum (especially dressed the way he was) who went to openings only to slurp and burp. She began to move over to the next picture.

"So what do they say?"

"Some are in English." She moved back. "That one is in Arabic. It is a sura from the Koran. It says, translated, 'Reclining therein, calling therein for many fruits and drink.'"

Thank you Allah. "Would you like to go get some fruits and drink, or a snack or something?" Somewhat abrupt (I hate people when they're not polite [Talking Heads]), but divinely inspired.

She turned and looked at him. "Now?"

He shrugged. "I'd love to look at your paintings, but I'm dying of thirst," he waved the fingertips of his right hand against his throat and stuck out his tongue, "I'm as dry as a camel." Christ, of all the stupid things to say.

She shook her head and laughed, imitating his gesture. She had a nice laugh, clear and honest, and he noticed her fingertips (unpainted, chipped nails) were smudged with (what he assumed was) ink. "What does it mean, dry as a camel?" She stuck her tongue out again.

He shook his head, smiled. "I don't know. I think I heard it as a kid."

"I do not know many camels, but they are not dry, they spit."

"I've never seen a camel up close."

"No? They are mean animals, they like to spit and bite." Enough with the fucking camels already. "If you hire a camel at the pyramids in Egypt you must be careful, because the drivers will take you away, and you will have to pay much to return." He stood there, mute, like a Darryl (This is my brother Darryl, and this is my other brother Darryl.) She looked at him (stunning green eyes [although her lenses were thicker than he first realized]), cocked her head to one side, then frowned, "What about your friend?"

"He's working. I'll catch up with him later."

That didn't seem to satisfy her (she was no fool), but what could he do? Still frowning she stepped back, and nodded to the picture on the wall. "These are not paintings, like you said: I do not use paint. I use ink, and sometimes I make the ink alone."

He had to say something. "I like it very much, 'Eat, drink, for Allah is good and great.'"

They stood there staring at the picture for a few minutes (an hour at least). "Ok, we will go," she stuck out her hand. "My name is Reham, and my family is from Al Quds, what some call Jerusalem, in Palestine."

"I'm Peter, and I'm from Bel Air. Near Los Angeles. In the United States."

The food and drink tables (paper tablecloths, napkins and plates, plastic utensils and glasses) were located just off of the textile gallery (the opposite cross of the T), near to where he had seen the Amazon and the General gawking at the rugs. The food (assorted Turkish [the exhibition was partially sponsored by the Turkish consulate] mezzes [Reham pointed out the names], included dolmas [stuffed grape leaves], sigorta [meat filled pastries shaped like cigarettes], borek [pastry with spinach], biber [assorted peppers], caçuk [pickled vegetables], helim [fried cheese], kuzu sis [lamb kabab], pida [pita bread], thick yogurt and lokum [Turkish Delight]), was plentiful and good (Peter especially enjoyed what he called a kuzu burrito, a pide stuffed with lamb, yogurt and peppers. He ate two [the first almost embarrassingly quickly {after he pounded a bottle of Evian (to support his thirst fib)}] while Reham nibbled on some pickled carrots, pide and yogurt, and spoke in another language [a language Peter didn't recognize {Arabic? Palestinian?}] to one of the women who was helping straighten the dishes and replenish the food [when the serving woman laughed Peter wondered briefly if she was laughing at him]).

When he had almost finished his second sandwich (he hadn't meant to eat two but he was very hungry), Reham smiled and asked, "Would you like to drink some raki?"

"Rotgut?"

"No, Rahhhhki."

"What is it?"

"Raki is liquor that tastes like anise. Black licorice. Would you like to drink some?"

"Sure." He watched carefully as she walked to the drinks table, took two clear plastic cups half full of clear liquid from the bartender and placed an ice cube from the styrofoam container into each of the drinks, returned to where he stood chewing the rest of his second sandwich, and handed him a glass. He noticed the ice was beginning to cloud the transparent liquor, like that French drink (that turned snot yellow) Wanda and her art friends liked. She smiled, and brought him his glass.

"I should give you some water: Raki is very forceful."

He liked the way she said that: he found her phrasing and accent (when he could understand it) exceedingly charming. The food made him feel much better, and he was becoming more than a little interested in this woman: he was no longer motivated solely (or even primarily) by revenge (on Wanda). She seemed strange, foreign, that was obvious, but at the same time, weirdly familiar, as if he had met her somewhere before. Perhaps he had (although he couldn't for the life of him remember where [he grephed quickly his memories of art openings and other similar events {including a grass-growing, phone book reading reception for the Japanese trade consulate} but no items were found]), but he hesitated to ask (Haven't we met somewhere before? would be too cliché [even for him]).

As he raised the plastic to his lips and tasted the fiery anise liquor, he noticed Bryan's spotlight precede him (camera glued to his face) into the lounge area. Where was Yashika? they were supposed to be working together: Yashika talking and Bryan taping. Christ, did he have to watch them every single minute? Fuck it — it wasn't his problem (although it was) if they couldn't follow directions. Maybe Yashika just went to the lady's or something.

"Do you like it?"

"What?"

"The raki. Do you like it?"

"It's ok. I think it will take some getting used to" (like drinking bong water, or having his foreskin pierced). Where the fuck was Yashika? He wiped his mouth with his napkin, took another drink of his rotgut (the second sip went down easier [doesn't it always]) and surveyed the room quickly. Although Bryan knew never to approach him while he was talking, Peter began to feel crowded and watched (and guilty [although it was perfectly natural and expected {part of his job} that he would be talking to people {including attractive women}, he still didn't want his conversation with Reham captured on videotape {like that lard-ass skeez dick-smoker, Monica Lewinsky}: although he couldn't conceive of any contingency

where Wanda would view the tape, nor could he imagine that anyone {Bryan, Hector, Karla, some faceless
client} who would see the tape could assume he was
doing anything other than working, and even if they
{Bryan, Hector, Karla, some faceless client} did, in the
furthest corner of unlikely possibility, suppose he was
genuinely flirting with this woman, he couldn't imagine them possibly caring {or informing Wanda}. Still,
he didn't want to be videotaped]). He began to raise
his hand to his face to block the camera but luckily
caught himself in time and merely scratched his forehead. What was wrong with him?

"Are you well? You look somewhat nervous. Is
the raki too forceful?"

He smiled. "No, I'm fine. I just saw someone I
thought I knew." He took another sip of his drink.

"The friend you are supposed to meet?"

"No, someone else." He suddenly wanted to
leave, at least this room, at least for a while (if he'd
known that this sand-eater art soirée would cause him
so much anxiety [and possibly get him into trouble]
he'd have stayed home [or gone to the Lakers] —but
then he wouldn't have met Reham [was that good or
bad?]). Maybe it was time to wander around, look at
the stuff on the walls (although to be honest, he had
yet to see anything resembling a camel or bearded
crazy firing a rocket launcher — in fact, he had yet to
see anything resembling anything else at all; just rugs,
tiles and that weird, elaborate chicken scratching). He
looked at Reham: she was very attractive (in an odd
[exotic, alien, foreign] sort of way), although the feeling they had met before wasn't as strong as it was earlier. He wanted to hang with her, although not in this
room. The food was restoring his strength (he was no
longer lightheaded), and the drink was cutting
through his paranoia just enough to where he could

act. "Let's go and look at your work."

"Sure. Have you finished eating?"

"Yeah."

"What about your friend?"

Jesus, let it go. "It's okay, I'll catch up with him later." He quickly (unsuccessfully) scanned the room for Yashika (where was she?), and then nodded slightly to Bryan as they left the room.

On their way to Reham's calligraphy, they stopped in front of a huge (26' x 32') bokhara (Salor, with symmetrical blue and magenta silk güls [medallions] and a madder red background): Reham's shoulder briefly and lightly brushed Peter's arm.

"I have one just like this, only smaller."

Reham frowned slightly. "Have you been to Turkey?"

"No, but my mother and father have. Had."

"These rugs cost very much money. Especially if they are old."

He couldn't help himself. "How much?"

She shrugged her shoulders (she almost shrugged her face, if that were possible). She stepped forward and took the carpet between her thumb and finger. "This one is not old, but very big. I do not have a price paper with me, but maybe, I am guessing, maybe two hundred, maybe two hundred and twenty five thousand dollars."

He almost whistled. That was some serious change. He'd have to take his out of the closet, get it appraised (not to sell it [he didn't need the cash, and besides, there was the {the possibility of the} house] but to see what it was worth. He didn't think his parents ever carried enough of a wad for an A-list magic carpet — still, you could never tell). He backed away from the wall and positioned himself to see how Reham's black hair, white skin and green eyes (spectacles removed) might look against the deep reds and blues of his rug (laid out in his room). She was lovely: he wanted her (me so horny, me love you long time), although how badly and how he would act on this desire remained unclear. This was a strange situation for Peter: while he was accustomed to (even adept at) sexual flirtation, such sport (while he was involved with Wanda) until now had been confined to the theoretical, and therefore harmless, variety. He had bought and been bought drinks, received (never given) phone numbers (never called), and had once or twice even participated in (farewell) spit swapping and face munching— but he had never been so genuinely interested in hooking up with another woman as he was in hooking up with Reham. It was almost as if his desire for Reham and his fealty to Wanda were engaged in some sort of struggle (some weird oleo wrestling match [a nice image]) in which he was merely an innocent spectator or witness, or prize for the winner (like that Star Trek where Spock had to fight Kirk in order to mate with this Vulcan hoochie). Still, he had no definite plan: she would look fine on his carpet, that was for sure, but he didn't know what kind of attempt he would make (or risks he would take) to try to arrange that scenario. He finished off his drink and rolled a half-melted ice-cube in his cheek.

"Let's look at your work now."

"Yes. It is over here."

She turned abruptly away from the carpet and walked quickly out of the textile exhibit, past the intersection to the corner walls displaying her ink and paper drawings. Her pace surprised Peter, and it wasn't until they had almost reached her work that he caught up. He stationed himself (arbitrarily) in front of the third one from the intersection on the longer wall (there were eight altogether: three on the longer wall and five on the shorter), and stared intently at what looked like a bunch of squiggles, doodles, commas and loops, all jumbled together, and rubbed his chin with his right hand. This was writing? Who the hell could read this?

"This is fascinating. How long does it take you to . . . create one of these?"

She made that gesture with her face and shoulders (palms turned skyward at sides, shoulder hunched up and forward, chin and lip stuck up and out, brows furrowed) again. "It depends. Sometimes it requires a day, sometimes a week. I'm glad you like this one: it required a very long time, almost a single year. It is my favorite."

It took an entire year to do this huh? No wonder you people are still living in tents, squatting in the sand (he suddenly thought that perhaps she was too foreign, too exotic: his sexual interest became slightly weakened, contaminated, tainted [it was almost as if she had just loudly farted]. Kirk had won). Maybe he should just chill, let the conversation die, then excuse himself and try to locate Yashika: he was supposed to be working after all. "Yes, I like it very much. What does it say?"

"It says 'And round them shall go boys of theirs as if they were hidden pearls.'"

So someone was a friend of Dorothy, huh? "Show me with your finger."

They both stepped closer to the picture. She began to trace in the air with her index finger. "This part says 'around them,' 'boys,' and 'hidden pearls.'"

"What do these things mean?"

"These make these into verbs —'shall go,' and 'were.' And this is 'like,' or 'as if.' You have to read from right to left, backwards from English." She continued her tracing, but Peter was having a difficult time correlating her finger movements to the black lines and various hamza and vowel points on the paper. Not that it mattered. She let her hand fall to her side and looked at him. "Do you truly like it? Or are you acting kind?"

"No, I do really like it."

"Would you like to see a pricing paper?"

" A price list. Sure."

"I will return." She gave him a nice smile and walked back toward the larger gallery. His heart beat faster: was he being set-up (how absolutely charming — Spock had risen to his feet and the battle was still on!)? Ah commerce! He loved art: it was the making and marketing of totally useless (in the long run) commodities. Pure buying and selling, pure market capitalism: this was something he could understand and admire (maybe Reham wasn't so foreign after all). It was bullshit about artists being less interested in money than anybody else, as all of the artists he knew (through Wanda) were the greediest, most self-serving, materialistic money-hungry pigs imaginable (with most of them it was the only thing he could tolerate about them). Different drummer my ass, they just didn't want to have to work at real jobs. At least they could be honest about it, like the traders or film people he knew (who made no bones at all about digging the do re mi [It's all about the Benjamins, baaaby]), and not mask their greed behind some bohemian outlaw refuse to conform d'ya like my tattoo I'm better than you are crap: everybody was looking to sell out, it was just a matter of finding a buyer. He was interested to see how Reham would play this, if she would be honest or not. Who knows, maybe he'd even buy something (Kay might go for one of these ornate scribbles, although he wasn't sure how it would fit her decor. Wanda might appreciate a drawing, but she wouldn't appreciate where it came from [that would probably be a bit sleazy]): one exchange (cash for art) possibly

leading to others (more intimate)—although everything depended on how much the damn things cost.

Reham returned, took his empty cup, handed
him the price list, and then, instead of strategically
retreating to a discreet distance (like those salesgirls
from Barney's, who always assumed the perfect separa-
tion [within earshot without looming]), she moved
closer, to his side, as if to read over his shoulder.
$5500, $8000, $4200, $9000, $4500, $3000, $2300,
slightly lower (cut-rate) than he expected (somewhat
disappointing): he could feel her breath on his cheek,
and he caught a faint whiff of her hair, a combination
of oranges, cheap shampoo (Suave) and cigarette
smoke. The skin on his shoulder and arm seemed to
expand, to try to reach out for her, to touch her — was
he being worked? If so, her working was working,
Spock was winning and Wanda's memory fading: he
hadn't felt like such a slut in a long time. He looked at
her — would $2000 (he would never pay $2400 [on
principle]) be worth the possibility (Peter wasn't crude
enough to think he was actually buying the girl) that
he might, as the song said, "make her sweat till she
couldn't sweat no more?" He wondered how she
would sound, with that accent of hers, and if she would
call out, Oh Allah, Oh Allah, instead of Oh God, Oh God.
He wondered what the word for fucking was in her language, and if she would talk dirty to him. He wondered
what kind of underwear she wore, what her tits (especially her nipples) looked like, and what kind of weird
positions she knew and would teach him (he was thinking of some vague combination of that Kama Sutra film
and a porn video he had rented (with Wanda) based on
the Arabian Nights, replete with belly dancing, harem
pants and an eunuch who really wasn't a eunuch [he
was a she with a buff boy body and an extremely solic-
itous and skillful {from all that watching} tongue]). A

couple grand might be worth trying to find out (plus he'd get this drawing, a souvenir, as it were, of his own arabian night). He looked back at the price list, then at the picture on the wall. Screw it, why not? "I'll give you two thousand for it, right now."

She smiled, then bit her lip. She looked at the picture, then at him. Then she smiled at him again. "For you, I will take two thousand dollars."

This was too easy. He took his checkbook out of his jacket packet. "Will you take a check?"

"Yes. I will deliver this to you after the exhibit closes, at the end of next week. Your check will clear by then." She began to write out his receipt. He tore his check out and handed it to her. She took it, looked at it and frowned. "You say your parents were in Turkey. When was that?"

"My father was there quite a bit between 1975 and 1982. He and my mother died in 1982."

"I am very sorry. How did they die?" Her frown deepened.

What do you care? "They were killed in a plane crash in Turkey."

"I am sorry to have to ask you this, but where did their plane crash?'

"Their plane crashed outside of Ankara in June of 1984."

Her frown deepened further and she bit her lip. What the fuck was going on here? How could the death of his parents possibly upset this total stranger? Maybe she witnessed it or something, but she said she was from Palestine, not Turkey. "Why are you asking? Do you know something about this?"

She quickly looked up at him. "No, of course not. I have to go now. I will deliver your picture to the address on the check. Next Friday." She walked past him toward the intersection, then turned left and was gone.

So that was it, the sale was over, and adios Abdul. Somewhat cruder than he was used to: bedouin closing techniques obviously weren't as refined as they were here in the big city. Dumb bitch (his desire completely snuffed by her nosy questions [what was that about?] and abrupt [and mysterious] departure [what made him think they had met before?]): he could always cancel the check (he only bought the fucking thing to help him get in her pants). He looked at the picture he had just purchased — it was actually kind of cool, with all the dots and squiggles and shit. It was not, however, twenty Frankies cool (he certainly didn't want the fucking thing around [either in his own, Kay's or Wanda's space {maybe Pavo would like it}] to constantly remind him of the crazy cunt). He would cancel the check tomorrow (he'd be two grand richer [plus the satisfaction of dicking her over] and she'd get an important lesson she could fly back on her carpet to Baghdad with — Do not fuck with Peter the Great). Okay, that was over, no blood no foul: he wasn't going to bug about it all night. Anyway, he needed to get back to work. Where was Yashika?

CHAPTER THREE

"She was whack, man, crazy. She started out acting like that chick in Clueless, all warm and moist and ready to get stinky, but ten minutes later, man, she was frozen solid, preserved in frost, like that ho who dances with the baby, Ally McBeal. God I hate that bitch." A heavy, Germanic melody (Wagner or Beethoven, probably Wagner) could be heard coming from the next room (Hector was in the house). Were they talking about Reham? Did Bryan somehow spill the beans or show them the tape? What the fuck was going on? "Who are you talking about?"

"Which Clueless, the tv show or the movie?"

"The tv show. If I was talking Alicia Silverstone, I would have said so. Man, it was like the Titanic out there, just cruising along and then pow, right into an ice cube." Lapp (faded grey Osh Kosh baggies cut off just below the knee [$50], an old white Howard Stern Private Parts tee shirt [swag from Random House {Peter gave his to Wanda's half-brother}], black Sears socks [$5], black high top Chucks [$25], two large silver hoop earrings in left ear [$50 each], Swatch with the original Joker face [$125], twelve assorted silver bangles on his right wrist [$10 - $300] and a Canon Powershot 350 Digital Camera [$550] with hard case [$49.99] around his neck) guffawed and high-fived Tino (blue Yankees cap [$15], unbuttoned red [cayenne] plaid Eddie Bauer light flannel overshirt with sleeves removed [ripped off, $45], olive green JC Penney wifebeater [$12.99 for 3], too-long purple Pauline's [$64.95], black and white checked high top Vans [$75], three small gold hoops in right ear [$30 per], a snake tattoo crawling up his belly from his crotch [$275 House of Pain], a greyhound on his right shoulder [on the house from House of Pain], an 18k gold Gucci watch [$7000], and a Sony MZ-F40 minidisc player [$300 {headphones (minis) wrapped around the back of his neck}] on his Gap black web belt [$12]).

"How many times you see that flick?"

"I ain't seen it once, man. I know the story, I ain't stupid."

"Who are you talking about?"

"Hey Pete" (he hated being called 'Pete'), "sup? We're rapping about Tino's love life, or lack thereof."

"Hey, I ain't no Rico Suave. I get my share."

Lapp and Tino laughed, and Peter (skinny black jeans from Sandy Dalal [$250], peacock blue Calvin Klein silk short sleeve [$350], black leather belt from Coach [Grandma present], sky blue silk boxers from Charvet [$126] and tan Teva Sidewalks [$75], plus a squirt of Gucci The Postmodern Condition for Men [eau de toilette, $52 3.4 oz]) chuckled to himself (at least they weren't talking about his own sinking last night). He took a sip of his (now lukecool) Starbucks venti cappuccino ($3.89), put his sunglasses in their case, and placed hard copies of his acid jazz and Islam art reports, along with his Mont Blanc Gold and Silver Meisterstruck Solitaire ($700) and black lizard Glaser Designs memo book ($350) on the conference table in front of him. He had left his PocketNet in the Saab's glove compartment. "Rico Suave?" Lapp made that hourglass motion with his hands, "where the fuck didja get Rrrrico Suaaaaave?"

"I heard him on the radio as I was driving over."

"I hear he's still pretty hot in your hood, amigo."

"Hey, fuck you ese. At least we ain't still creaming on Dee-Lite or the Go -Gos."

"Who's still creaming on Dee-Lite or the Go-

Go's?" asked Karla (Nike Tailwind Clima FIT Jacket [Chlorine Blue and White $124.99] over Alpine Blue Nike Swoosh Sport Top [$43.99] and matching Sport Short [{great fucking legs} $27.99] with white Peds [$3.99] and white and silver Nike Air Max Astound Lo [$109.99]), walking in (Peter usually hated active wear, but anything that showed off those getaway sticks was hard to dislike: he felt little Pete harden as he sat there [my God]). She set some manila folders, a video tape (last night's?), her PDA (Everex Freestyle Executive II, $475), cell phone (Nokia 6160 Dual Band $199), cassette recorder (Sony TCM-80V, $179, all official meetings were recorded [some even videoed]) and (personal) microcassette (Panasonic RN-502, $59.99) on the table and sat down.

"Lapp, over there, loves em."

"Hey, Belinda Carlisle's still phat. I saw her on RuPaul the other night."

"She was always fat. We like to eat we like to eat we like to eat, yeah, we like to eat. The woman moves like a truck."

"What's her Q, anybody know?"

Tino guffawed and Lapp grumbled. "Aw c'mon, they crashed like ten years ago; her Q must be one flat line."

"If she was on RuPaul, she must have something. Peter, will you holler out to Yashika to look up Belinda Carlisle's Q rating for me?" (Karla didn't like [to put it mildly] Yashika [friend of Hector's brother {whom she also couldn't stand}], and in order to avoid being a Total Obvious Bitch [TOB] about it, refrained from speaking to her directly).

Peter couldn't stand immediately (little Pete chunky style), but he also wasn't going to sit there and bellow through the plate-glass (even though Yashika owed him big time for covering her ass after she left the art opening early [with some cocktail length abalone sequined Gaultier {so ten-minutes-ago ($4500)} with cool Ann Klein lizard sling backs {$450}, and a shaved head handle-bar mustached Odd-Job {a size-queen if there ever was one} wearing what looked like a bluish black Caraceni {Wanda's stepfather's suit of choice ($6000 [Peter recognized the weird, almost oblong buttons])} and dark brown Edward Green tie-shoes {$500}]), which created a bit of a dilemma (didn't he see this on Spin City or something?): he couldn't be absolutely sure his jeans would mask evidence of the effect Karla's outfit (and Wanda's absence) was having on his system (who was the size queen now?), so he chose to err on the side of caution and stall. He needed to say something, anything: he could feel Karla's expectant stare boring into him (which didn't help [neither did his silk Charvets {a lightening flash of Reham writhing (with pleasure?) on his carpet}]) — this might take awhile. "I'm sorry, whom did you want me to ask her about?" Weak.

"Hello. Who were we talking about? Belinda Carlisle, ex of the Go-Go's. Please ask Yashika to find her Q. Sometime within the next hour, if possible."

"Let Lapp go, he's the one who brought her up." Better.

"Hey, Tino brought her up. And you're closer to the door, dude."

"For Chrissakes!"

"I'll ask her." Tino got up and walked out of the office. Peter looked down at his acid jazz report and pretended to read. He could hear Yashika in the next room, "Who?" and "How do you spell that?" and could feel Karla's stare on the side of his face. His (mild) anger toward Karla (her fault) inflamed little Pete even more, and he strained against the silk and denim (although both his anger and his lust were only partially directed at [his boss in] the Nike outfit sitting across from him).

"What are you on the rag for?" Karla's voice was not unfriendly.

Peter looked up at her. "Nothing." A few seconds passed, then "Sorry."

Tino returned. "Yashika says the system's down and she can't get through. She'll keep trying and let us know when she can."

"Whose system, theirs or ours?"

"I dunno. Theirs."

"Are you sure?"

"No, I'm not sure."

"Find out."

"Hey Yashika, who crashed, them or us?"

"They did. We're fine."

"They did, we're. . . "

"I heard. What the fuck do we pay them for? Sit down, and let's get started. Hector will be late, Susan is still in San Fran, and Bryan's screwing around with his equipment, so it'll be just us four for a while. Everyone ready? Ok," she pushed the Sony to the middle of the table and turned it on, "the first priority is getting the caliente y frio list together. That's why I wanted to check on Belinda Carlisle, maybe there's some action there. Well, anyone have any ideas? Who or what is caliente this week?"

"Smoking. I think smoking's in."

"Smoking what, reef?"

"No bro', cancer sticks, cigs, coughin nails. Bacco is bomb."

"Ciggies. Unfiltered. That heavy stuff too man, Camels and Marlboros and shit. You hang out near high school man, everyone's puffin up, like a goddam factory. Edgers were doing it months ago, but now its spread to influencers, big time. Even conformers are there, lighting up. We could do something with that."

"What about pipes?"

"A few edgers, but no, no pipes. Cigarettes."

"Good. Anybody else think smoking's back in? Peter, what do you think?"

Little Pete had gone back to sleep. "I think Tino's right, people seem to be lighting up more and more, probably because it's illegal in most places. I heard some high school in Ventura is trying to get Camel to buy them some band equipment or something. They want to become the official Camel High School, like those Coke and Pepsi arrangements. I saw it on CNN, but I don't remember what high school or anything. They want cigarette vending machines in the cafeteria."

"Anybody have any objections? Lapp?" Lapp shook his head. "Okay, I'll put it down, smoking esta caliente. Ok, if cigarettes are caliente, what's frio?"

"Cigars."

"Where the fuck you been, Nebraska? Cigars have been dead for years."

"Okay, Kurt-fucking-know-it-all-Loder, if cigarettes are in, then what's out?"

"I dunno."

"What about reefer?"

"Na, reefer's never out. Everyone loves la mota."

"What about sex? If smoking is in, then sex could be out."

"You trying to tell us something 'bout you and Hector?"

"No, apretado, I'm just trying to find a comparable activity to smoking cigarettes."

"Sex is always out with Tino."

"Just cuz I don't talk to Rosie Palm every night, pajero," Tino made an up and down motion with his hand.

"You oil your shorts more than I do, Pancho."

Tino laughed. "Pancho? Where the fuck didja get that? Pancho. No way ese. I am Chico, of Chico and the Man."

"Chico and the man? What's that?"

"Before your time, bro. Freddie Prinz, the original spic comic."

"What do you mean, before my time? We're the same fucking age."

"I liked that song: bum, bum bum bum, bum bum bum bum bum bum bum bum bum bum" (theme from Barney Miller).

"That ain't it. That's Barney Miller."

"No. You sure?"

"Yeah, that's Barney Miller. Right Lapp?"

"I don't know."

"Karla, that bum, bum bum bum, bum bum bum, that's Barney Miller, right?"

"I don't know, we never got the gringo channels. I was always watching mi madre's and my telenovelas, like Los Ricos y el Hermoso. We did watch Dallas, though. Why don't you go ask Bryan, he knows all that shit."

"Is Freddie Prince the guy who says 'dy-no-mite?'"

"No, man, you're thinking of Jimmy Walker on Good Times. All us darkies look alike to you cholos? And his name was Prinzzz, not Prinssss, ese: he ain't the artist formerly known as."

"Hey, wasn't there a Freddie Prinz in Wing Commander?"

"That was his dad."

"Whose dad? This dude was young."

"Fool, the Freddie I'm talking was the dad of the Wing Commander dude."

"Ain't we lucky we got 'em, Good Times," Peter sang to himself.

"How do you know all this shit? We didn't grow up with this stuff."

"Doesn't your trailerpark have cable? Mi hermana and I watch it all the time: we pop open a couple of forties, fire up la morisqueta and tune in Nick at Night. You should try it some night ese. C'mon over, and I'll school your ass."

"I'd rather go out. Feed the beast."

"Yeah right. Your beast is starving."

"Quit the swordfighting and let's get back to the list. If cigarettes are in, then what's out?"

"What's the opposite of smoking cigarettes?"

"Taking care of yourself. Running, buffing up, working out."

"Everyone works out, man. They smoke while they're pumping, or after their run."

"Hemorrhoids!"

"You mean steroids."

"Yeah, steroids. If smoking cigarettes is in, then steroids could be out."

"That's not bad. Anybody have any idea about steroid consumption in the city?"

"Boring. Boring. Let's just say it: steroids is out."

"No, we need to find out for true. You never know, bacco and roids could be new cocktail, right after you lift. Smoking cigarettes is muy caliente, but we need to find out more about this steroid business. Tino, what are you working on now?"

"Nothing. I just finished that piece on spats Hector gave me, so I ain't doing nothing now."

"Ok. I'll have to run it by Hector, but you should think about doing something on steroids and smoking. You and Yashika can check out Peter's high school lead." Karla brought her Panasonic to her mouth, "Memo to self, ask Hector about assigning Tino to steroid and smoking report. What else? Hot or cold, in or out, doesn't matter."

"X-Files."

"Hot or cold."

"Cold, stone cold."

"I dunno, they still seem to be going strong. High Q's last week, and the flick still has strong b.o.. Besides, you know how tight Hector is with the Fox suits, and how much they throw our way. Unless you got something concrete, I can't see killing it yet."

"The plots are boring and hard to understand. It's like Star Trek re-runs."

"The smoking man is bomb."

"Yeah, smoking is bomb, the smoking man is bomb, the X-files is da bomb. Let's make it caliente."

"No, Peter does have a point: it's not fresh, so it can't be caliente, but everyone likes it, so it can't be frio. Let's forget it and go on to something else."

Peter shrugged his shoulders; he wasn't going to argue. He wished he hadn't left his Pocketnet in the Saab, although he couldn't really phone up anybody in the middle of a meeting. Maybe he could go to the bathroom. He took another sip of his (now cold) cino. The background music faded out. Peter stared at the Sony TCM-8oV on the middle of the table. The over-ture from Der Rosenkavalier started abruptly.

"Everyone's wearing eyeglasses, even if they don't need them. I saw one of the Baldwins the other day at Mimi's, don't ask me which one, and he had on these thick geeky oval wirerims: he looked like Mr. Magoo."

"Poetry is out again. There was a slam at The Whisky last week, five people showed up. I hear Bertelsmann cancelled Kiefer Sutherland's three volume complete works, man, not enough prepub noise. Dead again, man, dead again."

"Blood drinking's muy frio, ever since that 60 Minutes story. I heard some mokes been setting their pubic hair on fire, but I ain't seen it yet. I could check it out if you want."

"I heard Beavis and Butthead getting back together. Huh huh huh huh huh, huh huh huh huh."

"What about Casper?"

"Yeah, Casper is way hot, ese. You've heard of the friendly ghost, right?"

"Who's the friendly ghost?"

"Which Casper?"

"I didn't know there were two."

"Yeah, one with a 'C,' and one with a 'K.' The one with the 'K' plays sort of deep house jungle techno loungish instrumentals, while the one with the 'C' does R & B be-bop acid pop, with a lot of vocals. The one with the 'K' might know something about barbequing, as I think that pubic hair burning thing is called. Wanda's tight with one of them, I'll ask her about it when she gets back."

"When is she getting back?"

"Next week sometime."

"Which Kaspar you mean?"

"I dunno about no house, instrumental techno bullshit. The Casper I'm talking about does that song 'I just wanna be inside you all night long, I won't do you no wrong, please listen to my song, I just wanna be inside you all night long'" (All Night Long, from the CD The Ghost with the Most [Geffen, 1997], Caspermusic ASCAP). "Everyone listening to that tune where I live."

"That's Casper with a 'C.'"

"Anyone else hear Casper?"

"Yeah, I've heard them."

"Me too."

"Memo to self: have Tino check Caspar's Q and Billboard Accutrac for sales. Call our usual contacts. Tino, I need this by four, get Yashika to help you if you need to. Okay, if they're hot, then who's not?"

"How 'bout Madonna?"

"Cuz we living in a material world." Peter liked Madonna, had even met her at one of Wanda's stepfather's Sony receptions. She had been wearing a white silk dress from Valentino ($4335), cheap John Bartlett sandals ($175), and huge Harry Winston diamond earrings ($400,000). Peter was charmed to see that the Valentino didn't fit her that well. He continued to sing to himself.

"No, we don't touch Madonna. She's always both, caliente and frio, always both at the same time. Every time we've put her on the list, something happens that makes her the opposite of what we've said: she's impossible. Who else?"

"Hey, you know what I been hearing? that macarena song, Hey Macarena. Remember five or so years ago, that song was everywhere, man; you couldn't do nothing without hearing that tune. Somebody made a remake or a remix of it or something, and I swear to God, it's coming back."

"But what's out? We need something that's out."

"Can't we just check Accutrac, see who's falling?"

"Any asshole can do that. We, you and I, all of us, are in business because we can gather, package and market something special, something unique, something rare: inside info. If our clients could get this information by simply looking it up for themselves, we'd have nothing to sell, and so we'd be out of business, which would mean no more toys like that digital camera. You're not stupid, you know this. You also know that every Friday we do next Monday's hot and cold list, so you know that you need to come up with things we can put on the list. So I'm going to ask again: what's the word at the mall, what's the edge not wearing, not doing, not saying, not watching, not listening to, not eating any more? Fuck, I'd even settle for an influencer trend. What the fuck is going on, what the fuck is going out?"

"Who's that band that does that Nike ad?"

"Which one?"

"The one with Jerry Springer."

"Bone, Thugs 'N Harmony?"

"Na, they're with Arsenio Hall for Intel."

"Bone, Thugs-N-Harmony. Yeah, they whack."

"Nike's been whack for awhile."

"Yeah, but Bone and them usta be hot. Remember Breakdown? They were phat."

"You just like Mariah Carey and her two friends."

"What about Mind of a Souljah?"

"Nike sucked ever since they changed slogans. Just do it, that was da bomb."

"Yes I can, that blows."

"I got skiiiillls. That was cool. Was that Nike?"

"I don't remember. That's way better than I got game."

"I like I got game. I got game, you got game, he got game, we got game" (Public Enemy, from the Spike Lee joint I Got Game, 1998).

"No Whiners,'I like that one."

"Who's that, Timberland?"

"American Express?"

"No, it's some beer. Black Dog, or something."

"I dig those Absolut ads. Absolut Paris, Absolut Plunkett, Absolut Sherman, Absolut Au Kurant, with that purple garter snap — that was great."

"Who's Sherman?"

"That's not really a slogan, is it? It's more a pictoral thing."

"How much do they get for those ads?"

"I know whose leg that was."

"I love garters."

"All men love garters."

"Si, all men love garters. Los garters esta muy caliente."

"How do you know whose leg that was?"

"Remember two or three years ago, when we did that special report on parts models? I followed this woman, Greta Brooks, around New York for a couple of weeks, and she did this shoot in some guy's studio, close-ups of her thigh. So, next time you chilitos shoot mecos all over your left hands, at least you know she has a name, Greta Brooks. Nice face, but she's only got one breast."

"Only one hoot, huh?"

"Yeah, she's proud of it too. Wears tight sweaters shirts all the time, with no fake boob or anything like that."

"Parts model, what a gig."

"Parts is parts. Who was that?"

"I dunno, some car repair store or something, like Goodyear or Goodrich. . ."

"Mr. Goodwrench!"

"No, not Mr. Goodwrench. It was a chicken restaurant."

"Remember that song, Who wears short shorts? We wear short shorts?"

"Short shorts are back in, man, Daisy Dukes. Saw a couple of influencers, white chicks, on Rodeo, both with legs up to their earlobes, one with neon pink velvet hot pants, I swear, and the other with these micro denim crotch huggers so tight you could see the yeast growing, topped off with big white plastic buttons, thought I was living some Austin Powers flashback. Serious booty call, tastefully done." He looked at Karla. Those Lisas had some serious back: it was straining that cloth.

"Can't you think of anything but dipping junior?"

"What else is there? Tell me you think different."

"Think different. That sucks."

"Yeah, big-time. Be like Mike, that sucks, or sucked. Haven't seen it in awhile."

"That motherfucker had some game. He used to kill the Lakes."

"He used to kill everyone, Knicks, Cavs, Jazz, Sonics. Isn't Magic doing Amex now?"

"Yeah, for that Pozzie-with-coin niche market. He's doing shit for Coors too. Wonder what his Q is."

"Coors sucks. I hate that piss-water."

"KROQ sucks, listen to us anyway."

"Gigabyte me."

"Short shorts, they're caliente."

"I agree."

"Yeah, put it down."

The Strauss had stopped a while ago, and heads turned as Hector's door opened, and a youngish, heavy east-coast styling black man (brown light wool suit [Richard James $1300], buttoned up Egyptian cotton Oxford [Ike Behard $150], dark wine tie with small ivory polka dots [Venanzi $90], English suspenders [Hackett and Company $125], brown Gucci loafers [$399], a gold Rolex President with Onyx dial [$17,500] and a soft bankers green leather brief case [Asprey, $2000], along with a whiff of YSL How to do Things with Words [$55 2.5 oz]) followed Hector (bone white linen jacket [Oscar de la Renta $300], slightly lighter [snow?] white linen pants [Perry Ellis $145], tan or dust silk and linen short sleeve shirt [Barneys $165], Tag Heur Kirium [$1000] and huaraches [Kenneth Cole $110]) into the room. The black guy was definitely not from around here.

"Listen up, everyone. Karla, turn the recorder off, please. Where's Bryan?"

"Where else? With his gear."

"Ask him to come in here please. And Yashika as well." Once again, Tino bounded up and went to fetch Bryan and Yashi (did Tino have wood for Yashika? [not always smart to poke the boss's niece]). Everyone surreptitiously (or not so surreptitiously) checked out the new guy while they waited. Peter disliked him almost instantly. He was hard to place — too uptight for California (a fucking half-Windsored Venanzi??!!), yet too relaxed for New York (suspenders went out with Gordon Gekko [Tell me something I don't already know, Bud Foxx], and what was with that [very, very cool] green brief case?)— maybe from Asswipe Texas or something, Atlanta, who knows? And what the fuck was he doing here; they weren't going to hire him, were they? He was an arrogant looking son of a bitch, that was for sure, but so was (almost) everyone in LA. Bryan (black Levis cut off at the knee [$30], multi-colored Grateful Dead tee [$6], Teva Desertrunner sandals [same as Peter's $75], Timex 1996 Olympic watch with plastic band [$60]) came in, looking dazed as usual (too many carbon life forms here, eh Bry?), followed quickly by Yashika (black and white cotton and silk mini with artificial zebra stripes [possibly worn to piss off Bryan {Anna Sui $150 used}], unbuttoned faded black long sleeve light cotton sweater [Susan Lazar $100, used] over an oversized black Old Navy [Gap] pocket tee [$12], medium heeled Isaac Mizrahi black velvet pumps [$150], agnes b. Shimmer Plum eyeliner with Cilissime Super Thickening mascara [$12 each], Revlon LavenDare lipstick [$8], and a spray of Fendi Phenomenology of Perception [Eau de Parfum, $175 per 4 oz]) and Tino. Yashika sat next to Peter, Bryan next to her and Tino returned to his position near Lapp. The Fendi smelled nice.

Peter's vagarious antagonism toward the man with no name (High Plains Drifter), interrupted by his coworker's entrance, soon returned. What was it about him that rubbed Peter the wrong way? Was it his dark, almost bluish purple (Midnight Plum) skin color (Peter had a couple of friends of color, Suarez, for example, and he had dated [and enjoyed {experienced} rather unremarkable sex {a few quick dorm room missionary explorations with Saturday Night Live in the background} with] an African-American princess [Janel] from Santa Cruz for a couple of months in college)? Or was it his shaved, oversize head? Or his sleepy, almost Asian looking almond eyes? Or maybe it was his posture, slouching, aggressively relaxed, arrogant, liked he owned the place, or at least knew something no one else did. Or even the deep green butter soft (you could tell from here) leather briefcase. Whatever.

"Okay, is everyone here? Who's missing?"

"Susan's in San Francisco."

"Right, Susan's in San Francisco. Okay, everyone, listen up, I want you to meet Mr. Jonathan Trojan" (Jon Trojan? Reality bites, Hector, he's x-laxing you. What's his wife's name, Ortho Gel?). "Mr. Trojan has his Masters in Business Marketing and Research from the London School of Economics, and is new to the Los Angeles office of Anderson Consulting. I'm bringing him in here to help us become more robust, and to work closely with us on a few projects."

"What projects?"

"That's what this meeting's about. Mr. Trojan . . ."

"Call me Jonathan, please." Ah, the sweet baritone of a British public school accent, emanating from a man named after a (perhaps faulty, hence his existence) scumbag. So he came from the old world, no wonder Peter couldn't place him. He'd have to tell Kay about this, although she'd probably want to have him to dinner, or at least cocktails, and British racing (not banker) green Asprey or no green Asprey, he was still a bloody wanker, what?

"Yes, Jonathan. Jonathan here will be working both sides of the street, as it were. We hope to use him as a sort of . . . "

The front door buzzer rang loudly. Yashika jumped up immediately, "I'll get it." It rang again.

"Who could that be?"

"UPS, Fed EX and snail mail all came this morning. Maybe it's special d."

"UPS, Fed EX and US mail already came. You expecting anything, Bryan?"

"Just those Harry Connick proofs. But they won't be here til Friday."

"Your Harry Connick proofs aren't due until Friday. Anyway, as I was saying, Mr. Trojan, er Jonathan, will be working . . . " the intercom interrupted, "Jesu Christo, what now? Yes?"

"Package for Peter."

"For me?" He wasn't expecting anything, and he never received anything at the office. He half-rose out of his chair, then remembered protocol (Hector could get extremely pissy if he felt his authority was being questioned), and looked up to meet Hector's eyes.

"Go ahead, but please hurry."

He hurried through the office, excited and a bit frightened (had something happened to Kay? or Wanda? Maybe a gift from Wanda?), but stopped when he saw Yashika supporting a large flat rectangle covered in brown wrapping paper. What the fuck could it be? He desperately hoped it wasn't the picture from the Arab: he had stopped the check and wanted to forget the entire scene. He hurried over.

"There was no delivery person or anything, it was just propped up against the door."

"Did you see anyone?"

"No." Keeping an edge on the floor, she leaned the top of the package over to him. He saw his home address in elaborately scripted in black magic marker, with the office address, in a much simpler handwriting (Pavo?), scratched underneath: there was no return address. "I should get back."

"Thanks. Tell them I'll be a few minutes." He picked it up, carried it over and set it on the nearest desk (Susan's), where he sat, facing the front door, his back to the window of the meeting room. It must have been Pavo who sent it over, because Louisa (Kay's housekeeper/secretary [$48,000 a year]) would have just signed for it and put it in his room. It was definitely the picture (or drawing or whatever). He could feel Hector and his coworkers looking at him through the glass, and so he hesitated. He didn't want to open the package in front of everyone. The (small) possibility that it could be something other than that scribbling briefly entered his head, but no, it was the perfect size and shape: it could be nothing else. He stared at for a few moments, trying to gather himself (why was his heart racing?), hoping that his audience would lose interest and go back to their meeting. After a while, he took scissors from the top of the desk and began to cut carefully along the top. It was the drawing, nicely framed and mounted, just as he had seen it in the show. Keeping it partially covered, he turned it over and looked at the back (although he wasn't sure what he was looking for — a name, an address, a phone number): it was blank. He peeled the brown wrapping paper slowly down the back of the picture until a plain white envelope appeared (he was right), taped to the bottom edge, his first and last names traced in that delicate, elaborate hand. He carefully and slowly unstuck the envelope from the backing, and then turned the picture over and set it on the desk.

He opened the envelope and looked inside. There was his check, along with two or three pieces of heavy looking beige paper, probably a letter. He removed his check and turned it over to examine it: there were no bank markings on it, she hadn't tried to cash it. Why not? Perhaps the letter would explain (he wasn't sure he wanted to know). He felt light-headed, almost giddy (was she interested in him?), and at the same time slightly guilty, as if his harmless and innocuous (to him) flirtations had somehow taken too strong a hold (perhaps his playful gestures carried more weight in her culture).

One thing was for damn sure, he wasn't going to sit there and read the letter in full view of Hector and Mr. Trojan and the crew, but he didn't want to have to wait until the meeting was over either. He picked up the phone and punched 3, then swiveled around to face the meeting room.

"Hi Hector, I'm sorry, but I've got a small personal problem. I need to go to my car and make a phone call, if that's ok. I'll be back in ten or fifteen minutes."

"You have a small personal problem and will be back in ten or fifteen minutes. Okay. Is it anything serious?"

"No, I just have to make a phone call. Thanks."
Click.

He put the picture in the trunk and sat in the front seat, looking at the envelope. It was humid, so he removed the keys, engaged the car battery (Da Funk [beeeoow, beow beow beow beeeoow, beow beow beow beeeoow] from Daft Punk boomed out on the radio [he quickly switched it off]), and pushbuttoned the front seat windows down. He thought back to sitting in the car before the art exhibit and how hungry he was. He removed the sheets of thick, expensive looking paper from the envelope.

There was writing on only one side of one of the three pieces of paper. The script was extremely hard to read (she probably couldn't help it):

> Dear Peter,
>
> I would like you to accept my picture as a gift to you, a gift of friendship. I do not know how to say this, and I am sure I will say this badly, but it is very important that I meet with you again. I am going soon to Harvard University, and then I fly to Japan, before returning to Turkey. I will be at the Los Angeles airport next Saturday, May 14th, from one to four (thirteen to sixteen hundred hours). I will wait for you then in the Ports of Call bar, near gate 25, Concourse number C. Please, please, meet with me there. Your friend, Reham.

As he finished reading and separated that sheet from the others in order to turn it over, a small scrap of paper fell out into his lap. He picked it up and looked at it: it was not a scrap at all, but a torn and blurry photograph of a man's face, a man who looked a great deal like Peter's father.

BOOK II

CHAPTER FOUR

So she did know something. Peter felt as if the (Oriental) rug of order and comprehension had once again been pulled from beneath him, and once again he was freefalling in space (Peter [without Wanda] had gone through a bungee-jumping phase in and after college: he was jumping three times a week for a short period, until the inevitable exemplary fatality [a fifteen-year-old cheerleader from Phoenix {the harness somehow detaching itself from the support cord}] had served as cautionary tale); hurtling through his emotions (anger, excitement, hope, dread, intrigue, fear), memories (his father's immense [to him] shoes lined up neatly in two rows in the walk-in closet, the smell of his father's towel after he had showered and shaved, his mother's spinach salad with bacon dressing, the back of both of their heads as he sat on the sticky back vinyl seat of that third or fourth hand cornflower slate Volvo stationwagon) and questions (what had happened to them? what and how did this person [Reham] know anything about it?).

He closed his eyes, and took deep breaths, deep breaths, and swallowed hard. After a while, he slowly began to regain his equilibrium, and the falling sensation began to dissipate. He opened his eyes. There he was, sitting in his car in the afternoon sun, and, and what? What could he do, telephone someone? Kay? Wanda? (the first would be hostile [I told you before I do not wish to speak about my sister and her husband] and the other inquisitive [How did you meet this girl? Is she pretty?]). No, there was nothing he could do at the moment. Besides, he had to get back to the meeting (this might be already stretching things with Hector [while it could never lead to any serious trouble {through Kay he was pretty much untouchable}, his boss was easily torqued and could be imaginatively vindictive {he once gave Susan (a jock-dyke who hated kids) grade school duty (often by third grade one can already discern edgers, influencers, conformers and geeks, although at this young age the boundaries are pretty fluid) for three goddam months, and he sent Tino to five or six bullshit interviews (Marv Albert, after your trial, you joined the church of Scientology, is that correct?)} and assign him absolute crap for a year]). So he needed to shut his mind down, bracket all of this confusion and discomfort off, and go back inside. Hector's meetings seldom lasted very long, and then he could go home and think in peace.

He looked at the (half) photograph. The face did seem to resemble the face of his father in the photographs he had found in the trunk (his real memories of his father's face were too vague and insubstantial [and were in fact filtered through the photographs] to be of much help), although he needed to compare them side by side to be sure. And where would Reham get this? How would she know about it? That was the real mystery. He would meet her at the airport; she needn't worry about that. Anyway, he couldn't think about this now, he had to get back inside. He placed both the letter and the photograph back into the envelope, put the envelope in his shirt pocket, and returned to Mr. Trojan (Señor Impermeable) and the others.

He kicked his Tevas off and sat on the edge of the bed. It had taken him much longer to get home than he had planned (a long and redundant introductory meeting with Jonathan Trojan [Peter felt slightly uneasy and threatened by the newcomer {what did they need a consultant for? they were consultants} as their areas of interest {fashion, music, marketing, alternative culture} overlapped], and then a longer session finishing the caliente y frio list [caliente — smoking, frio — maybe steroids; caliente — Casper, frio — new lounge hard-bop and narco-corrido; caliente — penal transplants, frio — Viagra; caliente — recordable cd's, frio — mini-disc; caliente — monk straps and oxfords, frio — platforms and wedgies; caliente — smuggling, frio — day-trading], which had caused him to hit the early rush, turning his usual commute of twenty-five minutes into a journey of an hour and ten [thank God for tunes and AC]) and he was exhausted (the back of his Calvin Klein, despite the Saab's efficient climate control, was soaked).

Focusing on traffic (slow but treacherous), work (both the previous meeting [he should have pushed harder for X-Files as frio], his new assignment [he was do to a market analysis of those who barbequed {barbeque'ers?}, what they wore, drank, smoked, ate, listened to, etc.]), music (KROQ [retro-rush] played a long set of B-52's [Love shack baby yeah!), his computer decision (there was tons of software for PC's, but he'd have to learn a new word processing program, and was his printer compatible? he'd love a flat panel) and Wanda (he'd pick her up at the airport [moms could take the stretch], take her home [if they could make it that far] and go right upstairs [he loved her bedroom {BIG-ass Sony 41' KP-41T35 ($2500 [retail, all the Sony stuff was from dad]), 8mm Camcorder (Sony CCD-TRV52, $1099 with tripod), Sony DVP-S300 DVD ($599), nice Bose system (Lifestyle 8 $1399), strangely comfortable Guglielmo Berchicci original Isotta (Terence Conran Tokyo) armchair covered in yellow leather ($2750), large flokati rug (12' x 15'

[$4500]) and a real fucking Warhol on the wall (aqua and yellow Marilyn $12 million even)}, especially her bed {king size cherrywood sleigh (La Grange $3400) with black Ralph Lauren silk sheets ($450) and large Nord Norwegian goose down pillows (4 x $150)}], where they'd fuck quickly, on the chair or the flokati, with most of their clothes on [all men love garters], then kissing, they'd undress, move to the bed and start again, slowly, tenderly [to what's-his-name's Bolero or Everything but the Girl {Wanda's choices}]), he had managed to keep Reham and the photograph on the periphery (for the most part) of his consciousness on the drive home.

But now the drive was over and there they were. He removed the envelope from his shirt pocket and set it next to him on the bed, then unbuttoned his CK, took it off, and threw it hard against the door of his closet (where he kept his dirty clothes [for Tina]). He stood up, removed his Dalals and hung them on his dressing chair, then leaned back on the unmade bed and put his hands under his head. He had been so eager in the car to study the photograph and compare it with those he found in the trunk to determine its authenticity, but now he just wanted to avoid the whole thing, like when after an operation or head injury, you hesitate to look into the mirror to assess the damage. But eventually, because of something more than curiosity, you look. In order to exist, in order to start getting better, you have to know what has happened to you. And so, sooner or later, inevitably, no matter what, you look. Perhaps a quick swim would refresh him, or a drink. He didn't move. He stared at the smooth white ceiling above.

What did he know for sure? First of all, he was fairly certain that he was alone on this, except for possibly Reham. But leaving her out of this for a minute, there was no one he could go to and discuss this with — Kay was absolutely out of the question and Wanda, well, it would probably cause some friction with Wanda if he were to divulge this to her. He could ask his grandmother (among his entire family, only Isabelle talked freely [if sadly] about his parents), depending on how she was feeling and if he wanted to drive all the way down to Diego. That was a possibility — if things got too gnarly he'd drive down and talk to Isabelle.

Who was this woman (he wished he had some bud to take the edge off [he'd have to get in touch with Suarez soon] — did he have any beer? A few Heinies in the fridge)? What could he be sure of? First, he knew absolutely nothing about her, other than she was some sort of artist. She didn't try to cash his check, and she did give him that picture, so if there was a money angle involved it wasn't immediately obvious. Still, he didn't completely (or even partially) trust her. Why couldn't she tell him what she knew the night they met, why go through this Chinese fire drill bullshit? Why she'd split on him like that, only to beg to see him later in her note? Why didn't he try to cash the check? And where did she get that photograph?

He licked his lips. He was thirsty. It was weird, whenever he thought of Reham he wasn't able to shake the feeling that he had met her somewhere before. Maybe at college, although he didn't hang with the art farts there and he probably would have remembered meeting some nice-looking harem hootchie from Turkey, or Palestine, or wherever the fuck she was from. This wasn't the really weird thing though (although for Peter it was weird enough). The really weird thing was that she had or was something that he wanted to understand (even Peter realized that understand wasn't exactly the right word) better. This desire to know wasn't primarily sexual (that would be easy) or emotional (he certainly wasn't in love with her [he was in love with Wanda]), although he could only begin to think about this bizarre (to him) desire as a variation or combination of these two (sex and love) more familiar types of feelings (it would be hard to say how much of these intuitions, these vague and nebulous intellectual and emotional impressions Peter was able to articulate to himself. He was lying on his back, thinking about Reham, and was bothered by his feelings for her, of this we can be certain, but as to the extent of his comprehension, who can know?). This desire to understand or to know was disconcerting for three reasons; first of all, while he was curious about many things (his parents and their demise of course the prime example), he had, until now, never desired to really know or understand another living person. His relationship with Wanda was comfortable: they had shared, for as long as he could remember, a sort of easy familiarity, a kind of passionate affability, and their relationship was, to a large degree, defined primarily by the agreement of their interests and tastes, and divergence was somewhat troublesome. This is not to say that their views on everything coincided perfectly (Wanda was much more adventuresome in music, food, fashion, art, acquaintances and technology, while Peter tended toward the experimental in politics, sexual positioning, drug use and, strangely enough, architecture), but their disagreements were more along the line of minor squabbles between old friends, where one takes a contrary position just to have something to talk about, rather than chasmal, irrational and unbridgeable differences of interpretation (like Israelis and Palestinians, to give one example among many). Oddly enough, there had never been a time, as long as Peter could remember, when this had not been the case. Their relationship had never undergone the frightening, tentative, wondering what the other was thinking would they call tonight stage: they had bypassed all of that and had moved almost immediately into the collective pronoun phase (marriage would be a mere formality). To Peter, this (enjoying the same things, appreciating the same clothes, music, art, etc. and fucking each other every chance they got [like Nicholas Cage and Laura Dern in Wild at Heart]) was love. This feeling of wanting to penetrate the defenses of an other and genuinely understand another person was as foreign to Peter as some Turkish republic potentate.

The second reason he felt slightly unnerved by this desire was that he sensed, right from the beginning, that it could very possibly get him into trouble (perhaps this was part of the attraction). What kind or how much he didn't know, but he knew that if he were to act on his desire (meet Reham at the airport), it could definitely destabilize (but to what extent?) one or both of the two most important relationships of his life (Wanda and Kay [When everybody loves you, it's as funky as it can be {Counting Crows}]). He had to be careful. Wanda would not be at all upset if he were to go to someone, even an attractive woman, searching for information about his father, while that would likely anger Kay (You talk to a total stranger about our family, and what's more, you believe her?); on the other hand, Kay would not be at all devastated if he were to have some sort of fling with another woman (if it didn't fuck up the wedding [and how could it, she was going back to Turkey]), which would certainly piss off Wanda (who, instead of getting weepy or depressed, would retaliate [exponentially] in kind [probably starting with Eli, that coke-whore PR2 {both

Puerto Rican and Public Relations} sleaze {she'd make sure he (Peter) found (smelled) his (Eli's) stains on her Ralph Laurens (she might even tape it)}]). The smart thing to do, the safe thing to do, would be to burn the letter and the photograph, and bury the picture in the closet, or better yet, sell it (or even give it away) to someone at work (get it the fuck out of the house [it was in the trunk of the Saab]). Still, no matter how much trouble and difficulty this meeting might possibly cause, he had to do something: simply chilling and forgetting wasn't really a possibility.

But why not? He'd carried wood, serious wood, for other women while sleeping with Wanda, and had always managed to sublimate (for a couple of weeks last summer he had fantasized fucking Mila [half Vietnamese, half Irish, one of the most beautiful women he had ever seen: grey eyes, buffed butt, great hoots and faint air of Fear and Trembling {Elizabeth Arden $35 2.4 oz}], this new intern at work, while he got busy with Wanda [not every time, but enough times to remember almost a year later]), resist or eventually forget his attractions: was this really any different? Didn't this have more to do with his immediate situation of sexual deprivation, with the fact that Wanda was currently away, rather than with any genuine emotional and sexual passion (he remembered his stogie for Karla that afternoon), with any true desire to know Reham better? It was all just chemicals, it was all just little Pete, the general, standing at attention and ordering him around. And big Pete could (usually) control little Pete.

But this wasn't only about little Pete. No matter how hard he tried to pretend that it was, no matter how much he tried to force his feelings for Reham into some sort of sexual container, he was certain that there was something else there. Even if he disregarded (as

much as he could) her (alleged) knowledge of his parents' death, there was still something which both puzzled and attracted him. He suspected (believed was
too strong) that Reham possessed (or in fact was) an
answer to many of his questions (questions he as yet
might not know how to ask [questions he could know
only in the asking]). The question now was not what
that answer or those answers might be, but how much
equilibrium and shelter (what he considered happi-
ness) he was willing to risk finding out. What exactly
did he want from this meeting? Knowledge about his
parents, sure, but what else? An airport bar was probably the worst place in world for meaningful conversation (he remembered one time waiting for Kay to
arrive from London at some terminal joint and a middle age nordic woman [You are the Dancing Queen,
young and sweet, only seven-teen {Abba, Dancing
Queen, 1976}] with bad teeth, thin cigars [Cafe Créme]
and a Raiders nylon track suit [$350] had sloppily but
unmistakably tried to pick him up with stories about
what a bitch Kirstie Alley was to work for [free beer
was free beer]) — what with the blaring televisions,
endless PA announcements (Johnson, please meet
your party at gate seven), ugly chrome, glass and fake
wood (not to mention excruciatingly uncomfortable
chairs), and jagged out travelers wandering in and out,
back and forth, like the living dead (including a few
bored businessmen who'd be sure to stretch their ears,
eyes peering over their Tom Clancys). Plus, there was
the real (if extremely slim) chance that someone he
(or Wanda) knew might see them. No, he'd try to take
her somewhere else, somewhere where they could talk
quietly (and safely), although it was doubtful that LAX
(one of the most public places in the entire fucking
world) contained anything resembling a private
alcove. The Marriott across the way was a possibility;

at least they could talk in the lobby or bar (possibly encountering similar problems as in the airport), although a room would be certainly be more intimate. But getting a hotel room would change both the game (between himself and Reham [what did he expect or envision from this meeting? {Peter half imagined (fully hoped) that Reham would bring more photographs, and documents (something she'd have to spread out on a table or bed)}]) and how the game would be perceived if discovered (by Wanda [especially] and Kay).

And then there was his family, and he was going to have to think about that now. While he had to make all of the decisions on his own, his actions had the potential for affecting everyone (alive or dead) he really knew and cared about (perhaps a slight exaggeration). And what was even stranger was that this simple meeting with Reham also had the potential of radically altering not only his present existence (how he got along in the everyday world with Wanda and Kay), but also his future (would Wanda get so angry she'd break up with him [call off the {as yet unscheduled} wedding? probably not]) and his past as well (would he learn something new about his parents? Would he view them in a different light?) This could be an important moment, a turning point in his life. Is this what he wanted? He was happy the way he was. No wonder he was fucking upset.

He sat up on the edge of the bed and looked at the envelope. Was that even his father in the photograph? He stood up and walked over to his dresser (a reproduction [by L.A. Haute] of a semainier in elm and oak, after a design by Dufrêne [$2500]. Kay's ex-husband, Robert Johns, had been quite a collector of art-deco furniture and accessories [both originals and reproductions] and had insisted that both houses, main and guest [Peter's current residence {he had moved from his two rooms in the main house after the divorce, when he was twelve}] be decorated almost entirely in that style [reproductions were banished from the guest house, the library, living room and office of the main house, to be scattered liberally throughout the remaining rooms {the master bedroom was furnished almost exclusively with (relatively inexpensive) copies}]. After the [amiable] divorce, Johns removed the [valuable] originals, and Kay evicted those frightful reproductions to the guest [Peter's] house, replacing them with Stickley [all bedrooms and her office] and Frank Lloyd Wright [dining, living, library and game rooms]. In addition the semainier, Peter's bedroom consisted of a nice metal desk with insert leather top, and matching chair in lacquer and tubular steel [from Century Furniture Industries, after a design by Mallet-Stevens {$1700}], a monstrous armoire, lacquered in green with gold trim [from J. Robert Scott, after a design by Renaundot {$3700}], a small ebony dressing table and stool [from L.A. Haute, after a Lady's Writing Table by Montagnac {$1850}] with an oval gilt framed mirror [La Barge {$400}], a matching long chaise lounge [Wanda's favorite piece {she loved to sprawl out on it, dressed or not}, although it was often covered in Peter's half-dirty clothes {depending upon how energetic Tina was}] and armchair, in dark red silk and black lacquered oak [from Monique Savarese and Dialogica, after a design by Chareau {two chairs (the other broken) and chaise $10,000}], and a low slung, almost Japanese, gray sycamore bed [Guy Chaddock, from a design by Chauchet-Guilleré {$7000}], that, even with a Serta box spring and mattress [$1000], was never that comfortable, and three Erté prints [Wanda hated {pronouncing them cheesy}] that he was rather fond of. There were also three large [five panel] and one smaller [three panel] decorative screens [including an original but damaged Franck {$65,000}], that Peter kept folded up in the storage closet) and opened his teak and Chinese jade jewelry box (a gift from a grateful client to Kay) in the first drawer to check out his empty brass Protopipe ($33). He poked around in the bowl: nothing but ash. He put everything back and closed his drawer, then walked into the kitchen over to the fridge and grabbed one of the dark Heinekens. He opened it and took a deep pull (Life's too short for cheap beer or Wouldn't you really rather have a Heineken?) and wondered what kind of beer his father liked, or even if he liked beer at all. Whatever. He needed some tunes, and maybe he should get that drawing out of the Saab.

He was aware (on some level) that he was stalling, that these ruminations on Reham, Wanda, Kay and his relationships with them were largely exercises designed to avoid facing the possibility that he might acquire some new information about his parents, and therefore about himself. Regardless if he were going to meet Reham or not, his next move was to make certain the face in the photograph was the face of his father. And the best way to do that, indeed the only way he could think of, was to compare that photograph with other photographs in his possession, photographs of which there was no question as to the identity of the subject. So he should go to the trunk in his closet, remove one or two albums from it, and compare the torn photograph (why was it torn?) with one or two in the album to see what, if any, resemblance could be confirmed (or discounted). So why was he standing there in his kitchen, calmly drinking a beer?   The image of the mutilated accident victim looking into a mirror again came to him. He stood in the kitchen drinking his beer for some time, and when he did move, it was into his bedroom to put Bach's Anna Magdalena Notebook for harpsichord (Nicholas McGegan $15.95 [Tower Records]) on his Sony.

Ok, well, it was time to see what he would see. He set the beer on his bedroom floor, then went to the studio's storage closet, where he dug through his computer and electronic equipment cartons and manuals, as well as his skis (Salomon Driver 997 [190+ cm] with Marker M51 bindings [$635.00]), snowboard (Option Signature 162 with Elysium bindings [$474.99 {he wouldn't mind doing big air with Wanda at Snowmass again}]), ballglove (Rawlings Ken Griffey Revolution [$169]), motorcycle helmet (Lazar Attack Racer [$159]) and a box of old textbooks from college until he uncovered the Vuitton footlocker. He dragged it out of the closet and into his bedroom, next to the Chaddock. He sat down on the Chaddock, looked at the envelope, hesitated, then opened the trunk and sneezed twice (the dust). He took the top photo album and set it on his lap, then opened the envelope and removed both the picture and the letter, placing the photo face up on the bed near his left hand and the letter on the floor, to the (right) side (he'd wait to reread the letter, trying to avoid the distraction that [possibly pleasant though annoying] thoughts of Reham would bring).   He opened the album to the middle (he had no idea where to begin) and focused on a snapshot in the right corner of the left page, a snapshot of a woman (his mother[?]), looking like a twenty-something Kay, holding a toddler (him[?]) and staring off camera (stage right and down), while a man (his father), his back turned three-quarters to the camera, extends his right hand up above the child's face, partially obscuring the child's face with his arm and elbow. Peter sang to himself over the harpsichord, "I love you, you love me, we're a happy fam-i-ly." There they were, in all their glory, although the only identity he could be somewhat certain of (disregarding the hazy unreliability of childhood memory, which, for Peter, would always be a problem, having no one who was able [his parents or a sibling] or willing [Kay, to some extent] to verify and corroborate his remembered history [he thought about Blade Runner {Wanda's all-time favorite flick} when Decker tells that Sean Young character that the photograph of her and her mother was bogus and her memories were implants]) was his mother's, as his father was turned away from the camera (in one quarter profile) and the view of his own face blocked by his father's arm (can anyone be certain of one's own childhood features?). His mother wore an avocado (not a good color for her and not one he ever remembered her wearing) dress or blouse (the photo was cropped at her waist) of indistinguishable material, his father some sort of casual black or dark blue jacket, and he Venetian red shorts with a tangerine tee shirt. The background was brown, and the caption, in block print (his mother's hand [his mother always printed and his father always wrote in cursive {with a backward slant}] on a strip of paper underneath), read ABBY AND ISAAC WEDDING CARMEL 6/77. Peter didn't know Abby or Isaac.

He couldn't see his father's face, but the hair (fine, brownish and collar-length) did seem familiar. He took Reham's torn photo and placed it next to the one in the book: neither print was sharp and focused, and the quality of the developing was quite different, as Reham's was faded and bleached next to the one in the book, although it too was old and not as vivid (maybe he should get a digital camera like Wanda's Nikon [CoolPix 900, $850 {he'd get Adobe Photoshop on his new computer (he was leaning toward the Dell) and do some cutting and pasting}]) as it probably once had been. He wasn't sure why he was wasting time with this particular photograph: his father's face was almost invisible, and his hair in both photos was too generic and vague of both color and style to be comparable. Still, he liked this picture: here was evidence (such as it was) that he had once belonged to a family, here was evidence that he had come from somewhere. Here was proof (not incontrovertible) that his father did love him, and had played with him, and his mother did love him, and had held him, at least once.

He removed the torn print, and, without looking at the other pictures (and their explanations) trapped beneath the clear plastic, turned the page. Here were images, evidently taken by his (unseen) father of himself and his mother on the beach. A bright sky, a skinny white child (no longer a toddler) with baggy white trunks lying on a Mexican blanket beneath a Campari umbrella, next to a (suddenly) stylish looking woman in a dandelion yellow one-piece with a straw Breton hat and Ray-Ban (Wayfarer) sunglasses. No sign of his father. Without reading the legend, he turned the page again. More of the same. His father, if that's who was taking the pictures, had some sense of composition and color, as these beach scenes were much more aesthetically accomplished than the first snapshot. There were two on the bottom of the right hand page where he was featured solo, playing in the sand in his now dirty white trunks, sandwiched between the primary red bucket and yellow shovel in the foreground, blue water in the back. PETER ON THE BEACH HUNTINGTON 7/78. What was his father thinking as he arranged the props, adjusted the shutter speed and aperture setting, and framed him, his son, through the viewfinder? Was he thinking about posterity, about passing his genes, knowledge and name, his self (or part of it anyway) down to the next generation? Was he proud of his son, pleased with his past progress and hopeful about his future development? Did he feel a powerful bond, an empathy, a love for Peter, made especially poignant and acute now they were spending the day together? Did he (Peter) bring his parents closer to one another, creating a blood connection and strengthening their emotional commitment, sheltering all three within a magical sand castle of perfect familial affection? Or maybe his father just wanted a good shot, and his white limbs and trunks, together with the blue sky, the yellow shovel and the red bucket, created especially nice effects. What was he (father) thinking? What was he feeling? What difference did it make now? And what about the caption? Was it his father's carefully constructed title (did he write or even think about naming his photographic work?) or simply his mother's descriptive label? Did his father even look at this photo after he had (so carefully, it seemed) taken it?

This wasn't easy, and it wasn't helping. He could watch the vid of his father teaching, but the quality wasn't great, and besides, if he remembered correctly, his father sported a facial lawn and a pony tail, proving beyond a shadow of a doubt that he was too cool for school, one hip mofo (as if poking and then marrying a grad student wasn't hip enough [he knew he wasn't a bastard, but perhaps his imminent arrival had helped them settle on a date]). Daddy-O (from Wanda's performance Daddy-O vs Jackie-O, imagining a meeting between Jack Kerouac and Jackie Onassis, narrated by a bitter Frank Sinatra).

What the fuck was he doing? Why was he wasting his time? Both his old man and his old lady were dead, gone, buried, hasta la vista baby, except he wouldn't hasta la vista them, they were just gone: gone Daddy-O gone (Gone daddy gone, love has gone away, Gone Daddy Gone, from Violent Femmes, Add It Up [1981-1993]). And here he was, sitting on his bed on a perfectly nice spring evening, breaking his own (blue) balls over two people who didn't love him enough, or who couldn't get their shit together enough, to manage to stay alive (fuck Travolta and fuck the Bee-Gees) past his eighth birthday. What did he owe them? Or more precisely, what did he owe to their memory? Kay was right (she usually was): let the sick bury the dead (or whatever). These people were strangers to him, he didn't know the first fucking thing about them, not what they felt, not what they thought, not even what they liked to goddam mother-fucking eat, so why did he insist on digging around try-ing to resurrect their sorry, J.C. Penney wearing, used car driving, domestic (Bud Lite, Almaden and Gordon's) drinking, two bedroom Riverside apartment dwelling, snaphot taking, bohemian loser (Cruise's bitch in Jerry McGuire [great movie] making that 'L' sign with her thumb and index finger) asses? What did he care? He was lucky, fortunate (with their death) to be delivered from a life of (relative) poverty and material mediocrity, happy to be alone and free of responsibility to honor and obey (whatever that was from) two people who seemed like such Eugenes, two chumps who would be stuck in Riverside until their bodies withered and they'd forget their own names (Dad first), when they'd have to be packed away some-where (still in Riverside) and Peter would be awarded the opportunity to receive that magic phone call detailing a broken hip, colon cancer and/or acute respiratory failure (Is there a chance? There's always a chance, but it doesn't look good. Pull the plug, doc, pull the plug). Only then would they be allowed to leave the Valley, to be planted alongside G-pa and G-ma in the family plot in La Jolla. Not to mention his own limited options. While Kay or Isabelle might kick in for school, the Saab, along with (most of) the rest of his stuff (especially all the Sony shit he got from Wanda) would be well beyond his means, would be well beyond even his power to imagine. And Wanda, would she be at all interested in a Structure shopping, used car driving Zima sipping smog monster from Mission Boulevard? He smiled: somehow he didn't think so, little Pete wasn't that large. It would be, well, it would be like him going out with Reham (although he didn't want to think about her now and that was different besides). She'd be friendly, and they might even chill together for a while, but there was no way that anything serious would ever come of it. She did hang with her skeez art fags and musicians, but they were art fags and musicians, they at least pretended to make or do something, and Peter wasn't sure he could ever pull that off (for one thing, most of them [besides Wanda and one or two others] lived communally in various fluid combinations, and Peter required his own, personal, private space [he wasn't that fond of shared bathrooms, and the idea of a communal kitchen almost made him retch] where he could keep his own personal, private stuff [although if he didn't have any stuff maybe he wouldn't need the space]. For another thing, Peter didn't consider himself that clever. While he desired money as much as the next person [maybe more], he didn't really know how to pretend to work for anything else [fame, notoriety, artistic success]. It wasn't that he was necessarily honest, or that he refused to dissemble, it was just that his talents lay elsewhere). So, without the 'rents, a pretty good life. With the 'rents, no bucks, no stuff, no Wanda. No fucking thanks, Homie don't play that game.

And what about Reham? Where did she fit into all of this? Without Daddy-O and Mommy-O, the Muslim Princess was less than a one night stand; she was a flirtation, a passing fancy who didn't even have the sense to sell what she gave away. Who the hell was she, causing him all this trouble and heartache? Fuck her and her ink-stained fingers, her thick accent, her weirdass writing and her bushy armpits (she probably had a hairy pussy too [he was only guessing here {he hadn't seen her armpits either}, but he had heard {never experiencing for himself} that European and Middle Eastern {non-north American} women let the hair of their nether regions grow wild, and Reham was probably even less concerned with convention than your average Euro babe {Wanda had fine, light brown pubes, and kept her legs, underarms and snatch hygienically and meticulously groomed}]). And fuck her for running out on him. She wasn't honest, wasn't on the level, and this was all bullshit. He should stop feeling sorry for himself, burn the letter and the photo, put the drawing in the closet, and forget about meeting Reham at the airport, forget about Reham completely. Wanda was coming home, and they still had to buy Kay's birthday present. Not to mention the purchase of a new blazing fast Pentium III or Mac G3 computer with a flat panel display thank you very fucking much.

He set Reham's photo back on the Chaddock, closed the album and placed it back into the footlocker. Now what? He was tired, and his mouth dry. He could slam the lid, drag the Vuitton back to his closet, have a few beers, or maybe drive out to Wiley's for a couple of (Conmemorativo and Cointreau) margs ($9 a pop but worth every cent), and try to forget the whole fucking thing. That's what he should do, he should close the lid, put the footlocker back, tear up the letter and half photo (where was the other half? what was that about?) into tiny pieces (so he wouldn't have to do this all over when he returned), put some clothes on (his almost new [only worn twice] Helmut Lang pale gray cotton v-neck [$390], his Nautica [David Chu] rust linen pants [$125] and his Barbara Shaum brown leather sandals [$225]), get into his Saab and drive to Wiley's, order a coyote marg, see if anyone was there (Suarez, Judy and her seriously buffed friend [what was her name, that amazon fitness instructor, who did an Iron Lady or something?] hung out there sometimes) and maybe have some dinner (excellent ceviche [$12] and crab enchiladas [$22]). He looked down into the footlocker, and then picked up the photograph from the Chaddock: it would be so easy to rip it up into a hundred tiny, microscopic paper fragments, just tear it up, rip it up, forget the whole thing.

But who was he kidding? He had to know if this was truly a picture of his father, and how Reham had come to possess it. From the moment he had first seen the torn photograph flutter from the envelope, he had been reminded of an image from one of the video tapes, a short, blurry fragment from his fourth or fifth birthday party. He leaned over into the footlocker and searched through the tapes until he found the one with the words PETER'S B-DAY & XMAS 1979 printed on the side in his mother's stiff hand. He walked into his studio and placed the tape in the Sony VHS, which immediately powered on. He flicked on the XBR, found the universal remote, and stood there as, after a few seconds (quickly muted) of Beethoven's fifth (his parent's [father's probably] idea of a joke), the images jerked into color, shape and motion. There he was, in a light blue striped cowboy shirt (maybe pajamas), eating his breakfast of Lucky Charms (how ironic [he remembered the taste of the marshmallow bits and how the milk would get rainbow colored and sweet]), and as the camera reverse zoomed, the frame encompassed his mother, in an almost colorless rose housecoat or nightgown, shyly (didn't she ever look at the camera?) buttering a piece of toast beside him. His mother looked pretty, in a sort of disheveled, early morning way. He froze the picture as the camera focused on her face, her hair mussed, pulled to the (camera) left off her cheek and out of her eyes, her mouth opened slightly, her eyes down, the corner of her toast in bottom right corner. She did look remarkably like a younger, more reserved and sheltered Kay — he had forgotten how striking the similarity was. He looked at the still image for awhile, the harpsichord playing softly.

Fuck it, he didn't have all day. He pressed Play, then FF to find that section where his mother was videoing and his father was in the front of the camera, playing or organizing or doing something (those weren't his pajamas, but his birthday shirt, topping off a pair of [faggy] sky blue shorts, dark socks and small white low-top Keds). He fastforwarded through images of his mother (still in her nightgown) blowing up neon yellow and purple balloons; himself jumping with excitement (or fear) on the forest green, fifties sculpted orlon/rayon/nylon sculpted sofa (he recalled the scratchiness of that artificial fabric and the raised piping on the cushions [he hated that couch]); his mother emerging from their bedroom in a smart cream (probably linen) sleeveless blouse with matching drawstring pants (she looked into the camera briefly, her hair tied back with a French knot); Kay and his grandmother (no grandfather) emerging from the white

Lincoln, and there, there, his father stringing up a (rather small) piñata in the garage. He rewound, and then slow-motioned forward until his father's face appeared . . . there, freeze frame. Because of the darkness (his mother obviously hadn't adjusted the aperture when they moved into the garage) he couldn't make out much detail (what kind of camera did they have, Pixelvision?).

Dear old daddy-O. He looked rather goofy (trying too hard to be casual or playful), with what appeared to be khaki Dockers (was that before their time?), topsiders and a denim work shirt. He was standing on a small stepladder, gazing up, his head framed by his arms holding the piñata above his head, his face (further) distorted by the low camera angle. Peter advanced the tape a few more frames, there was really no better image, so he quickly returned. There might be something later on the tape (he couldn't remember), or on other tapes, or in one of the photo albums (there were other photos, he had many pictures of his father), but this was the image that had first come to mind when he saw the photo in Reham's letter. He stepped closer to the screen and held the half of the torn photograph next to the arrested electronic picture. The angles were completely different, as was the scale, the clarity (one distorted by motion, the other posed), quality (one pixellated, the other glossy and yellowed) and the light (one shaded, the other bleached by bright sunshine). It was like comparing apples to oranges (one of Barbara's [Wanda's mother] favorite sayings).

There were similarities and differences between the two figures: while the mouths and chins seemed particularly analogous (strong chin, thickish lips and a wide mouth), the eyes (one pair thick and hooded [piñata], the other pair clear and small [Arab]) and postures (the piñata seemed awkward and ill at ease, the Arab strong and graceful), seemed almost totally incongruous (because of the darkness and the angle, the hair was invisible in the birthday shot, while it was longish and windblown in the photo). Peter again backed up and went forward a few frames, then returned to that shot. He looked a while and sighed.

There was no absolute (or even partial) revelation, no certainty as to either the identity or the diversity of the two images. There was no doubt the possibility existed that the two figures were the same person, just as possibility existed that they were two completely different men. The percentages of each possibility were still unknown (30/70? 50/50? 95/5?). The only thing Peter had learned was that he was not going to be able to confirm or deny Reham's possible involvement with his father from the scrap of photograph she had given him. The beginning of her story was impossible to verify without meeting and talking with her. If he was interested, that was what he was going to have to do.

He switched off the XBR and VCR, and moved back to his room, where he placed both the photograph and letter in the envelope and placed the envelope in the first drawer of his desk. He turned off his cd player, went to his kitchen to grab another Heineken, and returned to his Chaddock. He was tired; maybe he'd take a nap before dinner. Wiley's still sounded good. He'd lean back, have a few Heine's, and take Dr. Dre's advice and "chill til the next episode" ("Ain't nothing but a G' thang"). He picked up a computer catalogue from the floor near the Chaddock: he was going to pull the trigger and buy something soon.

CHAPTER FIVE

It had been a wonderful day. Lying between Wanda's sheets (her red silk Chanels [a special night] $600), wearing nothing but a post-coital grin (Wanda turned away on her side, sleeping or just about to, her ass against his hip), Peter thought back to the previous twenty-six or so. He loved everything and everybody. Wanda's plane (United, First Class) was an hour late, as was he (he had worn his favorite Prada [black stretch linen suit $1295] with a gray rayon sweater [Byblos Collection $325], black Coach belt, his Barbara Shaums [$495] for moms, who didn't show [had decided to stay another week], and his cotton Gucci bikini [nothing much more than a nut pouch with a string {$65}], with a splash of Totality and Infinity by Alex McQueen [$25 6 oz spray] for Wanda), and so he had managed to meet her (neon pink Todd Oldham raw silk mini [her legs took his breath away {$300}], Felina cotton bikini panties [$46], her Enzo Angiolini high heeled sandals [$300], a weird greenish brown, almost dull olive leather jacket from Ted Lapidus [$780] over a BOSS Hugo Boss man's sleeveless tee shirt [$12] dyed black, a [Victoria's Secret black lace demi {$40}] bra [My nipples get hard when I fly. Even coach? I've never flown coach.] and her trademark Van Cleef & Arpels one carat sapphire nose stud [$3500]) at the gate. A quick hug and a deep kiss (Face Stockholm Cherry Pop Lipstick [$18], shu uemera Thickening Mascara [$13] and just a hint of Glas by Thierry Mugler [$65 per 3.4 oz]), then it was down to baggage, where, as soon as her luggage (one large Belgian carpetbag from Rula [$350] and a smaller Hermès weekender [$2400]) arrived, she presented him with his gift, a pair of way phat sweet round toe crocodile loafers (Lorenzo Banfi $600 on sale).

They hurried to the Saab where they made out for awhile (I missed you. I missed you too. Thanks for the shoes. You're welcome do you like them? I love them I really love them.), but not wanting to drip all over everything, my panties are already soaked"Wanda insisted that they wait until they got (to her) home. She took off her coat, put her feet up on the dash (giving Peter a relatively unobstructed view of her moist Felinas) and placed her hand oh so nonchalantly on his crotch as soon as he started the car (keeping it there for the entire ride [Highway 1 {fucking crowded, they should have taken the 405} up to Sunset]), all of which caused little Pete to strain mightily against his bikini, like a dolphin caught in a tuna net.

After handing the keys to Avery (he took car of the car and the luggage), and a quick welcome home drink (Lagavullin, 16 year old $49 per 750 ml) with step-dad (And how are you, Mr. Peter?), they walked quickly up the stairs into Wanda's room, where they fucked pretty much as Peter had imagined they would a couple of nights before: first a quickie on the Guglielmo Berchicci (he sitting with Wanda facing him, her Felinas off Oldham hiked BOSS raised and the zipper of her Lapidus rubbing against his forehead), followed by (hanging up clothes) a small blunt (some nice generic Marin county [$50 an oz] and a more extensive session (although truth be told, it [even the sixty-nine] seemed rather perfunctory to him [maybe he expected too much or perhaps they were tired]) to remastered Miles Davis Kind of Blue ($15) and most of Sketches of Spain ($12) in the background on the Lifestyle.

The morning, however, was glorious, like that Canon commercial with the greyhound (A color called morning — one of the colors between the colors from Canon): first (a little bud, then) breakfast in bed (strawberry crêpes with clotted cream, croissants, cappuccino and Clicquot Yellow Label [$35] mimosas [with fresh squeezed {Jaime (the cook) would insist} blood oj]), then, to Mozart's Concerto for Two Pianos (Alicia de Larrocha and André Previn [RCA Victor Red Seal]) Wanda put on her newest outfit, an exquisite Elisabet Yanagisawa thistle dress $9500 (a present for me), over tiny, white silk thong underpants (a present for you [BCBG $65]). Little Pete was mighty interested, standing straight up to get a better view, but Wanda insisted they take showers and go shopping: Kay's birthday was only a couple of weeks away, after all.

"What are you going to wear?"

"It's too early in the day for this: besides, I'd like to save it for a special occasion. I dunno, I'm a little tired of Oldham, maybe my Michael Kors pants or Anna Molinari blue dress, although it's a bit tight for the day, I'll look like a Hollywood ho. Those salespeople can be such bitches, we should wear something nice. What about you?"

"I don't know, what do I have here? Where are we going, anyway?"

"Let's go to Rodeo. Have you seen my sapphire?"

"Did you take it out before we went to bed?"

"I don't remember."

Wanda (sapphire found and reinserted) ended up in a nice aqua and teal Rei Kawakubo lizard print summer dress ($595) with Isaac Mizrahi sandals ($250), Lancôme Creme Powder Eye Color in Chocolate Brûlé ($14), Le Crayon Kôhl in Black Coffee ($10), Bobbi Brown Professional ($20) mascara, M.A.C. Matte lipstick in Diva ($18), Annick Goutal's Visions of Excess ($145 per 2.4 oz), Revo® City Metal Rectangle Black/Blue Mirror sunglasses ($240), slathers of Clinique Nightshade 45 sunblock ($48 per 6 oz) and a long black (I don't feel like fucking with my [shoulder-length, straight, platinum blonde] hair) theatrical wig (Wilson Theatrical Supply, from Polkadots and Moonbeams $75), while Peter sported DKNY black jeans ($225), Coach belt, a Valentino Dahlia print linen shirt ($200), his Shaums sandals and a spray of Giorgio Armani Early Greek Thinking for Men ($75 6 oz spray). When he saw the wig, he thought back to his gallery flirtation with Reham (was Wanda mocking him?) and felt slightly disconcerted (an unease quickly dissipated by the short drive to Wilshire).

They had planned to go to Sotheby's to see if they were having an estate sale (it was Wanda's idea to get used jewelry. We could find an estate sale at Sotheby's or Christies or Harry W's. This way you might be able to get something unique, something old that isn't the same old same old, for cheap, or relatively cheap), but they were holding an auction (Elizabeth Wurtzel's [Prozac Nation and Bitch {Wanda had liked Prozac Nation}] letters, manuscripts, pillboxes and sextoys), so that was no good. Right next door they noticed a jewelry store that specialized in estate sales, Frances Klein Estate Jewels Inc., but it was closed on Saturdays.

"This looks like a good place."

"How can you tell?"

"I dunno, it just does. We should come here Monday or something. Does it have a phone number, maybe we could call, set up an appointment."

"We could look in the phone book. If we're going to come here later, what do we do now?" He of course knew the answer to this question before he asked.

She smiled. "I really think we should keep this Frances Klein Estate Jewels Inc. in mind for Kay. We could go to Christies, or Cartier, or Harry's, although I'm not sure they do estate sales. Why don't we just walk around, do a little shopping, maybe we'll find something we like for Kay . . . or for us. D'accord?"

"Sure." They considered going to Ted Lapidus, but, after crossing the street and looking in the window, decided to bypass it, as Wanda was kinda sick of all those animal prints, belt buckles and ballpoint pens. They looked at the gallery next door. "Did you ever think of getting her a drawing, or a statue or something?"

Peter had a brief and rather frightening flashback to Reham's picture, which was still in the trunk of his Saab. Could Wanda know anything about this, or was it just pure coincidence? Not that it mattered, as the Arab wench was out of his life for good (he had just decided). "I wouldn't know what to get her, I have no idea about her taste in art."

"Hey, you could get her a first edition."

"A first edition of what?"

"Duh. A first edition of a book. Brad gave Winona a first edition of Catcher in The Rye, she dug the hell out of it. Johnny Depp collects rare Beats like Ginsberg and Kerouac. Kay's kinda smart, she might go for stuff like that."

"I dunno. That really doesn't sound like her. Fuck it, let's go to Sonia Rykiel, it's only a couple of blocks away."

"And then Prada."

"Of course. And then Prada."

It was warm, and a bit smoggy, even in Beverly Hills, even on Rodeo Drive. As they walked, Wanda kept taking her sunglasses off, rubbing her eyes and complaining about the pollution (she looked great in that black wig and Peter felt fortunate that he had a girlfriend who would do things like that). They crossed the street again, past Battaglia's, Bardelli's and Bernini's (The Italians are so stylish — have you ever been to Italy? You know I haven't. We should go sometime. If I want to go to Italy, all I have to do is come here, and then Spago's for lunch.), and Wanda lingered in front of the united colors and Cartier (I wonder if they do estate sales). Peter checked out the traffic (Saturdays were really no more or less busy than other days of the week [except Sundays]: if you could afford to shop here, you could afford to miss work [as if], and if you were a tourist, it didn't matter what day of the week it was). There seemed to be fewer Armanied, Blassed and Hilfigered Asians (both Asian men and women tended to avoid their own designers [Yamamoto, Watanabe, Kawakubo, Kenzo, Yanagisawa {even if their work was strictly Euro}] who seemed to be particularly popular with western women), although he did notice a gaggle of K-Marted touristas (either midwestern American or eastern European [they looked exactly alike]) milling around slightly slack-jawed. He remembered the parking lot had changed as well from the good old days, as there was nary a Jag, Benzo convertible or stretch in sight: it was Hummers ($70k +), green Range Rovers ($50-$80k), ugly Cad Denali's ($64,000) those huge, tank-like Lincolns (Escalades $67,000) and Excursions ($70,000 [the one Boxster {$87,000} he saw was dwarfed by a Denali on the left and a Lexus RX300 {$49,000} on the right]).

Wanda appeared (he didn't recognize the black wig out of the corner of his eye), "See anything you like?"

"Not really. Let's walk."

"No, no, man, I totally disagree. Lang is totally

beat, the dumps, beached whale, washed up. No one digs that bullshit minimalism anymore, that severe silhouette and those goddam v-necks."

"I dunno. Look at Donna Karan, Jil Sander, even Steven Sprouse — all still doing skin-tight, bare bones greyhound looking stuff. It's a good look, timeless."

Peter and Wanda crossed the street, the male voices following. "That's New York, man, that ain't LA. LA's phat now, man, east coast is doornailed, too conservative. D and G, man, give me D and G. Dolce and Gabbana, that's where it's at in LA, or Badgley Mishka, or Narciso Rodriguez."

"What about Anna Sui?"

"Sui sucks, man: I hate that pseudo Apache look."

"Keep your voice down please."

As they reached the opposite curb, Peter slowed down so the two voices would pass, and as they did, he was surprised to see two short, rather overweight middle-aged men (one wearing a black Starter Bulls jacket [$65], with old black and red Champion Replica shorts [$29], Gargoyles Nitro sunglasses [$65], a white Starter 6-peat Bulls cap [$12], white Nike cotton Swoosh peds [$6], black and citron Brooks Tsunami Crosstrainers [$110], with a scent of Bally Pour Marx pour Homme [$45 3.2 oz], the other in blue polyester and nylon track pants by Tag Rag [$60], white and blue nylon reversible tank by Polosport [$40], a navy Adidas laundered golf hat [$20], Killer Loop Pandemania sunglasses [$130], white Champion Cross Training Quarter Socks [$18 per 3 pair], Asics® Gel-Marko-Crosstrainers in White, Midnight and Lime [$110], with a slight smell of Zents The System of Logic [$235 2.4 oz]) walking a nervous looking off-white miniature poodle thing (Bijon Frise $700), with painted pink toenails (Greta's Grooming of Beverly Hills $175), a rhinestone encrusted leather leash

(Chez Chien $160) and a green collar from Harrod's ($85). Wanda nodded at the trio as they passed, and Peter smiled. "Do you think they're gay?" he asked after they had ambled out of earshot. Wanda shrugged her shoulders.

"I like their dog," she said.

They finally reached the entrance to Sonia Rykiel's tiny shop, and walked through the heavy gilt doors into the rather stark but cool rectangular room (he loved the smell of fine boutiques; a combination of cultured wool, worked and polished leather, acrylic paint, metal, chrome and efficient air-conditioning, a smell that created the feeling not so much of money, but of luxury and certainty, of safety and desires that would likely be satisfied [I smell sex and candy, Marcy Playground]), where they were immediately sized up by a youngish (20?) salesperson (merchandise consult-ant) who looked something like an adolescent (Out of Sight) Jennifer Lopez (with nice pins in a two year old [at least] Mark Eisen tiger print mini [$150 {so much for avoiding zoological patterns}], a new black sleeve-less Massimo Mattetti shell with oversize zipper [$485], Robert Clegerie sandals [$150], dark Persol shades [$200] pushed on top of her brunette head and a hint of Diane Von Furstenberg's Je Tu Nous [$20 per 2 oz] — Peter wondered why if she worked at Sonia Rykiel she wasn't wearing Sonia Rykiel), who eventu-ally beeped off her Nokia NS 450 ($179) and asked, with as much sincerity and charm as her 'tude would allow, if she could possibly be of any help (it must be difficult to work in such a shop: while you needed to be somewhat snobbish [else why not work at the more egalitarian Gap, Banana Republic or Benetton] because the customer would expect it [couture being the antithesis of popular democracy, people bought expensive clothes {and objects} partially {mostly} to differentiate themselves from the masses], you depended on commission [he doubted {correctly} that base salaries for these fashion advisors were very substantial] so you also had to be somewhat friendly and helpful [the customer, in addition to buying a piece of cloth with a label attached {as well as the opportunity to prove that in fact they could purchase this piece of cloth with the label attached (the purchase being both an exchange [credit card number swapped for cloth, design, workmanship, etc.] as well as a performance [by buying you demonstrated that you possessed both money {the means to purchase and own} and taste {the means to appreciate and desire}], was also procuring service [people with money will only stand for so much discomfort before they get pissed], and so a good merchandise consultant earned every penny [both he and Wanda had this friend {Gwen} from college who started as an assistant {not even a} salesgirl at Christian Dior, making $14 grand a year, and worked her way up within two years to six figures, which was cool, but what was the bomb was she became this social fucking butterfly, the short chick from Chula Vista who was now invited to the AAA-list soirees, openings and shows, and who was helping Marcia Clarke pick out drapes, jetting to Milan and Paris with one of the Arquettes, and partying at Orso with Dineh Mohajer]. He wasn't sure he could do it himself — it would be too much of a tightrope walk between arrogance and obsequiousness, between fuck-you and fuck-me), and if she could, her name was Miriam. Une Very Stylish Fille from Dmitri From Paris (1998) played in the background.

He moved over to finger the rubber, nylon and leather of these baggy and multizippered trousers ($1300) on a rack near the door, while Wanda talked to Miriam about a gray cashmere ensemble (pleated slacks, sweater shell, single vented jacket and necktie $7000).

What were you buying when you plunked down (you didn't really 'plunk' anything down, it was more a discreet slipping of the MC or Amex from one hand to a machine, a silent, electronic movement of digits from one column [account] to another. It was all incredibly quick, clean and painless. No one used [dirty] cash anymore, except perhaps gangsters and rap stars, but even they were becoming more and more civilized [this wasn't Miami or Dallas]) $25000 (or $2500, or $250) for a bright, red and yellow and green flower print silk dress with a rainbow striped cable-knit wool scarf? You were buying the material, sure, and the design talent and experience, plus the time it took to cut and sew, and then transport and market; he understood all of that well. You were also buying the advertising, the marketing of the image to go along with the dress; he had no problem with any of this. Wanda stirred in her sleep, and then turned over, her breath softly blowing in his face. He turned over on his other side, and buried his face in the cool Chanel silk pillowcase and the Nord Norwegian goose down pillow. He loved the (silky) smoothness of the silk, and the cloud-like softness of the pillows: quality was important. It was what you paid for. But was that all? No, it wasn't. Not to him. Not to anyone he knew.

He moved on to the other rack (there were only two small racks in the entire space, with one or two outfitted mannequins and three or four dresses on hangers hanging on the walls), where he began to examine knit mini-skirts, low belted dresses and short and sweater suits ($1299-$3800), all the hue of a flesh-colored crayola, when a stylish euro-looking couple (he in a black velvet two button suit from YSL [$1500], a Versace white cotton shirt [$400], an Armani blue silk tie [$160], black Ferragamo Oxfords [$600], a Patek Philippe Chronograph [$25000], Calvin Klein Fade framed sunglasses [$300, quickly removed] and a more than subtle scent of On the Sublime by Helmut Lang [$75 per 2.8 oz]; she in a sleeveless Marc Jacobs [Louis Vuitton] white silk shirt [$350], black, skintight spandex pants [Veronique Branquinho $600], scary looking black stiletto half boots [Manolo Blahnick $750], a white silk toque [rather subdued for Philip Treacy $300], brilliant 1.2 carat [each] diamond studs [Cartier, Good, F WS1, $40,000], shu uemera's Colorless Face Powder [$40 per 4 oz], Lipstick in July Lunar Frost [$12 per stick], Chanel Instantlash Mascara [$18], Aveda Cobalt eye shadow [$20], and the ever so slightly thickened perfume of Akris Nicomachean Ethics Pour Femme [$90 per 4 oz]) entered the store, carrying two rather large Mila Schön shopping bags. The woman smiled, kissed the man hard on the lips (they were about the same age [30?], which was to say that he wasn't her sweet and old), said something to him in European (it wasn't Spanish, Peter knew that) and began to look through the rack he (Peter) had just abandoned. The man then reached into his shopping bag, removed a video camera (the Sony CCD-TRV52 [$1099], same as the one in Wanda's room) and began to shoot the woman as she examined the clothes. As soon as the camera was on her, she began to ham it up, doing the grind and shimmy with a rubber and leather jumper [$6000] and zipping and unzipping a red leather Mao vest [$3000] in time to Dmitri's swinging synths. Wanda guffawed (whether with derision or amusement he wasn't sure) and Miriam looked on nervously. The woman began to prance (remarkably well considering those heels and pants [they both commanded that effortless tenuity of the well-bred {or at least not-so-recently monied}]) around the store, the jumpsuit with hanger at her chest, the camera tracking from the corner by the door. It was hard to say whether they were influencers or conformers (they were probably foreign arrivistas, a term Wanda had run across and used for awhile) as such distinctions tended to disappear in the stratospheres of the upper economic brackets (he did still think that edgers and geeks existed everywhere, even among the very rich [they were often combined within the same person {Bill Gates et al}], although these two were no edgers): while he wasn't sure that conformers would dance around a high fashion boutique, he also didn't think influencers would videotape their shopping trips. She was sashaying toward the counter where Wanda and Miriam were standing, which could be dangerous because Wanda seldom participated in other people's art projects (hated being photographed spontaneously) and was liable to give them the finger or demand money or something, and so he was anxious and slightly apprehensive to see how she would react to the whirling Natasha and her video Malcolm McClaren. Without missing a beat, as if they (she and Miriam) were alone in the store (in the world, the universe), she slipped her sunglasses over her face and continued speaking to Miriam.

This snub seemed to take the life out of the strangers: the woman quickly scooted over to the dressing room to try on the jumpsuit, and the man let his camera-hand fall to his waist. Wanda turned to face him (Peter), her eyes peering seductively over her Revos, and smiled, then abruptly turned back to Miriam and continued their conversation. He felt slightly in awe of her then, as well as hungry (Spaqos was close by, but he was in the mood for something different, maybe trout at the French Laundry). He returned to look at a long sleeved flesh-colored ribbed merino wool sweater ($2000) and thought about lunch (trout before Prada or Prada before trout?) until the woman burst out of the dressing room, the door whacking the wall behind her, and without a sideways glance or foreign word, marched stiffly past the man (who was forced to awkwardly step out of her way and then recover to hold the camera, grab the bags and follow in her wake, closing the door behind him) and out the door. Miriam immediately went to the dressing room, where she emerged after a few moments, ashen faced (she looked like she was going to cry), carrying the jumpsuit in a crumpled heap in front of her. Dmitri from Paris abruptly finished, then after a short pause, began again, from the beginning.

"Did she ruin it?" Wanda asked.

"I don't know." Peter wandered over as Miriam set the jumpsuit on the counter, and carefully and gingerly began to smooth it out with her hands. Wanda removed her Revos. "I don't see any rips or anything, but look how wrinkled it is."

"You're not going to get in trouble, are you? It wasn't your fault, and we could tell your boss that."

Miriam stopped fussing with the material and looked at Wanda. "I don't know, I don't think so. I didn't do anything."

"We'll come back in an hour and a half or so, after lunch, and I'll look at that gray suit again, okay? And don't worry, it's just wrinkled, that's all. I guess she didn't like the way she looked in it, huh?"

"Fucking cow," said Miriam.

They engaged in a longish lunch (at Spago's after all [he enjoyed an exceptional seared yellowfin tuna salad with Oaccata jalapeños and cilantro {$24} while Wanda found her spring lamb, rosemary and mint pizza {$18} disappointing {they split a rather mediocre Pouilly Fume (Laudoucette Chateau du Nozet, 1990 $40)}]) and returned about two and a half hours later (after Prada [Peter almost bought another {a bluish gray stretch wool three button} suit {$1520} but decided to wait], Chloé [Wanda did buy a strapless lavender muslin cocktail dress {$1700 on sale}] and Charles Jourdan [nothing]), only to find the door locked and the shop darkened. They went to Peter's for a swim and a quick shower shag, then to Wanda's for a light dinner (Navajo chicken tacos [one of Jaime's specialties], chipotle and agave salsa, arugula salad with a Valtellina balsamic and domestic garlic dressing, Dos Equis Amber and Patron tequila shots with Veracruz sea salt and Argentinean limes), a movie (Gridlock'd [I'll let the bitch die] with Tupac [That's just the way it is {Greatest Hits}] and Tim Roth, which he found funny but depressing, and which rekindled Wanda's dilettante desire to snort heroin again) and more (dope and) sex (Wanda insisted on wearing the wig [and her leather thong {Hard On Leather SF, $65}], which both Big and Little Peter liked a lot [he took her from behind and they came extremely hard {to Brahms Piano Sonata #1 (Sviatoslav Richter)}]).

He was having a hard time getting to sleep, which was quite unusual for him (he was usually out like a light [and awake just as quickly {Peter's transitions between different states of consciousness were almost always immediate}], especially after sex). He couldn't help thinking about that couple that had videotaped their shopping adventure: while, on the surface and at the time, he thought it ludicrous and in bad taste, there was something (he realized now) about it that he understood quite well, even sympathized with. Shopping and buying at these fine stores (at any store? he didn't know) was more than the simple detection, selection and acquisition of objects, it was really the construction of a personality, the creation of a self. If people recorded the miracle of birth (the gowned husband trying not to faint, nervously jiggling the vidcam as the bloody head emerged through that tiny slit [would they ever fuck again?]), why not record the acquisition of an outfit, a look, a style, a self (Clothes make the man, as Kay used to say whenever she took him shopping [when he was younger, before she opened his Amex account for his middle school graduation] and he had never found reason to disbelieve this)? His first solo outfit purchase (black wool Prada slacks [$250], a textured cotton and silk BOSS Hugo Bass sport coat [$475], a Pink custom made white cotton Oxford [$175], Dior red silk tie [$50] and his big mistake, ill-fitting [and ugly] Allen Edmonds loafers [$275]) was, for Peter, his bona fide rite of passage, an event marking the transition between the unformed and generic personality of the child and the individuated particularized psyche of the adult.

Clothing gave him security and confidence, a mode of behavior and a way of seeing the world (he felt and behaved much more alive and spontaneous the better dressed he was, and became uptight and sullen only in more casual attire [he felt incredibly inadequate and paranoid {like an orphan} when underdressed in public {when alone he was indifferent to what he was wearing at the time, and would focus only on what he would put on to be seen by others (including Wanda [it wasn't so much that he dressed to please others, it was just that in dressing, the difference between how he saw himself and how he imagined others would see him did not exist])}]): in short, an identity. And so, buying clothes (which was much different than buying other objects [jewelry, cars or objets d'art {although he never purchased off-brands, and when faced with even the most trivial choice, would inevitably select the most luxurious or dear}]) was an important and (self-) creative act.

But what was it about his clothing that affected or even determined (produced) his self (-image)? Was it the material (he was especially fond of Egyptian cotton, light stretch wool, rayon and fine silk)? The cut and drape (he preferred the tight, slim Euro silhouette)? The workmanship and tailoring (he adored hand basted lapels, hand sewn linings, horizontal buttonholes and mother of pearl buttons)? He loved quality (Quality is cheaper in the long run [Isabelle], and The good is the enemy of the best [Kay]), that was easy to say, but what exactly did that mean? Was he attracted to the abstract knowledge that he was wearing something well-made, stable, dependable, something that would never let him down? Or was it more sensual than that: did it involve the actual feel of the luxurious fabric on his skin (the soft silk of his Charvets, the airy suppleness of his BOSS Hugo Boss linen slacks), the immense pleasure of the deep, carefully dyed colors (the absolute purity of Prada black, the deepest royal blue of a DKNY linen shirt), that wonderful smell of the freshly laundered cotton (or brand new cashmere), the hushed brushing sound of silk against wool? It was all this (the various abstract [intellectual] and material [sensual] pleasures) certainly, yet there was something extra, something more obscure and more difficult to understand.

It was more than mere cloth (material) and thread (workmanship); more than drawing (design) and cutting (execution); more than even the glossy photographs (advertising) and tiny, gallery-like exclusive boutiques (marketing). The idea or feeling he was trying to understand was at once more ethereal and primitive than these relatively mundane concerns. To Peter, there was something undeniably fascinating and absolutely elemental about the names of the houses of the clothes he wore, and it was these words, and all they represented, as much as (perhaps more than) the clothes themselves, which helped create (to his own mind, which [here, anyway] is of primary importance) Peter's very identity (this was more [much more] than snobbishness [greed or the acquisition of status], as snobbishness [especially in fiction] is usually considered almost a secondary characteristic, or, to be more precise, the manifestation [symptom] of a more basic character flaw [say insecurity or bitter disappointment]. With Peter [and perhaps with us all] the judgment, discernment, establishment of hierarchies and creation or recognition of difference was [one of] the primordial activities of his consciousness, and it would be as useful to ask him to abandon it as it would be to ask Jerry Lewis to abandon his kids. Lucky for Peter [Lucky Pierre], he derived a great deal of joy and pleasure from this discrimination [and this is where he was truly blessed]).

There was something magical in the names, something almost alchemical (the addition of a label could transform a rather drab handbag into a minimalist masterpiece, an ill-fitting jacket into an ironic comment on body-shape, an uncomfortable and ungainly pair of shoes into the envy of all cognoscenti, a tacky polyester blouse into the newest kitsch retro must-have, and a camouflage jumper from a deer-hunter hick-suit to the life of a Balthasar party) and incantatory about the labels, something virtually spiritual (the belief that the addition of a single word to an object could create such desire, a desire based almost totally on trust [if Tom Ford or Donna Karen says that this looks good, then it must look good] is akin to religious faith), and he would often daven the names to himself (Prada, BOSS Hugo Boss, Alexander McQueen, Anna Sui, Gianfranco Ferre, Salvatore Ferragamo, Elisabet Yanigisawa, Gianni Versace) in liturgical fashion, as if he were trying to find the secret name of God.

So, like captions that hold the key to understanding a photograph or painting, he found the labels (the names, the words) attached to the clothing he (and others) wore to be more important than the clothing itself (he had known this for quite some time, and his reluctance to shop for and wear vintage [or even new] clothing of obvious quality yet uncertain origin was evidence of this [his sharkskin suit and Hackett Tuxedo were exceptions that proved the rule, as both were presents from others {suit from Wanda, tux from Kay}]; the few times he [with Wanda] had found himself inside a vintage clothing store [smell of must and broken toys], he had confined his browsing to women's clothes and other paraphernalia, refusing even to wander near the men's racks). Conversely, he could easily desire (or appreciate) a suit, jacket, pair of shoes or other piece of apparel (imagining it as his own or on someone else) without ever having seen it either in person or in a magazine (or catalogue), as the words themselves created exciting possibilities in his mind (a Prada suit, a Comme des Garçons jacket, a Versace dress, Ken Cole oxfords, a BOSS Hugo Boss shirt, a Hermés necktie, a Fendi bag, a Michael Kors coat, a Galiano dress): the clothing (thing) required a label (word), but the label (word) required only the possibility of clothing (thing).

Peter's style, therefore, was not a symbol or metaphor for something else — his clothes did not function as signifiers pointing to deeper meanings, his appearance was not the key to understanding his interior personality — rather his style *was* his personality, his appearance indistinguishable from his psyche, his clothing identical to his self. It was as if he had been turned inside out, with his most basic and fundamental characteristics exposed to the world, and his less important, easy to understand, superficial qualities hidden away (Peter's clothes did not dress or clothe anything more important than themselves: his clothing was no clothing). Peter truly wore his soul on his sleeve.

So in some ways, Peter's fashion sense transcended materialism: while he was enchanted and could almost be seduced by the sensual enjoyment of the wools, cottons, silks and leathers, these corporeal delights constituted only a small part of their appeal (as evidenced by his aversion to unnamed articles), and his true fascination (desire, need) was centered on the spiritual or emotional confidence, the authentication (justification, confirmation, legitimation) the names (of the designers, the houses) of these things gave him. The material goods were, in a sense (and not completely), mere vessels for the abstract power of the words and the spiritual aura that truly clothed him.

Peter did have some comprehension of the vital role expensive clothing played for him, and he did realize that his personality was built on a sort of deep and fundamental superficiality. He mistakenly attributed this to his orphanhood: since most people had two parents, and one or two siblings, and shared memories of at least some sort of family life (hunting squirrels with dad for dinner in the Appalachians, helping mama clean out the hut in the Congo, or putting on those big-ass hats and hitching the horses to the sleigh with his brother in Moscow) and he had not, he needed something to provide him with the self-confidence and courage (the self-esteem) that a normal family background would and should have given him. His clothing provided him with a past, a past he was cheated of, a past he was forced to purchase. He was the only person he knew who had to buy his own history, and so he would spare no expense to provide himself with a nice one, and feel no guilt for doing so. And if his past was better (prettier, more glamorous or luxurious) than others, well, that was part of the point, wasn't it? Again, he was doing nothing but restoring the balance (as best he could). He was doing nothing but taking care of himself.

He yawned and turned over on his back: he was getting sleepy. He and Wanda had nothing planned for tomorrow, so maybe he'd ask her about Kaspar, try to arrange a meet. He thought briefly about Jonathan Trojan, but managed to purge that negative vibe out of his head quickly by thinking about driving to CompUSA and trying out the new Macs (if he got Photoshop, a DVD and some extra memory he'd probably have to drop at least $2800 whereas he could pick up a Sony through Wanda for half that) and I smell sex and candy segued into Everybody wants to be naked and famous, I'm naked and famous (Tricky Kid, off of Pre-Millenium Tension, Tricky) just before he fell asleep.

CHAPTER SIX

Peter (Gap paisley cotton boxers $12) opened his eyes, looked over at his Lenin Cowboy Swatch (9:25) and sat up quickly: today was the day! He was going to pick up Wanda, drive down to CompUSA in Beverly, try both the 450 Mac and the 600 Sony or IBM with that bad-ass slim 19 inch Sony monitor (the Dell was dropping out of contention: Peter didn't do mailorder [not that he needed immediate gratification, far from it {he loved the anticipation (although he did tend to obsess) separating the fitting and delivery of his suits for example}, it was just that he wanted to test drive these fuckers]) and, finally, buy one (or get Wanda to order the Sony for him). It was time to shit or get off the pot: no more hemming and hawing, no more checking web sites for specs and reviews, no more mak-ing hypothetical pro and con (caliente y frio) lists, no more scouring the ads for deals. At the moment, despite Wanda's admonitions (Why do you want to be like everybody else? Fuck Bill Gates, he's a fascist, and They're too goddam hard to use), he was leaning towards a Windows box, but could (and probably would) still change his mind. This would be fun, although not quite as exciting as buying clothing (com-puters were, after all, simply machines or tools [and the names merely labels pasted on nearly identical beige or dark grey boxes {which is not to diminish the very real and chasmal epistemological, ethical and ontological differences separating Macintosh (not to mention Linux) from Windows (although Microsoft owns both)}: flat, lifeless words {Dell, Compaq, IBM, Macintosh} which failed to resonate in the least in

Peter's consciousness]). They still had Kay's present to shop for and buy, so maybe they'd follow up CompUSA with a trip to Fashion Island, or they could give that estate sale place a call and head back to Melrose. And then, a little celebratory lunch at Valentinos (he could use some veal scaloppini with baby peas and Lake Country Asiago) or Midori (they both dug Bento). Whatever, it would still be robust, phat-o-matic, def, nasty and nude. He sprang out of bed, rifled through his cd's (noticing a little dust on the Sony CVC [when was Tina getting back?]) until he found Aaliyah's Are You That Somebody on the Dr. Dolittle Soundtrack (WEA $16.98 Virgin Superstore), which he put on and cranked the volume. A pee, a quick shower and then clothes (he could wait until Wanda's for java [Jaime made killer cino, with free market Tanzanian]) and he could be on the road in thirty, although he probably should stop by to see Kay, which could cost him ten to fifteen if she was chatty (affectionately loquacious or, if she could see he was in a hurry, insistently garrulous): maybe he should just phone from the car. No, he'd have to suck it up and stop by (Sometimes I'm goody-goody / Right now I'm naughty naughty [he wouldn't mind getting naughty naughty with Aaliyah and her nasty nasty g-string peeking over the top of her skirt {the only reason he bought the album (successful marketing)}]). She was probably in the tea room (her word) having scones and coffee, while Pavo sucked down his third gin and juice of the a.m. Okay, vamoose motherfucker, I'm burning daylight.

After pissing, showering, drying, shaving (around his goat) and brushing, he walked into his walk-in (opened his Renaundot copy) to decide what to wear. He didn't want the salesgeeks to think he was a suit, treat him like a moron (This is your floppy drive, this is your hard drive. Your hard drive stores much more than your floppy) and jack the price up on him. Still, the better he would dress, the better he would feel, and the better he would be capable of dealing with the crater faced pocket protector crowd (although it had been three years since he had visited a computer store, and the floodwater Lees with little brother's WalMart shortsleeve had probably been replaced with something more corporate [Royal Knight or even Izod]. Still, stereotypes died hard [see Bryan]). So a compromise was needed: something cas enough to avoid intimidating the green badges, and yet fine enough to give him the confidence he would require to be a well-informed consumer (plus he didn't want to have to come home and outfit upgrade [to avoid looking the punk] before they went to Fashion Island or V's). He wondered what Wanda would be wearing: cas, funky or semi-formal, wigged, Chanel chapeaued or au naturel; Manolos, Walgreen flip-flops, thigh-high Docs or Evergreen roller blades; Oldham mini, Daryl Kerrigan bell-bottoms or Narciso cigarette slacks; carefully tied Versace leather vest, Molinari tube top or Nicole Miller cocktail length silk frock; she could look good in fucking anything (even last year's Hervé Léger dirt-colored bandana monstrosity [$5000, I kid you not]). Maybe he should phone her up and try to suss out her outfit (not in order to match colors or fabrics [I'm with Stupid and Stupid] but to coordinate moods), but that might be too faggy. He thumbed through a couple of sportcoats and suits (he should have hit www.cductive.com and burned his own anthology cuz other than naughty naughty Doctor do do sucked sucked sucked [although Ain't Nothing but a Party wasn't bad]): fuck it, he'd go with his unlined gray cotton sportcoat from Issey Miyake ($450), and if it was clean (if Tina took care of it before she left), his cream colored semi-sheer silk shirt from Jil Sander ($140) over his black DKNY (the official jeans of New York) jeans ($120), BOSS Hugo Boss cotton semi-briefs with a Yorkshire Terrier print ($18) and crocodile loafers (Vali's wouldn't frown on denim during lunch). Ok, now for the accessories (the Sander was clean): his croc belt from Bergatti ($198) . . . no, too much, better go with the simple black Hard-On (indeed). Gray socks (Bloomingdale's from g-ma), shades, phone, wallet and, after a quick shot of Critique of Judgment from Marc Jacobs ($30 per oz), he turned off his box, locked the door, and was ready to roll.

Sony had a great software package and DVD with S-Video out, but both the HP and NEC had a bigger hard drive and scored faster on the Wintests. Maybe he should close his eyes, open his wallet (like George Jetson) and shell out for a big motherfucking strawberry Mac with fries (he could still get that slim Sony monitor, although the color schemes wouldn't match), something he knew and wouldn't have to upgrade for five or six years (if Mac were still around). That dark purple tiny little Sony box looked cool, and it might be fun to do some image manipulation (like morphing Wanda's face onto Tyra Banks' body or sticking his own mug onto Kobe B.) with Photoshop. He'd have to see them in action before he decided — still, it would be hard to beat Sony's software and graphics card. Louisa was in the hallway near the kitchen.

"Hello Peter."

"Hello Louisa" (wine colored Chanel pantsuit [$2200 {Kay hand-me-down}], Le Tini flats ($175), Di Bernardi pantyhose ($24), Maybelline Volume Express Waterproof Mascara ($12), Nars Blue Lagoon nail polish ($20) and matching Hermés watch ($2000), with Cratylus ($55 per 4.2 oz) from Céline. "Is Kay in the tea room?"

"Yes."

"Is Pavo there too?"

"Excuse me?"

"Is she alone?"

"Yes, I believe so."

"Thank you."

"Peter?"

"Yes, Louisa "

"This came for you yesterday, FedEx." She handed him a large cardboard envelope. "We weren't home, and so I didn't know about it until this morning."

"What is it?"

"I don't know."

He recognized the handwriting immediately. This was not what he needed: he had a life to live, a computer to buy. He accepted the envelope and looked up as she spoke, ""Will you be joining Kay for breakfast?"

"Just orange juice, please" (Louisa made shitty coffee). "I'll be there in a minute." What the fuck, was she stalking him or what? He should have never gotten involved, never spoken to the bitch, never accepted the painting and never read the letter. She knew where he lived, that was obvious. While he hadn't exactly forgotten her, even since Wanda returned Reham (and her likely story) had been relegated to a seldom used broom closet of his consciousness, close to the stairs in the basement. Now she was out again, upstairs in the foyer, demanding to be let in to the sitting room with the white folks. He turned the large white envelope over in his hand, it was sent from Harvard on Thursday, with the Harvard Art Department as the return address. He supposed he could send it back unopened, that might teach her a lesson. But she was coming back here (soon), and then going away, so the lesson might not reach her. He sighed, and began to return to his house to open the envelope and read the letter, but once he reached the kitchen, he hesitated and stopped. Fuck her — he wasn't going to waste his time reading her asswipe letter and brooding over it alone in his room with the photographs of his parents spread out all over like David Caruso on some goddam missing persons crusade (when was Dennis Franz gonna call it quits?). He tore the protecting cardboard off and quickly opened the smaller envelope within. There was another photograph, or rather half a photograph, or, more precisely, the other half of the photograph she had sent him earlier, enclosed in a letter. This half, as blurry and faded as its mate, showed the face of a woman who looked something like Reham, holding a thin brown faced infant in a tattered yellow blanket (for just pennies a day you can make sure that Fatima Khan will receive breakfast and a chance to go to school), with a darkened shape of what could either be (have been) a large doll or a small dog on a wall or shelf in the background. What was going on? Time stopped. He was unable (or unwilling) to say exactly what the photograph meant. He moved over to the (green Italian marble $200 a square foot) counter and leaned against it. He glanced at the photograph again, and then read (the now familiar handwriting of) the letter.

> Dear Peter,
> I am afraid that you will refuse to come to meet me at the airport, and so I am telling you why this is so necessary. This piece of the picture is of my mother and me when I was a smaller little girl. If you do not know yet, the other piece is your father, who is also my father. Now that you know, I am hoping you will come to meet your partial sister at the

Ports of Call bar, Gate 25, Concourse C,
between one and four o'clock (in the after
noon), on May 14th, Saturday.

Reham

P.S. I do not want any money or anything
from you, I want to speak with you only. If
you do not come, do not worry, I will never
phone or write you.

An entire lifetime (both past and future, regressive and progressive) of possibilities quickly opened up before him before his mind crashed, went down, offline, error message # 176849B Temporary System Failure, central processor toasted.

May 14th was today.

"Good morning Peter."

"Kay" (a red silk kimono tied carefully at the waist from Rei Kawakubo [$1000], two large South Sea cultured pearl stud earrings [Harry Winston's $1400] and Ecco Homo by Cerruti [$75 2 oz.]). He (involuntarily) snatched the letter and photograph behind his back and tried to put his body between the envelope on the counter and Kay's line of sight (with a subtle Who's the Boss or There's Something About Mary [he'd like to eat Cameron Diaz] motion). He had a sister, he had a fucking sister (if she were telling the truth)! "How are you?"

"I'm fine Peter, and you? You look pale."

"I'm alright. Just a little tired."

"Are you sure there's nothing wrong? Pavo told me there was a package for you. Did you get it?"

"Yes, Louisa just gave it to me." Reham was his sister (which explained the rude spazz act and the photograph [but how did she know about him?]).

"And everything's alright?"

"Yeah, it's just something from work."

"Why didn't they give it to you at the office? Weren't you just there yesterday?"

"I don't know. It's from Boston." He had a family!

Kay nodded. "Will you be joining us for breakfast? Louisa and I are alone this morning."

"For a little while: I'm supposed to meet Wanda at ten-thirty."

"Wonderful. I'll have Louisa set a place for you." Somehow, Peter managed to wait until Kay quit the kitchen before collapsing into one of the Stickley-style bar stools (Heritage Design $700). His entire world was rocked, nuked, anthraxed (Baby got an atom bomb, Fluke, 1996 off of The Saint Soundtrack): nothing was left intact.

Although, to tell the truth, he did have his doubts. He had to see her, had to find out if her story was believable. She could be his half-sister, meaning he wasn't alone in the universe, but she could also be a con artist, trying to get something from him. But what? Money was the immediate answer, but why not try to cash his check? Duhh, because she was after bigger game (how many movies had he seen that emphasized this?). But was he big game? In actuality he only owned clear about a hundred grand, which really wasn't much. Although maybe it was to her, and besides, how could she know that? Maybe she was after Kay's bread, but if that were the sting, she was barking up the wrong tree: Kay already had (at least one) charity case, namely himself, and he doubted that Reham, even if truly his blood kin, would have any claim, legal or moral, on anything of Kay's (except her undying resentment). There was something fishy going on, something that wasn't quite right (weren't those people [Arabs] notoriously untrustworthy?), and he needed to keep his guard up while Reham dropped some knowledge.

Fuck, he'd almost forgotten about Wanda: he'd have to think of some excuse and call her to cancel their day. And Kay; what about Kay? He had to be super super cool for ten or fifteen minutes, made of stone, poker faced like Commander Data: he couldn't give her any clue as to what he had just learned. He had to expunge everything else out of his mind and focus on concealing the possibility (story) that his (dead) father had perhaps cheated on his (dead) mother (Peter was afraid that Kay might treat him very differently [infinitely worse] indeed if she were to find out that his father had fucked around on her sister, and while there was the chance that she might [unknowingly] either corroborate or refute Reham's tale [perhaps she'd gotten over her acrimony {perhaps his father's infidelities were the cause of this bitterness} by now and would, if not welcome the chance to unburden herself, at least be willing to talk to him about his parents {she might even want to know about Reham (yeah right)}], until he learned more about it and was able to make some sort of determination for himself, he would need to keep it secret from his aunt). He looked at the photograph again: the older woman did seem to resemble (what he remembered of) Reham. Jesus, he had a sister (maybe).

What did that mean? It meant a lot, but he couldn't deal with any of it at the moment, he had to steel himself for Kay. There was simply no way he could let Kay know anything about the existence of the letter or the photograph or Reham — she would be oh so pissed and forbid him (the punishment for disobedience, although undefined, would be certain and painful [even though he was of legal age Kay signed the checks {although he did have his job (Kay as silent partner) and trust fund}]) to pursue the matter further. Okay, he had to gather and brace himself, calm himself down: he couldn't tell her anything until he met with Reham and found out if she were telling the truth (although exactly how she would prove her story he had no idea).

He needed some water. He took one of the Orrefors rocks glasses ($25) from the (Cuveé custom) cabinet, opened the Subzero 6000 ($4700) and took a bottle of Volvic Spring Water with Essence of Lemon ($2 liter) out, poured, drank quickly, then poured another. He couldn't calm down, couldn't really keep his mind focused on one image or thought: it was as if his entire existence (self-image [he had since the age of seven thought himself an orphan, alone in the universe]) had been shattered into tiny pieces, like silver (for some reason) confetti, and he would have to examine and configure each tiny piece to reconstruct his self. The second glass of Volvic went down, but he couldn't catch his breath. Did he have a sister or not? How could he keep Kay (and Wanda) out of this for long as possible? He couldn't do this. He'd have to.

"So, dear, please sit and tell us about your day. What have you and Wanda planned for this lovely spring Saturday?"

Peter looked down at the two dozen white roses ($75 per dozen at Les Fleur Beverly Hills) in the Waterford vase ($550), three settings of Tiffany Padova flatware ($900 for eight settings plus extras), Grateau Venetian water and juice glasses ($45 each), five or six blue and white (he hated that cornflower blue) Wedgwood plates of different sizes ($25-$100), all except one (his) with various amounts of food (scones, croissants [$1.89 each], bagels [from the

Champagne Bakery {$6 dozen}], eggs [free range {$3 a dozen}], ham [Black Forest {$12 a pound} and Prosciutto di Parma {$20 per lb}], preserves [a rather odd collection including Nutella [$1.89 4 oz], Judyth Mountain Hotter Pepper Jelly [$7.50 10 oz] and McCutcheon's Amish Country Blackberry Jam [$6.99 18 oz], along with Philadelphia Cream Cheese [$1.89 8 oz] and Tori's Finnish Lox [$40 a kilo]), three Wedgwood saucers and coffee cups ($250 for set of four), a large silver thermal carafe from Stelton in Sweden ($125), a Danish wooden bagel and bread cutter with knife (Kis $80), Calvin Klein Country woven straw placemats ($35 for four) and white linen napkins from the Beverly Hills Hotel (gift from a client), all on a plain Stickley cherry breakfast table ($3700) with green caned Brighton Pavilion chairs ($200).   Schubert's Trout Quintet (Steven Lubin, fortepiano) played in the background. As he sat, Peter flashed on the image he had had of Reham, with her head tilted back on his Turkish rug: that would probably never happen (and it was too weird to think about now [or was it?]).   He had to focus on trying to appear cheerful, upbeat, perky — Fred Schneider rather than Trent Reznor, Conan O'Brien than Larry Saunders — and so he had better answer quickly.

"I think we'll go down to Bev. I might buy a new computer today.   And then Valentinos for lunch, followed either by Fashion Island or a drive up One to Santa Barbara." So far so good. "How about you?" He looked at both Kay and Louisa (to be polite) and without thinking he reached over to the carafe and poured himself a cup of coffee as Kay answered.

"I have to show a couple of oceanfronts in Newport.   And then I was going to drive up to Palm Springs and go to the Givinchy for a sauna, body wrap, massage — the whole nine yards.   I should be back

Sunday evening. Meanwhile, Louisa will be typing up contracts. I just closed two properties: a co-op in Marina del Rey and a big estate with two guest houses in Brentwood."

"Congratulations." The coffee was terrible. He added another two teaspoons of sugar while Louisa looked on. "So you're going to the Givinch to celebrate?" (that must be where Pavo was, docked at the Givinch pool bar, sniffing the botox, eyeballing the tucked gummers and dreaming [plotting?] about another cafeteria lady). "I hope you have a nice time. And your birthday's coming up. Any hints about what you want?"

"No, you have to think about it yourself. That's the fun of getting presents. Why don't you try a scone, Louisa made them herself."

"From a mix."

"Or a croissant; they're from Ivan's." Was she telling the truth? Was that his father? Where did she get that photograph?

While he might be capable of carrying on a conversation without betraying his secret, his stomach (body) was less accomplished at dissembling, which was to say that even the idea of food (especially Louisa's) was enough to make bile (mixed with the rancid, almost salty coffee) rise to his throat and spill over to the back of his tongue. "No thanks, I'm not hungry."

"It will be a long time until lunch. I know I'm playing the nag, but you really should have something to eat. Here, if you don't want a scone, Louisa will fix you some eggs or waffles. You should have something to eat Peter, you really should."

"No, no thank you. I'm really not hungry."

"I am sorry to pester you, dear, but are you sure you're feeling okay? You do look a little pale. Doesn't he look a little pale, Louisa?"

"A little pale, yes."

"There, see, you do look a little pale. Maybe you have a fever. Where is our thermometer Louisa, maybe we should take his temperature. Do you feel hot or dizzy?"

"Or cold."

"Yes, or cold?"

He couldn't take this. "No, I do not feel hot, dizzy, cold, feverish, epileptic, cancerous, constipated, nauseous" (he did), "jaundiced, sickle-celled anemic, demented or dysenteric. I do not have AIDS, TB, Hepatitis A, B or C, toxic shock, head trauma or hemorrhoids, eczema, acne or emphysema, scurvy, scabies or rabies, and I am not pregnant. Nor am I bulimic, anorexic or diarrheic. I also am not, in the very least, hungry. However, I am beginning to feel slightly annoyed, and, more importantly, guilty, because I'm going to be late to pick up Wanda. So if you'll please excuse me." He nodded to both Kay and Louisa, put down the Wedgwood cup, rose from the Brighton and wiped his lips on the BHH linen.

Where'd that come from? On the one hand, this did provide him with a viable exit, but on the other, Kay was probably angry (rudeness was never tolerated), which was always dangerous. She was staring straight ahead, holding her coffee cup with both hands near her mouth. He sat back down. "I'm sorry Kay, but really, I'm feeling fine. It's kind of stressful at work: they hired someone who does the same stuff as me, and so I'm not really sure what's going down" (that was inspired, might as well make some use of the bastard. Plus, I just learned I either have a sister nobody ever told me about, or I'm being stalked by a con artist, so yeah, things are a bit frantic at the moment). "Actually, you'd probably like him, he graduated from that British School of Finance or whatever."

Kay smiled. "The London School of Economics."

"Whatever. So, anyway, that's why I'm not hungry. And I'm sorry. To you and to you," he turned toward Louisa and back to Kay. He wasn't sure how much longer he could pull this off: he needed to get the fuck outta there as soon as possible.

"Apology accepted. Louisa?"

""I have no problem": she was a bit miffed.

"Okay you charmer. Now go, pick up that exquisite girlfriend of yours, and have a wonderful time. And don't forget lunch on Tuesday — I'll send you either an email or a voice mail from Palm Springs. And you have my cell phone number, right?"

"Of course." What was this all about, this out-pouring of affection and concern? This mother hen routine occurred sporadically, but (usually) only when she was changing gigolos: maybe Pavo's absence was more than temporary, although she seemed cheerful enough before his outburst. Against his better judg-ment (she would either tell him what was wrong [delaying and distracting him further] or she would resent the intrusion) he decided to ask.

"Everything all right with you, Kay?"

She looked at him strangely, almost angrily. "Why yes, why do you ask?"

Right again. "No reason, just wondering how you're doing."

"I'm fine, better than fine: I told you, I just closed two deals."

He stood up again smiled, and kissed her on the forehead. "That's great. Congratulations again, and I'll see you Tuesday. Louisa, I'll probably see you Tuesday too."

"Goodbye Peter."

"Ciao dear."

He should have called Wanda from the house a half hour ago, but for some reason, he wanted to get on the road as soon as he could (the way traffic was easing up he'd be at least an hour early for his appointment with destiny), and now he was afraid, because she was certain to be pissed, whereas if he had called right after breakfast, it would have been much easier to break their date. What was he going to tell her anyway (he'd turned the Blaupunkt off while still in the driveway so he'd be able to think [of an excuse]), that he was going to meet his half sister? That might somehow return to Kay (although Wanda and Kay seldom addressed each other directly, and he couldn't imagine them having [even] a [telephone] conversation without him present). Family problems would be much too vague, she wouldn't buy that, and would insist on more details about this woman who knew his father, although she probably wouldn't be as sexually jealous about his half sister as she would be about non-kin. And if he were sick, why was he driving around in his Saab? Maybe Isabella was ill and needed her grandson, although Wanda might conceivably try to contact Kay to see if she could help (and the fact that Kay would be in Palm Springs for the weekend, which, at first offered Peter a modicum of hope, due to Louisa's everpresence quickly disappeared into irrelevance). Work was a possibility: Wanda enjoyed little if any contact with the Fortunato crowd (other than accompanying him to comped concerts, industry parties and the like [stuff her dad could probably get her into anyway]), and had only been to the office once (where, as fate would have it, she struck up a rather long and involved conversation with Mila [later informing Peter that I think that

Mila girl wants you. Are you serious?]). But work had never caused him to miss anything with Wanda before, and so she was bound to be annoyed and inquisitive (he could deal with annoyed). He'd better think of something: he was already almost forty-five minutes late, which far exceeded his previous record of twenty minutes (some poor fuck committing suicide on the Five) for keeping his lady waiting (although Wanda was constantly, almost inevitably tardy, both at home [a twenty minute shoe stare at this kennel ugly room in her house was standard] and out [once she had kept him waiting an hour and a half at Turandot with some lame {I couldn't find my nose stud or my keys} excuse {making it up to him in spectacular fashion (mutual crotch munching in the Saab later that night)}]). Maybe he should just tell her the truth, and that he'd call her again that evening, the first chance he got. He had to (make himself) dial right now.

"Hi, it's me."

"Hi yourself. Where are you?"

"Listen, something's come up with my family, and, I, uh, well I'm going to have to cancel today. I'll call you this evening."

"What's come up with your family? Is something wrong?"

"I can't talk about it right now. I'll call you tonight, okay?"

"What do you mean you can't talk about it now? You can't just phone up and say 'I can't make it and I'm not going to tell you why call you later bye.' What's going on?"

This was exactly what he had feared, the fucking third degree. He took a deep breath. "Peter, are you there?"

Another deep breath. "Yeah, I'm here. Where

would I be?"

"I don't know where you'd be, because I don't know where you are." Then gently, and slowly, "Where are you? What's happening?"

She deserved an answer. "You can't mention this to Kay, you promise?"

"I know this is going to come as a shock to you, but Kay and I do not meet every morning and talk about you behind your back. Jesus Peter, of course I won't say anything."

"I'm going to meet this woman who says she knew my father."

"What? I can't hear you."

"I said I'm going to meet this woman who claims she knew my father."

"I still can't hear you. Are you on your Pocketnet? Switch to analogue." He had a hard time understanding her.

Fucking AT&T, they could reach out and touch this. "There, can you hear me now?"

"Not really. Hang up and try again." Maybe this was a blessing in disguise (he should buy AT&T stock).

He shouted into the mouthpiece, "I'm going to meet this woman who says she knew my father in Turkey. I'll call you later." There was a funny noise on the other end (almost like a scream, or a laugh), then static. He pressed a couple of buttons (beep beep beep), then switched the phone off. He was almost at the airport.

BOOK III

CHAPTER SEVEN

He had almost finished his second big beer ($7 for a 20 oz Becks) when he spied her long black hair under an embroidered blue cap (his sister!) coming down the concourse on the mechanized walkway. Immediately he was certain (somehow) she was telling the truth (they were [half] brother and sister), but as he studied her for a second or two before she noticed him — dark eyes, pale skin, high cheekbones, large nose, fragile looking neck, posture neither rigid nor relaxed — and tried to compare these images to faint recollections he had of his father (or to the physical conception he had of himself), his certainty quickly crumbled. When she noticed him she waved, and he waved back. She had to pass by on the walkway (well-worn faded blue Levis 501s [$35] with a blue, red and yellow Missoni knock-off sweater tied around her waist [The Limited $95], a black sleeveless cotton oxford [Old Navy $25], six small gold hoop earrings [two new in left ear, Piercing Pagoda, Boston $65 total] and her Timberland boots, carrying an old North Face black vinyl backpack [$28]) and then double back, and so, as he stood, drinking his beer and waiting, he had time to think more about how to play this: skeptic or believer, agnostic or initiate, apostate or convert, infidel or mullah.

One thing was for certain, they'd have to go elsewhere: the Ports of Call Bar at Concourse C was a magnet for doomed young business louts (a telemarketers convention) in casual Fridays Dockers ($59), Van Heusen Polos ($50), Tommy Hilfiger and Nautica sportcoats ($99-$129), Hush Puppy and Dexter loafers

($89), with 3Com Palmpilots V ($379), Cassiopeias PC E-20's ($289), Ericsson Omnipoint CH388 Digitals ($49), Sony Dual Mode Sprints PCS ($249) and Structure's Consequences of Pragmatism for Men ($16 4 oz) loudly cheering the Supersonics against the Rockets. Reham would be the only female in the joint. The rest of the airport was just as crowded, as the software salesmen were either returning from or embarking on their coach class $150 per diem junkets to Tulsa, Pittsburgh and Omaha. He'd have to steer her out of here as quickly as possible: a quick cab to the Marriott and then the big conversation (he wondered if she was carrying more photographs and papers in her North Face) in private (although it might look bogus, getting a room for a couple of hours with only her small backpack between them [But we're brother and sister followed by the knowing nods]).

As she approached, he wondered what he was going to say to her. He had been sitting at the bar for almost an hour, looking at the photograph and reading the letter, going over various plans and possibilities (ranging from the wealthy long lost sister interpretation to the desperate terrorist grifter scenario) in his head, but none of that seemed appropriate or adequate to what he was feeling now. She was beautiful, that was for sure (he noticed several pairs of Docker eyes tracking her as she walked through the small bar), but he really had no other programs or scripts to help him play his part. He had no lines to memorize, no gestures to copy, no familiar music to help set the mood, and even his costume, which he could usually rely on to situate himself, was designed for a much different play (when he dressed this morning it was with an eye to buying a computer and enjoying an expensive lunch with his girlfriend, not to meeting his possible half-sister in an airport bar and taking her to a hotel room).

He would keep his guard up. It was important not to play the fool.

She (she uemura sheer Rose #172 Lip Rouge [$15], Clinique Darkest Gray Eye Pencil Eye Shadow [$20], she uemara Mascara Basic [$27], Revlon Midnight Eyebrow Pencil [$12], Face Stockholm Neutral Foundation Cream [$35], Sally Hansen White Colorfast Nail Polish [$15] and Emanuel Ungaro Philosophical Investigations [$80/oz]) walked up to his table and they stood there: their eyes met (she wasn't wearing her glasses) and then they both looked down. He smiled and looked up at her again, "Hello Reham, how are you?"

She looked at him nervously. "I did not think you would come."

"I wasn't going to until I saw the second picture and read the second note." A roar went up from the crowd, and the bartender increased the volume of the tv, "In a stunning turn of events Gary Payton. . ." Reham winced and looked around.

"Why don't we go somewhere else?"

"Pardon me?"

"Why don't we go somewhere else?"

"Yes, yes."

"Do you have any other bags?"

"I'm sorry?

"Is this your only bag?"

"Oh no, I have two big suitcases, but I checked those in Boston, and the university is shipping my art. Where should we go?"

"Let's just get out of here for now."

She nodded, turned quickly and walked rapidly out of the bar, while he had to gather his things and catch up. Reham had dropped her knapsack, and was lighting a Marlboro ($2 per pack).

"I don't think you can smoke here."

"I am sorry. Does it bother you?"

"It doesn't bother me" (although it did), "but it's against the law. If you want to smoke, we have to go back in there," he turned back toward the bar," or find one of those glass-enclosed smoking areas." He hesitated. "Or we could go somewhere else."

She dropped the cigarette to the floor and ground it out with her heel. "This country has many rules." She looked at him, "Where do you wish to go?"

"We could get a cab and go to the Marriott nearby." She was wearing a lot of makeup.

She looked away quickly. "The Marriott is a hotel, yes?"

"It's a quiet place where we can talk."

Still looking away, "I'm not sure this would be clever."

For some (unknown) reason it was important that at least this (the Marriott) part of his vague plan work out. "Jesus Reham, what do you think I'm going to do? You asked me here to tell me about my father, and now you won't even talk to me. You weren't even straight with me from the beginning, sending two halves of the photograph and a couple of cryptic notes. If I'm really your brother, or half-brother, as you say, you owe it to me to tell me the whole story, and not in some goddam airport bar with the tv blaring, surrounded by assholes trying to overhear."

"In my culture it is meaningful if two people go to a hotel together. Other people talk."

"No one's even going to see you, let alone talk about you. Los Angeles is a big city; it's easy to get lost. Besides, we're brother and sister, so what could they say? C'mon, we'll get a room where you can smoke."

The last statement seemed to sway her. She hesitated. "My airplane departs in three hours."

"I promise you'll be back in time."

She hesitated, then nodded. "As you wish."

Hotel rooms (Marriott Airport LAX, $149 a night) always made him horny, and despite her heavy pancake job (an exaggeration: California Pete was familiar with and attracted to only the most subtly applied [that All-American girl next door look {although he did like piercings}] cosmetics [except when Wanda {or someone like her} went punk {spiked hair, kohl eyes and tomato red lips}]), so as he closed the door little Pete stood up to get a better look. She took off her cap (nice hair), put her pack on the bed, turned away and lit a cigarette. The room smelled of previous smoke, and he could hear water running somewhere above. The floral print curtains and matching bedspread were hideous, as was the desk and television armoire (this certainly wasn't L'Hermitage [$320], the Bev [$1350 for a suite] or even the Avalon [$240 a night]), although the king-size bed was nice and big.

He stood near the door for a while, then moved into the room and sat on the edge of the bed. She stood still, her back toward him, smoke rising slowly above her head. He thought about putting his arms around her, or at least touching her shoulders with his hands, but he (wisely) did nothing. He sat on the bed and waited.

She slowly moved toward the window and shut the heavy hotel drapes. The room went dark, and as his eyes adjusted, he focused on the orange tip of her burning cigarette (she must have turned around). The soft sound of water running continued above. He was almost afraid to breathe too deeply.

"I did not come to the States to meet you. I knew about you, had heard stories about you, and knew that you lived in Los Angeles, but as you say, Los Angeles has many many people, and I did not come to see you. I came because of my art: meeting you was only a strange accident.

"When I was a smaller little girl, I used to wonder about you. I thought that you would be handsome, and would come and take me away from where I was, take me with you to the United States, and we would live like they live on the television they let me watch at the fruit market. When I first met you, I did not know it was you, but when I heard the story of your family, and then saw your name on the cheque, I knew that fate had led me to you. I was upset, and did not know what to do, did not know what you would want me to do. I finally decided to inform you, tell you about my family and about myself. I thought that because we are related, I should give this thing, this knowledge to you, but I am not certain that this is the correct thing to do."

As his eyes became accustomed to the darkness, he saw that she wasn't facing him, but had her face and body turned toward the side wall, so he was looking at her profile. He started to speak, to reassure her, but his mouth was dry and nothing came out but a scratchy cough. He swallowed and said, perhaps too loudly for the darkness of the room, "You did the right thing. Thank you."

"Perhaps, and perhaps you are answering too soon. I read a proverb in an American book once, that a free lunch does not exist. I did not understand what that proverb meant until I asked my teacher, who explained it to me: every gift has a cost. This is true, every gift has a cost."

He followed the arc of the burning tip as she lifted the cigarette to her mouth, took a deep drag, and dropped it to an ashtray on the desk, where she tapped it twice and set it down. He pinched the cheap nylon cotton blend of the bedspread (at least the murk obscured the too vivid crimsons, citrons and flamingos of the floral decor) and wondered what had happened to his pre-meeting resolution of keeping his guard up, of playing the skeptic and forcing Reham to prove to him the truth of her story. At the moment, his guard was a high as Bruno's or Botha's (or any pale canvas chewer), and he had about as much detachment and doubt as Leesa Gibbons (da da da da da da Up next, the real story behind Air Bud, Ben Stiller and Hershey Chocolate Kisses. After this). His sister was enchanting (more like Fairuza Balk [nice name] or big-lipped Neve [We are the weirdos, mister] than Sabrina), and he would have to keep reminding himself that she hadn't proven anything yet, that this whole thing might be some sort of (as yet unidentified) Usual Suspects fuck-job, so he'd better watch his own back.

He remained staring at her silhouette (which was a demi-shade darker than the curtains in the background), as if somehow he could look through the darkness, obscurity and murk and see what he wanted to see, see the truth laid out before him, unambiguous and clear, crisp and sharp like a freshly pressed Brooks Brothers suit. He stared (trying [and failing] to cut through the veil of memory, language [silence] and desire) and waited (in anticipation and dread of what she might say), squinting through the gloom, for some unidentifiable amount of time (a minute? an hour? day? lifetime? two lifetimes?), until finally she spoke again. He leaned forward to hear her low, dark voice.

"I do not remember my mother very much. I have heard she was an educated woman, not a peasant. It was not easy for her to bear a child without being married. It was worse because the child was the child of an American, an American Jew. In the

Palestinian part of Ankara, where my mother and I lived, they do not love Americans. They, we, do not hate Americans, but we do not love you either. We do not love you when you lie with our women and then go away.

"I do not know what I think about my father, our father. It was not right for him to lie with my mother and then go away. I understand about the sex; I know what it feels like to want to sex, to have sex with someone and then want to go away, but our father should not have left my mother with me. She was poor, she had nobody, and then there was me. And he was in America. With you.

"My mother taught school, English and Turkish, until I was ready to come out, to be born, and then they would not let her teach school anymore. We did not have enough to eat. I do not remember my mother very well — I do not think about what she looked like or how she was to me — but I do remember many times not having enough to eat. And then she died.

"It is not for certain how she died. I remember a man, a Turk, perhaps a policeman, coming to our apartment and taking me in his car to a tall building, where a big woman took me into a dirty yellow room that smelled like animals, and there she told me my mother was dead. She asked me in Arabic who my father was, and if anyone was related to me, or if we had any friends in Ankara where they could take me. I did not know what to say. I did not know what had happened to my mother, and I did not know what was going to happen to me. I did not know my father, and we had no friends or relations where I could go: the children I played with in the street, their mothers would not let me come to their homes, because I was an incorrect child, the son of an American, a Zionist. I began to cry. The woman became angry, and yelled at me in Turkish to stop crying, but I could not. She came toward me, and I thought she was going to beat me, but she left the room and slammed the door. I thought she was going to leave me forever in that yellow room, that room that smelled of goats and horses, and I cried even harder. But after a while, the woman returned with a Coca-Cola and a piece of lamacan, which is Turkish pizza, and put it on her desk in front of me. I like Coca-Cola and lamacan very much, but I did not want to be impolite. The woman told me to eat, and after a while I stopped crying and ate. I am not certain it truly occurred this way, I could have dreamt some of it; this is how it seems to me, not real, like a dream. But I have no other memory of my mother's death, and so I believe that at least some part of this must have truly occurred."

She took another drag of her cigarette and stubbed it out in the ashtray.

"I don't remember much about the time that followed this. I remember this building, which was made out of cool concrete and large gray blocks, where I was taken and where I lived. There were other girls there, but they were Turkish, and unfriendly to me. They did not hit me or say anything to me, but they would not talk to me or play with me. There was not much to do in this building: I think that some of the girls went to school, but I was too young or not allowed, I do not know. I remember taking my bowl of food and going back to the room where we slept, and eating alone on my bed, but I do not remember what I thought or how I felt. I remember there was not much to do, for we were only allowed outside into the court-yard, and we had no books to read or papers to draw on inside. I remember that one day a little girl, about my age, came into the room where we were ready to sleep, and that after we were supposed to sleep some of the other girls went to her bed and quietly beat her. I saw her the next morning at breakfast, and her face was bruised, but she looked proud. She too brought her bowl into the sleeping room, and ate in the corner with her back toward me. That night, the girls beat her again, and that morning, she took her bowl into the sleeping room and ate with her back toward me again. This happened many times, and I don't remember how it began, but soon we started talking, and then playing. She told me her name was Güler, and she was a Kurd, that was why these dirty Turks beat her. I told her I was not a dirty Turk and would not beat her. One morning soon after that, she was gone. I remember how proud she looked, even though she was blue and purple with the beatings. After that I was alone again, and do not remember much."

Peter, who was usually inured (he was from LA) to sob stories (very few tales [according to him] could match his own for sheer pain and suffering [although Kay would sometimes regale him with narratives starring unremembered high school acquaintances {his}, progeny of distant clients {hers}, or former hired help {theirs}, accounts that usually began with too much to drink or smoke, and ended with graphic descriptions of twisted metal, padded rooms or AIDS hospices {one of Wanda's good friends had contracted HIV, then full-blown AIDS and had died last year} followed by a shaking of the head {hers}, signifying {he supposed} that God could be a mean son of a bitch]), found himself strangely moved by Reham's story: she was even more alone, more of an orphan, than he was (Peter always had a soft spot for girls in trouble). Still, he retained enough self-consciousness to realize that it was somehow possibly no coincidence that she was pushing all the right buttons.

"That time was vague for me, unclear, and I remember only flashes, images, surrounded by blankness. I remember Güler, and her beaten and proud face; I remember being bored, but how I escaped that boredom I do not know; I remember eating the lamb and pide by myself on my bed, but I don't remember being full, and I don't remember being hungry. I remember the coldness of the concrete floor and brick walls, but I don't remember the feel of the blankets on my skin, the sunshine on my hair, or the mud from the tap where we washed but did not drink. I was like a dog, with no memory of feelings, and the days passed for me like they pass for a dog, one day after another, each day filled only with eating and sleeping. I did not speak much, and as all I heard was Turkish, I began to forget my Arabic. I am not sure about this, it was told to me by the man who called himself my uncle, some time later, when he became angry because I could not understand his commands. I learned Arabic again, and English, but I am mixing things up and not telling the story as it happened.

"As I said, that time for me was vague and unclear, and I do not remember much about myself at all. One day, after some time, I do not know how long, a man with a thick long beard came to see me, the man I mentioned earlier. He did not look at me, but spoke Arabic to me, and told me that he was my uncle, and that Allah, the great, the merciful and the just, had punished me for my mother's sin, but the time of punishment was finished, and I was to come with him to a new place, a place far away, where I would be with my own people.

"I was happy: happy that I would leave this place, and happy that I had an uncle, someone who was a relation of mine. I was a little frightened too, because the man with a beard, my uncle, was not the type to gather affection from small girls. I did not understand when he said Allah was punishing me for my mother's sin, but I did not like that thought. I was happy too because I thought he was going to take me back to my old neighborhood in Ankara, and I would be allowed to play again, and maybe go to school. He handed me two bags that were like nets, and said that we would go as soon as I gathered my things.

"I did not have much, and so used only one bag. He nodded to me, and then stood as if to go. I remember this very clearly: it is really the start of my clear memories. Before, I can remember only a few things, but beginning with my uncle's visit, I remember very much better. Anyway, he stood up as if to leave, but he did not know how to go, he did not know the way, because there were three doors in the sleeping room, and he did not remember which one to go back out of. I crossed near him, and walked to the door which led out to the courtyard and out to the street. He walked behind me to the door and then struck me on the side of the head with an opened hand. 'You have lived too long in the city of Ash-Shaytan, and have forgotten the fiqh, the laws of the Prophet, peace be upon him. Never walk in front of me, child, or you will be corrected.' My mother never struck me, and the people who supervised the concrete and brick building never struck me, but the man who said he was my uncle struck me after only a few minutes. I remember very well how his hand felt on my head: it did not hurt my head so much, but hurt something inside of me much more. When I was living in that building after my mother died, I did not think about myself, about what had happened to me, about what would happen to me. When the man with the beard came, my uncle, and told me he was going to take me from this building, I had the hope of a child that my life might perhaps be better, that I would be able to play and go to school, but when he struck me on the head, he struck away that hope, and I knew that he was not going to take me back to Ankara, but to a new and perhaps even more harsh life, someplace far away. I became very sad. My uncle struck me more times after this, always as corrections, but this was the most important time.

"I followed him outside into the courtyard and out of the courtyard into the street. I had not been outside into the street since that woman who gave me Coca-Cola and lamacan brought me after my mother was buried. It was hot outside and he motioned for me to get into a big brown truck, the kind men sometimes bring fruit or animals in from the country. We drove quickly out of Ankara, and my uncle did not look at me or speak to me for many kilometers."

Reham stopped speaking and coughed. Peter swallowed hard: the uncle (his uncle?) was a real bastard (Peter hated religious fanatics in general, but anybody who'd hit a kid because she wouldn't walk behind him was sick). God, what a life — he thought he had a shitty childhood, but he never had an uncle smack him for anything (his uncles [Michael and David and even, by marriage, Robert Johns] had thankfully never felt the duty to step in [after his father died] to try to establish themselves as some sort of masculine authority presence in his life, and so had neither opportunity nor cause to hit him. He had never even imagined getting hit, although now that he thought about it, Davey might clip him one if sufficiently provoked [but he had no idea of how such a provocation might be accomplished]), and that cement building with those snot-nosed bullies sounded fucking bleak (what was the name of that flick he saw in school, with those Mexicans or whatever? Pixote, yeah it was like Pixote). And this was his sister, at four or five years old, eating and playing by herself, Christ. How old was she? "How old were you?"

"I do not know. As I've said, I cannot remember much about that time."

"How old are you now?"

He saw her profile shift. Perhaps she was looking at him (finally). He heard the water running above, then suddenly stop. In the silence that followed, he thought he could hear her breathing heavily. Was she crying? Or maybe she was pissed because he asked her about her age. Someone bumped against the wall in the next room, and he thought he heard a bed creak. The water began again in the same place. When she spoke again he could barely hear her.

"Because my life has been so unsteady, it is very difficult for me to tell stories. I do not remember many things, and some things I do remember are like dreams to me, and I am not certain they truly happened. Even with things I remember clearly, I sometimes do not know where in the story they belong, and sometimes, unless I concentrate strongly, I put things I remember in places they do not belong, and so the story I am telling gets mixed up, and does not create much sense.

"I am grateful that you are listening, but please, do not stop me, for I will get lost in my telling, and my story will not create much sense. I cannot tell my story another way, and so please, please, do not stop me anymore. I am not certain my story will satisfy you, but I have hope it will help you know a little about me, and a little about our father, but if my story is not told correctly, then it will not help you know anything. I realize this is a strange way to tell a story, and I wish I could tell it easier, but I cannot."

She stopped abruptly, like a paused cd, the reverberation of her voice swallowed by the curtains, carpet and bedclothes.

"I will finish here if you wish."

He was certain she was looking at him now. "Please go on."

She laughed. "I am even worse in Turkish or Arabic: my stories create no sense at all. I will first get a drink of water." He remained on the edge of the bed, listening to the tap behind him echo the water above (what were they doing up there?), thinking about a small alone Reham eating (with her fingers) beans out of a (broken) bowl on her (narrow) bed, while he parked himself by the prawn boat at the Sea Cliff buffet for his grandparents' fortieth anniversary (he wasn't sure about the time frame) and chowed (each shrimp almost as big as his hand) until he made himself sick (ruining his new Buster Browns with a spray of half-digested reddish cocktail sauce and pink chunks of crustaceans in the parking lot [he never saw those shoes again]). It wasn't fair.

She opened the door and light spilled into the room, illuminating a slice of bedspread, carpet and curtain before being extinguished. He felt her move back into the room, and then sit on the bed, near the pillows: half brother and sister now separated by only a couple of feet of bedspread, sheet and mattress. She shifted around on the bed, and his mouth got even drier.

"I remember our journey very well, with much detail. I remember that after we left Ankara, after a while, my uncle began to talk to me. That is not exact, he did not really talk to me like I am talking to you, rather he talked as if to the air, and I was there in the truck with him, and I listened. He talked about my mother, and about how she had been punished for her sin. He said, and I do not know if he was telling the truth, that my mother had been put out of her family, her friends, and her religion after I was born. It was a sin to lie with a married man, that was certain, but it was an even greater sin to lie with a Zionist, and American, our enemy, one of the devils who were killing our people. Such a sin could only be forgiven by the Prophet, peace be upon him, and my mother had received what she deserved. It was still light, and I remember looking out the window at the dusty roads, and the villages where covered women with colorful scarves led donkeys with big loads of sticks into the stables, as my uncle kept saying, again and again, that my mother had been punished, thrown out of her job, her family and friends, and that perhaps, before she died, she had learned her lesson, and I remember then beginning to hate. I did not hate my uncle, or I did not hate only my uncle, but I hated many things, a big hate that included many things. I did not hate my mother, but I began to hate the truck with the torn seat that hurt my bottom, the dusty roads with bumps, and those women who were so ashamed of their own faces they covered them up. I even hated the donkeys that walked behind, carrying those big loads of sticks. I told myself I would never cover my face, even with pretty scarves, and I told myself I would never walk behind.

"After a while, before it became dark, my uncle became quiet. He drove off the road and parked on the side, and told me that he had to pray, and that I should leave him for an hour, but when I returned, we would have something to eat, and then sleep. I did not know what an hour was — I have never had a good idea of time — but I had to go to the toilet, so I walked far away, over a hill where my uncle could not possibly see, and went to the toilet. I then walked back to the top of the hill, sat on a big rock, and watched the truck while the sky got darker and darker until I could no longer see the truck. I sat there on the rock until it was very dark: I do not know what I was waiting for, but I remember I was waiting for something. I know that I was not frightened. I knew that if I wanted to go to the truck, I only had to walk down the hill until I got to the road and then follow the road up or down until I found it. I knew my uncle, although he might become angry, would not leave me there in the dark, because he had driven very far to find me. I sat on the rock and I waited in the dark, and I prayed. I did not pray for forgiveness, because I had done nothing wrong. I did pray for my mother, but not for her to be forgiven, because she too had done nothing wrong, but I prayed that Allah had taken her, and she was sitting close to the Prophet, peace be upon him. I did not pray to be put in a better place, because perhaps it was Allah's will, the great and merciful, that I should be sitting on that rock and praying. I did pray that Allah would allow me my hate, would let me keep it as mine, as the only thing I owned. I was young then, very young and not wise, but I knew that the hate I felt for those who had injured my mother was very important to me, and it would help me live in the hard ways I knew I would be made to live. I also prayed that Allah, in his mercy and wisdom, would leave me, would go away from me for a time so I would not be able to hate Him, Him who in my ignorance and stupidity I blamed for permitting the others, like my uncle, to hurt my mother. I asked Him, the great and merciful God, for a sign, a sign that he had heard my prayer and was leaving away from me, and that sign would be silence and darkness. I sat there for a very long time, praying and watching and listening, happy that I heard nothing but my own breath in the air, happy that I saw nothing but darkness like ink all around. I know this may not sound meaningful, but I have never felt as close to God as when I sat on that rock that night, and knew He was leaving away from me.

"I sat there on the rock for some time, until finally I became tired, and hungry as well, and I walked back in the darkness to my uncle and the truck. I believe he had been sleeping, but had wakened when he heard me come. He was very angry and asked me where I had been, but when I told him I had been praying he was not as angry as before. He said I would have to learn how to behave according to the laws given to the Prophet, peace be upon him, and that he would teach me. He gave me a pear, some grapes and bread, and half of a bottle of water — it is funny how I remember everything so well — and told me to eat and then to sleep up in the front of the truck, while he went to the back. I ate, and then I went to sleep.

"In the morning we ate more grapes and bread, and drove without saying much, and we came to a big town and then to a border. I had no papers, but my uncle had the papers of someone else, some other little girl, and then, and even today perhaps, the soldiers do not check the papers of small girls very carefully, and so we had not much trouble. All of the signs and language was Arabic now, not Turkish, and my uncle seemed to feel better. The land became more flat, and much hotter, and there was not much to see out of the window. We stopped for many times for petrol, and my uncle would not let me leave the truck, even to straighten my legs. Once when he stopped, I saw a man say something to my uncle, and when he returned to the truck, he was very angry again. When we arrived at Al Quds, I heard him tell my aunt that we did not go through Lebanon because of the Zionist airplanes, and had to go the way around through An-Nabk. Anyway, my uncle was angry we could not drive the way he wanted to drive, and his mood became even worse.

"After we drove a little while more, I had again to go to the toilet. My uncle was in a very bad mood and I was afraid to ask him to stop the truck, and so I said nothing. I said nothing for a long time, but the truck bounced, and the chair of the truck was very thin, really only metal and plastic with a piece of cloth tied over it, and soon I could not wait, and I had to ask my uncle to stop by the road so I could run out into the sand. My uncle was angry about having to drive, he was angry about having to stop, and so he wanted to punish me, or correct me, and because he wanted to punish me, when I returned to the truck he told me a story. A story about my, our, father, and you.

"I had always been taught not to think about my father, not to wonder about him or question why he was not together with me. I knew that he was an American, but I did not know much else, and did not much care. I did not think about him when my mother died; I did not wish for him to come and take me from that building with the Turkish girls. He had left from my mother and me: why would I think about him? But my uncle, because he wanted to make me angry, told me of the big house my father had owned in Los Angeles, California, where everyone was rich from the big movies, and everyone had a swimming pool and drove three cars. He told me my father had once lived there with his Zionist wife and his Zionist child, and they ate the sweetest fruit and the richest and softest lamb every day, while I was alone in that Turkish prison, as he called it. My uncle said that you, my brother, had gone to a good school, and had a bright red bicycle that you rode after school, and that you had many clothes and played sports with your friends, and then had watched a big television at night with your mother and my, our, father. My uncle then said that Allah had decided to punish my father for lying with my mother, and had put his hand out and caused his airplane to crash and burn, not very far from where my mother was buried. This is how I learned that my father too was dead. This is how I learned about you."

Peter started to ask a question, but then stopped, remembering the warning. So she never even met him (their father), and had nothing more tangible, as far as he could tell (as far as she had told), than that stupid blurry photograph, which she had ripped in half to convince him to meet with her: so much for hard evidence and incontrovertible proof. The only other thing she had, they had, was the half-remembered at least second-hand tale of some goddam Islamic nut told fifteen years ago to a little girl to punish her for having to squirt. So this is it, this was thing that was changing his life, jeopardizing his relationships, threatening his stability and destroying the way he had always (for the last eighteen years anyway) thought of himself: the badly recalled (didn't she admit she couldn't always remember things in order) broken English rerun of a story told by some malicious towel-headed prick how many years before, to a little orphan girl who didn't even know how old she was. Who knows if the uncle was even telling the truth, that bastard, he could have made the whole thing up just to scare or hurt the girl. Christ, what a joke, it was like a bad episode of South Park: Who Killed Kenny's Dad?

She never even met their dad: he had better memories of the old man than she did. After conception, she was never even in the same room as their father. What could she tell him? What could she offer? She had even less to go on than he did. He should be telling her of that time on the beach, or his seventh birthday party when his dad (why did the fucker look so vague all of the time, all grays and beiges, the walking definition of nondescript) took him to see the Dodgers play the Giants, and while they did eat hot-dogs and his dad had a couple of beers, unlike that MasterCard commercial (baseball — $9, box seat tickets — $50, program — $7, talking with your son — priceless), they didn't share a lot of precious conversation (Do you want another hotdog? No thanks. Nachos? Sure. [did he even like baseball {Peter didn't}?]). Or he could narrate (straightforward, no bullshit, like fucking Hemingway) the time his father took him to the Young People's Symphony (his mother was on the program), and Peter, who had a cold, couldn't stop coughing. Instead of gracefully and smilingly removing him from the auditorium, his father stared straight ahead, eyes focused and jawline rigid, leaving Peter to receive alone the dirty looks, shhh's and whispered admonitions. He'd started to cry, and he remembered quite vividly (one of his few detailed recollections) the smell of his father's breath (dinner coffee and tuna salad) and the painful grip on his arm as dear old daddy dearest threatened to sell the goddam tv if Peter wouldn't shut up and sit still for a goddam half an hour so at least he, his father, could enjoy the music. Who was this man? Who was he?

So what was she dropping on him? What was she telling him that he didn't already know? Their father was gone and no one could even be certain what he looked like. That was it. His father, their father, was dead and buried, mourned (missed, wondered about) by his two children only, half a world apart: one who had never met him and the other who couldn't recall a single conversation they had had of more than five minutes' duration. Although his image faded easily and quickly, the man must have possessed something while alive, some spark or charisma. Moms was quite a catch and if Reham's mother looked anything like the daughter, well, let's just say he wouldn't kick her out of bed (she wasn't his stepmother or anything like that). My father the swordsman, hung like a stallion, Big Paul and Little Paul, Paulie. Maybe, or maybe not: it really didn't matter now, did it?

So what was he doing there, sitting in the dark listening to some sob story that happened half a world away and half a lifetime ago (if he wanted to feel depressed he'd watch the news), killing (or making) time with a dark head hootchie when he could be macking on his American blond girlfriend, or buying some kick-ass computer (maybe the teal and silver Mac was the way to go)? It was a mistake to come, and was becoming more of a mistake to stay. He should split, fold up his tent and cut his losses, he could probably still catch Wanda and they could make Valentinos by two, two thirty. Enough with this experiment about recreating his past: from now on he would just accept who he was (an orphan), and try to live his life the best he could. Kay was right, leave sleeping bitches alone. Okay, he'd take her back to the airport, buy her a magazine, and say sayonara (or whatever) for ever. Later sis, this ain't no Brady Bunch (and didn't Greg boink Marcia every chance he got?). He had no business here (nothing to gain). It was time to go.

And yet he wouldn't, couldn't leave, even though (or because) he (strongly) suspected Reham's narrative wouldn't take a dramatic turn for the better anytime in the near future. Despite his disappointment, anger and impatience, he (somewhat) believed they were, after all (if everyone was telling [at least the partial] truth) half-brother and sister, and he owed it to her to allow her to narrate her life to him, no matter how difficult (spooky) the narration or uncomfortable (twisted) the events being described. Compared to her life, his was Disney, and the very least he could do was to let her finish.

But why was this so important to him? What

did it mean, that she (if everyone were telling at least the partial truth) was his half sister? What was he staying for? Just to prove to himself that he wasn't alone? Why was that so important? What if she really was his sister, what then? Would his life be changed? Fuck no, she'd go back to Turkey, he'd stay in Bel Air, a couple of letters and cards, maybe even a small check or two once in a while, that would be it. And he was wasting the entire afternoon (more if you counted all that worrying and anxiety) for this? This was bullshit; it was time to get back to his life. He sat absolutely still.

"After he told me about my father and you, my uncle was not angry any more, but quiet. Perhaps he felt regret about telling me these things, perhaps he thought that it would have been better to keep silent. I did not know what to think about my father, for I could not feel sad about someone who was never with me; I could not feel grief about someone I did not know. I did, however, think and question to myself about you. I had a brother! That was very exciting. I did not know before about you, my mother never told me: perhaps she did not know or perhaps it would have been more shame upon her. And then, before I could think much about you — what you looked like, how old you were, if you were big and blond like I pictured Americans in my mind — I thought that maybe you had died in the plane with our father. That idea did not make me feel sad for you, because we had not met, but for me, because I wanted to have the idea of you, the idea of you that would say to me always that someone else alive in the world shared my blood. I so wanted you not to be dead, but I dared not ask my uncle, for I knew that such a question would make him furious. But I needed to know, I needed to know more than anything, and this need overcame my fear, and as we drove through the outer part of Dimashq, I finally asked my uncle if you had died in the crash of my father's plane.

"He turned to look at me, straight, for perhaps the first time, and then quickly his eyes returned to the road. He did not speak, and I thought perhaps he might strike me. We drove, and the town became thicker and thicker, and there were many cars, and I remember seeing a camel for the first time and thinking at first that it was some kind of horse that had been injured, and then understanding and saying to myself, so this is a camel, and still my uncle said nothing. I thought that you must have been killed, and my uncle did not want to tell me and hurt me anymore; but then I thought that you must be alive, and my uncle did not want to tell me to give me hope. We drove into the center of town, past the big Ommayed mosque, and still he said nothing. Finally, as we were leaving the city, he spoke, again as if to the air, and said that it was Allah's will that you remained alive, praise be to His mercy.

"I felt great joy then, not for you, but for myself. I knew that you were alive, you existed, and so I could dream and think about you, and these thoughts and dreams about you were my own, like my hate, and could not be taken from me. This is funny to say, but my thoughts of you have always been close to my hate for others, they are like cousins who share the same room. We shared a father, blood, and this blood allowed me to have a strong imagination about you, and this strong imagination helped me keep living through hard things and times. I did not always think good thoughts about you. Sometimes, when the time was bad, I would curse you for failing to come to help me, and my hate for others almost became a hate for you. And sometimes I was certain that you would come, and I would see it in my mind, as I would walk home from school, I would see you getting on an airplane in California, and flying to Tel Aviv, and then taking the bus to Al Quds and bringing me new Levis jeans and a bicycle from a big American store, and we would go to California and live in your big house with a swimming pool. This is why, when I was young, I always tried to learn and practice my English, so you would not be ashamed of me when we lived in California — of course, that was not the only reason. You were very important to me, my brother, especially when I was smaller. As time passed, I did not think or dream about you like I did at first, but the idea of you has been my friend ever since my uncle told me about you in the truck.

"My uncle drove us to his home in Al Quds, where I lived with my aunt Munnever, who was my mother's sister, and her three children, my cousins Fatma, Zehra and Ali. My aunt was younger than my mother, and because my mother had gone to university and learned bad ways, my aunt was punished by her parents and was made to marry my uncle, Emad Ellali, at a very young age. My aunt was meek, and did everything she was supposed to do, everything the shari'ah, the fiqu, the Koran and my uncle told her to do. She loved my mother, and when she died, I believe she felt the free part of her also died. She was very strict with me, but would also try to shelter me from my uncle, who wanted me to behave more as a servant or housecleaner, and who thought that it was not important for girls to go to school, especially stupid girls who should stay home and help their aunt who was kind and generous praise be to Allah. I would sneak out to go to school, and my aunt would not tell my uncle, and would not answer his questions clearly when he asked if I had helped her around the house. Finally, after a little while, he saw me walking home and asked where I had been. I did not lie to him, and he was angry for a while, but not as angry as either my aunt or I expected him to be. From then on, I went to school with my cousins.

"One night after dinner, after my uncle went to drink tea with his friends, my aunt called me into their room and presented me with a book, the book you put pictures in. She told me that a few weeks after my mother died, it had come inside a valise full of dresses to the post office in the old city, where, out of pure chance and kindness, an old Jewish man who knew my grandparents saw it in the pile, and delivered it himself to my aunt. The book was only about half full, and it had some pictures of my mother and father, like I gave to you. There was also one or two letters from my father to my mother, but she would not allow me read them then, for I was too young."

Peter couldn't help himself. "Where is the book now? Do you have it?"

The silence that followed took on a physical presence, surrounding each of them like separate blankets. Even the water had stopped running. Jesus Christ, here we go again. So there was evidence, a book of photographs and letters — better than nothing he supposed, although he was sick of knowing his father (and mother) only through semigloss snapshots and had hoped for something more concrete and intimate, something three dimensional and definite, although what that thing might be he had no idea. And now the waiting game, as if he were waiting for her page to download so he could get the rest of the story, although, truth be told, he didn't mind at all sitting alone on the bed in the dark with her (don't go there Peter).

He needed to have a look at that book. There had to be at least one picture there that would more closely resemble one in his footlocker (and therefore provide more convincing proof that he wasn't being Busta'd [Who do I look like, Montel Williams? Do I look like Montel Williams to you?], because no matter how much he wanted to believe her story [sad though it was {for her}], he was having a hard time shaking [or ignoring] the feeling that he was being played). He doubted that she carried the book with her (she would have shown it by now): maybe she would send it to him when she got back to Istanbul or wherever she lived now. He would pay for it, FedEx, although he couldn't suggest that now or she'd clam up for a month. He tried to look at the clock, but couldn't see it from where he was sitting. The water above started running again. After a while she spoke.

"I realize that this book is most important to you, but as I've tried to say, I cannot tell my story unless I can continue without distraction. This is very difficult for me, as it is for you, I am sure, but if my story is to create the sense you desire, my story must be allowed to be told in its own way, in the only way I am able to tell it."

Okay, okay, Christ.

"After my aunt showed the book to me, we looked through some of the pictures together, and I saw the face of my father for the very first time. I was not very interested, as I've told you before. I thought to myself, this is my father, this is where I come from, I should pay more attention, but I did not: he was not important to me. After we looked at the book, my aunt showed to me my mother's dresses, dresses my mother had worn and now my aunt sometimes wore under her chador. My aunt let me put some of the dresses on, then she called in my cousins Fatma and Zehra, we all tried the dresses on and played together for a long time, and we had very much fun together.

Every time after that when I looked at the picture of my mother and father, I think of those dresses, and how much fun it was to wear them with my aunt and my cousins that day. Even now I am thinking about them, as I tell you about our father.

"These times were hard, but they were good for me: I went to school, I played with my cousins, my aunt was kind to me, and I tried to be quiet and unnoticeable around my uncle. Often when my uncle did notice me, he would correct me for some reason or another, but soon these corrections became less, and then they finished. I was not becoming more pleasing to my uncle, but he was thinking of other things. There was beginning a battle, a war in our country and city, in Al Quds, and this war was between my people and the Zionist monsters, the Zionist bastards who wish to drive us from our land. The Israeli soldiers came and closed our school, and many families were exiled from their houses. When they tried to keep some men from going to the mosque, we fought back. The soldiers were strong and had many weapons, and we had only rocks and bottles, but we fought bravely. My hate, which had become small when playing with my cousins, was again growing big and strong.

"One day my cousins and I went to the market, one far away because the markets near us were closed or destroyed by the soldiers, and when we returned, a neighbor said that soldiers had come and taken my aunt and uncle to jail. Ali was with the neighbor, and he was crying, and we went inside, the four of us, and we waited for my aunt and uncle to return. But they did not. And Zehra and I made some food, but still they did not come. And then we went to our beds, still waiting for them to come home. At night, someone knocked at the door, and we were frightened, because we knew that our aunt and uncle would not knock. We were correct to be frightened, because at the door were Zionist men, not with uniforms but regular clothes, who told us we had to leave our house, and if we did not leave by the following night, they would burn it to the ground. One of the men gave me some money, and they left.

"We did not want to leave, because when my aunt and uncle would return they would have trouble finding us. The next night, the men came earlier, almost before it was dark, and did not knock, but came into our house and began to throw our things out into the street. When I told the man, the man who had given me the money, that we needed to remain there for when my uncle and aunt would return, he looked at me, and then looked down, and said they would not return, they would never return, and that we must go before we were injured. He spoke to the other men in a language we do not use, and they stopped and went out into the street, and the man said to me that they would return at noon the next day, and we should be gone by then. I knew that Allah had left me completely then, and I also knew I would never forgive this man, these men without uniforms, for putting us out like dogs in the street.

"We packed our things, and left the small house. Ali was crying, and Fatma too began to cry. I did not know where we were going to go, and all I could think about was my hate, and hoping it was big enough to keep me strong enough to . . . "

"What happened to the book?"

She stopped, with a dead, flat silence, a silence with absolutely no reverberation or resonance. The water above seemed to gush out, then subside, then gush even stronger. After a while she said, "What time is it?"

He turned, reached and swiveled the alarm

toward him. "Almost three thirty."

"You must take me to my plane."

"What about the book?"

"Please, I am tired. I am not sure where the book is— it could be with Fatma in Al Quds, or with Zehra in Istanbul."

"Will you send it to me? I'll pay."

"No. It is mine as well, and I do not wish it lost. You must understand, the Turkish postal system is not good."

"You could FedEx it or something."

"Please, I am tired of talking, and I wish to go to my plane. I left my address and telephone number on the back of the drawing I gave to you. Perhaps you could visit."

Yeah right. He needed that book, and needed to think of how to appeal to her (a check probably wouldn't work [at least not immediately]), but before he could say anything, she leaned over and with one hand on his cheek kissed him quickly on the lips. She grabbed her backpack and ran out of the room. Peter sat there in the dark for a while, and when he finally hurried down to the lobby, she was gone.

CHAPTER EIGHT

Peter's preoccupation with his sister's kiss (was that her tongue or upper lip [maybe it was just a cultural thing]?), book and story (vague images or thoughts of his father now intertwined with images of the bearded uncle, the bruised Kurd, the men without uniforms and the sound of running water) began to dissipate after a few days. He had returned home immediately (light traffic) from the airport, cued up pops on the VCR (he wished he had a hard copy of the still [he could probably do it on his computer if he had the tape decks hooked up {he'd definitely have to figure it out on his new one (the bondi blue or strawberry Mac 500?)}]) cracked open another Heineken and attempted to decide once and for all whether Reham was giving him mierda (like everyone he knew he suffered through a couple of years of high school and college Mexican) or not. He switched on the Yamaha and JBL (Bach's Anna Magdalena Notebook started up [Hi Mom {can't think about you right now}]), slumped down in the orange and black bean bag (LA RetroStyle $99), stared at the electronic image of his father and, although he tried to concentrate on Reham and her story, (inevitably) found himself focusing on the physical sensations and memories of his encounter: the dark smoky odor of the hotel room, the sag of the mattress as she sat on the bed, the touch of her fingertips and heat of her breath just before she kissed him. He was having a great deal of trouble concentrating, and he didn't know why.

He needed more information. He needed that book. She said she left the address on the back of the picture: he should probably check (was it still in his trunk?). She was going to Japan, and returning home when? He got up, went out to the Saab, removed the drawing and brought it inside. His Pocketnet rang but he ignored it (probably Wanda, he'd call her back when he could). He carefully removed the brown wrapper and without glancing at the front, read the inscription and address (that weird writing again) on the back: To Peter, with Love, Reham. Reham Al-Safia, No 24 Yeni Tuzla Caddesi, Sultanahmet Istanbul, Turkey; (90) (212) 2269734. How would he get there? He booted up his computer, went to Travelocity and checked out flights to Istanbul — $800 on Delta, $1100 on British and Lufthansa, $5000 First Class on KLM (a long fucking flight but a serious chunk of change [dear old daddy, are you worth a fiver? {maybe he could upgrade: he had a few and Kay thousands of miles}]) — then looked up Turkey on the Britannica (Republic of Turkey, Turkey Cumheriyeti Population: 62,484,478, Ethnic Groups: Turk 80%, Kurd 20%, Religions: Muslim 99.8%). He could take a little vacation (maybe do a piece on Turkish trends so he could write some of it off [and show Jon the Yawn Trojan who the fuck he was dealing with]), scope the picture book, and pick up a present (something exotic) for Kay (a silk rug or something [he remembered that general and the blonde at the art show]). Too bad he couldn't bring Wanda. As if.

He needed to call her, but not yet. He replaced the brown paper around the picture as best he could (all the tape was in the big house) and put it way back in the storage closet, behind the Ken Griffey and Option Signature. He closed the closet door and moved to the front of the XBR to look at his father. The tape deck had disengaged, and the screen reverted to that clear IBM blue. He couldn't or wouldn't do this: he was sick of thinking about his father, his mother, his aunt and his sister, sick of trying to reconstruct a past he wasn't sure he had — fuck, he was better off without a family, with just Wanda to screw (much more than that), his friends to hang with and his job to keep him occupied. He had always hated history in school, so why was he so interested in his own? Kiss or no kiss, sister or no sister, book or no book, he wasn't going to Turkey, he wasn't going to stare at (or try to remember) the fuzzy, indeterminate shapes and lines that were supposedly his parents, and he wasn't going to hang here, pout around and drive himself crazy. He pounded the rest of his Heinie (Rondo style), switched off the XBR, Mitsubishi, Yamaha and JBL (the Bach had to go), grabbed his Pocketnet and the Saab keys, and started outside, back to his life. And then stopped, just inside the door.

Try as he might, he couldn't ignore or repress it, the feeling of obligation, of owing somebody, of being in the red — submerged yet irrefutable, enduring like a vodka (Belvedere, Stoly Crystal or Grey Goose [$16, $16 and $20 frozen shots {they came in these little test tube like glasses, each with their own tiny ice-bucket} at Diaghilev]) hangover in the late afternoon. But who was it, exactly, that he owed? His (dead) father? His (dead) mother? Himself? Reham (he couldn't shake the image of her eating alone in her bed or arguing with the men who were putting her out in the street)? And what was the amount, or even currency, of the debt? What could he do to pay off his balance, amortize his note (Kay talk), clear his account and move the fuck on? He could go to Turkey (who was he kidding?), that was true, but that might be too much, or too little, that first step obliging him to continue to make payments over time, with some big balloon due when he least expected it. Even though things were way messed up, he believed that if he chose not to act he could still extricate himself from the situation with minimal damage (he might feel guilt and speculate as to what he might have learned [for a day or two tops]), while if he actually did something (go to Turkey) he would involve himself in something too complicated (he wasn't sure what) to easily escape from (he was certain it would be neither painless or cheap). Yet he absolutely hated the feeling of being beholden to, a discomfort made greater by the fact that A) the identity of the creditor was, if not unknown, at least scattered among a number of possibilities (his dad, mom, himself, his past, Reham); B) the amount of the debt was unclear (what he owed and at what interest); and C) the tender of the obligation was indefinite (should he pay in blood, time, money, or would the act of fucking up his life for the near future be adequate compensation?).

The phone rang again, this time the chirp chirp of the (Bang and Olufson) Beotalk 1401 ($149 [gift from Wanda to replace his vintage Bell Pacific OfficeMate black dial job {$15 Salvation Army}) near his Chaddock. It was probably Wanda, and he moved to answer it, grateful for the interruption, then hesitated again — what would he say? As yet he had no story to tell her, no explanation for his absence; therefore an immediate conversation might be disastrous. He stood there, listening, not really thinking, as if something important depended on the identity of the caller (could it be Reham?), but the answering machine's greeting drew only an inscrutable dial tone in response.

What would he tell Wanda? Maybe the truth (at the moment he had no energy to concoct a plausible fiction). He'd leave out the part about the hotel room and maybe forget to mention the blood connection, at least for now (There's this woman who knew my father and she had a photograph to give me. Why didn't you tell me? I dunno I was upset. No wonder you've been acting so weird.).   Four thirty. As a rule he tried to avoid making major purchases when upset or distracted, but this time it might be a good idea to pick up his new computer (that fine flat panel RastaOps screen with either the strawberry Mac, the sleek silver Sony [he was desperate and so might even pay retail] or the black and powerful Compaq [maybe he should see about one of those DSL lines as well]); that would at least take his mind off of all this bullshit and he and Wanda could have some laughs hooking it up and fucking around with it (and each other [the anticipation of fresh tech often awakened Pete Junior]). That might be just the ticket:brand new toys, all clean and crisp, neat and perfect, unlike his life. He chuckled. Buying a new black box (smell of virgin plastic, styrofoam and silicone, the feel of bubblewrap), having some dinner (maybe Jaime would rustle something up for them [grilled trout or Bangkok shrimp {garlic, lemon grass, Thai chilies, gallons of Tahitian lime juice and turnip greens}] or they could do Jap take-out [tuna sashimi from Koy's]) and knocking boots with his girlfriend (a little Wanda sashimi) would certainly be more fun than a sixteen hour flight to Istanbul. Okay. Okay. Okay. He could call her from the car.

The next few days flew by pretty much as Peter imagined they would: his new Pentium plaything (he went with the Sony box and monitor, figuring Windows 2000 would be more difficult to learn and thus keep him better occupied than the Mac [he was right]) and Wanda's (she never questioned him about his Reham detour) attentions (her libido also sparked by the PIII, the BX chipset, the atp graphics card, the superfast DRAM and the 100mgz bus [she even brought over her new Olympus D-620L Digital camera {$1099} and tripod]) crowding out all memories, speculations and plans (about his father, Reham and his [extremely unlikely] trip). He also did a little work on barbecuing, arranging through Wanda to meet with Kaspar after one of their gigs the following week, and with all the photoshopping, surfing and fucking, the weekend disappeared (they didn't even take time out to shop for Kay's present) and before he knew it it was Tuesday (he blew off work Monday [Monday's were always dead]) and Marinetti's time again (he hadn't seen Kay since the Reham Saturday).

As he (charcoal Armani relaxed cashmere [it was cloudy and cool] sportcoat [$1,000, hung up in the back], matching wool baggy trousers [$400], a simple light gray [Mist] Perry Ellis cotton oxford [$125], a black silk tie [Ennio Capasa $110], his Kenneth Cole belt, A. Testoni black ankle boots [$375], CK silk hose [$22 a pair] and a splash of Neil Barrett's Postmodern Fables [$65 4 oz spray]) drove (Pico to San Vincente [he didn't mind the Five but was in no hurry], Sheryl Crow All I wanna do on KROQ) from the office (after a rather perfunctory appearance) to Marinetti's he was feeling, well, almost peaceful. Peter, bathed in post-coital contentment, was actually thinking about marrying, or at least moving in with, Wanda. Shacking up, settling down, maybe it was time. It wasn't like he was interested in anyone else (his consciousness skipping so quickly over Reham she almost didn't register), and Wanda certainly wouldn't cramp his style (the nights out with the boys were getting rarer and rarer [not that Wanda kept him on a tight leash or anything like that {she was no Kathy Lee who hired a dick to trail old

Frankie Giff}]) and, truth be told, he was getting a wee bit tired of the guest house (he had been living there for almost fourteen years) and could use something new. There was also the attraction of the (possible) loot: Kay would probably (had better) kick in with the crib in Samo (Seventh and Colorado), and her stepdad, fuck, maybe a HDTV set-up or a new set of wheels (those four wheel drive Cedes were sweet [ML-320 with EVERYTHING $70,000 {He's big, he's bad, he's my big bad dad}], but Wanda called them belly-button cars, cuz everyone had one), and her father, a way enabled rainmaker who was some sort of crunchy venture capitalist or something in Seattle, would probably be guilt-tripping all over hisself to bestow the new couple something special (a cruise [finally to Italy], another Warhol, or a nice little portfolio of their own [Amazon and Cisco were going through the roof]), while his one g-rent would probably come through with a nice fat Bennie collection (he had to get down to see her soon or maybe she'd come up for Kay's birthday). He wasn't sure about this, and no telling what Wanda would say, but maybe they should talk about this some day soon. He didn't exactly know how to bring it up, and he would have to think about it (a lot) more, but hell, maybe it was time to at least consider possibly moving in together. He smiled, he was more than a little bit surprised at himself for even entertaining the cohab idea (All I wanna do, is get some loot. . .).

As he turned off of Santa Monica on to North Beverly and stopped to valet the Saab, Peter was in a pretty good mood (it's all good). He was young, well dressed, looking forward to a tasty lunch — he was hungry, maybe even for cow, and Marinetti's did fine surf and turf (12 oz Tuscan t-bone and a 10 oz Maine lobtail for $35 [and it was Auntie's dime {she wrote it off anyway}]) — and Kay was usually in fine spirits after her Palm Springs weekends. Besides, after lunch he was going to pick up Wanda and they were going to take a drive up One (it might be a good day to pop the top) to Santa Barbara (they had rented a boat and done some THINGS with popsicles on the deck [he remembered her lips {upper and nether} smeared purple and the taste of grape popsicle, Jo Malone sunblock and Wandajuice as he licked and licked]), then to the Camino Real for a movie (he was hoping for Glamshot, based on the Bret Easton Ellis [great writer] novel, with Ehrinn Cummings, Maya Shoa and Adam Sandler, while Wanda, he was sure, would hold out for The Eye of the Needle, another junky come lately by Larry Clark, with Gary Oldman, Boy George, Drew Barrymore and Hanna Schygulla (We have to see Hanna Schygulla, we have to), so what did he have to complain about (except the possibility of a yawner flick [although supposedly Drew and Boy got naked together])?

The joint was jammed as usual (there was what's his name Dylan McDermott [classic navy Brooks Brothers {$2000}, blue and white striped cotton shirt by Lorenzini {$275} with a red silk faille tie {Calvin Klein $80} and To Boot captoe shoes {$375}] with his wife [Shiva Rose {nice name} in a beautiful light jade green Clements Ribeiro kimono with matching slippers {$5800}]. And that guy in the big green and gray plaid cotton and silk Paul Smith suit [$3500] with bigass Docs [$200] looked like that bald guy from Smashing Pumpkins [Billy Corgan]), but Kay (soft brown, beige and ivory linen Lilly dress by Voyage [$3500], simple brown Ferragamo flats [$275], with a string of small white pearls with unobtrusive matching earrings [Tiffany $3500] and just a little makeup [Clinique Moisture On Call $30 3 oz, Double Coffee Quick Eyes

$14.50 and Clear Red Masque by François Nars, $35 2 oz pot], her hair severely swept back in some Eugene Souleiman chignon) was sitting at her usual table, where, as usual, she had already started eating (cold duck salad with oyster mushrooms [$18]). He moved closer to kiss her on the cheek and caught a subtle whiff of Cartesian Mediations ($125 2 oz) by John Rocha. She looked relaxed, well rested and ever so slightly tanned.

"Hello Kay. How was Palm Springs?"

"Hello Peter. Palm Springs was divine — you know how I adore the Givinchy. I'm almost sorry I had to come back so quickly. I do apologize for having to eat so early, but I have to meet a very important client at two. A very important client who is, how should I put this delicately, a bit of a Tory. Hence the Kennedy outfit. Rose, not Jackie." She chuckled to herself as she took a sip of her water (San Moritz Wasser mit Gas [$6 12 oz]). "You'll notice, dear, that I'm even forgoing my customary glass or two of wine; not because I'm suddenly avoiding the grape after a weekend of excess, but rather because I'm afraid this Orange County deacon will somehow smell it on my breath and scotch the whole deal. And a very big deal it is too, my love." She buttered a piece of bread as Peter looked around for the waiter. "I'm really not that crazy for their business. It's not that I'm prejudiced, necessarily, but as a child of the sixties, well, early seventies anyway, I don't enjoy dealing with them and all their self-righteous bigotry and intolerance. Not to mention pure greed. People in glass churches shouldn't throw anything. I'll find them property, I'll show them buildings, I'll broker deals and I'll take their checks, but as far as I'm concerned they can go fuck themselves. They all smell like hairspray too. Especially the men."

A waiter arrived with a menu. "May I bring you something to drink, sir?"

He was tired of Sierra Nevada. "What kind of beer besides Sierra Nevada Pale Ale do you have?"

"We have Heineken light and dark from Holland; Kitzmann, Becks light and dark, St Pauli Girl, DAB and Bitburger from Germany; Adler, Blanche des Neiges, Gueuze Lambic Mort Subit and a Triple Trappistbier from Belgium; Kopparbargs Fat, Hallsta Birka and Zeunerts Pils from Sweden; Beamish and Crawford, Guinness and Harp from Ireland; Corona, Corona Light, Dos Equis Light and Amber and Tecate from Mexico; Brahma and Colorado from Brazil; Victoria from Nicaragua; Kohaku, Doppo, Asahi and Kirin from Japan; Singha Gold from Thailand; Fosters Tien Gang from Vietnam; Pyramid Lager and Pilsner from Egypt; Macabbee Premium and Goldstar from Israel; Pilsner Urquell, Budvar, and U Flecku in the big bottle from the Czech Republic; and we have a number of local micro brews, including Long Beach Crude and Top Sail Ale from Belmont Brewing, Blind Pig Pale Ale; Wind and Sea Wheat and Pump House Porter from La Jolla Brewing; Rhino Chaser Bock and Amber Ale; James Brown, Rat Beach Red and Manhattan Beach Blond, all from the Manhattan Beach Brewery; and . . ."

"Do you have Fat Tire from Colorado?"

"No sir, I don't believe we do. We do have something brand new, just received this morning, an Efes Pilsner, sir, from Turkey. In a sixteen ounce bottle."

He thought of Reham (evil uncle, bruised child, book of photographs) and looked quickly at Kay, whose attention seemed riveted by the forkful of duck breast and Pernod vinaigrette she was bringing to her mouth. Dare he chance it? No; there was nothing to be gained by stirring up sleeping dogs. "I'll try the, uh, what were the Manhattan Beach selections?"

"James Brown, Rat Beach Red and Manhattan Beach Blond."

"I'll try the Rat Beach Red."

"Very good sir. Our specials today are a miniature baked butternut squash almond sliver tort for an appetizer, freshly smoked oysters over shaved Napa cabbage, with a warm champagne shallot vinaigrette with focaccia croutons, a fresh artichoke puree with wild rice for our soup de jour, grilled venison with chipotle sundried blueberry rioja sauce, which comes with grilled Japanese eggplant, zucchini, and Israeli cous-cous as an entrée, and eclairs with Bavarian cream and chocolate mousse for dessert. Would you like an appetizer to start?"

"Do you still have the lunch Surf and Turf? With the Tuscan beef and the Bar Harbor lobster?"

"Yes we do."

"I'll take that. And your New Zealand spinach salad, with purslane and roasted Portuguese garlic vinaigrette."

"Very good sir. And how would you like your beef?"

"Medium well."

"Medium well it is. And the salad is fine, madam?"

"Very nice, thank you."

"I'll return with your beer shortly."

He was glad he hadn't ordered the Turkish brew: the further he could push Reham (who was she anyway?) and everything surrounding her out of his mind the better (he hated feeling guilty). What was he thinking about before lunch that had made him so happy? Ah yes, Wanda, and the possible houseplaying scenario. Perhaps it wouldn't hurt to drop a small hint to Kay, maybe she'd loan him the keys, and he and

Wanda could check out the new crib this afternoon, before they headed up the coast. It would be hard for Wanda to say no in (to) that house (not that she would anyway), and so a change in plan might be in order — it might be better to secure the pad (or at least its promise) from Kay before he brought up any sort of mutual mailbox with Wanda (she was certain to dig that crib, no worries there).

He looked again at Kay, who looked back at him and smiled. He needed to do this carefully: he needed to phrase his comments so anything he said to Kay could be denied later in case things blew up in his face (Wanda might have other ideas [he knew she was tired of LA and had mentioned Manhattan, Boston and Aspen]), and he didn't want to appear too greedy. And although Kay sometimes found his boyish lack of sophistication charming (Kay realized that Peter was, to some degree at least, the consequence of her own values and attitudes [the apple not falling far from the {proxy} tree]), he knew it would be a mistake to just bull ahead (do an Earl Campbell) and approach her directly. A subtle approach was called for, one with much more subterfuge and irony (cunning) than he was capable (at least at the moment) of providing. He needed to think about this, develop some sort of plan, maybe ask Wanda for some advice (although he'd then have to disclose the impetus for his scheme, which would render the whole point moot). Anyway, he wasn't ready to bring it up, and so he'd (they'd) have to find some other topic to discuss during lunch.

"What are your plans for today, dear? Are you going back to work?"

"No, I was going to take Wanda up to Santa Barbara for sailing, and maybe a movie."

"How lovely. I haven't been to Santa Barbara in ages."

"How about you? Where are you speeding off to?"

"I have to go down to Santa Monica to drop off some keys." A tiny alarm sounded in the periphery of Peter's consciousness.

"What are you showing in SaMo?"

"That little Tudor that I took you to. And I'm not showing it, not any more. I'm closing, it's gone. Bought it for six fifty, sold it for a mil. To those Christian fanatics I was just raving about." Kay looked up from her salad (Peter was so seldom interested in her work). "Why do you ask, dear?"

No fucking way! Goddam it to hell! "No reason, I was just curious."

The remainder of the meal degenerated slowly: at first Kay chatted on about her Palm Springs weekend and Peter responded with the absolute minimum of grunts and monosyllabic words, until Kay eventually grew tired of carrying the conversation, and after a few half-hearted jabs at the born-agains, uncultured youth, Wanda (she even called her Wendy just to get some response [none] and asking him if that was Renée Zellweger [cropped silver mylar jacket {Alexander McQueen $1100}, periwinkle blue cotton tube top lycra tube top {Tommy Hilfiger $110}, jade green stretch capri pants {Bruce $200}, matching high heel sandals from Diego Dolcini {$700} and D&G sunglasses {$250}] who had just come in with Dana Giachetto [ivory linen suit {Corneliani $1800}, beige linen shirt {Ascot Chang $350}, black silk tie with blue stripes {Ralph Lauren Purple Label $110}, with beige and brown oxfords {Gucci $400} and a vintage Jaeger-Lecoultre Reverso {$4000}]), she too fell quiet and focused her concentration on her wine (she decided that one glass [Bonneau du Martray 1992 Grand Cru {$14 glass and worth every penny}] wouldn't hurt and fuck them if it made any difference) and her food (a delightful Chilean sea bass with ginger and shallots). Peter, after quickly finishing his first beer, ordered one, then two of the rather large Turkish brews.

    The interminable (from hell) lunch finally over (a spritz of watery green lobster guts had squirted out onto his Perry Ellis, leaving a pale greenish silver [sea mist] half dollar mark just above the pocket), Peter stood on the curb, waiting for his Saab (as he handed his ticket to the valet he discovered he only had a ten spot for the tip), fuming (and yawning). Every time a chance for stability, every time an opportunity for normalcy or a possibility for conventionality presented itself, it was indifferently snatched away by some one or some thing. Life was not fucking fair (he hoped the Ellis was not totally ruined [he had a good dry cleaner {NonParail on Samo Blvd}]). If he deserved anything, he deserved that house. He was relieved he hadn't mentioned anything to Wanda. What a bitch Aunt. What a selfish bitch Aunt. He hoped that she had noticed (and questioned) his choice of brew, hoped that she had caught the significance of the Turkish beer (the second better than the first). Maybe he should go to Istanbul anyway, that would show her. Fuck fuck fuck: he and his plans were hosed, big time.
    Here was the Saab, easy there Pancho, it ain't no Chevy. Yeah, you're welcome, hope the fucking wheel isn't greasy. Why did she lead him on like that in the first place? What did she have to gain from practically promising him the crib and then jerking it away like that? Maybe it was Wanda; maybe Kay really didn't like her (what about that snotty question, How's Wendy my dear?). And it wasn't like there was anyone he could ask either (By the way, Auntie Kay, why'd

you'd sell that house you promised me? Whatever are you talking about, deary?). Why'd she take him there if she had been planning to sell it all along? She was freaking, that was it, probably menopausing or something. Or maybe she was having troubs with Pavo. Fuck, now what was he supposed to do?

Peter cranked the radio (Garbage Push It from Version 2.0 [do do do do do do do do]) as he turned up Wilshire, and continued to rag as he made a right on South Beverly Glen, and then left on West Sunset to Bellagio Road, then a sharp right on Roscanne, another sharp right on Chalon, then zigging and zagging up Sarbonne, Stradella and Airole Way (Air, La Femme D'Argent from Moon Safari), back to Stradella Way, Stradella Drive, Stradella Court (couldn't they come up with any other fucking names?) and finally to Wanda's house. He opened the iron gate with his remote (he had lost his about four months ago and they had to redo the code [Pops was pissed {in that quiet way of his} and only last week had he received a replacement]) and up the driveway to the door. Of course she couldn't be waiting for him; of course he would have to get out of the Saab, walk down the path through the freshly trimmed (by young Koko or old Koko) Kitsuni bonzai forest, climb up the Italian (Chiampo) marble steps, knock on the massive Chinese teak door, wait a couple of minutes, then knock again, then be let in with feigned surprise (his remote identified him when he opened the gate) by Jeremy or Caitlin (the forty something Irish twins whose exact status in Wanda's household remained mysterious [more than servants yet slightly less than family {second cousins types (but to whom? —Wanda's mom was Italian and Greek and stepdad [who seemed to surround himself with blondes and redheads] was pure Shikoku)}], as if every Bel Air household came equipped with a pair of six-foot green eyed red haired assistants [the opposite of leprechauns]), who would coldly open the door, reluctantly lead him to the small reading room — where Caitlin would oh so grudgingly offer him a drink and Jeremy a seat — where he'd wait among the Caroline chairs (4 x $4000), the Seventeenth Century French Settee ($9000), the small Berber rug ($5600), the tiffany lamps ($2900 and $11000) and the 18th century dark walnut sideboard ($7600) with matching bookcases (filled with books chosen and arranged by mom for cover color and aging [$50-200/yard {Wanda was the only (nominal) reader in the family and she kept her books in her bedroom or in the music room}]) until Wanda decided to grace the room with her presence. Which is pretty much how it happened, and he didn't even get the drink (Jeremy [grayish blue {slate} wool and cotton suit {Vestimenta, $1200}] with a BOSS Hugo Boss white cotton shirt [$250], a tomato red with small gray grayhounds Joseph Abboud silk tie [$120], black Ferragamo wingtips [$400], a Rolex Datejust [$12,000] and more than a hint of Anti-Oedipus by Sandy Dalal [$30 4 oz spray]).

This was bullshit. He hated waiting in this room, and Wanda knew it. It was some weird power trip or something. She should put a Sony here, or at least some magazines: he had even once been driven to trying to open one of the bookcases, but was unable to do so (I think they're locked so the books don't get dusty). He had been shown to this room (was every guest brought here, or just him?) without fail, ever since he had started hooking up with Wanda, and always had to wait a minimum of ten and a maximum of forty minutes. He rose (the fucking Carolines were assmurder [the settee was even worse]) and put his hands in his pockets (he wasn't going to pace and he had already examined, in minute detail, the three art-works [a small drawing of an upside down eagle {Keifer}, some stick figures and squiggles on brown paper bag colored canvas {Basquiet} and an English landscape with lots of green {a restored Smithson}] on the almost olive [French Forest] colored walls before). At least they could put a comfortable chair in this room, a Roche Bobois or something, fuck. He would never create a room as uncomfortable as this.

If he ever got the chance thank you Kay. He tried the settee and leaned back (as best he could). This was salty. For at least a year now, ever since Kay had shown him the Tudor (she had taken him there, given him the tour, had even asked him questions about how he liked it and what he might do with the different rooms [What do you think? Do you think this is big enough for a bedroom, or would it be better as an office?]), Peter had dreamed of blowing the guest house and moving down to Samo with Wanda. Whenever he got sick of Pavo, annoyed with Tina, irritated by Louisa or tired of Kay, the promise of his own (shared with W or not) joint had allowed him to chill, to put things in perspective, to look at the long run (Ain't no thing, I'm tailights motherfuckers). But now he had nothing: once again, Life had screwed him big time (Spike Lee's You got nothing echoed in his head).

Fuck it, he'd move out anyway. He had some bucks, a good job; maybe he could even sell some stock, or borrow from g-ma or Kay (she'd probably charge him vig). He'd need all the do-re-mi he could find, because he wasn't going to live in ghetto (renting was feathering someone else's nest), and Wanda was used to a certain lifestyle (as was he). What was he looking for? How much could he afford? Where did he want to live? How much down payment did he need? Maybe he should start thinking about this, start making a few calls (he'd go through someone besides Kay, that would really yank her chain [didn't Hector and Karla just buy?]). Christ, what a pain in the ass.

And another thing: since Kay wouldn't give them the crib, the extravagance of the other wedding presents would most certainly diminish — they'd be lucky to clear a Carnival cruise and a domestic (Fox Chapel or Ethan Allen) leather couch (they had seen a beautiful butter yellow sofa from Nicolliti [$6500] in the window of La Casa di Mobili the other day). Adios HDTV and sayonara M-320. Wouldn't even be worth it. Where the fuck was this woman?

He should just walk: he was sick of always having to wait for her (although he did owe her one for the Reham airport expedition), and was really in no mood for a long drive (and the conversation that would demand), a beach excursion or a movie. He wasn't even anticipating a shag (although with certain techniques little Pete could almost always be persuaded), which meant he really must be upset. Why didn't anything ever work out for him? First his parents, and now this. Look at Suarez, he had a nice crib on Balboa (and a nasty new wench as well, some model friend of that Spawn or Species chick, what was her name? [Natasha Henstridge]). Or Hector and Karla, with their new Pasadena place. Even loser Bryan had a bungo near Silicon Beach (still wasn't getting any). What did he do to deserve getting dumped on all the time? He wasn't a bad guy: didn't sell drugs to kids, didn't beat his dog or cheat on his girl (he had even tried to help that salesgirl at Sonia Rykel's); he wasn't cheap (he spent a lot on presents [a Diamond Rio MP3 Portable Music Player for Yashika's birthday {$155}, a four hundred dollar gift certificate from Louboutin for Kay for the birthday before last {she creamed for those red soles} and a thousand dollar check in Wanda's name to the Santa Monica AIDS Hospice {how was that for generosity!}] for Christmas [their family did that all gifts to charity in our name thing this year {when he had attempted to present W with a pale blue Norell mermaid dress (from Decades on Melrose [$1700]) she had steadfastly refused and had forced him to take it back}]) and was a good, no great, tipper (always 20% and a Lincoln to Jesus the valet), so why did he have everything taken away from him? Maybe he was some asshole (a banger or Huggy-Bear) in a previous life; that might explain his run of bad luck in this one. He looked down at his shirt (at least the stain wasn't on his jacket [but then it wouldn't show]) and bet himself that it would be the first thing Wanda noticed. He had some shirts here; a copper DKNY linen ($295), a beige Jil Sander cotton ($325) and a white Helmut Lang ($250), but the DKNY and Sander wouldn't match, so maybe he'd keep the Ellis on to piss Wanda off.

If she ever decided to show. Which she did, after a while. Peter had returned to one of the Carolines, and was staring down at his Testonis when she (bright yellow and fuchsia daisy print cotton Gucci bells [$600], black and pink cropped sleeveless BodyGlove neoprene vest [$80] under a Jean Paul Gaultier crimson gypsy blouse [$1000], T. LeClerc Midnight Mascara [$22], Mary Quant Oblige Lipcolor [Spandex Red, $18], Jo Malone Sunblock #35 [$50 3 oz] with Ann Demeulemeester black sandals [$300], Jet Set red nail polish [hands and toes] by Get Nailed [$140 full set] and the scent of Being and Time by Bally [$175 2 oz]) burst into the room. He stood to face and kiss her.

"I'm so sorry I'm late, but my Tae Bo class ran over, and I didn't want to shower at the club. Let's take the Saab, I don't feel like driving. What's that on your shirt?"

Bingo. "Just some lobster jizz: I had surf and turf with Kay."

"Come on up and you can change."

"Let's just go."

"What's wrong? You don't want to go out like that, do you?"

Out of nowhere Caitlin appeared from behind Wanda's shoulder and handed Wanda a J.P. Tod white canvas beach bag ($700). "Here's your bag." She turned and Peter waited until she cleared the door.

"What difference does it make? We're just going for a drive and a swim."

"I thought we were going to the movies."

"It'll be dark in the theater. Don't worry, no one will see me."

"What if we want to stop for drinks or get something to eat? What if we want to go shopping or something, for your Aunt? What's your problem?"

"I dunno. I guess I'm tired. Whatever."

"Well snap out of it dude. I got my new Gideon Oberon bikini in my bag, which should perk you right up." Wanda arched her eyebrows and leered (Peter [big and small] usually found the spoiled sex kitten act extremely effective [there was just something about the juxtaposition of uninhibited, almost savage sexual exploration {the raw} with exquisitely luxurious situations and objects {the cooked}], but today he [big] was more annoyed [and almost embarrassed] than aroused [Junior remained asleep]). "Remember the last time we went to Santa Barb? Remember the popsicles? So the quicker you change your shirt, the quicker we're there. Dude."

What was wrong with him? Even without the lobster attack, a fresh shirt was not unreasonable, given the stress of the lunch and the smog and humidity. So why was he hesitating? All he had to do was climb the stairs to Wanda's bedroom, open the door, step into the walk-in cedar closet and take his freshly laundered Lang from the hangar and put it on. He'd changed clothes here dozens of times before, so what was stopping him now?

"Peter, did you hear me? What's wrong?"

"Nothing. Nothing at all." As he turned toward the hall, the staircase, Wanda's room and cedar closet, his shirt, he heard "I'll wait outside" over his shoulder.

"So, you want to talk about it or not?"

They had passed Carillo Beach and were just outside of Solomar (My Name Is [Eminem, extended remix], What It's Like [Everlast], Song II [Blur {Ooo-hoo}], You know things are bad when cheerleaders are bumming, Go starbursts go, 10 10 345 Long Distance, The Bridge [Red Hot Chili Peppers], People don't dance no mo [Goodie Mob]). The soft Egyptian cotton of the Lang felt great, which annoyed him even more (Ten Things I Hate About You).

"What? Do I want to talk about what?"

"Whatever the fuck is bothering you. You've been sulking since you came over. Bloody hell" (Bloody hell? where'd that come from?) "if I wanted to hang with mutes, I'd go find Rita and Satchmo and watch them nod off. So what's eating you, Gilbert Grape?"

"I hate that movie."

"Something at Fortunato? Is it that guy, Ramses or whatever?"

"Trojan, Jonathan Trojan. And no, it's not him, and it's not something at work."

"He's black, right?"

He turned to look at her. "So?"

"Just curious. Well if it isn't him, and it isn't work, then why are you pouting?"

"I'm not pouting."

"Pouting, sulking, moping, scowling, call it what you want, you're acting like a spoiled child, and it's boring me."

It required some self-control to refrain from pulling the Saab onto the shoulder and, and what? Slapping her? (not likely). Walking home? (again, not likely). Turning the motor off and sitting silently on the side of the road? (perhaps). He should do something, he was within his rights. There was no more insulting word in Wandaland than boring: it was absolutely her most radical cut, her most extreme dig. The word boring signified that she was not amused (of course), but it went beyond that, beyond anger (she was no longer angry), but beyond even indifference into something approaching pure forgetfulness (not only was she no longer angry, not only did she no longer care, but she could not even remember caring): the word boring signaled that her memory of you, if it could be recalled, never mattered in the first place. He drove on (courageously), trying not to think. He turned up the volume on the Blaupunkt as (the ubiquitous) Will Smith began his Welcome to Miami Bienvenino á Miami (he wished he were in Miami right now, or even Turkey, anywhere but here).

Her left arm struck quickly, like a snake, killing the radio. "So?"

"So what?"

"So if you're not going to say anything, turn around and take me home. I didn't hurry through Tae Bo so I could sit here on my ass, listening to Top fucking 40 and wondering what if anything is on your mind, wondering what if anything is making you act like a dick. And not an interesting dick either, a limp dick, a small, flaccid, pink, silent, limp dick who is not amusing, not engaging, and who probably just needs to be alone for awhile to sulk."

"So I'm a boring dick, huh?"

" I didn't say you are a boring dick, I said you are acting like a boring dick.   There's a difference."

"Yeah right. Whatever."

"Yeah right whatever." She was looking at him; he could feel her stare on the side of his face. He knew he should probably let her know about the house (he wouldn't have to mention his [now defunct?] plans for their cohabitation), about how Kay had all but promised him the Tudor (not in so many words it was true) and then welshed on the deal, but he was pissed about the Lang, about how she had (possibly) embarrassed him in front of Caitlin, and about how (relatively) easily he had given in and gone upstairs and changed. He wasn't going to give in this time; he wasn't going to tell Wanda about his anger at Kay for selling the (his) house. He was going to keep his resentment hidden (like Clint), private, like a man should, like a man had a right to.

He knew she wouldn't let it go. As much as he wanted to keep it a secret, Wanda, through a combination of curiosity and competition, wanted to know.   It didn't matter what the secret consisted of (Wanda wasn't a terribly empathetic person by nature, and while she would certainly show [feign?] concern and offer succor and advice, she as certainly wouldn't lose any sleep over his distress [except that this time his affliction concerned property, and Wanda usually respected real estate, so the possibility did exist that her solicitude might be genuine]), it was the mere fact that he was hiding something that simultaneously annoyed and stimulated her. No, she wouldn't let it go, he was certain of that, and it would require a great deal of strength and concentration on his part to keep his anger hidden.

And yet he didn't want to piss her off too much. He sensed that they were heading toward uncharted waters here, toward experiences they hadn't yet approached. They'd fought (one bitter, drunken row with under the breath mutterings about Kurt vs. Courtney had turned into a raucous, Joseph Cole throwing waterfight about Mila vs. Eli [the waterfight adding an element of play into the vitriol]) sure, and said mean things (he replied to her clumsy, boring, noodle-dicked jerk with a spoiled coke-ho cunt after sideswiping a Taurus LX [97 {$12,000 blue book} with her Beamer [98 Avus blue with gray interior 2.0 liter Z3 $32,000}] on North Bev near Carmelita [he dropped $3500 for both cars to keep State Farm stupid]), but this seemed different, this seemed quieter, subtler and more possibly damaging, although he couldn't exactly say why.

Maybe he should just chill, insist it was nothing more than a crunchy mood (on the rag, the cotton pony) and try to change the subject, maybe discuss the upcoming flick, although she probably wouldn't let him off that easily. And fuck it, why should he give in? Why should he have to change his mood to match hers? He had a right to his bad mood, he had a right to feel angry and depressed, and he had a right to pout, sulk or mope if he wanted (needed) to. She was correct, he did need some space, and he should just turn around and take her home. Apologize, no big deal, I need to be alone right now, I'll call you tonight and then buy her something nice tomorrow, maybe some orchids (roses were frio) at Dietrich's or something. There was a turnoff, should he do it? She'd be pissed for sure, but more pissed than she was now (or if things continued as they were)? Did he have the huevos? She was still looking at him; he could feel her stare boring into the side of his face, through the skin, flesh and cheekbone, trying to get inside his head. He did need to be alone (maybe a hundred in the pool), and here was another turnoff, but she would be torqued big time. Maybe he should give it one more shot; if only to try to pry her eyes out of his fucking cheek. He turned to look at her and smiled.

"So who was at Tae Bo? Did you see Corbin Benson again?"

She met his eyes for a second then turned away toward the passenger window. He kept one eye on her for a few miles, then propped his left elbow on the door and rested his head on his hand, both eyes on the road. Ah yes, the silent treatment. She had never done this before, and he wasn't sure how good she was at it, although he guessed he was about to find out. On the one hand, he could use some peace and quiet; it would give him some time to think. On the other hand, this silence was not quiet, this pause was not peaceful. On the contrary, it was frightening in its insistency, and the longer it continued, the more frightening it became. He considered turning the Blaupunkt on, but immediately thought better of it. He remembered Reham's story (it had been a while since he had thought about Reham), about how she knew that Allah was listening to her because He refused to answer, how that silence was an answer to her prayer. This silence was not from God.

So now what? Was this important, important enough to risk a major explosion? It was nothing, stupid, so he didn't get what (the house) he wanted (needed, deserved), so what? He should just tell her, get it over with, and begin the reconciliation process. But no, not this time, he was tired of giving in to everyone and everything. He had been humiliated twice today (so far), once by Kay and once by Wanda, and he'd be damned if he would let her win this time. He could keep quiet just as long as she could; he could be just as stubborn as she.

They *had* humiliated him today. Fuck em both. Maybe he should split for awhile: he could get some distance, some space, sort things out (get over his disappointment), and at the same time teach Wanda and Kay a lesson, show them that they couldn't take him for granted. He could go to Turkey (where'd that come from?), check out that book, and maybe, depending on how he was feeling, pick up some cool stuff (for himself and others). Yeah, that's the ticket (Jon Lovitz for the phone book [poor Phil Hartman {a cautionary tale}]), Turkey. Yeah, Turkey, right, that would show them, show them good. Show them what dumb fuck he really was.

Still, whenever Wanda would leave (she was always going someplace [Boston, Manhattan, Rome, Aspen, San Fran, Tokyo]), he missed her big time, and looked forward eagerly to her return, so maybe his absence would have the same effect on her. Especially if he brought her something nice. It wouldn't have to be Turkey, it could be someplace cool, like Paris or Ireland (he had been to neither). But Turkey was funky enough (or at least he imagined it was, he really had no fucking clue to what it was and only a vague idea of where it was) to suitably impress Wanda, and it had the added bonus of carrying enough family baggage that Kay couldn't help but understand the significance of his visit. He could kill two birds with one stone, plus look at the book, three birds (that vague feeling that he owed something surfaced again).

Work, however, could be a problem. Although no one ever minded if you took a tour (Hector and

Karla were always driving to Vegas), he wasn't sure he wanted to abandon the field to Jonathan Trojan — he might return to an internal exile of costumed cat shows, Hansen interviews and frozen yogurt tastings. He could write something up that'd be exotic (caliente) enough that Karla would dig it and Hector, fuck Hector'd kick in some expense dough, if not for his plane ticket then a hotel and a meal or two. Might not be a bad idea, not a bad idea at all. He'd give Reham a call soon to scout things out. He might not actually go to Turkey, but he would check it out. He was almost excited. Who was he kidding? He hated flying, he hated dirt and he hated weird food: the closest he'd ever get to Turkey would be at Thanksgiving.

He glanced over at Wanda's (the back of her) head, still staring out the window. She could probably go on like that, silently staring out the window, for miles, fuck, for hours, days, weeks, months. She was right this was boring. Maybe the popsicles would be worth it after all; at least it'd be something to do. He didn't want to tell her, but he didn't want to drive all the way to Santa Barbara surrounded by some truly gnarly vibes either. She was spoiled, willful, vindictive, and she had won. She wouldn't always win (he hoped), but this hour was hers.

He looked straight ahead and took a deep breath. "I guess I'm bummed because I thought my Aunt was going to give me a house, a fucking house in SaMo, and she sold it instead. I just found out."

She made a little grunt and turned slowly toward him. "When did she tell you that?"

"At lunch."

Another little grunt. "No, I mean when did she tell you she was going to give it to you? When did she promise it to you?"

Whose tip was she on? He should have kept

his trap shut. "I don't know. I mean it's not like she ever came out and said 'Peter I want you to have this house in a couple of months' or anything like that. It was more like unspoken. She took me there a couple of times, and she's never taken me to any other of her places. It's not like she handed me a goddam contract or anything."

"Where is it?"

"Seventh and Colorado."

"Nice location. Good shape?"

"Great shape."

"How many rooms?"

He quickly counted in his head. "Two bed-rooms, two baths and an upstairs loft." He suddenly remembered a detail that would impress Wanda with the seriousness of his (and by extension their [her]) loss. "It's got an Aga."

The grunt was longer, more like a short laugh this time. "Peter, that house is probably worth seven fifty easy, maybe even a mil. What made you think Kay would give you such a gift?"

What was she saying? "What are you saying?"

"Nothing. I'm just wondering if there was any-thing real, anything tangible, why you would think that she'd give you such an extravagant present. Is this some tradition in your family, giving away million dol-lar houses? You've already turned twenty-one, and Kay's got enough tax shelters to hide Santa Barbara, so unless she was feeling extremely guilty, or doing some Ecstasy, I can't see her giving you a million dollar crib."

He stiffened. So that was what this was about. Now he'd have to defend Kay. "My aunt's been gener-ous to me."

"I know she has. I'm sorry, I'm not trying to fight, I just can't see Kay giving you an expensive house like that. For no reason."

He couldn't tell her that somehow he felt the house was owed to him, that it would somehow, in some way, (begin to) make up for the loss of his parents. He couldn't tell her how important the house was for him, how important it was to him to have a place of his own, a place no one could kick him out of, a place in the world where he could be untouchable, safe. It wasn't just a million dollars, it was shelter, a home, a place, a space, defined by real walls and fences, unassailable and fixed, definite and sure. There was no doubt about a house, no vagueness or questions about property (that's why they called it real.) There were no fuzzy edges to stare at, no faint memories to try to bring into focus, no pixilated images to interpret, it was all cut and dried, clear as day, and no one (dead or alive) could fuck it up.

To be truthful, he hadn't really wanted the house that much before today, before it was taken away (it wasn't that he hadn't wanted it, it was just that he hadn't wanted it *yet*). He didn't think about it all that much, and when he did, he thought about it in the future, as a sort of bond that hadn't quite matured. But now he realized how important it was for him, and how much he missed it, and how little Wanda understood (him), and how difficult (impossible) it would be to make her understand. The day, which had started out so promising, was diving right into the crapper.

Maybe this was some sort of jealousy thing between Kay and Wanda. Maybe Kay somehow guessed that if she gave him the crib he'd want to ask Wanda to live with or even marry him. No, she'd always been psyched about the wedding: if anything, giving him the house would speed things up. There was something else going on, although he had no clue as to what it could be.

Wanda patted him on the leg and kept her

hand on his thigh. "Now let's talk about something else. What film do you want to see?"

He didn't want to talk about something else; he didn't want to talk at all. He wanted to escape: escape from Wanda, Kay, the house, Karla and Hector, everything. He wanted to get away, to Turkey perhaps, where nothing could bother him and he could clear his head and relax. That was stupid: Turkey would be the last place he could kick back and chill. He'd see Reham and have to listen to her goofy and interminable stories, he'd think about his father (and mother too), he'd have to write something up for Hector and Karla (not to mention the flight and the food etc. [what did they eat there anyway?]): it'd be a real fucking mess. So the question was, did he want this mess here or that mess there?

Probably the mess here. Although there was dear old dad. Can't forget him. Laying pipe around the world and then crashing and burning, leaving a couple of kids (at least [maybe]) and a fuckload of questions. He wondered if he'd screwed around regularly, and if he, Peter, should be checking out the cheese girl at Treasure Island or the car wash kid at Chuck's Texaco for that largish nose and high forehead (his own forehead and nose tempered, softened by the Connor genes). He was a professor, after all, and even in the PC world of Peter's schooling there were always stories of locked offices and mutual tutorials (it was a fairly consistent rumor that his Advertising prof gave oral finals to select leggy grad students), so it wasn't difficult to imagine that back in the early seventies old pops could do some serious liver scratching with impunity. And did moms take it? Was she too busy practicing to notice? Or did she poke around on her own, maybe with one of her students, laying herself out on the baby grand, her feet on the keyboard, while pimple-faced

Chester folded his glasses, pulled down his sweats and shot his load all over Für Elise (some Playboy thing he had seen or something).

What was their relationship like? He had no memories of fights (whispered or screaming), no memories of couch sleeping (dad) or bed sobbing (mom), no memories of slammed doors or silent dinners, but then again no real memories of welcome home kisses, unexpected gifts, joyful duets or midnight moans (no real memories at all [that wasn't quite true, he had a number of memories of music {either moms practicing or pops listening}]). Not only did he have only the vaguest idea of how they functioned as parents (how they related to him), he had even less knowledge of how they acted as a couple (what they felt toward each other). There was this big gap, this big wound at the center of his life, and when things were going well, he could almost forget about it, almost smooth it over in his enjoyment of the now. But when things fucked up, it was there like clockwork, rising to the surface and screaming at him what a loser (literally) he was. Maybe it was time to face the music, maybe it was time to try to find out more.

"Still pissed? Oh Peter, you're so cute when you're mad." Her hand moved up, and little Pete awakened. "And so predictable. That's why I love you." He sighed heavily.

That night, after dropping Wanda off (after popsicles and Boy George), he sat at his computer, opened a Heineken (new 12 pack), and bought a refundable ($250 to change or cancel but so what) round trip one stop (change in London) ticket to Istanbul ($1200) on United (not enough miles for an upgrade) on the net for the following Tuesday (he couldn't remember but was pretty sure Reham would be back by then [he'd try to call her in a day or two to set this up]). The next day he went to Andiamo on Melrose before work, where he bought a black leather shave kit from Burberry ($275), a crocodile leather money belt from Anna Conda ($98), a nice vintage 4 oz. Cartier replica sliver flask ($200) and a funky, relaxed all weather Panama travel hat from J. Peterman surplus ($80). He was going to Turkey.

ISTANBUL, JERUSALEM, AND GAZA CITY

BOOK IV

CHAPTER NINE

About forty, make that twenty, minutes into the flight Peter (dark dark burgundy Jil Sander boiled wool sweater [$525], off-white D&G silk and cotton tee shirt [$175], gray with flecks of red light wool and cotton blend slacks from Kiton [$450], his Banfi lizard loafers [still a bit painful {not yet broken in} as he had figured he'd mostly be sitting so they'd be okay], Prada cotton socks [$30], a Tanino Crisci black leather belt with money pocket [$200], his Raymond Weil and a spray of The Powers of Horror by Chanel [$129 4 oz]) wondered what the fuck he had done. He'd had second third and fourth thoughts even before boarding, but jammed between a butt-ugly, slightly overweight ho momma (or g-momma) in those seriously homely blue hair photogray (although seventies retro was making a comeback these were whack) bifocals (gold temples attaching to the bottom of a clear plastic frame) and a gray and pink Adidas track suit (matching jacket, pants, tee shirt and sneakers [with white ankle socks]) on one side (window) and a skinny, nervous looking Abdul (probably sitting on a case of plastique) in a pale yellow short sleeve oxford (unbuttoned at the top revealing white cotton undershirt), brown nylon and cotton blend Dockers (one knee slightly shiny) with no belt, brown wingtips and black hose with a gold Timex, a fucking huge bushy stache (matching eyebrows) and the (not quite uvula tickling but certainly inescapable) smell of roofing tar and onions on the other (aisle), he wondered how the holy fuck he could have gotten himself into such a totally gnarly beach ball of death (he'd reserved an aisle seat but they'd lost his reservation and by the time he got on the plane it was too late [sorry Charlie {when he got the chance he send someone a nasty email}], plus he'd forgotten to buy a zine or anything and so had absolutely nothing to do [he didn't want to drag his Powerbook {Zero Halliburton DZ7 gun metal gray case} down between smelly and skanky {he only had Quake on his Mac but had brought a couple of cd's (Kaspar Mute [from Wanda], Los Angeles Critical Mass Compilation [from work], Glenn Gould's French Suites [long ago present from Kay] and Mazzy Star Among My Swan [$17.99 at the airport {where he had picked up a small bottle of L'Expérience Intériure by Kenzo $75 .4 oz for Reham}])}, besides he didn't think he had much juice left] except stare at the seat in front of him and try to avoid that foul wind from the aisle, although gramma's mug was just as bad. Maybe he should put on his Cutler and Gross's and try to catch some z's [where the fuck was the drink cart?]).

Anyway, this was one stoopid idea: probably the worse he had ever had (his Todd Marinovich, his Waterworld) and there was not one goddam thing he could do about it except sit there with his eyes closed and nostrils pinched, trying not to go agro (pull a Cunanan) until he could down a couple of Jacks —even though it was just barely noon and his flight attendant (fine straw blonde hair, nice green eyes and full lips although a little wide in the caboose [should have opted for the skirt rather than the slacks {who designed those outfits that Drew Carey hawg?}]) would proba-bly give him crusties for the next eight or whatever but fuck her (not a bad idea [10,000 mile club] although he probably couldn't fit both her and her ass into one of those johns — he looked around trying to spot a trim-mer collaborator [no Calista {or Kate Moss}: he didn't dig the skeleton trade], someone like Ehrinn Cummings [or Jenny McCarthy] he could stand against the door, lift up her skirt and do the nasty while gramma here hopped on one leg and stared at the occupado, but all he saw [besides an Earl with a flattop and the cutest gold earring] was a small, forty-something bird working in the far aisle with streaked bleached hair pulled back so tight it looked like it was holding her nose in place [not a bad frame but he'd be afraid to loosen her 'do and see her face collapse]). He wondered what Wanda was doing now (he'd left her a voicemail saying he had to go someplace for work [weak, very weak] and would call her in a couple of days [he had sent an email to Kay {ask me no questions I'll tell you no lies}]): it was Saturday so she was probably enjoying a late breakfast with moms (Jaime made primo habañero huevos with free range eggs and Belgian pork) or riding with Caitlin (thigh high custom-made Mantelassi riding boots [$1200] with Bridgely jodhpurs [$400]), or maybe windsurfing with her surfer buds (Bodyglove long sleeved wetsuit top [$250] with Eres [$400] or Bruce [$200] bikini bottoms [she looked excellent in swimwear {in anything (and nothing)}]). What was he doing now? Thousands of feet over fucking New Mexico (or wherever), flying halfway across the world to see some dark-haired playa-hater using him up and down like Jordan on a white guy (any white guy [thass right even Bird]). And for what? For the promise to recover something he never had. Or had but couldn't remember. Looooser.

He hoped he wasn't screwing things up. He'd try to email her from Heathrow. No, I don't want headphones I want a fucking drink! Faint whiff of Experience and Judgment ($60 .4 oz). Might as well, "Sure, thank you." Not as bad as he first thought: it looked muscular and high, like a black woman's (the bigger the cushion the better the pushin'). Maybe when they dimmed the lights to show the flick, he could scope her out some more. What was the flick anyway? He skimmed through his copy of Friendly Skies: flights to Europe — Kenny G as the featured artist, Rachmaninoff's Romantic Melodies, where were the movies? Here we go, Father of the Bride III with Steve Martin (a wild and crazy guy), Hugh Grant (the king of [Benz blowjobs {or was it a Beamer?}] airplane movies), John Travolta (again), Jennifer Lopez (speaking of booty) and Bette Midler (she still alive?). He looked at his Raymond Weil: ten more to London, three hour layover, then another four (he had better have an aisle) to Istanbul. Jesus fucking Christ.

Peter's flight from London to Istanbul, although shorter, was, if possible, even more unpleasant than his flight from Los Angeles (the tedium of an uncomfortable seat, unwatchable film, uneatable food [two meals from LA to London: the first a bone-dry scone, weak coffee and cream that had lost its clot and run all over the plate covering his two .22 caliber bangers, followed five hours later by some sort of mystery wrap in brownish gray gravy] and unbreathable air was more than matched by the fear of actual physical danger [in addition to the uncomfortable seat, uneatable food {an unspeakable quiche with a thin greenish tomato wedge and an almost translucent slice of green pepper} and unbreathable air]). Full of raucous and bitter (and variously attired [everything from Armani to Old Navy to {no designer, no bullshit} camo]) Turks returning home from seeing their national soccer team suffer a controversial one nil defeat at the boots of the Brits (the only goal an Alan Shearer penalty [fucking racist referee]), Peter (in his aisle seat) put his Weil in his pocket and scrunched down (as best he could) as the hairy and smelly (you guys ever hear of Mitchum?) horded around him, and, in both public school and broken English, ordered drink after drink and mercilessly abused two small (one boy one girl) and rather (under-standably) frightened looking flight attendants (You British, you don't own the world any more. You think you do, but you do not. This beer is not cold, please replace it.) until the pilot came back and spoke to them in their native tongue, after which they contented themselves with murmuring their guttural, phlegm producing syllables (the flight attendants having quit the field, leaving Peter high and dry). This mumbling soon grew in emotion and volume, however, and a couple of guys suddenly got up from their seats and began clapping their hands, stomping their feet and singing. Soon Peter was surrounded by Turks on the warpath (?), praising Allah and calling for the death of the America the Great Satan (they were actually singing football [Fenerbaçhe and Galatasaray] anthems and Black Sea folksongs). A friendly looking twenty-something college boy with bad acne, a Michigan cap, tight Tiffany and Tomato jeans, a brown Marks and Spencer sweater, a thin (looked penciled on) stache and sad, sad eyes, turned and without speaking offered Peter his unopened Efes. Peter, a bit flustered by the racket, his spine screwing Heathrow nap and his early and frequent (five all told) Jack Daniels', shook his head (it was too loud to talk) no, after which Homeboy shrugged (the same gesture as Reham — the top of his head tilted toward the side, while the corners of the mouth turned down and his shoulders twitched upward, with palms upturned) and resumed singing.

The attendants eventually returned to direct everyone back to their seats to prepare for landing. Finally, finally, they landed, and Peter was surprised (and a bit disconcerted) to hear applause and cheers ring out from the cabin: was a successful touchdown such a rare occurrence? Well, here he was — exhausted, stiff, a little drunk, a little hung, constipated, anxious, regretful, dehydrated and slightly angry — in Turkey (big deal).

And now, yeah, let's stand here for a fucking goddam hour while we all try to get out of the fucking plane. Passport and return tickets inserted (he had checked four or five times) in his Coach travel wallet (present from Kay's ex before the split [he had transferred all his stuff from the Ghurka because the Coach was larger and heavier and therefore {he reasoned} harder to pick {besides it was a travel wallet}]) in the front pocket of his Kitons, hand firmly on Mac case (not that he would miss it that much [what files he did have he had translated and transferred to his new Sony] but he sure as hell didn't want to provide a complimentary laptop to some thick-fingered sheet wearer with a beard down to his belt sitting in some temple or mosque [whatever] downloading a recipe for anthrax or fucking nerve gas or some such crap). What the fuck was the holdup the door wasn't even open yet Jesus Christ. He swallowed hard, fought down a moment of panic: one week, one fucking week, seven days, he could do this. Seven days (what time is it anyway? He checked his wrist, where was his RW? Oh yeah, in his pocket. The time didn't really matter: it was dark and besides, he wasn't sure he had set it right). So he'd chill with Reham, maybe get some sleep, and tomorrow, or the next day at the latest, he'd collect the book. Fuck, he wouldn't even have to stay the whole seven: he'd check out the book (dear old daddy), play el tourista for a couple of days, take Reham for some good grub, and blow town (back to blonde Wanda) by Friday. It would cost him some small change to leave early (plus he'd have to upgrade to business no matter what), but those were the breaks. He yawned nervously.

Reham. He had avoided thinking about her for

most of the flight. He would see her in a couple of minutes (if this motherfucking, cocksucking, cuntlicking door ever ever opened and these greasy, beer swilling, deodorant avoiding maharajahs could ever find their way out). He would be on her turf now, which meant he would really have to watch his nuts. He was only there to find out about his dad: gather some info, scope out the book, and, if she was helpful and they hung without too much friction, maybe slip her a few bucks (at least pay the two grand for the drawing). This wasn't going to be a Family Ties reunion (and didn't Alex have a thing for his fictional sister, what's-her-name, in real life?) where they all lived happily ever after. A few emails once in awhile (did she even have a machine?), maybe a check or two (at first), and that would be it. The weird vibe he had felt for her when they first met and after the kiss (what was THAT about? [probably just some cultural thing {or maybe she was playing him}]) had quickly been erased by Wanda's attentions and other immediate (first) worldly concerns (like losing that crib and wondering where he was going to live). Still, he would have to watch his back — he was in her house.

    Finally the door opened and the line began the two-step shuffle toward it. C'mon, c'mon, what's the hold up? He noticed the stiff frozen smiles of the flight attendants as they deplaned the passengers (Fuck you for flying United, Fuck you for flying United [who could blame them?]) and gave one of them (a sweet, dewy-eyed thing with freckles and platinum hair [Sweden or California]) a sympathetic (we're both white) smile. Then it was down the stairs and on to a bus (don't they even have regular ramps and shit?), where he stood and waited some more (he now had to pee), and watched while this ninety year old sixty pound refugee-looking rag-rack half yanked half pushed a suitcase the size of a new Volkswagen down the steps while some of the soccer buffs (hey Ayatollah why don't you give her a hand) milled impatiently behind. Finally one of the bright orange jumpsuited ground crew (a wiry dude with a big cigar) came to her aid (he also had trouble with it) and soon the bag was grounded where it could be dragged to the bus. And then some more waiting (as the bus filled the air became close [sweat and stale cigarette smoke], so Peter turned his nose away and saw a LOT Polish Airlines jet [Polish Airlines sounded like the first line of a joke] taxi by slowly followed by an Air Ukraine 737) and more loading until the bus was packed, when whoosh the doors closed and it lurched away.

After a few fun-filled minutes of speeding, swerving and dodging (the bus) and trying not to (breathe or) slam dance into his fellow passengers (Peter), they came to a stop, the doors opened, and (gentlemen start your engines) people dashed out, across a sidewalk, and into a set of double doors, some literally sprinting (a bomb in the bus?) to get inside (take it easy there slick the airport ain't going nowhere). Although he had to piss like a racehorse, he wasn't going to run like one, and so, the last one, he stepped nonchalantly off the bus and took his time to get to the double doors.

After he entered, he saw the reason for the haste. Lines. Actually not individual lines, but more of a formless mass facing and perhaps, if one could only watch long enough, moving toward three small openings at the far end of the room. Fucking motherfucking motherfuckers. He moved to where it appeared he would have the most acute angle to one of the openings, set the Zero Halliburton down, and stood, but, feeling little Pete in need of relief, found the door marked WC and hurried in to drain the main vein.

When he returned, another planeful of passengers had arrived and had joined the throng. After finishing one line (good thing he peed) only to be sent to another to procure a visa (Where is your visa? I'm from the United States. You need a visa sir [fifty fucking bucks].), Peter finally (his heels beginning to hurt) made it past the passport booths and into the baggage room, where he stood just inside the doors, amazed at the thick nimbostratus of cigarette smoke floating about a foot above his head. He was almost surprised it wasn't raining large black tar and nicotine drops. Fuck, he needed an iron lung just to hang, so the sooner he grabbed his Samsonite (he hadn't wanted to take his Vuitton set [to which the footlocker belonged] and so had crammed everything into an old Samsonite Dublin [Kay's emergency purchase in Hyde Park to carry home a set of fabric samples from Miguel Cisterna]) and split, the better. He swam through the thickened air over to the carousel to wait (more waiting) for his luggage. He hoped Reham wasn't getting impatient and didn't blow (leaving him high and dry [he had her phone number {it did work he had called her before he came (he wasn't that stupid)}] and coughing up a lung while he limped around the airport looking for her in the thickened air). Of course his Samsonite would have to be the very last fucking bag.

Except it wasn't. As the crowd thinned, successful in their assignations (lucky assholes) and Peter was able to move closer to where the slide or chute met the carousel, there was still no emerald green four-wheeled hard-sided Dublin Samsonite suitcase. No matter how hard or for how long or with how much desire he stared up the ramp to the cusp of the sleek silver chute, no Irish green rectangular case with four hidden wheels came sliding down into his waiting embrace. The slide had been barren for a while (the carousel conveying a single, forlorn brown cardboard box tied with string around and around), and he stood alone, waiting, hoping, trying not to let his anger (fucking fur lipped motherfucking towel head sand eating camel jockeys can't even move a single suitcase off a motherfucking airplane) somehow disqualify him (karma) from being reunited with his bag. Finally even the carousel stopped. His right heel throbbed. His Samsonite was missing. He refused to think in terms of lost.

He looked around but the baggage room was almost empty: there had to be a desk or something where someone from United could help him. He saw a group of porters hanging out in a corner by the customs exit, as well as an unmanned desk at the far end of the room, and deciding on the desk (hoping to avoid human contact until he could speak to someone who could actually help him) walked toward it (noticing as he approached the inch-thick Plexiglas window [what were they afraid of?] and a sign that said United and Alliance Baggage Claim in five different languages). He thought there would be a bell or buzzer he could ring for help, or that someone would notice him and come out to speak to him, but he noticed no buzzer, and no matter how loudly he sighed or how conspicuous he tried to make himself, no one emerged from the door behind the glass. He turned to the porters, who were leaning against the wall and smoking. He hesitated (it was either try the porters or go back toward the passport desks), gathered himself and walked (as) confidently (as he could [his right heel was stinging]) across the baggage area.

The porters were big men. Peter chose one who was less big and said "Is there a baggage agent here? They seem to have lost my bag." He assumed they spoke English, or he was really fucked.

One of the bigger ones answered, "Back where you were."

Peter turned his head. "There's no one there."

"Yes." He turned to his companions, said something in that guttural language of theirs, and they all laughed.   Peter set his case down and waited.   The laughter stopped quickly. Well? He considered greasing the wheels a bit, but he had just dropped a fifty for a visa and all he was doing was asking a simple question. Besides, he didn't want to immediately reach for the Coach to solve problems (besides that he hadn't bought any Turkish money yet and the lowest he remembered having [from the visa purchase] was a ten). Okay, dickface. He turned back and faced the desk. "What flight did you come in with?"

He turned back. "United. Twenty seven something. From London."

"You are English?"

Did he sound English?   He remembered the fight songs. "No, American."

"American. Yes."   He said something and the men laughed again. "Would you like a cigarette?"

"No thank you." He shifted his weight to the other leg. "I don't smoke," he added for some reason. He had a headache. He waited. He turned and looked back at the desk. He waited some more. Okay, fuck you. He picked his Zero Halliburton up and began to pivot away from the men.

"Knock strongly on the window. Someone will come."

Yeah, fuck you anyway. "Thanks."

"I'm sorry sir, but there is no record of your bag arriving in London." Short black hair, round face (looking like it had just awakened), thin peach lipsticked mouth, large blue eyes surrounded by gray eye-shadow, all set on a large, five foot eight two hundred pound frame with tits that almost overflowed the gray and maroon United uni's, with that upper crust Brit accent (even through a set of small holes in the Plexiglas) that he associated with class and so was constantly being surprised by the discrepancy between voice and appearance (sound and vision).

"What does that mean?"

More keypunching. "As far as the computer knows, your bag was not on the flight from Los Angeles to Heathrow. So obviously it would not come from Heathrow to Istanbul."

"So it's lost."

"It is not in London, and it is not here. I will try to check Los Angeles, but that will take some time."

"What do I wear in the meantime?"

"You will need to fill out this form, with a telephone number where we can reach you. We will attempt to locate your bag. A bag is not considered lost until three weeks have elapsed. If we cannot locate it within three weeks, we will issue you compensation." She slid a form beneath the glass and punched some more numbers in her computer. "We do not have to deliver it to you within three weeks, we simply have to locate it within that time frame. We will of course make every effort to deliver it to you as soon as possible, but we do not guarantee delivery within this time."

Three weeks? Fuck. "How much?"

"Our compensation is limited to twenty US dollars per kilo. Six hundred and forty US dollars total."

Peter coughed. He had been breathing crap for about twenty four straight now (although he did live in LA). He was angry, sure — they had lost his stuff — but in an odd way, he felt almost gratified, vindicated in his suspicions and paranoia. Not only had he decid-

ed not to take any of the Vuitton, but had also made
sure to pack only clothes he wouldn't miss and which
he could (emotionally and financially) afford to lose.
So instead of his D & G blue jeans ($299), he had opted
for his black silver button Levi's ($79); rather than the
Charvet silks [$126], he'd gone with the assorted GAP
cotton paisley's (3 for $25); and instead of the Armani
dark brown cardigan ($750), he had chosen the Zegna
turtle ($400). The one irreplaceable article or articles
(besides his new shave kit [luckily he kept his Chanel,
Mitchum, Oral B and Crest Ultra in his Zero
Halliburton] and flask, fuck!) was his sharkskin rayon
suit (Wanda's present from LA Retro, but he had
almost worn it out anyway. Six hundred wasn't much,
but it might be fun to pick up some Turko threads
(none of those sheets and shit maybe something
leather [he'd heard about Turkish leather from Lazy
Susan {one ugly dyke but she knew her skins (and he
seldom said no to shopping)}]). Still, it was a huge
pain in the ass, the fucking imbeciles. Maybe he
should bitch and try to get some more cash. Neither
Wanda nor Kay would settle for a flimsy six: they'd be
on the horn to someone, threatening lawyers and shit.
He didn't have time for this. He felt his anger rise (he
needed some air).

"What is this I'm signing?"

"This is to say that you recognize that our lia-
bility is limited to six hundred and forty US dollars."

"And if I don't sign?"

She shrugged (a slight hunch of the shoulders).
"If your bag is located, it will make no difference. If it
is not, then your compensation may be delayed."

He wasn't going to fuck with this all night, or
day, or whatever the fuck it was. He scribbled his
name and slid both the pen and form back beneath the
barrier. She looked it over, then up at him, then back

at the form. "This is the telephone number where we can reach you?" (he had given Reham's number).

"Yes."

She punched the number into the computer. Then looked back at him. "Will there be anything else?"

He shook his head, picked up his Zero, and walked through the customs to the greeting area. Time to meet his sister.

The main lobby, although higher ceilinged and sparsely populated (it was late), was, if possible, even more polluted than the baggage area (the nicotine cloud dropping down to chest level [stinging his eyes slightly]). Fuck, if it was this bad at midnight (he saw a clock [12:15]), it must be a white out at noon. He looked around for Reham, and saw only a few various figures slumped in chairs, a few broom-pushing ciga-rette-smoking janitors, and a couple of fat men in ill-fit-ting cheap suits with paper signs reading Bodrum, Ephesus and Vasilinky smoking in a corner. No Reham. At least the moneychanger was still open, and he quick-ly picked up some Turkish greenbacks, or whatever the fuck they were. He counted the bills carefully. Some weird looking money, ese. And what was with all those zeros? Seemed like quite a wad. He'd figure it out later. Where the fuck was she? Where was his sister?

He wandered around a bit more. This was per-fect—thousands of miles and about a thousand bucks (and counting) later, unknown damage to his relation-ships with his fiancé and aunt, hours of worry and con-cern, and here he was, alone, standing like some Eddy in the middle of the airport, feeling quite the (consti-pated, exhausted and dehydrated) chump. He had her number, time to give her a call: he hoped she was asleep and that he'd wake her from pleasant dreams.

As he looked around for a telephone, he noticed a man in a Burberry raincoat, covering a nice taupe Pal Zileri lightweight wool suit over a gray knit Versace tee, with soft brown leather lace-up boots (possibly Duffendorf) walking toward him.   Maybe they had found his bag (but those boots were not the boots of an airline employee [unless they fell out of someone's suitcase]). "Excuse me sir, are you Peter bey?" Slight whiff of Donitella Versace Das Kapital, and Peter noticed the gold Tissot Millenium with a rather large gold and opal ring on the ring finger of his right hand.

"My name is Peter, yes."

"I am a friend of Reham. She had to go away. I am to take you to your nice hotel, where she will tele-phone you" (this guy was smooth — not oily, not greasy, more like mercury than 10-W40).

He was almost too tired to be pissed, but not quite. "Where'd she go?"

"She did not tell me. This letter is for you." This was too much like James fucking Bond, and he was sick of these games. He took the letter, noticed the now familiar script on the envelope, opened it and read:

Dear Peter,

I regret very much being unable to meet you tonight. Please go with Murat to the hotel (not the Marriott) and I will ring you tomorrow or possibly the next day. I know you have many questions and not much time, and I am sorry that other duties have interfered. I feel much joy that you are here. This is not my country, but welcome. Gratefully, Reham.

Christ! "So she'll call tomorrow?"

"I do not know. But I am to give you this." He handed Peter a bulky Ericsson Z-240. Peter took it (it was heavy) and stared at it for a while, then placed it in the Zero where it just fit. "Where is your baggage?"

"Your guess is as good as mine."

"Excuse me?"

"They lost my bag."

Murat shrugged. "Please, follow me. Have you been to Istanbul before?"

"No, never."

Murat stopped and took an antique art-deco sliver cigarette case from the coat pocket of his Zileri. "Gaulois?"

"No, thank you. I don't smoke."

He smiled at Peter at he lit up (matching lighter). "Have you injured your leg?"

"Just a blister on my heel."

"I am sorry. Anyway, welcome to Turkey."

Yeah, right. Welcome to Turkey.

CHAPTER TEN

Was that the phone? Fuck, where was it? It was dark in his room, more of a deep purple (Smoke on the Water) than a pitch black. He reached over to the nightstand and lifted the receiver off of the hook. Must be Reham. "Hello?" The telephone kept ringing. "Hello?" What the fuck? "Hello." Goddam phones didn't even work. "Hello." Stupid ass place. He replaced the receiver. The telephone kept ringing. It was the Ericsson (sounding exactly like his Beophone) Slick had given him last night. Where did he'd put it? In the Zero Halliburton. Which was where? He stumbled out of bed, following the sound of the (muffled, he now realized) ringing. Under the bed — no thief would ever look there. He opened the case; he was excited (a telephone call from his [half] sister [although she would have some splainin to do]). "Hello?"

"Hello, Peter bey."

Fucking Murat. "Hello."

"I am sorry I am not who you are expecting. I am thinking that maybe you are by now hungry, and would like some lunch. If you please, I can take you to a place where they have a very good kitchen."

"Lunch? What time is it?" He looked around the room: the clock radio on the opposite nightstand read 2:15. He'd slept late.

"It is after two o'clock. I did not break your sleep, did I?"

"No, I was just getting ready to take a shower. Have you heard from Reham?"

"No. But you will bring the mobile, so you will not miss her call." He ran his hand through his hair.

Shit, why not, he could use some grub. "Okay, sure, let's do lunch."

"Yes, let us do lunch. I am in Sultanahmet." So? "It will likely require around one half an hour to get to your hotel, so you may take your shower as you planned. Let us meet downstairs at three o'clock. Is this fine?"

"Three is great. See you then."

"Goodbye."

Peter beeped off the Ericsson and stared down at his Powerbook. He hadn't had the chance to check his email (or his quotes [he wondered how his great his Cisco {Cisco S 170} was doing {probably fucking great} and was more than a bit concerned about his Sprint PCS {110 7/16, which had dropped almost a quarter before he left (last time he took a tip from Hector the financially challenged [If your broker's so great why is he still working?])}]) during his layover at Heathrow, and wondered if either Wanda or Kay had written him, asking where and how he was (he wasn't concerned about anyone else). He could try from the room, but didn't know if the hotel was analog or digital (probably closer to diesel, but it was the Hilton [$145 per]), and he didn't want to fry his modem. He could phone home (at $10 per second), but wasn't sure what time they were on (probably way too early), and besides he wasn't sure he wanted to answer the questions that would probably (Wanda) or certainly (Kay) be asked. So maybe Murat could lead him to a cyber café after chow. He rubbed his head again. He had a headache, and he was still constipated (he felt like he would never, ever, ever dump again: it was as if his body lost both the cellular requirement as well as the muscular memory of excreting solid waste): he needed some cino bad, for both his head and his butt. He wondered if there was a Starbucks around, although the Hilton might have some passable java. He should probably get dressed and find out, but turning to sniff his left pit, he realized that he would have to wash first. He remained on the edge of the bed.

He could call Reham: he had the number, and he had a cell phone. Her number was in his Coach (he had to get a Palm), which was in his Kitons, which were where? He got up (his neck was still stiff [from Heathrow nap]) and opened the heavy, dusty drapes. Jesus Christ: what was it with the lilac, gray and teal (he almost closed them again). He looked around. His pants weren't draped over the chair, so he must have hung them up. Oh yeah, lost Samsonite (Jesus fucking Christ [maybe an omen {Damien, I'm here for you Damien} of something nasty]): the Kitons might be the only pants he'd have for awhile (which is why he must have hung them up [he'd have to get Murat to take him somewhere to pick up some Levis or some-thing {he'd also have to call United before they did lunch}]). He walked over to the closet, where he removed the Coach from the Kitons and punched Reham's number in the Ericsson standing up. It was busy (he remembered the funny busy signal from call-ing before). Who could she be talking to? Or, more importantly, why wasn't she talking to him? He beeped the Ericsson off, and sat back down on the bed.

Did she have a boyfriend? Or a husband even? Children? He had never even considered the possibili-ty that she was connected with anyone. She seemed too angry, too strong, too set in her ways and self-suf-ficient (and there was that kiss). But it was possible that she could have a family, a husband anyway, or at least a lover. Maybe that was why she couldn't meet him at the airport, and couldn't call him immediately. How old was she anyway? If he was twenty five, then she was what? Twenty, twenty two? When did his dad screw around on his mom? Peter hoped he waited at least a year until after he was born. The fucker.

Anyway, she wasn't your average veil-wearing, belly-dancing sand eater, so she'd probably be a good catch for some four-eyes, some teacher or something who'd been to the States and seen the civilized way we treat our women. She certainly was no conformer, and was probably too far out to be much of an influencer either. She might even be too weird to be an edger, if such a thing were possible. He thought back to the airplane boys singing their angry songs — Reham was as foreign to them as she was to him. Life had probably not been very easy for her here (so far).

So hopefully she did have someone to hang with, someone to do the horizontal with when she needed to. He could ask Murat if she was hooking up with anyone. Although maybe he was the guy. Peter shuddered involuntarily: he didn't want to imagine that (although the briefest instant of Murat's dark greasy head buried between Reham's white thighs on some oriental rug [his?] flashed through his consciousness). Dude was seriously slick. Galwhaw? Asshole. If he was the dude who was sexing her silly, maybe he should sit Reham down for a friendly, brother to sister; she'd certainly appreciate the fraternal concern. Not. What was Slick doing in the middle of this? Was he just friendly, or nosy? Or did he have some other motive? Maybe he was her scam partner, and they were in this together, 'this' being a game of let's dick the American. He'd have to watch himself, that was fer sure. Every time he'd thought he had it handled, thought he had his defense set (like Da Bears of '85 [Peter was ten]) some image from that story or something came floating back into his mind like some strand of rank seaweed washing up on the beach, and he started feeling sorry for her and shit and got all sentimental (the fact he was here was proof enough of that).

And what time was it? Fuck, Murat would be here in ten, he'd better get into that shower. He looked down at his bloody Pradas — he'd have to locate some new pads today too, some cheap Chucks or something he could walk around in, although Chucks would look el stupido with the Kitons. He'd also have to find Band-Aids for his heels, or else he wasn't going anywhere. He'd get some from the desk on the way out. He yawned. Need. Caffeine. Now. And where the fuck was his sister? He punched redial on the Ericsson. Still busy. Chatty bitch. He got up to take a shower.

He had jumped (not literally) again when the Ericsson rang (again Murat [not Reham]), informing him that he was very very sorry, but that he would be unable to meet Peter for lunch as he had promised, and would telephone him this evening to perhaps make plans for dinner. He had given Peter his cell number in case he needed anything, and had spelled out the name of the restaurant (Peter [heels bandaged], sitting in the lobby with a cup of American coffee [he had tried a Turkish {medium (orta)} and although he liked jet fuel as much as the next guy had found it a bit stout {put some har on yer chest (filter the fucking grounds)}] without anything to write with, had merely repeated the seemingly random sequence of letters [i-n-n-o-g-u-l-u-a-k-d-e-n-i-z], having absolutely no intention of going anywhere near the joint) where he had planned to take him (Any taxi will know). He was very sorry. No sweat Jackson, TTYL. So Peter was on his own: no sister (he called again [still busy]), no Samsonite (he called), and no one to show him 'round the hood. And he was hungry, and since the Hilton didn't lift his skirt (favorite saying of Pedro [Wanda's gay friend {one of many}]), it was time to go out into the wild.

The air outside was a slightly diluted version of the airport smog, with gasoline and industrial fumes replacing the almost pure cigarette pollution of the terminal (he wish he'd worn his Nick Ashley or even his old Marc Jacobs instead of his Jil Sander [which was warm enough but both the Ashley and the Jacobs had more pockets {the Ashley would have been perfect}]). According to the Hilton map and desk clerk, if he walked down Cumhuriyet Avenue past the Intercontinental, he'd come to an area called Taksim, where there'd be a number of fine restaurants featuring both Turkish and international cuisines. He wasn't yet sure what he was in the mood for: a bowl of Tet Soup (free range chicken breast, oyster shrooms from Osaka, tons of Cambodian lemongrass and Bangkok chilies, plus homegrown fresh basil) from L'il Saigon (near Los Feliz) sounded tasty, as did a fresh (they had their own boats) snapper (marinated in Korean soy, Bermuda onion and Cointreau) sandwich (baguette from The Bread Man, local arugula, red leaf and Belgian endive, topped with their extra hot [habañero and chipotle] homemade mustard) from Marcolini's Bait Shack. Fuck, he was hongry. But for what? He seriously doubted there was a Marcolini's Bait Shack II in Istanbul. Maybe a nice New York Strip would be the ticket: even the Brits could cook beef (although there was that crazy cow disease thing a few years back [he didn't want to end up in a straightjacket in Parkwood with his dick flopped out, his fingers up his nose, dribbling on his shoulder just for some Turksteak sandwich], so maybe fish would be the way to go [they were, after all, by the sea]). Maybe he'd just walk along until he came to something that looked halfway decent and clean and chow down. Then give another call, do some clothes shopping (maybe he could find a Gap [those high top sneaks weren't bad]), and hopefully get ready to meet with Reham (he didn't want to have to hang with Murat all night).

There was always Mickey-D's. Two all beef patties special sauce lettuce cheese pickles onions on a sesame seed bun. It was phat the way the Mickey-D's was everywhere: no matter where you were in the world it would take you ten minutes at most to find those golden arches. Not that he had the jones for that cardboard crap — he avoided all fast food, especially McDonald's (Peter had an irrational fear of either being spotted by someone he knew [Gawd] or by being gunned down à la C. Vista [the televised news reports of that massacre were embedded in Peter's psyche {even now the words Chula Vista brought to mind images of helicopters, smeared blood on polished chrome and French fries mixed with broken glass}]) like the plague. He weren't no sprout eating, protein lacking, bean farting, pasty faced, stick armed, bird chested, Dave Matthews quoting how-could-you-eat-that-don't-you-know-how-they-murder-them veggie (two or four legged, vegan, ovary, lactose, macro, organic only, grainarian, fruitarian, citrusian, liquidian, clear liquidian, soft mechanical, etcetera etcetera [fuckers made him want to eat veal]), nor did he have a weight problem (he didn't overeat, he swam and worked out [both weights and ball] regularly, plus he was only twenty five): it was just that he found that type of food and atmosphere, well, pathetic (skinny old men nursing fifty cent coffees [free refills] half the day, obese white twenty something newmoms with bewildered faces and milk stained blouses chewing and swallowing among piles of happy meal debris, and sullen homies smoking up in the lot before school). Still, it was nice to know that if you absolutely had to (actually a couple of weeks ago, on a road trip to Vegas, he and Wanda had made a 2 am stop to use the [always clean] restrooms and they had dope [big blunt of M-county sinse] -dined [I'm starving fucking starving] on Big Macs, fries and cherry pies), you could fill your belly with something, something that if not all that tasty (not tasty at all), was at least dependable and filling. And cheap. America was a good country (no irony here).

As Peter drew level with the Intercontinental on his left, the crowd (assortedly dressed, from nice Brooks Brothers to that head to toe veil thing) began to thicken, and suddenly he was assailed by a clambering posse of scrawny (and filthy), obnoxious and relentless brats (a tiny dark haired and skinned girl in a torn Nile-green plaid school skirt with a hideous over-size quince blouse and basic red and white Keds; a slightly taller skinny red headed boy in a sleeveless tee shirt underneath a navy blue windbreaker with tight highwater Lees and sloppy galoshes; a chunky, round faced fellow [possibly the girl's better fed brother] in khaki trousers with holes in the knees, a University of Miami sweatshirt and some ancient duct taped Pumas [like his]; and another girl, slightly taller and older [perhaps fourteen {Peter could never tell with kids (she looked like she would soon be peddling other goods)}], in a faded lilac and white sundress with a tomato red sweater tied around her waist, four thin gold bangles, once white ankle socks and fairly new and bright Mary Janes) sucker-hawking little packages of Kleenex, Crest, Scope, and even Trojans (too bad your daddy [daddies] didn't use one). They followed him for almost half a block, pleading ("Please sir, only one dollar," "Please, for my mother sir," "Please, gentlemen sir, we are hungry, only one dollar") and pulling on the sleeves of his

Jil Sander (which he did not like at all [where have those hands been?]), until he broke away and started to run (jog really, his heels hurt and the Banfis weren't made for sport [besides he didn't want to look like a total geekbot]), dodging both Armanis and veils, until he stumbled and almost turned an ankle in front of a small flower stand, his Cutler and Gross's clattering to the pavement. Fuck! Jesus fucking Christ (or Allah fucking Mohammed or whoever). He steadied himself, turned around and picked up the shades. No scratches he could see. He blew on the lenses, looked through them again, and replaced them on his face. That was the last fucking thing he needed, to scratch his sunglasses. He looked down: Miami had followed him and was snickering (the rest of the pack moving on to easier marks). No-neck monster (his Uncle David's pet name for him). What the fuck you looking at? Peter threw up his right hand quickly and lurched forward as if to chase, but Miami didn't move. He simply continued to stare and snicker.

"Go home. Get outta here. Get outta here."

The boy stopped laughing, but did not stop looking at him, staring at him, staring through his dark lenses, staring him down. Peter stared back —he didn't care where he was, he wasn't going to let some baby fat twelve year old ass-wipe piece of dog feces without his first pubes make a dick out of him. An old woman (the flower lady) in a bright sky blue scarf on the edge of his vision to his left was shaking her head and making a loud clucking sound (the sound his Gramma [all Grammas?] made) with her tongue (whether at him or the boy Peter couldn't tell). What was he doing? Rumbling with some twelve year old? This was ridiculous. Good thing Wanda couldn't see this (if Wanda were here he wouldn't be in this mess [if Wanda were here they wouldn't be here {they'd be sharing a pussysickle on the Santa B beach}]). He continued staring — better not screw with me Burt. Finally the boy, without dropping his eyes, pivoted slowly and walked (didn't run) away. Peter turned to the flower lady, who immediately looked down and busied herself with an arrangement of bright pink and white jasmine.

Li'l fucker only wanted a buck (although it looked like he got enough to eat his pals could use some change). How much in funny money was that? Probably feed his entire crew for a Lincoln. And they weren't begging, they were selling: unlike ninety percent of the scum in LA, they were at least offering something in return. He should be rewarding their entrepreneurial spirit instead of yelling at them to go home. What an asshole he was, staring him down like that. Peter took a single step to follow, and then stopped: if he gave them a shekel or two, they would never leave him alone, and the last thing he needed was a pack of braying brats stalking him, those shrill little voices sticking in his brain and those grubby little paws mucking up the Jil. This wasn't a pleasure cruise — he was trying to find his sister, and his father, and make some sense out of his life — he didn't have the time to be screwing with every street punk who wanted change. Where the fuck were their parents? Where the fuck were his parents? Where the fuck was his sister? Where the fuck was he?

Okay, okay, he needed some fuel. He'd feel better after eating. Besides, that litter wasn't going anywhere and he'd have a chance (probably five or six) to catch 'em on the rebound. He'd study his money at the restaurant, figure out how much to give them (maybe a little extra cuz he had acted like such a prick) and walk by the same way after lunch. Plus he'd get some Scope in the bargain (and maybe some Trojans too [although Turk condoms might not be the most dependable protection if you know what I mean Vern {those kids were proof of that}]). What was he thinking about? Wanda was on the pill. It was all that coffee and no food — the last time he ate (if you could call that eating) was on the plane. How long ago was that? Seemed like weeks. Time to find some grub.

After he had eaten (carbo-loading on mediocre pasta Bolognese [couldn't touch Marinetti's or Pasqueli's let alone Jaime's even Louisa made better sauce], a beat cuke and tomato salad and a Heineken at a place called Trattoria Montana across the street from this old looking church) and tried to call Reham once again (still busy, something was wrong with the connection — maybe he wasn't doing it right), Peter looked at his map and decided to take a walk down to the Bosphorus (since he was here, he might as well try to see something, and the idea of MTV in his Hilton crib did not appeal to him in the least [although he did want to email and check his quotes, that could wait], and besides, ignoring the thickened air, it was a pretty nice day [not unlike the three B's when the mountains were out {although the light was all wrong}]). He felt better, stronger, more capable of handling things (he still couldn't dump), although he remained disturbed by the memory of those kids screeching and grabbing at him while he ran and almost fell, his C & G's skidding along the pavement. Which reminded him — he needed to find some new threads, although for some reason he wasn't exactly in the mood for shopping (how whack was that?). Still, if he spotted a Gap or Old Navy or even a Marks and Spence, he'd pick up some Levis, boxers, Chucks and socks (his Banfis were just starting to hurt him again). And he'd keep the receipt (fuck United). As he turned right from the Trattoria Montana (That's right, look at me, I'm the focking bad guy here. But you need me, motherfockers and Say hello to my leetle fren [he loved that flick]) and began to walk down the hill, two odd looking dudes (possibly Istanbul edgers) with Yankee caps, coke-bottle horn rims, some way cool denim baggies, plaid work shirts and big ass queer stomping Doc Marten rips came goofing up toward him (an interesting combo of skin-head and neo-Teddy although a bit last year for LA). He felt a slight moment of panic (his pepper spray was in the Samsonite), as their gait showed definite signs of a major buzz (he pictured himself comatose, legs-broken, in some Turkish hospital [Coach {ID, money} and Ericsson long gone] with absolutely no one [Wanda, Kay, Reham and even Murat] knowing where the fuck in the world he was), but as they approached, he saw that instead of some Turkish gangers, they were tards, mongos (Mongoloid, he was a mongoloid), maroons. And they were holding hands. Mongos look the same the world over. He swerved to his left and let them shuffle past. It was weird: here he was, walking down a street in a city he never in his wildest dreams imagined he'd visit, with a language, customs and food totally strange to him, and yet somehow it wasn't entirely unfamiliar (it was more than just the mongos). It wasn't that he'd lived here in another life, or any such bullshit, nor did he feel some sort of mystical blood con-nection to daddy dearest, it was just that he imagined he would (and should) feel more alienated, more estranged or unsettled (disconcerted). It wasn't that he felt comfortable, not by a long shot —no way this was his barrio ese — it was just that after a twelve hour or whatever plane ride half way around the world, to a country where they believed in some other God, he was a bit surprised to see advertisements for AOL, Dolly

Parton (upcoming concert and new cd [he guessed]) and Smith and Hawken (a large billboard of a tranquil garden, a white gazebo and a large wheelbarrow full of spades, rakes and other landscaping accessories with the words Smith and Hawken in white scripted English on the bottom). Coke, Pepsi, Levi's, Macs, Nike, okay, global capitalism, market penetration the world over and all that, that he expected (although the Taco Bell was a bit much), but Smith and Hawken?? It was weird, too, the way there was so much English around. For every three shop signs or billboards (something called Organik Gübre made by someone called ATT Tarim Urunleri Sana, Yi Ve Ticaret Ltd.Sti, showed a nearly naked young thang lying in a field of corn; Remak Araclar Endustry Vi Di TYCA made something that caused a fifties looking family of four to smile into their soup [or whatever] and Dunya Goz Hastansi was either an apartment building or office filled with a number of those red curved swords) with those fuck- ing bizarrro letter combos, there was at least one in good old readable American, and although sometimes the lingo was a bit off — Menthol Travel, Gravity Gold and Silver, Munnever's Hair Chick Saloon (he'd have to remember that one for Wanda) — it was kind of cool in a way.   He turned the corner (of Backarogiuloa- laoaoaoaoa caddii) and came upon a forty foot tall Marlboro man trimmed in neon, lying on his side in the street, Brandi's The Boy is Mine (at least it wasn't that Elton John Princess Di noise [how many times had he heard that song the past year?]) blasting out of jury rigged car speakers (Soundesign) slung over the extended tip of the big man's cigarette. Peter looked around: except for the big man and him, the street was deserted. He chuckled to himself. This was surreal man, pure LA (I love LA). Even when some dude with a slicked back pony and bad acne only partially covered by a straggly beard pulled up in the oldest VW van he had ever seen and asked him questions in two or three languages, none of which he understood, he couldn't shake the (rather disappointing) feeling that this wasn't strange or unsettling enough, that he'd seen it all before (how many times in No Hoe or Samo had he been addressed, questioned or yelled at in some language [all the slope tongues, Arab, Russian, turbaned Indian {or Paki}, Italian and of course Mexican which he could almost comprende] he couldn't follow? Plenty). In some way, it felt as if he'd never left home. It was strange how normal this all seemed. So much for breaking out of his boring dick routine (although Wanda would never have to know how mainstream this really was, especially if he brought back some extreme kick-ass gift). It's all LA. It's all good.

He continued walking down the hill toward the water: Here I am now, entertain me. Poor dude. That guy had it all: superstardom, a foxy wife, a kid, artistic truth, critical admiration, and pow, shotgun to the head, brains splattered on the wall. Nirvana. Nevermind. No wonder our generation's so cynical, our gods are dead: Kurt, River (Wanda met him a couple of times at the Chaos Club, thought he was kind of an ass-hole), Tupac, Biggie, and even Gianni. And Reagan (whom Peter rather liked, doubtless in reaction to Kay's hatred), poor old fuck, dribbling down his shirt while Nancy spoon fed his oatmeal. It's all about the Benjamins babeey, cuz there wasn't nothing else. He didn't completely believe that (although dinero was dinero). After all, he was here, wasn't he? What was the profit motive now? It was costing him some big bucks, not to mention his time and the fact that he was seriously pissing off his girlfriend and aunt. He was taking a chance here. And for what? For the possibility he could suss out something about his father, his dead father, from a woman who claimed to be his long lost half sister. Better change the tape, dude, because this story was sounding dumb and dumber. Maybe he should stick to show me the money. That's why I say hey man nice shot.

The street was becoming narrower and more crowded, with tough, wiry looking men in striped sailor shirts, blue denim pants and brogans, smoking (of course), drinking beer or what probably was tea (in small, clear glasses) and milling about on the side-walks, in doorways and sometimes spilling over into the street. A few women hurried by, many with their heads covered, some with that entire head to toe body wrap deal. Now this was a bit exotic, although not necessarily in a good way (he was definitely being stared at [cased?]). He was on the shady side of the street (it was suddenly almost chilly), and the build-ings, close in, blotted out the minarets he was using for a landmark. He walked to the corner (not hurrying), found his minaret things — instead of in front of him, they were slightly to his right — then looked down at his map. He must have taken a wrong turn some-where, possibly by the Marlboro Man. He'd still get to the water this way, and it looked like there was a park or something dead ahead, but he wondered if this was a hood he wanted to walk through. Some Ren and Stimpie and Johnny Bravo (Whoa Mama) back at the Hilton (wish he had some weed [no way Jose Midnight Express]) was looking better and better. Well, he did not want to continue to stand on the corner looking at his map (might as well carry a big sign Tourista Please Mug), so it was either push on, turn right toward the minarets, or back to the hotel. Back to the hotel.

But he didn't want to simply turn around and retrace his steps, looking like a real take-my-wallet Melvin, so he decided to turn right toward the minarets for a block and then see if he wanted to continue to the water or go back up the hill to the Hilton. This street was definitely livelier (and safer): the sun was shining, and he could see bright red Coca-Cola and slightly darker Campari umbrellas dotting the sidewalks, with better dressed (wide leg Kenzo pants, Farhi jackets; Armani, Brooks Brothers, YSL and Zegna suits; Pink and Boss shirts, Kenneth Cole and Paul Smith shoes; Paul Smith and Canali ties; Rolexes, Cartiers, Brietlings and LeCoultres; Manolos, Le Boutoutins and Sergio Rossis; Lagerfeld and Ungaro dresses; Michael Kors suits and sweaters; Byblos and Kookai separates; Chloe and LaRoche hats; Suarez and Prada bags; Bobbi Brown and Urban Decay makeup; and gold gold gold [Buccetelli, Kathy Waterman and Kentshire]) westerners either clustering around the outdoor tables or chatting on their Nokias as they hurried by. Not a headscarf in sight. It was like he'd turned a corner and rejoined the twentieth century. I love it when a plan works out. Maybe he should stop somewhere and have a drink, although he didn't want more coffee, and another beer might do him in (his clock was all off). He'd just take a stroll down the boulevard, check out the scene, and see what he wanted to do when he reached the end of the block. Maybe he could get some new duds. Cool man cool.

    "Hello. Would you like some apple tea? Or coffee?"

    "Excuse me?" He was looking into the greenest (female) eyes he had ever seen in his entire life.

    "You are American, yes?" (There was that proper Brit accent again).

    "Yes, I am." How did she know? What the hell, did he have a big 'A' tattooed on his forehead? There must be something that marked him, but what?   And what was she selling (she had to be selling something)?

    "Would you like some apple tea? Or coffee? It

will cost you nothing."

She was hot, definitely. His C & G's let him examine those big green eyes (surrounded by kohl liner [Trish McEvoy], mascara [Brenda Christian] and light gray shadow [Tony and Tina], all expertly applied) at length, light brown, almost reddish hair severely bobbed, burgundy lips gloss, large gold earhoops, a sexy Hussein Chalayan (wasn't he from around here? Or maybe he was Greek) long hooded dress with a very high very charming slit, brown suede Gucci spikes (clashed slightly with the dress) and a thin gold (right) ankle bracelet. He also noticed the rather obvious perfume of Time and the Other by Issey Miyake (not so expertly applied).   She was too well dressed to be a ho (at least one that he could afford), and so there must be some other game involved. Whatever it was, she was a fantastic advertisement: she could generate some serious eyeshare.   Now would be a good time to walk away.

He remembered Reham in the Marriott a free lunch does not exist. "A free drink, huh? What exactly do I have to do?"

"All you must do is come inside and look at beautiful things. That will not be so difficult, I am sure."

"Are the things inside as beautiful as the things outside?" Ouch. He couldn't believe he said that. What was wrong with him? He felt himself blush.

She smiled. "You will have to come inside and see."

This probably wasn't a pussy palace; she was too classy (although you never could be sure). It must be some sort of swank strip club, but again, she seemed too clean and western for that (although if he ran a posh tittie joint she'd be exactly the bait he'd put out, as she'd attract both the western suits who wanted a taste of back home [at least to get them started] as well as the Lexused locals who believed heaven was a white meat lap dance). Either way, he should probably bag it, as some vaguely remembered warning came to mind (from who? [maybe Robert, Kay's ex, or one of his uncles]) about the dangers of foreign gentlemen clubs, where the drinks were a C each and if you didn't cough up you ended up with something broken.

He turned. "I should probably get going."

She leaned forward and touched the shoulder of his Jil Sander with her fingertips (he noticed a gold pinkie ring and another, even larger, ring on thumb). "Please."

Run away.

He hesitated.

"Where are you from?"

"The United States."

"Yes, I understand, but what place in the United States?"

Better not tell her exactly. "Outside of Los Angeles."

"I have been to Los Angeles." Of course you have. "Have you ever been to Sarajevo? I once saw Reese Witherspoon there."

Maybe she wasn't bullshitting. "Yeah, I used to go there all the time."

She smiled again (she had a cheerleader's smile, a California smile). "There is also The Raw and the Cooked, which is across the street. My father once took me there, but I do not think he liked it — the people were rude and the food was very expensive."

"Yeah, they're rude to everyone there. I think that's why people go."

She smiled that smile again. They stood there for a moment (little Pete yawned and stretched), and then he said, "I really should get going."

She leaned forward just a bit, and touched his shoulder again. "Please, come inside, meet with my father. You do not have to look at carpets." A carpet joint! Not a tittie bar, not a pussy place, a carpet joint. "Just meet with my father, have a drink with him. He loves America, especially Los Angeles; he has a brother there. Please, come inside."

The Ericsson rang. He looked around. It rang again.

"Hello?"

"Allo. This is Reham."

"Reham!" He turned from the eye-candy. "Where've you been? I've been trying to call you."

"You have been trying to call me? Where?"

"The number you gave me. I dialed it about twenty times, but it's always busy."

"The telephone number I gave you is for the phone you are now using."

Duh. "Oh. Where are you?"

"I am in Üsküdar. Near the Fatihi Pasha Park. Where are you?"

"I'm at this carpet shop somewhere."

"Pardon?"

"I'm at this carpet shop. Near some bars and restaurants."

"Are you near your Hilton? What is the street you are on?"

"No, I walked down a hill. I can't see the street name."

"Ask someone. Ask someone for the street name."

He lowered the phone. "Excuse me. What street is this?"

"Is this your wife?"

He smiled. "No, my sister" (maybe).

She smiled back. Jesus what a smile. "Tell your

sister we are on yedi Babiali Sokuk. Seventeen Babiali Sokuk."

"I'm at seventeen Babiali Sokuk."   .

"Peter, please go back to your hotel. I will meet you tomorrow at nine o'clock in the morning."

"What? Why?"

"The carpet shop you are visiting is not honest. If you are interested in carpets, I can bring you to a more truthful market. But now, please go back to the Hilton. Or go somewhere else. But that carpet shop is not honest."

Okay okay. Christ, he wasn't going to buy anything anyway. But he didn't like to be bossed around, especially in front of an audience. He turned toward the curb, away from the carpet lady. "Why can't you meet me today?"

"I cannot see you today. I have other obligations."

"You have other obligations. I come half way across the world to see you, and you can't even meet me at the airport." Fuck this.

"I am very sorry Peter. I have other obligations in my life."

"I'm tired of being jerked around like this. All these notes, all these phone calls, all this bullshit. I want to see you and I want to see those pictures of my dad."

"Please, I am sorry. This is difficult for me as well. I will come tomorrow morning and tell you what you wish."

"I'm leaving tomorrow."

"Peter, please, no. You've come all this way. I will come tomorrow morning. Please do not make this any more difficult than it already is."

"Difficult. Difficult for whom? You're the one who hasn't even come to meet me yet."

"Difficult for both of us. Please, go back to your

hotel. I will meet with you tomorrow. I make a promise. Please."

Peter hesitated. What a sucker. "Okay, okay. You'll come tomorrow? Alone?"

"Of course."

"What time?"

"Nine or ten."

"What time exactly?"

"I cannot be exact — Istanbul has many cars."

"Okay."

CHAPTER ELEVEN

Whenever he woke up, Peter never had any trouble remembering exactly where he was. From the very first split second of consciousness, the circumstances of the previous night (or morning) that placed him in that particular bed came flooding back to mind. It wasn't that he recalled every detail necessarily (especially after drinking or drugging), it was just that the memory of his location (and, in college [pre Wanda], his companion) was (for some reason) always non-volatile, immediately accessible upon booting up the next morning (as it were). So he never had to waste time looking around his room, gaze fastening on every object (window, dresser, bed, nightstand, adjacent head or body), trying to attach a memory (or at least a fragment of one) to each, thereby (re)constructing a narrative which could explain his presence in that specific environment. Along with this instantaneous awareness of both present (where he was) and past (how he got there), Peter also awoke with an implicit knowledge of the probable future (what he was going to try to accomplish, and what would likely occur in the day). He was always a man with a plan. In short, upon awakening, Peter always possessed context, and he never had to work to try to establish one for himself.

This morning was no exception. Even after a night of fitful and sporadic sleep, the second the eight o'clock wake-up call rang, he was instantaneously aware, on some level, that he was in the Istanbul Hilton (phone call, carpet shop, Marlboro man, nasty brats etc.), that his supposed half-sister was meeting him in an hour or so (she'd fucking better), that he had to call United (he'd wait until after the meet to avoid having to make two calls [in case he wanted to split]) and that he desperately needed to buy some new threads. He also realized that he could postpone his calls or emails to Wanda and Kay (although he would like to check his stocks), as there was a real possibility he would be returning to Kay's house and Wanda's bed (he stroked little Pete awake — he'd been weeks without the furry [he thought about Wanda's thighs streaked purple and the taste of salty grape popsicle as he muff dived in the Saab {Yves Delorme beach towel on the back leather seat} and then his stomach growled and he remembered he hadn't dumped in what felt like weeks {he regretfully released (the still interested) Junior}]) imminently.

It was time to rise and fucking shine. Reham was coming in an hour, and he had to shower (and hopefully shit), maybe trim the goat (that was out no tools), coffee up and dress (same old same old [fly the totally fucked skies {he'd have to get some new cloth in a hurry}]). And if she didn't show in sixty, he'd pack up the Zero and taxi to the airport (leaving the Ericsson at the desk): sayonara sis, see you in the funny papers, don't call us, we'll call you (he'd change his phone number but she did have his [Kay's] addy although he'd most definitely be outta there soon [to where? Not Samo thank you Kay {this was all too goddam random as if he would alter his lifestyle just to escape some dark eyed Mulan with a (impossible to follow) story}]). Before he went into the bathroom, he sniffed the Jil and the D & G: the Jil was okay but D & G tee was getting a bit nasty (the Dolce was not so dolce). Fucking United. He didn't sniff his Gaps.

He heard the telephone (not the Eriksson) ringing as soon as he shut off the shower taps. He grabbed a (nice) towel and carefully (didn't want to slip and end up in some David Lynch) walked over to the bed. This was it. No more bullshit or he was history, taillights, on the plane with a GQ and a double JD. "Hello?"

"Hello Peter, I am Reham."

"Hello Reham. Where are you?"

"I am downstairs." So she showed. "They will not tell me your room number and so I cannot come up."

"Room 2637. Give me five before you knock, okay?"

"Pardon me?"

"I'm sorry. . . you're a little early, and I just got out of the shower. I need to get dressed, so please wait five minutes before you come up."

"I will see you in five minutes."

So this was it, this is why he had come, this was what he had waited almost fifteen years for. Maybe. All through this whole fucking thing, he could never quite escape the very real feeling he was being played. Although the kidnapping scenario seemed slightly ridiculous in the (teal and gray) light (what didn't?), there did exist alternative possibilities (like robbery or extortion or even blackmail [this was the second hotel room he'd been in with Reham {how'd Wanda like that?}]). He'd have to keep his guard up (he'd said that before). And even if she were on the level, her plot was bent, crooked, twisted like a goddam maze (like Millennium), and if he'd try to straighten her out or hurry her up, he'd just fuck it up even more. Okay.

If her whole routine was at least somewhat dope, and she did have something he wanted, then he'd have to play by her rules to get it. He'd have to keep his mouth shut, his questions and prompts to himself, and let her do her whole song and dance at her own (Cowboy Junkies) pace. Otherwise, he'd never get what he wanted (before he turned thirty). He'd have to keep his temper, be patient, chill like a motherfucker, and just let her ride. This was her movie, and if she wanted to Greenaway it (boring motherfucker), he'd go along. He called room service for a pot of coffee and assorted pastries.

The first thing he noticed after she (loose [not baggy] black Levis, a plain Fruit of the Loom black sleeveless tee [her bare shoulders surprisingly cut {a swimmer?}], dark brown Cat work boots [spotted with dark ink], long black hair pulled loosely back by a light blue Byblos cotton scarf tied high behind the ears, two silver bangles on her right wrist and a silver armlet on her left, two small silver rings [pinkie and index] on her right hand, and three [pinkie, middle and thumb] on her left, eyes lined with agnes b Northern Dusk, lips with she umara Tuscan Sparkle, and the slight trace of A Thousand Plateaus by Estee Lauder [again, no specs]) walked into the room and set her jacket (black with fringe from Levant Leather) on the bed, was that she wasn't carrying any book of photographs, or a bag that could hold a book of photographs (although as she entered, the room itself somehow shifted, morphed, became less compressed and anonymous, brightened [the furniture grew less threatening, the colors less insulting, the odor {cigarette smoke under Pine Sol under new shower} less obvious]). This would be a real test of his plan: if he blew up, she might evaporate. He'd relax, stay quiet, let her take her time and explain. He could do this.

"I have never been in a room in this hotel, although I do not live very far from here and can see it from my window."

"You haven't missed much."

"And how was your journey?"

"It was okay, although the airline lost my luggage."

"Yes, I heard. That is bad, although it happens many times. Are you tired? Have you slept enough?"

"I'm all right."

"May I sit please?"

Peter motioned to the chair at the desk. "Or you can sit on the bed, whichever is more comfortable." She looked pale, tired, jagged, but not quite weak or vulnerable (not with those shoulders). "You can smoke if you want."

"No, thank you please. I do not wish to smoke." She perched on the edge of the bed and looked down at her jacket, stroking the fringe. This would probably take some time, so he'd best find a seat. He moved around her and pulled the chair out until it was facing the bed (he thought briefly about straddling it backwards, à la Mickey Rourke [Rumble Fish]), but even in the best of situations that wasn't his style (bent back, spread legs [look at my crotch] and dangling [unless you crossed them on the top of the chairback] arms), so he parked it normally, back straight and hands in lap, and waited for her to begin.

"When you rang me up and said you were planning to visit me, I was very surprised, and very nervous: I did not know what I should do. I thought that perhaps the story I told to you in Los Angeles would frighten you from me, and, to tell you the truth, that thought made me a little happy. I do not want to hurt your feelings, but I had seen you, and had informed you of my existence, and I believed nothing else would be necessary, or even desirable. It is true that I have had a difficult life, as has my family, but what has that to do with you? I mean to say you are not to blame for the past of my life, and I do not believe you can help me at present. It was enough for me to see you in front of me, and to know that there existed in this world someone who shared my blood. I see now that this knowing is not enough for you.

"I did not believe this would have so much meaning for you, so much meaning that you would come to Istanbul. I believed that Americans care only about their money or their stock exchanges, and do not care so much about their history or their blood. I believed you were happy in Los Angeles, and that you would not desire any more thoughts of me to break into your life. And so, when you rang me up, I had difficulty believing, and had much trouble organizing for your visit."

Room service interrupted (a so far rather pointless story) with a knock. The smell of fresh (American) coffee flooded the room, as the waiter maneuvered past the chair and set the tray on the desk. Peter waited until he had left before offering Reham coffee and a pastry, which she accepted.

"I enjoy American coffee: it is not as forceful as the Turkish."

"Have you had cappuccino?"

"Yes, of course, in Paris, Rome, and in the States. I enjoy American coffee the best."

They chewed and sipped in silence (the coffee was excellent, as was the sour cherry Danish [although not quite as good as what could be found at Ivan's Bakery, off of Mulholland {Wanda preferred Doughboy's or even Café La Brea}]). Peter sat and watched Reham. While not extremely fastidious (a croissant crumb glued by the umara to the crease of her lip with the first nibble remained until the last [its companions leaping off the roll to the side of the bed with every bite]) or graceful (perhaps due to her upbringing) she was beautiful (shiny black hair, clear olive skin, smallish [almost almond] brown eyes [surrounded by a few tiny crinkles {what had she seen?}] with large, strong [Semitic] nose, full expressive lips, shaped shoulders and arms, a nice if compact rack) or, if not exactly beautiful (there was something off about her [her teeth needed polishing {perhaps straightening as well}], something clumsy [although her shoulders were way cut she did not move with fluidity] and inappropriate [she didn't have the wild and yet calculated double sight {eyes both forward and back (how do you like this?)} of an edger, the supreme self-confidence of the influencer {I'm sure you will like this}, or the frantic antennae waving of a follower {I really hope you'll like this (Hector called them Sally Fields)}: Reham was, if possible, off the map]) then intriguing, alluring, enchanting. Maybe it was just that he wasn't used to Euro girls, but there was something dangerous and strong about her, forceful as she would say. Yes, Reham was certainly forceful. All the more reason to be extremely careful.

After his second cup of java (washing down a pain au chocolat in addition to the cherry Danish), Peter set his cup and saucer on the desk and turned toward Reham (who had declined a second pastry but was on her third caffeine). So?

After a while, she (the crumb on her lip gone) set her cup and saucer on the nightstand and turned to face Peter. They sat quietly for a time, looking at one another. They didn't attempt to lock eyes (when their gazes happened to meet one pair would immediately drop), nor did they undress each other with inquisitive stares; rather, they looked as if they were trying to situate the other, as one attempts to place the half-recognized face of a grocery store clerk viewed in line at the bank. Reham quickly rose and walked to the full-length mirror on the closet door. She (nice butt, long legs) stood there for a while (Peter could see his reflection looking at her [at them]), and then she moved into the bathroom. "Peter, please come here." What was she doing? He got up and slowly walked to the bathroom.

"I want to see if our faces have anything the same. The light is not good in the other room. Stand here and look at our faces: do you see anything the same?" Before he turned to face the mirror, she brusquely brushed his chin with the fingertips of her right hand, "There was bread in your beard."

The bathroom fluorescence was bright and unflattering, bleaching her skin tone into a cadaverous pallor (Clinique Winter) and his into some sort of neutral orangish beige, like a watercolor representation of a tan. Who could look good (or even animate) under such glare? He was surprised how Don Johnson he looked (he combed his fingers through his goat). He'd need some shaving gear as well as clothes.

At first glance, he didn't notice any striking similarities (any similarities at all [this was all a fucking joke and he was being played {but if this were a hoax why call attention to it?}]). Their hair and eyebrows were quite different: his light brown, hers jet-black. His eyes were bigger and rounder than hers, and his (WASP, according to Kay) nose smaller. Their face shapes weren't at all alike, as Peter's was more rounded or oval, and Reham's sharp and triangular. They shared nothing (except those rakis at the gallery). "What is this on the ceiling?"

"A heat lamp."

"How do you turn it on?"

"That knob. Twist it."

The small room almost instantly filled with heat, and their faces were now weirdly backlit (he was reminded of this mural on the side of a building in east LA where a bunch of homeys had dropped to their knees thinking a light from the sky was God when it was really only the searchlight from a police helicopter). "You are too much bigger than me; bend your legs so we are equal." He bent down so that his face was next to hers, the tips of his goatee almost touching her shoulder. His bowels began to grumble (finally [great timing]). He could smell her A Thousand Plateaus and his shower.

He still couldn't see anything in her face that reminded him of his, or in his that reminded him of hers. The sooner he was on that plane, the better. Her eyes (in the mirror) traveled rapidly back and forth from (the reflection of) his face to hers. She began to frown.

"Please stand behind me." He backed away as she moved in front of him. "Place your chin near my head please." He looked down at the crown of her head (no dandruff). "Move closer please, and look up, I cannot see your face." He raised his head to look above them, but the direct reflection of the light hurt his eyes, so he squinted and looked to the right. It was getting hotter and hotter. They stood like that for quite some time. Finally, "I do not see much that is the same. Do you?"

He looked at their faces in the mirror. "No."

"We both will smile. Perhaps our smiles are the same." They both smiled, and both smiles looked like grimaces. "There is some sameness in our smiles, but not much. Do you see it?"

It was hot, and he felt a little strange. And to tell the truth, there might be something similar in the way their lips curled over the teeth in front, and in the shape of their jaws. He needed to get out of the bathroom. "Yes, I think I see something. Although I'm not sure." She frowned, and turned away, her shoulder brushing lightly against his chest and her hip against his crotch. After she had returned to the living room, he looked at himself briefly alone, and thought of the photograph that had been torn in two. As he left the room, he switched off the fluorescent and the heat lamp.

Once out of the bathroom, he regained his strength and equilibrium (it was much cooler). She was sitting on the bed and he returned to the chair, but he didn't sit. He wasn't sure he wanted to continue with this — what would be the use? They didn't look at all alike, they weren't related in the least, and the sooner he could get her out of his room the sooner he could (take a dump and) be on that plane, back to Wandaland and its cold Patron margs, Marin blunts, Jaime's creole Brazilian langostino, smooth silk Dior sheets, and hot buttered furry, all he could eat (not to mention some different threads). He'd eat, drink, smoke, shop and fuck (he imagined a week solid of heavy decadence at the guest house maybe throw a party) Reham out of his mind for good (Bye, bye miss towel head pie). It was time to exit, stage right, see ya later alligator, make like the Diceman and disappear, or like Marcus Allen and (finally) split. He was sick of it all, sick of the long and scary plane rides, the stolen Samsonite (hey this is American, let's boost it), the stinky smoke filled airport, the secret agent phone calls (and slime boy Murat), the three or four times a day tower-wailing in the streets (he'd have to find out about that Ali Akbar for work), the Miami (he hated the 'Canes) shirted street brat, the ass-ugly hotel room, and another long opus from Reham, which he was probably only a third of the way through (she probably needed to go slow because she was making it up as she went [maybe she was just crazy {a fucking psycho from the Istanbul laugh palace}]), a story which finally he wasn't going to have the patience to listen to after all, because it wouldn't do him any fucking good (besides his bowels were squirming and he didn't want to sit on the can and serenade her with serious butt trumpet through the door while she sat planning her next move). It was time to put an end to this interview (one of Karla's favorite sayings). He should probably give her some dough but how much (at least a couple of grand for the drawing)?

He (knew he) was being rude by just standing there, but he was hoping she'd take the hint and say her goodbyes (or whatever), instead of sitting there frowning on the bed. After a while she turned her shoulders and head to look up at him. "I will tell you simply I cannot find the book." (That was quick) No shit. Maybe because there isn't any goddam book, you fucking loony, or fucking crook, take your pick. He kept his face and posture like stone (he hoped). He wouldn't say a thing. He focused his stare at the top of her forehead.

"I searched among my old belongings at my home: I do not possess much, and the search was not difficult. I could not locate the photographs, and I am very very sorry." Spare me. She dropped her eyes. Now what? Another sob story about little Reham in a Turkish prison? Or maybe the constantly interrupted retelling of the murder of her cousins by Israeli storm troopers, or Afghan rebels, or Chechen Serbs, or what-ever. Whatever it was, it would not be fast, he was sure of that. He remained standing. After a time she spoke again. "I believe I know where the book of pho-tographs is located." He remained silent, impassive. She looked up at him. He couldn't read her face. "I do not know if you will approve of this, you may think it is not at all intelligent. But I will say it: I think the book of photographs you desire is in Al Quds, in Palestine. I think we should both journey there."

He chuckled (couldn't help himself) and shook his head. "You've got to be kidding."

She shrugged her shoulders and looked away

(sadly?). "I am not joking. I did not believe you would like this plan, but I thought that perhaps, since you had already journeyed such a long way, that another small flight would not be such trouble. I also thought that because you are a Christian, you would like to see Jerusalem. In al makbah."

"Al makbah, what's that?"

She looked up at him and smiled. "The Sorrow."

What the fuck was she talking about, the sorrow. He lightbulbed suddenly. "Wait a second. If you didn't have the book of pictures, then how did you get that print of my, our, father you tore in half?"

"I bought tickets."

"You bought tickets? What tickets?"

"Airplane tickets. For Tel Aviv. From there we will go to Al Quds."

As if (he backgrounded [for now] the fact that she didn't answer his question). There was no way. The only plane he was getting on was the one taking him back to civilization (he'd upgrade no matter what): he'd be damned if he would visit her sand shack — can you say million dollar ransom? He shook his head. "I don't know about this. I've already" (he caught himself before he said wasted) "spent enough time and money on this, and you haven't given me a single thing. For two days now all I've seen is your cell phone and Murat: this is the first time I've seen you. And now you want me to go off somewhere else." He hesitated, but then continued, "Maybe I'd better go home."

She looked away. Silence. "Why did you come?"

"Why do you think I came? I thought you could tell me something about our father." And I

wanted some sort of adventure. And I wanted to punish my aunt and girlfriend.

"I did tell you something of our father when I
spoke to you in the hotel in Los Angeles. If you had
heard my story carefully, you would recognize that I do
not know much about him."

"Okay, okay. I wanted to see the book of photographs you mentioned."

"My cousins have had a difficult time, and this
book has little meaning for them. I am not sure they
have cared very much about this book: I do not even
know if it is still in their possession. But if you agree,
we will go to Palestine and search for it."

"But if you didn't have the book, what about
that photograph you sent me? The one you ripped in
two?"

"I have possessed that photograph for a long
time. I believe that it originated from that book, but I
am not certain."

This was getting more bogus (and the pressure
on his sphincter was increasing) by the second. He sat
in the chair. "I'm going home."

She turned and looked at him. She looked tired,
sad, the crinkles around her eyes dark. Some time
passed, then "You surrender too easily."

She was good, very good. She knew the right
buttons. But fuck her, he wasn't no hick from the sticks
— he was Peter the Great. He always knew the score
(although maybe, just maybe, she was right [echoes of
Wanda's boring dick accusation]). He wasn't going to
bite, not even nibble. He was going to go home.

"I have purchased the tickets: it will cost you no
money. You owe me nothing: your debt is to yourself.
We will go for two days and nights, and then return.
And if we do not find the book, then you may fly back
to your home and forget about me. Do not worry; I

will not make contact with you again. This will be only an unpleasant dream to you."

For some goddam reason (her eyes [what sadness had they seen?], her hair, the memory of Wanda calling him a boring dick, the accusation that he'd given up too easily, the fact that she'd bought the tickets [although if they were kidnapping him she would], the admiration of her skill [if she were playing him she was doing a magnificent job of it {he liked the part about owing himself}], the not incidental detail that he had to dump like a big dog and wanted her out of his room so he could, or maybe just pure perversity [or thrill seeking] or reawakened [or assumed] familial affection), he heard himself saying "Okay. When do we leave?"

"In four hours. We return on Friday."

Four hours? You don't waste any time. "I need to get some clothes. The airline lost my luggage."

"Yes, Murat told me. I would like to show you some of the city. Have you visited anything in Istanbul?"

"Only the carpet shop."

She laughed. "We will go to the Grand Bazaar today. I believe you will like that. And then when we return, perhaps Hagia Sophia and the Blue Mosque." She looked him in the eyes and smiled. "I am very happy you are coming."

Be careful here. "I'm going to need about twenty to thirty to get ready and check out. Would it be okay if I met you in the lobby at, let's say, ten after?"

She got up from the bed and he rose as well. "I will wait for you there." He thought (hoped?) she was going to hug him (and maybe a kiss?), but she didn't.

CHAPTER TWELVE

While it was a large relief to be wearing clean duds (his Sander, Kiton, D&G, Gap and Banfis [he left his bloody Pradas in the hotel room trash] stuffed in a plastic bag in Reham's left hand [the Zero Halliburton in his right]), he would have ideally chosen something a little more stylish than Marks and Spencer khakis (the Levis he had tried on were bogus [the denim thin and stiff {strange polyester blend} and the crotch rode up {and they were in a rush (he hated to be rushed [especially while shopping])}], so he had to settle for the army khaks), light blue cotton BVD boxers, a white Bundeswehr cotton tee with a white (Black will be too warm) cotton short-sleeve polo from someplace called Terra Nova (Italian Style for Less Lira), black cotton Bosphorus socks and (last year's [or the year before's]) black high top Vans (he had wanted to do some shopping in [they had a tiny Hugo Boss store] or near [he thought he saw a Gianfranco Ferrer sign on one of his walks] the Hilton, but Reham had insisted [You do not want to look like a too rich American] on taking him first to a sporting goods store [Sportmarkt], where she suggested nylon Puma warm-ups, and then to the Terra Nova next door [assholes had charged him an extra 2% for using his MC Gold]): he looked like a thirty-five year old ex-skate punk from Slimey Valley.

He was hoping to buy something (leather [Bally or even Coach]) other than a Reebok plastic bag to schlep his clothes around in. His dump had been less than satisfactory: a few small hard rocks (his considerable effort had cost him some time [which is why he was late {which is why they were in a hurry}]), and he felt full, bloated and sluggish (maybe he could take a few laps around the dunes when they arrived [he hoped there might be a sea involved he could use a swim {he should have gotten more than one pair of BVD's}]). The last thing he needed was another (anus-suturing) plane ride (he must be out of his fucking mind). So, all told, even though he was wearing new clean clothes, he was not in a particularly good mood.

This crowded narrow street (Reham had driven [{through thick traffic} in her old and sloppy white Euro hatchback {Renault 1610}, your basic mode of transportation that reminded him of a Vega one of Wanda's friends drove {actually a collector's item now and worth about 5 g's}] and pointed out the various sights [Aya Sofia, Blue Mosque, Topkapi Palace]) wasn't helping any (people chattering in about a thousand different lingos and no, two hundred year old man, I don't want a backgammon set). Reham was marching about five or six steps in front of him (he considered slowing down further but didn't want to lose her in the crowd [she was carrying his {dirty} Sander and Kiton's etc.]). At least it was shady.   He could do with a bottle of Volvic or San P. In Kay's pool (with or without Pavo). In Bel Air. In America.

The crowd (and the ice cream, souvenir, post card and backgammon vendors) thickened. Maybe if he stalled enough, pretended like he really was interested in these cheap dildo shaped spice grinders, these flimsy Aladdin lamps, these genuine onyx chess sets, they'd miss their flight. This was a bogus trip anyway (a bogus trip after another bogus trip before another bogus trip [home]). Even if he did see something he liked (except a nice [Bally] bag), he couldn't buy it now because he didn't want to have to carry it all the way to the Holy Land and back. So this was strictly window shopping, doing the tourista thang, killing time before the next flight, the next country, the next snipe hunt. Maybe he'd get Kay something in Israel: she'd be impressed (especially if he sort of left out the part about Daddy-dearest).

There was a knot of people (tourists [Turks don't wear shorts]) at the doorway of some sort of building, and Reham waited for him there. She faced him square. "Do you wish to buy anything?"

"I'd like to get a bag or something to put my clothes in. I already have enough stuff to carry."

"Leather?"

Duh. "Yes."

"Please, if you let me speak, you will get a better price. Do not be insulted, but you do not appear as if you are from Turkey: you appear like a wealthy American. I will speak for you. You should place your wallet and passport in the front of your pants. I believe you will enjoy this." She took his hand and led him through the crowd.

The Grand Bazaar was a bit dim, and he removed his C&G's. He was immediately impressed by the sheer quantity of objects for sale. Even at first glance, and even in the gloom only partially cut by the assorted lights (Chinese paper lanterns, tiny white and other assorted Christmas [including red chili pepper and Jesuses in red and green] lamps and bare 70 watt frosted bulbs) that hung in strings suspended from the low vaulted (ribbed groin) ceiling (which, as he only later [after Reham called his attention to it] noticed, was intricately tiled [soft porcelain ceramic with cobalt blue patterns over a cream white background]), Peter could see rows and rows of things to buy: everything from various carpets and kilims (some hanging from the ceiling, some carefully displayed in oak framed double glass shop windows, some stacked haphazardly on pushcarts) to assorted tiles (those which resembled the ones on the ceiling seemed popular) and glassware (hundreds of small clear fluted [tea] glasses, as well as more elaborate constructions, such as an intricately [luster] painted [copper over iron blue] fruit bowl); from rows of long leather greatcoats (natural brown, black, slate gray, dark forest green, pale tomato red, pale taxi yellow) on racks in the aisles to I Dream of Jeanie belly dancing outfits (short cut pink vests over cropped tight diaphanous long sleeve blouses, with matching harem pants [some with short shorts], complete with curled toe golden slippers); from little beaded bracelets (red, orange, blue, yellow, green) and peculiar peacock eye key chains ([nazar tasi] To ward of the evil eye) to wrist thick (Flavor Flav) gold ropes; from turquoise, silver, onyx and worked stone chess sets (including one set of solid amber and one of solid jade [both with rough cut ebony boards] to Philips and Samsung ghetto blasters [Lenny Kravitz Are you gonna go my way?]. This was one motherfucking mall! Wanda would be impressed (he wished he had brought her along). Yes, this was one motherfucking mall.

Except it didn't smell like any mall he was used to. Instead of the antiseptic smell of air conditioning (although individual stores did have their own peculiar and sometimes strong [and sometimes pleasant] smells [the exotic wax and strawberry smell of The Candle Shoppe, the spray-on rawhide and pelt of Wilson's, the rubber and astroturf of The Footlocker, the 60's incense and clove cigarette of Spencer's, the subtle worsted wool and fine Virginia tobacco of St. James for Men, and the air of alchemy and masked {by feigned (by both seller [to offer was to risk perusal and rejection {working in the Bev Hills Prada and seeing the jaspers from Iowa, Montana or Fullerton or whatever with McNugget grease on their fingers coming in and pawing through the merchandise you spent half the a.m. folding and arranging would be bad enough but then to have them toss it back all crumpled, shaking their heads as they walked away saying Four hundred dollars for this!? would be big time gnarly}] and buyer [to desire was to risk unfulfillment and disappointment]) indifference} greed at Prada [which {with its taint of dread and sex} was slightly different from the air of alchemy and masked greed at BOSS Hugo Boss {cruelty and amyl nitrate}, which was in turn slightly different than the smell of alchemy and masked indifference at Versace {secrecy and drooping (Crimson Glory) roses } etc.], smells that sometimes bled a few feet out into the walkway) or the sometimes nauseating smell of plastic (trays, utensils, cups) and frying grease of the food court (even in Fashion Island [although there the Plaza di Mange frites grease was cut by the sharp odor of Montressi balsamic vinegar and steam brewed Kenyan coffee]), the air of the Grand Bazaar was a complex bouquet of dust, worked leather, rosemary, human sweat, oranges, jasmine, cooking lamb and charcoal. No mall in America ever smelled like this. No place in America ever smelled like this.

    Reham turned to speak. "Do you enjoy this?'

    "Yeah, it's pretty wild."

    "Unfortunately, we do not have much time. Only about an hour. Let me take you to where they sell the leather baggage. And then we may look for awhile, but then must leave."

    "Lead the way."

    "Hello, hello. You speak English? We accept dollars."

    "Please, let me show you, beautiful, beautiful things."

    "Please, some apple tea. It will cost you nothing."

"Please sir, a moment of your time."

"Sprechen Sie Deutsch? Or English? You are American?"

"I love America. I have been to Chicago. Please, we will talk, I will practice my English."

"You need cold drink?"

He didn't mind the verbal hard barking, but he didn't like being touched (especially by the gangs of marauding children or the tiny tots crouching down by bathroom scales with a bowl for change [weigh your-self for 100 lira]), and so found the movement through the aisles of dark, ill dressed, over aggressive and under bathed point of purchase retail engineers more than slightly uncomfortable (he kept his hand on his Coach inside the right pocket of his Marks and Spencers [he didn't care how it looked]). This was the opposite of shopping in LA, where you couldn't attract the attention of a sales associate if you set your hair on fire (even if you'd been there before and dropped seri-ous change [he remembered the bitch at Barney's where he'd bought his Brooks [a grand and a half is nothing to sneeze at], went in there four days later to pick up the cuffed pants [and he was thinking about some sweet sunflower yellow Hermés silk tie {très cher which is why he had to think}] and the cunt [Marlene was her name] treated him like Fabian from Milli Vanilli, with a fucking look that shriveled little Pete for days: if he dropped a hundred in American dollars here he'd probably get a blow job from the whole family including uncle Abdul or whatever). Still, he'd have to say he preferred the LA way. There was no telling where little Mohammed there had been sticking his fingers (although the Terra Nova wasn't expensive it was clean [and who knew when he'd be able to change again {he was an idiot for only buying one outfit}]). He remembered the airplane serenade and kept his hand on his Coach, and tightened the grip on the Zero Halliburton.

Reham, on the other hand, seemed totally pissed by the clumps of touristas: she'd walk right up their ass and stay there, heavy breathing, until they noticed her and parted or moved aside so she and he could pass. One group of Nikon- (both analogue [F3, 5, FM2, F100 and F5], digital [D1, D1H, and Coolpix 550 and 675] with assorted lenses [20 mm f/2.8 AD, 17-35mm f/2.8D ED-IF AS, 80-200mm f/2.8D ED-IF AS, 105mm f/1.4 Nikor AI-S etc.]) wielding slopes didn't get the hint, and stayed clotted together by this genie lamp-and-dagger stand, yammering in that gook tongue, gridlocking an entire intersection. After a few polite attempts (accompanied by not so polite looks) to get by, Reham looked at him, shrugged and barged ahead, knocking a tiny little man (in a beautiful yellow and jade green silk Mao) into his tinier little wife (in a matching cheongsam). He smiled and followed. She looked good from the back.

What was all this stuff? People had been vend-ing here for hundreds of years, b 2 b, b 2 c, wholesale, retail, import, export, trade you a couple of chickens, my pig (well, not pig), my horse for your tent (or daughter, or rug, or whatever): this was the original mall, or even the original web. He'd have to come back here, maybe write something up on his Powerbook for work. This would also be a primo place to get presents, both Kay and Wanda (Kay didn't play chess but she might like some of that porcelain and Wanda, well he'd have to think about what to get Wanda [maybe some skins {although he couldn't snoop around for Wanda leather while he was hanging with Reham (but he would get his Bally)}]). No, he'd most definitely have to return: he'd go to Al Kudes (Zion), check out the book if it existed (if it wasn't vaporware), try to corner Reham to find out what the fuck was what the fuck, and then come back and spend some dough. This might work after all.

He stopped for a moment to scope out one of the harem outfits in a window and when he turned, Reham was gone. He hurried in the direction they had been heading, past a clot of Indis or Pakis or whatever (two women in brilliant gold and crimson silk saris with accompanying four males in various [blue and gold raw silk, crimson quilted silk, muted green silk and light blue cotton]) pajamas) and into an intersection. He stood up on his toes in the middle and looked up and down all four connecting aisles, trying to spot the top of her head in the crowd. No dice. Was this some kind of trick, some further headfuck? Or was he really being set up for some sort of kidnapping (or something)? Or was it just coincidence (there had been too much total weirdness for this to be just coincidence)? Fuck it and fuck her. He'd find his way out of here, take a cab to the airport, and that would be it. Except she had his Sander, Kitons and Banfis. Okay, he'd try to find her (he wasn't certain how to get out anyway, unless it was back the way he came, and there were no cabs on the street they had walked down to get there). But where was she?

She knew he was going to buy a Coach or Bally for his clothes, so he'd head to the Coach and Bally outlet, browse (he loved that word) and wait until she showed. No problem, except how would he find the Coach and Bally store in this maze, given that he had never set foot on this continent before? He could ask one of the shopkeepers (many seemed to understand American), but who knew if he'd get a straight answer (he remembered his airport adventure), and he'd probably have to have a glass of tea, a kebob and a couple of figs as the dude brought out every single rug or tile or whatever he had in his store before he'd learn jack (besides, he hated to ask for directions). And it would probably be a waste of time to try to get one of the (motor) coach cattle (assuming he spoka da English) to pry the minicam from his eye and try to remember if and where he'd seen leather bags. Ain't this a bitch. Shit happens. He should have stayed home.

He felt like a dick standing there in the middle of the intersection (of Lost and Pissed), and so he moved off to the front of a candy store (Turkish delight my ass) near the harem window. Lost in Space. She had to be around here somewhere: she must realize they were separated (and any delay would cost her more than it would him) and so return to the place where they had last been together. Which was right here, near the candy store. So he'd just chill and wait. He was still going to get his Bally (or something comparable [he liked Vuitton {of course}, Bally and Coach, but wasn't sure he wanted to drop the big bucks, given the fate of his Samsonite {he wouldn't let this one get out of his sight}, although he could use a nice morocco overnight bag]) even if they did miss their flight, that was for sure.

What was with her, anyway? Where was she for the last 48 (husband, kid, dyke lover, where)? And what about those phone calls and shit? She never really answered any of his questions (like if she didn't have the book where'd she get the photograph she ripped?). And where the fuck was she now? He shifted his Zero Halliburton from his left to right hand. This whole she-bang was bogus. And you'd think she would have discovered that he wasn't in her tracks anymore and started looking for him, instead of just abandoning him here (but that's what she'd done since he'd arrived) to pick his nose and goof on the bus livestock (they [he and

Wanda] would always see buses rolling through the 3 B's [Bel Air, Brentwood and Bev Hills] looking for the homes and/or graves of the stars [Monroe and Nicole Simpson especially popular], their beaks or telephotos pressed against the glass like they were in a submarine or something [you want to see something really wild you should go down to Compton or East LA]). He'd much rather check out some of the merchandise, assuming he could find a leather store, but he'd settle for scoping some of that amber jewelry (maybe for Kay, doubtful for Wanda) he'd seen before. But no, he was stuck here in front of the candy store, waiting like some kid without any allowance for his mom to come and set him up.

Fuck it. She'd eventually show (she had his clothes) and if she'd didn't, he'd call the not so friendly skies, see what time the next plane for the first world left, and write this whole thing off as a bad and expensive shroom job, like when his friend Danny ate some magic, started seeing little green men in the street and crashed his bike (nice Yamaha 500 Ninja) into a telephone pole: he walked away with only a butt cut (amazingly) but he had to drop big bucks to fix the Ninja (and pay off one of Bev's finest according to Wanda). No one was hurt (really), but the ticket and hotel were expensive, not to mention all of his missing (lost [stolen]) clothes (although he supposed he could claim the Sander, Kitons and Banfis as lost luggage). Screw it, it was only money. As if. He now noticed the proprietor of the Turkish Delight store had come out into his doorway and was giving him the once over twice. Yeah, watch me carefully, cuz I'm getting set to boost some taffy: I came all the way from Los Angeles California USA to rob this world famous legendary candy store. I'm just casing the joint now, but you'd better keep your fucking eyes open, cuz you never know when I might strike. This was ridiculous. He moved to the other side of the aisle, near a booth that sold postcards, honey, and strangely enough, pocketknives (Swiss Army, Lacota and Rostfrie).

He'd give her ten minutes, and then start to scope the place for a skins shop. He really couldn't understand why he just didn't blow this whole thing off and split. What did he owe Reham? What did he owe his father? What did he owe himself? Screw it. It had already been ten minutes: he'd start walking around now. He pointed himself in the direction from where (he thought) they came in.

He didn't remember even feeling that strongly about his parents, at least not while they were alive: it wasn't as if he rushed home from school every afternoon or anything like that. They had their own lives (his father, apparently more than one) for as long as he could remember. His parents were cool: took him on vacations (Disneyworld and Denver), visited museums and shit, and drove him where he needed to go. They had made sure he was comfortable and relatively happy, and then they were gone, and he was alone in the world (with Kay, etc.). Or at least he thought he was. Until the Arab came along.

Came and went. She was most definitely weird. And not just weird to him, not just weird because she (or he) was foreign, but, as he surmised before, she was obviously weird to her own kind as well (if you could consider her own kind to be people in Turkey, and Peter wasn't sure that was right). Maybe she wouldn't stick out so much when they got to her hood, although stick out wasn't exactly what she did, it was more like she didn't fit, like she was unattached, unconnected to the world, at loose ends as Isabelle would say. Like she was a pod person (Night of the Living Dead), an alien masquerading as a human (They Live), or a replicant. She was just fucking bizarre, that was all. And that's probably why he didn't high tail it back to the airport and LA CA USA.

Jesus, he had never seen as much stuff: carpets piled high in the air, racks and racks of strings of colorful (prayer) beads, dozens, no hundreds of those multicolored embroidered caps, along with shoulder high tottering stacks of black tassled red felt (tourist) fezzes, scarves of every conceivable pattern and color, some hanging from wall pegs, some folded and table displayed, others tossed haphazardly in bins, old and new books in scores of different languages, from cheap paperbacks and romance sleaze to dusty hoary tomes that must have weighed a ton, televisions, VCRs, satellite dishes, radios, boom boxes, turntables, mixers, amplifiers and speakers, large barrels of various spices with accompanying small, medium and large plasticine bags, spice racks, tea and coffee, pepper and salt grinders, mortars and pestles, he was beginning to feel nauseous, keyboards, guitars and other guitar-like things, drums of every size, various sizes and shapes of tambourine, more carpets, more fezzes, more postcards, beautiful ceramic tiles in many different shapes and colors, large and small porcelain bowls, some painted and some not, thin tall glasses and short small glasses, tiny ceramic mugs and small, medium and large long handled Turkish coffee pots, in both brass and stainless steel with black plastic handles, and a bit dizzy, silver and iron kebab hibachis, with various ornate kebab spears, suits and men's clothes, racks and racks of men's brown wingtip shoes, brass lamps and souvenir paper cutters, knives and more knives, wines and booze with bottles of raki and Cypriot brandy featured, gold rings and more gold rings, some with amber and some with dark rubies and startling sapphires, dark, somber, thick gold, more eye key chains and wall plaques, Turkish delight, what with the lack of sleep, trays of flat layered pastry and thin flat bread, and fruit, rich red cherries and pale yellow melons, large green apples and bright yellow lemons, and more cherries and more lemons and oranges, jars of dark almost black honey, jars and jugs of green viscous olive oil, more postcards, and the general weirdness, small dolls in native costumes, some on horseback and some kneeling or standing, more caps and fezzes, hookahs, pipes and water pipes, harem costumes, silver rings that dangled off the fingers, dainty toe rings and delicate waist chains, soccer balls and short-wave radios, travel books in English, pillows and intricate lacework, more carpets and televisions, cd's, cassettes and video-tapes, computer games, large and small flags of many nations, batteries and film, magazines and newspapers, cold drinks including beer, where was the leather, chess and backgammon sets of stone, wood, plastic and polished silver, men's ties, sterling key chains from Porsche, Lamborghini and Ferrari, perfumes, ointments, creams, lotions and powders, shampoos and mousses, women's belts, computer floppy disks, more hookahs, brilliant red poppies and huge artificial looking sunflowers, ivory cigarette holders, fine china plates, saucers, bowls and cups, some painted with elaborate designs, men's polyester shirts, thick wool gloves, ammo belts, crocheted samplers, copper plates with maps of Turkey, model airplanes and cars, where was his sister, more postcards, more carpets, expensive fountain pens, hand made bird cages, jade necklaces, discounted wrist and pocket watches, more carpets and kilims, more tiles, stuffed donkeys and camels for children, various cigarette lighters, sheaths and holsters for knives and pistols, dog collars, too vivid soccer shirts and scarves, straw hats, luxurious upholstery fabric and drapes, sheepskin rugs and mats, chrome toasters and blenders, vacuum cleaners, glass and wooden beads, gold and silver dipped roses, slippers of every description, more carpets, if she was his sister, more jars of honey and fruit preserves, more pastries, more batteries, film and blank video cassettes, cartons and cartons of cigarettes, leather, plastic and aluminum glasses cases, tee shirts and more postcards, puppets and simple wooden toys, more chess sets, brushes, combs, razors and mirrors, socks and tennis sneakers, pink, black and white pearls in bracelets, earrings and necklaces, decorated vases and urns, expensive analogue and digital cameras and accessories, saddles, blankets and bridles, travel alarms and walking sticks, more spices and jars of honey, an entire window of expensive used watches, more tiles, more apples, cherries and pears, large sacks of rice and flour, huge clear jars of various types of olives, bathing suits and beach towels, more old books and maps he needed to sit down, but where he turned and ran into Reham. Thank fucking God.

"There you are."

"I've been looking all over for you. Where've you been?"

"I've been searching for you. Where have you been?"

"Looking for you. So, we've been looking for each other."

"Yes."

"I haven't found a luggage store yet."

"We have no time. We need to leave right now. Perhaps you can purchase baggage at the airport."

"What time's the flight?"

"Sixteen hundred, I mean four o'clock."

His Weill was still in his Halliburton.

"What time is it now?"

"Almost two."

"So we have over two hours. It won't take me very long to find a Bally or something."

"We must leave now, the airport is not easy for me. I have only Palestine travel papers, and the Turks do not care for us very much. You have an American passport, things are easy for you. Please, come."

What could he do?

BOOK V

CHAPTER THIRTEEN

He was sitting in an ancient ('70's?) but clean Cedes mini-van, sailing down Highway 1 from Ben Gurion airport near Tel Aviv, towards Al Quds, or Jerusalem (How long is the ride? About sixty kilometers. How long is that in miles? I do not know about forty perhaps.). Reham was on one side, slouched against the window, possibly asleep. On the other side (he'd been stuck in the middle again) was a small, fine boned man with a pony-tail (tied with a bright blue ribbon), a thick five o'clock shadow, an (Israeli [flag on sleeve]) army jacket, a tomato red and white plaid long sleeved western (as in country [USA]-western) shirt with metal buttons from Lee Ranchero, faded purple Levis bell bottoms with fringe, a Dingo brown leather belt, brown leather Tevas, a Timex Time Master with a stainless steel twist-a-flex band, six assorted earrings (four in the left and two in the right), and a small (squirrel) monkey in Pampers (Petite Blanche), asleep in his lap. He had introduced himself (after giving Reham an appreciative once-over) as Señor Sonic, the hottest dj from Eliat to the Golan, from Allenby to Haifa, who was going to the States in a couple of days, Manhattan, to spin some wax at Beirut, not the country but the club, had we heard of it, and was going to drop off Petite Blanche here at his sisters in Jericho. Peter had a difficult time determining his age, as he was one of those people who either looked much older (because of the sun on skin [he didn't seem to have had anything lifted or tucked]) or behaved and dressed much younger (for a variety of reasons) than they actually were. Señor

Sonic had seemed pissed when neither he nor Reham (especially Reham [who had insisted on sitting near the window away from Petite Blanche]), unlike the scores of the curious at the service taxi (sherut) stand, had shown much interest either in the hottest dj from Eliat to the Golan or in Petite Blanche (chick magnet eh Señor), and so, after rocking the monkey back and forth and cooing at her, had twisted and hunched around toward the window with his pony-tail pointing toward Reham (Peter's hackles were up [some sort of {brotherly?} protective thing going here]). It was dark, and there was little to see. An Arab woman and her two small children occupied the way back seat. Alanis screamed (You oughtta know) from the speakers in the front of the cab, which smelled of sweat, chick peas (falafel) and Petite Blanche. This was not pleasant.

But it was a gigabyte improvement on the fucking airport. Reham was not kidding (for a change) when she told him there might be some trouble because of her passport. While parking the Renault she had told him to say that he was her boyfriend visiting her in Istanbul and they were going to Tel Aviv for holiday. This would make things easier (hopefully), but that he needed to expect the worse. He had no idea.

First of all, as they strolled (coughing [the cloud of smoke had grown and thickened in the duration]) through the atrium (bypassing the United counter [and the line of seven or eight]) before checking in at El Al, he had looked around for a Coach, a Vuitton or Bally, anything to haul his clothes in (Reham carried only her North Face), but could only find a couple of way overpriced pre Tom Ford Gucci carry-ons, as well as what he was sure was a bogus Fendi (sloppy stitching and a broken zipper). He'd keep the plastic bag before he'd pay that much for a Gucc, and besides Reham (who looked anxious and disapproving) was right: it might be a good idea to cut the volume a couple of notches in case some mullah started shooting or whatever, so a nylon (God forbid) EastPak or something would be smart. Which he found close by, and paid too much for (so what).

When they got to the check-in line, Reham repeated her instructions in a whisper.

"Should we hold hands or something?" he whispered back.

"No. If you were my boyfriend we would not hold hands. But please, take the tickets."

They walked up to the counter, Reham a pace behind, and he slid the tickets to the clerk, who looked about sixteen, across the counter.

"Passports?"

They slid them together across the metal counter. "Any luggage to check?"

"No. Just this."

"No. Just my backpack and computer."

"Did you pack your baggage yourself, Mr. Nicholas?"

"Yes."

"And was your baggage in your possession at all times?"

"Yes."

"And did anyone give you anything to bring on board?"

"No."

"And you, Ms. Al-Safia? Did you pack your bags yourself?"

"Yes. And no one has given me anything."

"Okay. If you'll please follow the signs down the corridor to your right, we need to ask you a few more questions. It's just routine. You'll receive instructions." He returned their tickets and passports with boarding passes, and looked behind them to the next customer.

He briefly considered complaining, or arguing or something (after all, he was American), but Reham touched his elbow and guided (herded) him away from the counter. Okay, he'd be cool, play the game. They walked past the counter through the doorway the clerk indicated, down one dimly lit (but still smoky) hallway, then another, until finally, he, his Zero Halliburton, his EastPak and his (possible [half]) sister came into a small waiting room and a small line (behind one of those solemn and smelly Orthodox Jews with the black unwashed suit, a white prayer shawl (tzit tzit), black unwashed beard, the funky Hamburg with tassled black velvet yarmulka (kippa) underneath and the side-burn dreads (peyos). Peter hoped they were on different flights, for the dude was surrounded by some serious bodily stink. He stood back.

"What's this line for?"

"I told you it would be difficult. Remember, you are my boyfriend. We met last month in America. At the art gallery. When we get to Al Quds, that should be our story as well. My cousins will be friendlier to you as an innocent American than as offspring of my Zionist father. Do not mention the book to them. I will look for it, and if it is there, I will find it. It is a mistake to have acquired tickets together."

Okay, boyfriend and girlfriend: he wondered where they would sleep. He also wondered why she seemed so nervous and agitated, and what the problem was about buying the tickets together (maybe there was some price break or something [airlines were whack]). If they found the book, he'd pay for the tickets, which would only be fair.

After a while in the line, they were allowed to approach another checkpoint, with a sweet young thing (blond hair, blue eyes, nice tan, light green army fatigues and an Uzi on her back [schwing]) sat stiffly at a raised desk. Two identically equipped (as far as the uniform and Uzi went) men, not large, stood behind her, smoking.

"Passports and tickets, please." The accent was thick, but not in that Brit English he had come to expect. It didn't sound exactly Turkish either. They quickly placed them on the desk.

"You are Mr. Nicholas, yes?"

"Yes."

"And you have no luggage? Other than what you carry. Is that right Mr. Nicholas? You came all the way from America with only a backpack and. . ." she leaned over her desk, then sat back down, "a computer?"

"The airline lost my Samsonite, my bag."

"And which airline was that, Mr. Nicholas?"

"United."

"And do you remember the flight number?"

"No, not really."

"Do you still have your ticket and itinerary? Can you check for me please?"

What the fuck: he wasn't going to argue with an Uzi. A vague sense of fear began to crawl up his back. He had seen Midnight Express, and didn't want to be fucked in the ass by some well-hung Turk. But he'd be cool in front of Reham. He kept his ticket in his Coach, so it was no big prob, but still, this was one serious bitch. Without speaking, he pushed the itinerary in front of her.

"Flight 1286 from LAX to Heathrow, and then 624 from Heathrow to Atatürk. Thank you, Mr. Nicholas." She dialed the telephone in front of her, and spoke into it in what sounded like Turkish to him. It was a brief conversation. "It seems like you are telling the truth, they did indeed lose your luggage. My sympathies, Mr. Nicholas." She returned the tickets to him.

"You are traveling to Tel Aviv with Ms. Al-Safia here, Ms. Reham Al-Safia. Is this correct?"

"Yes."

"How long have you known Ms. Al-Safia?"

"A month or so. We met in an art gallery in LA, in Los Angeles. And then I came to visit her in Istanbul."

"You have not been in Istanbul long. Why are you going to Israel?"

He didn't know what to say. "To see some friends."

"To see some friends, yes. What are the names of these friends?"

Reham stepped forward. "They are my friends. We are going to see my friends in Hebron, and Jerusalem. The Hebron friends are called Nadim Bouhari and Meryam Agi. Shmul Saba and Limor Sakhan are my friends in West Jerusalem. We are only going for two nights."

"Yes, I see from your ticket you are going for only two nights. What is the nature of your relationship, the two of you?"

"What?"

"What is the nature of your relationship? I am thinking you are not married. Are you engaged to be married?"

"No."

"Ms. Al-Safia entered the United States less than six weeks ago, and left less than three weeks ago, and so if you met in the United States, as you say, then you have known each other for less than six weeks, and since your passport, Mr. Nicholas, does not show any recent activity until you came to Turkey, you did not accompany Ms. Al-Safia to Japan, and so have not spent so very much time together. Is this right?"

"Yes."

"And you came all the way to Turkey to see Ms. Al-Safia? Is this correct? Is there any other reason why you have come to Turkey, and are now going to Israel? Any other reason than to visit Ms. Al-Safia and her friends?"

"No."

"Are you sure?" What the fuck did she want, details? Obviously. "Are you sure the only reason you are going to Israel is to see Ms. Al-Safia's friends?"

"Yes, I'm sure."

She stared at him for a while, then stood quickly. "Ms. Al-Safia, please follow me. Mr. Nicholas, please follow my colleague, Mr. Shamir."

Mr. Shamir, while somewhat less loquacious than the blond nazi, was a whole lot more frightening. Peter was led to a small room, with a desk and a small closet (changing room) with a curtain behind. Shamir (who had at least shed his cigarette) told him to put his Powerbook on the desk, turn it on, and type every letter on the keyboard, both small and caps (Turn on computer please and type. Every key.) Then he was made to shut it off, boot up and do it again (Again.). Then Shamir motioned for him to put his EastPak on the desk, where he opened it, removed and attentively examined every item (Peter mortified about how dirty his Kitons, Gaps and Sander were, although the funk would serve them right [at least he wasn't wearing them]). Peter noticed how unhurried Shamir was, and how gently and almost tenderly he examined Peter's clothes. His objects were carefully replaced in the EastPak, he was handed a basket, and Shamir motioned with his head toward the changing booth and said Clothes off, underwear on. After he stripped and folded his Marks, Bundeswher, Terra Novas, Vans and Bosphorus and placed them in the basket, Shamir came in and went through his clothes, piece by piece, in that same gentle, unhurried pace, while Peter stood there (asshole clenched) like Birdy in the corner. He looked around (here he was, [almost] naked [he suddenly wished he was less cut] in the bowels of the fucking Istanbul airport, no one back home knew where the fuck he was, with some sex starved Turkish soldier [although he didn't look Turkish] grubbing through his threads) and wondered how far his scream would carry. The curtain was thin, and the walls of the booth stopped a couple of feet short of the ceiling, but who would hear? This was not fun. He most definitely should have stayed in Bel. His clothes were soon nicely folded back in the basket. Shamir looked at him. Peter tensed.

"Turn please." Oh fuck.

"Thank you. You may dress now. I will return your ticket, boarding pass and passport outside. Your gate is G/9. Passport control is down the corridor on your right. Have a nice flight, Mr. Nicholas."

Reham was waiting for him in the corridor.

"Are you okay?"

"I am fine."

"Man, they don't want to let us out of Turkey, do they? Did you ever see Midnight Express?"

She looked at him. "Those were not Turks."

"Who were they?"

"Israeli soldiers. We are flying El Al, the Israeli airline. I am a Palestinian, and you are a young American with no luggage. They are very careful. If I had purchased separate tickets, you would have been spared this. And perhaps it would have been less difficult for me."

"I'm sorry." He didn't know why he said that.

"It is not important."

Except for the line, passport control was a breeze in comparison (the moustached soldier, guard or whatever looked carefully at his passport [including the fifty dollar visa], then at him, then punched a few numbers into a computer, looked at him again, then down at the passport, back up at his face. Do you have ticket? Yes. He looked carefully at the tickets, then at him, stamped both his passport and boarding pass, then repeated the sequence, although more slowly, with Reham). The metal detectors, however, were a true bitch. It used to annoy him how much shit (huge scrunched up duffle bags, computer cases the size of small refrigerators, purses and shopping bags as big as coffee tables, plus couples with all that baby crap carrying their entire goddam house on their backs) people would try to hump through on board, but he now could (almost) understand it. Still, too much was too much (the fucker in front of them had floor lamp with shade in his hand, and the jasper in front of him carried an opened case of [Betcha can't eat just one] Lays Potato Chips [don't they have snacks where you come from pal?]). Why wasn't this line moving? He leaned out to look ahead. An old man in faded green overalls, work boots and a red baseball cap was holding a nondescript brown wooden box about the size of two basketballs in his hands. Two guards, both big stocky men, were chattering at him furiously. They shifted him and his box out to the side, and things started moving (slowly) again. "You'd think they'd have more than two machines," Peter said. As they approached, the old man set the box on the ground, opened it, and out hopped a rooster. Christ.

Their luggage was searched once more, on the boarding ramp.

CHAPTER FOURTEEN

"Aaaaaaaaaaaaaaalllllllllllllllllllllllaaaaaaaaaaaaaahhhhhhh
hhhhhhhhhhhaaaaaaaaaaaaaaaahhhhhhhhhhhhhhhhhhhhh
Aaaaaaaaaaaaaaaaakkkkkkkkkkkkkkkkkkkkkkbbbbbbbbbbbb
bbbaaaaaaaaaaaaaaaaaaaaaaarrrrr."

Jesus fucking Christ. What a way to wake up
(Jerusalem Golden Walls Hotel, across Sultan Suleiman
Street [Paratroopers Road] from Herod's Gate [Bab as-
Zahra]). He could use some more shut but with Ali
Akbar (they should call them shrieks) screaming like his
pubes were on fire (bbq [even if he had to research
mooks who burned their crotches he'd rather be there
than here]) here there was no chance. He yawned,
threw off the sheet, went to the window and opened
the drapes. So this was Israel, Zion, al makbah,
Jerusalem, Al Quds, whatever. The land of his forefa-
thers (not mothers). He shrugged. All he wanted to do
was to collect some data about his own begatter, then
hightail it back to civilization. History could do what it
wanted. He yawned again. He was burnt, and definitely needed more z's. They had arrived late (about 11:30)
and he had had a hard time crashing (and once he did
the fucking buses or trucks or whatever in and out all
goddam night had awakened him periodically). He was
cranky. And tired. And impatient. And constipated.
And annoyed. Yeah, big time annoyed.

Reham was in the next room (supposedly [at
least he'd seen her go in last night]), so they hopefully
wouldn't have to play hide and seek again. He had a
slight headache. He needed coffee (what kind [Turkish,
Nescafe, American filtered, cappuccino] did they have

here anyway?) although he wasn't sure he wanted to be that alert just yet. He wanted to go back to sleep, covers over his head, and wake up between Wanda's Chanel sheets (and legs) back in America. Born in the USA. Maybe if he clicked the heels of his Banfis three times (his Vans did not seem magical) . . .

Ali Akbar finally shut up. The sun was rising over to his left, illuminating the dun brick of the square-waved northern wall and the tops of the trees and the buildings (towers, domes and spires) behind with a muted rose pink. Wanda would probably dig this (the view, not the room, certainly not the room [twin bed with dark mustard acrylic spread and faded ivory sheets, flanked by beaten and scratched {no bullet holes} oak shaker end table with a spooled buffet lamp, black forties telephone {like his old one}, a Philips digital alarm clock {no radio} and four books in the drawer underneath {Old Testament, New Testament, The Koran and Jerusalem yellow pages}, a rather bad drawing of Herod's Gate in a gold metallic frame over his bed and a small white metal cabinet, now in service as a combination armoire and media center {10 inch Elektra tv}, a dental silver wire mesh wastebasket, and a high backed red naugahyde covered barstool over which he had draped his Marks and Terra Nova {bathroom down the hall}]). He'd better not think about Wanda for a while.

He yawned, stretched, closed the curtains and returned to lie on the bed, his hands locked behind his head. He needed to piss (and dump [yeah right]) and he needed to sleep. He needed coffee, aspirin, his Samsonite and the book of father photos. He needed to buy gifts, and get on that plane (business class) and ride, back home, where he could get his life (Wanda, Kay, work and [new?] address) back together. He heard the airbrakes of a bus (or truck) scream to a halt just below his window, followed by the angry chattering (trouble in Paradise) of a po'd driver (or passenger or pedestrian), and then the laboring of first gear, the grinding into second and the gradual decrescendo of an exit. Good Morning Vietnam.

He was seriously bumming on the room. He needed to get out, take a walk, maybe get some breakfast (bacon and eggs [two sunny up like a twelve year old's bumps {Suarez}] with hashbrowns would be awesome [Captgo on Broxton had primo hashbrowns {with Vidalia's and guajillos}]) to go along with his caffeine. But if he split, he wasn't sure how he'd reconnect with Reham (and this was definitely the very last place in the world he wanted to be without a guide [can you say carbomb]). He could write her a note or leave a message with the desk clerk, but who knew if she'd get it, or read it, or whatever. Still, it might be way cool to give her some of her own shit, although if she got too torqued, she might leave his ass in the middle of this war, and Peter Nicholas, American, might get his dick blown off (bearded tableclothed suicide semtexan or babyfaced Shin Bet [where was he getting all of this dreck?] sniper it didn't really matter). Maybe inside with a native was the place to be.

What time was it? He checked the Philips: 6:15. Fuck. What time was that in real time? Didn't matter, he was beat. He yawned again. Maybe he could get some more shut for an hour or so, and then put his ear to wall and wait for the princess to wake up and, and what? Lead him to the promised land? He was already there.

He closed his eyes and breathed (sighed) deeply. A shower wouldn't be a bad idea (although why stand out more than he had to), but would eliminate any possibility of additional z's. A piss (necessary and imminent) and a dump (necessary and unlikely) were on the schedule as well, but if he got out of bed, he'd stay out of bed. And then what? Watch some tv? He opened his eyes. He stared at the table, telephone, lamp and Philips. 6:18. He had to get out.

It was warmer than he expected, and brighter (he immediately put on his C & G's) and dry (it smelled of bus exhaust and dust). He felt slightly better after his shower (although still no dump [maybe a walk would help although he didn't want to wander too far {Peter had a shy bowel syndrome (hated shitting in public toilets)}]). He stared out at the traffic (a few late model Mercedes [some taxis] but mostly Renaults, small Fiats and Opels of various ages) zooming back and forth (no wonder it was noisy the fucking bus station [Suleyman Arab] was right next door) on the street in front.

Well, screw it: since he was there (and up) he probably should see something (and get some chow) besides the bus station (he was in Jerusalem after all and likely [definitely] wouldn't return soon [ever]). He spied the gate (the drawing of which he'd seen in his room) and a crosswalk about a half a block to his left, and decided to go for it dude.

It was early (just after seven he guessed [he'd hidden his Weil in his Zero Halliburton {didn't want to lose a hand}]), but there were quite a few tourists (Americans he guessed [khaki and beige multi-pocketed shorts with the now ubiquitous Tevas {their omnipresence provoking the beginnings of an aversion (or maybe it was the [black or white] socks)}]) and workers (two young guys in what looked like gray and brown rags and matching Adidas Campus Supremes with bags of cement in some sort of sling on their backs, four nuns in light blue and white habits [nika

nika nika nika], two or three men in shabby suits and tablecloths, and your assorted black clad priest and black clad rabbi) milling around the platform and the gate (another amorphous line although slightly more orderly than he found in Istanbul). A couple of Israeli soldiers (the same units as the Turkish airport) were standing around, guns slung over their shoulders, smoking. Luckily he'd brought his Coach, in case they needed his passport, but he didn't have any money except a couple of Jacksons and some Turkish paper (he hadn't changed any dollars [Reham had paid for the taxi and had advised him against using the airport mon-eychangers {The mechanical banks give you a better exchange (he'd have to find one soon [breakfast])}]), so he hoped it didn't cost anything to get in (maybe dollars were universal).

No problemo (the soldiers barely glanced at him and there was no one charging cover). He was through the gates and into the (old) city (there was a Turkish coffee cart just inside the wall but he didn't have any local coin and didn't want to hand the boy a twenty American for a large caffeine). Now what? He didn't have a map (unlike Istanbul), much less a guidebook (his guide [hopefully] snoring back in the hotel): he had no fucking clue as to where he was, what he should see or where what he should see was. He knew the Wailing Wall was somewhere around, but he really wasn't in the mood to be the American at the moment (besides he didn't want to stray too far from the hotel [in case his dump started to come on and/or Reham woke up and wondered where he had wandered]). So maybe an ATM and some sort of snack (a bagel would work), and then back to the hotel (he'd probably have time to see the sights while waiting for Reham to [pretend to] look for that book).

He was standing on the side of a tree-lined

street, in front of a two story white stucco building (the Indian Hospice). All of the tourists, and most of the workers were flowing downhill, on the road to his right (Ha Tsari`akh), toward that golden dome (Dome of the Rock) and what seemed to be the center of the city (The Temple Mount/Haram ash Sharif).  He didn't think he wanted to be part of that stream (although where there were tourists there were banks [and restaurants] ), and so maybe he would go left (Sha`ar), hug the walls for a while, and go back and get break- fast in his hotel. Just as he turned left, he heard some animal noises behind him, and he turned around to see a flock of twenty or so fat sheep, jogging up the road in his direction, led by an older guy with a white beard in brown and black robes with that tablecloth on. He was followed by a straggly looking boy, in a once white tee shirt and navy blue shorts, fire engine red Starter cap (Chuck Durst) and sandals, and an even stragglier looking brown and white dog, who nipped at the heels of the sheep. Both the man and the boy had those curved shepherds sticks and bulky, old school Walkman cassettes (from the seventies [the old man's phones obvious over his head cape, the dude's likewise over his cap]). A couple of the tourists stopped and snapped photos, but neither the man or the boy paid attention to anything but their animals (Peter noticed a few lambs had neon orange streaks on their wool [to ID them?]). He was soon surrounded by the not unpleasant smell of sheep shit and wool, and stood and watched as the flock (or herd or whatever) trotted past him down the road he had been planning to explore.

That was picturesque all right, but he wasn't sure he wanted to follow the farm scene into the slaughterhouse (images of big oily fuckers with loin- cloths, no shirts and long knives doing some serious throat surgery [he loved lamb {he remembered a delicious rack with mint jelly at Citrus} and he wanted to continue loving lamb]) or wherever else they were going.

Walking between clots of sightseers (most rather quiet), he moved down the hill toward the spires, a bit to the right of the large golden dome. The crowd began to thicken: there had to be an ATM around somewhere. After a couple of blocks, he came upon a rather busy if narrow cross street (Via Dolorosa), with a large, three gated arch to his right (Ecce Homo). The first thing he noticed was a guy of about fifty, in a butt-ugly gray and light blue Merona (Target) plaid sport jacket with a matching light blue button down Arrow Broadstreet (opened at the collar), non-descript microfiber Pro Spirit slacks with brown Bass Oxfords, carrying a large wooden cross, followed by a number of Midwestern (US) looking men and women in various Iowa go-to-meeting checked farm frocks with sensible flats (or sneakers), assorted shawls and veils (women), and polo (small p) shirts, cargo pants, (those fucking) Tevas or suede Hush Puppies, and odd canary yellow straw cowboy hats (men), proceeding slowly down the street (to his right). All had small navy blue vinyl travel bags (Holy Land Travel) slung over their shoulders, and all carried books (Bibles or guidebooks he couldn't tell). Peter began to hum Losing my Religion and wondered how much that cross weighed (was he faking it or did it cause some serious lumbar ache? [did he hand off once he tired?]).

Tailgating the pilgrims (in white leather pants with a black jacket [Jezebel Leather] with a black Motorhead tee and looking like he did not belong) was Señor Sonic, the hottest dj from Eliat to the Golan, with a small fawn and white colored greyhound, prancing along on a thin leather leash. Their eyes met, and both hesitated, unable to quickly decide whether to acknowledge the other. The greyhound, however, broke the stalemate, and tugged on its leash to greet Peter's knees (Peter, infinitely preferring the greyhound to Petite Blanche, kneeled down on his haunches to allow it [her] to lick his face): there was no choice but to make some sort of communicative (if not friendly) gesture.

"Hi."

"Hey." Peter stood.

"What's your greyhound's name?"

"She's not a greyhound, she's a whippet. And her name is Twister. She belongs to my mother. I'm giving her her morning walk."

"She's beautiful. How old is she?"

"Nearly one year and a half. And how is your friend, your companion?"

"Reham? She's fine. Sleeping back at the hotel" (hopefully). Twister began to sniff around the walls and the street.

"I had better take her to another place." Señor smiled. "Once, when she did her toilet on this road, an Armenian priest chased us down the street with a mop for cleaning floors. This is not even the way Jesus carried his cross. He was tried at the Citadel, on the other side of the old town near Jaffa gate, and so he walked east, not west. Idiots." Peter must have looked puzzled, because Señor continued, "This is the Via Dolorosa, the Street of Sadness, where Jesus supposedly carried his cross from Pilate's house to Golgatha. Didn't you know that?"

Peter certainly didn't want to exhibit his ignorance in front of Señor Slut, so he looked Sonic straight in the eye and nodded knowingly. "Sure." Sonic shrugged (not quite the Turkish shrug but close) and began to move to attend to Twister's gastrointestinal requirements (lucky dog). "Wait a sec, is there an ATM around? A money machine?"

"There is not one for four or five blocks. You must go down this street until you get to Al Wad Road, and then turn right. Keep going for two or three blocks, and there is a Citibank on the left."

"Thanks. Any place you'd recommend to get breakfast?"

"American breakfast?"

"Yeah, American."

"There is no place close. The City Restaurant and the Coffee Shop both serve American breakfast, but they are far away, near the Jaffa gate. You must walk all the way down the Via Dolorosa, and continue even after it splits apart, past Al-Wad and Souq Khan al-Zeit, and past even the Christian Quarter Road until you get to, uh, Saint Dmitri Road. Turn left and walk for about 200 meters, and you will see both The City Restaurant and the Coffee Shop, they are next door to each other. There are many electronic banks nearby as well."

"Thanks."

"Shalom."

"Yeah. Shalom to you too."

When Peter (passable scrambled eggs with onions and peppers [no tabasco], excellent fresh oj and two cups of pretty good java) returned (8:45) to the Golden Walls, Miss Al-Safia, as far as the desk clerk knew, remained in her room. Peter decided to go up to his room and wait.

CHAPTER FIFTEEN

"Where are we going?"

"We are going to see a man whom you should see. I will leave you to speak with him while I go to my cousins to search for the book you desire."

"What was that all about back at the hotel?"

"They are cheating Egyptians. They saw your American passport and charged us double what I have paid before. They are worse than the Turks."

Reham (the same black Levis, the same North Face, the same Cat work books and black leather jacket with a fresh maroon silk and cotton short sleeved blouse [Diesel], the same rings and the same Byblos scarf tying back her hair [although this time it {her hair} was tucked inside the back of her jacket] and little makeup and scent [just a brush of the she umara on her eyes and a hint of Thousand Plateaus] looked almost dykish [Peter didn't mind]) walked quickly (Peter scrambling to keep up) down Sultan Suleiman Road, toward a plaza crowded with merchants and stalls (some covered with brightly colored umbrellas) and a mass of people facing the gate (Damascus [Bab al-Amud]). Reham suddenly stopped and jerkily removed her jacket. She was definitely pissed (there had been a small scene [raised voices and angry gestures] at the Golden Walls). Peter sincerely hoped it wasn't that T.O.T.M.

"Are you mad at me?"

"No. I do not like to pay too much for things. We will sleep another place tonight."

"I'll pay you back for the hotel. I found a bank this morning."

"No. You are my guest." She found her cigarettes and matches, lit one, and sucked in deeply. She
exhaled, and then smiled at him. "You have eaten
breakfast, yes?"

"Yeah. I got up early so I walked around. Got
some eggs at the City Café."

"You mean the City Restaurant."

"Right. The City Restaurant. I saw our friend
Señor Sonic at that road where Jesus carried his cross.
He told me about the restaurant. He said to say hi.

"Did he have that disgusting monkey?"

"No, just a little dog."

"That is almost as bad. I do not understand you
Westerners and your dogs. In Paris they are everywhere, even in the cafés. And their shit is everywhere
too." Reham took another drag and yawned. "I need
some coffee. Turkish coffee. There's probably a place
near the gate." She touched his elbow lightly as they
crossed the street.

He followed Reham through a maze of narrow
streets, alleys, courtyards, sidewalk markets and stairs,
dodging donkeys, cats, sheep, towelheads, furhats
(spodiks), dreadlocks (earlocks), skullcaps (yarmulkes),
headscarves (babushkas and the full Monty Yashmaks),
cowls, birettas, pillboxes, Gable and French hoods
(depending on the order), baseball caps (mostly
Yankees and 49'ers [all at either 12 or 6 o'clock]), zuc-
chettos, Tupac do-rags, garrison caps and berets (every
third dude [and some dudettes] under thirty with an
Uzi [some in Levis and tee-shirts]). It was getting
warmer, and more crowded, and the air thicker; a combination of cooking (chick peas, onions and bread),
shitting (sheep, cat and donkey) and working (the pop-
ulace in general could use a few [hundred] bars of

Zest). Reham kept urging him to keep up (You should not walk behind me), but he was having some trouble negotiating himself, his Eastpak and Zero Halliburton through the mob.

Somewhere through an alley they made a sharp left turn through an old iron gate into a court-yard, frightening about twenty cats from some sort of rotting garbage delight (what appeared to be a decaying donkey head was in fact just a green plastic bag full of foul smelling waste), and then (dodging some hanging laundry [red shirts and a camo jacket and pants], past a steel table with some nasty looking stains underneath a balcony with a wrought iron railing on which had been attached a couple of klieg lights) Reham started up some crumbling stairs. This place was old, older than shit, and it smelled like something dead (Jeffrey Dahmer?). Peter hesitated. This was it; this was the kidnapping (or murder or cannibalism, torture [in Jerusalem no one can hear you scream]). Reham turned around.

"Please hurry, we are now late."

"Where are we going?"

"I am leaving you with my friend, and then I will go to my cousins to look for the book. Do not worry, my friend is a good man, speaks good English. He is a physician, but the Zionist occupiers will not let him work, and so he is a physician for animals, I do not remember the word."

A doctor? Definitely not a good idea (Is it safe? Is it safe?) "A vet. A veterinarian."

"Yes. Hassan is a good, kind man. Please, hurry." Peter didn't move (he'd seen enough flicks to worry). "Please, you are being rude. What are you frightened of?"

"I'm not frightened; it's just that this wasn't part of the deal. When I agreed to come here, you said we'd get the book from your cousins. You didn't say anything about having some doctor baby-sit me or whatever."

"I did tell you that I would have to approach my cousins while alone, that you could not journey with me."

"So why can't I just bop around, see the sights? Why do I have to hang with your doctor friend? We could meet later, at some cathedral or something. Or mosque" he added quickly, "or church, doesn't matter. Or a restaurant: I'll spring for grub" (he was deliberately being obscure). "I just don't want to spend all day inside with some dude I don't know. I've never been here before, and I want to see some stuff" (there was probably good reason they wouldn't let him work [wasn't Hannibal Lecter a doctor too?]: he'd much rather find a bar or Starbucks or something [it was too early for that], scope out some furry [Israeli women were supposed to be hot {he owed Little Pete big time after this adventure (and what Wanda didn't know wouldn't hurt her [as if])}], and wait till Reham showed with the photos).

"Peter, please be more wise. You are an American, alone, with a computer and backpack, in a place that is not always safe for Americans."

"I was alright this morning."

"Yes, you were. If you stay with my friend today, I will take you to see what you wish tomorrow. We will visit the Christian monuments."

"I can do that today. I can buy a book, and see what I need to. And then we could meet later this afternoon, or even tonight, if you need more time."

"I have told Hassan that we would meet him. He is looking forward to seeing you."

Peter shrugged.

"Please, if you will not come, I will not look

good."

Peter looked at the ground.

"I'm sorry, but if you will not come, I will not look for the book. And you have wasted your time. And mine."

He looked up. Fucking bitch. All the way from LA, to London, to Istanbul and now Jerusalem, and now right in the fucking shorts. He couldn't believe it (yes he could). She had called his bluff (again [she was forceful]): it was either walk away René or follow the hootchie up the stairs to some evil ass doctor who'd probably connect Little Pete to a 50 volt generator with jumper cables. Thanks daddy: bite me. Ah, but what the hell, since he was already here (plus he wanted to prove he had the stones).

"You win."

"As you will see, it is you who have won."

Sure thing Yoda.

"Hello Reham," a kiss on each cheek, "it is so good to see you. And this must be Peter. Welcome, welcome, please come in and sit down."

Hassan was large (fat, Chris Farley fat, with one of those monster bellies on skinny legs), dark (deep oak), and older (perhaps sixty [anything between fifty and seventy Peter could only guess]) than Peter had expected, with one of those lilting, Masterpiece Theater British accents. He had thick, lightly tinted square, black framed glasses (think George C. Scott in The Hustler), thin, straight black hair greased back, and was wearing a clean if somewhat worn (two more wearings away from shabby) white doctor's coat, buttoned almost to the neck, a bright red with black swirls Michael Fish tie, a nicely laundered and starched pinstriped white and blue

Thomas Pink two ply slightly fraying at the collar, Henry Poole lightweight wool slacks and what looked like a pair of black John Lobb's English oxfords, in immaculate condition.   He was heavily scented in Blindness and Insight by Nino Cerutti, and didn't wear a watch (if you were that obese you were either impeccably dressed [John Goodman in Barton Fink] or a fucking slob [Matt Foley {You have plenty of time to live in a van down by the river, when you live in a van, down by the river!}] — there was no middle ground. Hassan had taste [more taste than money, obviously], but was beginning to go to seed. Peter began to feel somewhat sympathetic [although he usually hated fat fucks]).

He took off his C & G's (the guy could block out some serious light) and allowed himself to be gently escorted into the room (much cooler than outside). As Hassan turned, Pete saw that there wasn't much light to block, as the room's single source was a rectangular window made of wood in which holes and slats had been delicately carved (looking something like Reham's drawings): nice looking, but rather weak for illumination.   Music came from upstairs, Soft Cell's Tainted Love (?). When he was out of range of the Cerutti, he noticed the smell of incense and antiseptic, with something underneath, perhaps cat piss, perhaps frying olive oil. "Please, sit, I have tea already made."

Peter sat down next to Reham on some indefinable love-seat thing, covered with a thin (almost transparent in places) purple and white batik throw (he could feel her hip against his), and watched as the fat guy, who moved well for his weight (must be the shoes), dance around the kettle on top of a gas canister with a burner (like some sort of Coleman [didn't pay the electric bill?]), pouring here, stirring there, until he lightly glided back toward them with a tray and service, which he set on a low hammered copper table in front of them. Hassan poured, and Peter noticed the same manual dexterity and grace he'd seen when Shamir rifled through his clothes.

"I'm afraid I don't have sugar, as Americans sometimes prefer. I do however, have honey, but I suggest you try the baklava, as it will likely displace the need for additional sweetener."

The china was nice, although mismatched (Royalcrest and Colcough bone [Peter's saucer chipped and repaired]), and the tea was hot and strong. He wasn't really hungry, but when Hassan pushed the plate of pastry toward him, he somehow knew it would be bad form to refuse.

"Peter, you don't mind if I call you Peter, do you?"

"No, it's my name."

"Splendid. And you must call me Hassan. Peter, Reham tells me this is your first time in this part of the world. What do you think of our little tinder-box?"

The baklava was amazingly sweet. It was like injecting sucrose directly into his veins (he could almost feel his heart revving). And sticky too: it was impossible to answer with the honey and pistachio paste glued to his palate. He took another sip of tea to try to clear the roof of his mouth. He could feel Reham looking at him. "I really haven't seen all that much yet, we just got here last night. There are a lot of guns around here," he added helpfully.

Hassan laughed. "When a young man from Los Angeles USA says that you possess many guns, you possess many guns." Hassan laughed again and gestured toward Peter with his teacup. "You are right, my young friend. Palestine, Israel, we have many weapons. Although one side has more weapons than the other. Would you like some more tea?"

He was going to need more liquid to rinse his mouth and teeth of the honey, and offered his cup. "Thank you."

"The pleasure is mine." Was the Chunkster coming on to him? Was Reham pimping for Fats here? He looked across the table. Hassan was looking at Reham and smiling. Was that some sort of code or something? He knew he should have backed out, walked away, got out while the getting was good. Instead, he was trapped in this fat chicken hawk's studio (or office or whatever), while Auntie Em here waited for his mack to split so he could get down to some serious dicksmoking. No wonder there were no windows.

Maybe he was just being paranoid. He didn't want to get caught staring, so he shifted his gaze over to the left, away from Reham (although Hassan's large white mass remained in the corner of his eye, dominating in the gloom). To his far left, there was a once-white porcelain sink with accompanying towels and rags hung on pegs to the right. Continuing across that wall, Peter's gaze came to a couple of folding chairs, and what looked like bags of feed, stacked six high in the corner. On the far wall, next to the corner, was some sort of chart or diagram of what appeared to be sheep, although Peter couldn't be sure in the dim light. Against the far wall, almost directly behind Hassan, was a large glass book or display case, with a number of unknown objects inside, a stack of books and a small globe on top. Tacked above the globe was a map, a city map (it was too far way and too dark for Peter to ascertain what city).

"I see you are looking at London. I adore London. Have you been?"

Have you been? Have you been? "Yes I have. Four times" (not counting the recent stopover at Heathrow).

Hassan sighed. "London was the home of my youth, my idealistic, innocent youth. I went to school there, well, at Oxford: although I must add, while I went to school there, I was educated here, in Palestine. Reham doesn't care for London, do you dear?"

"Except for the British, I like it fine."

"You are right to distrust the British: they are simply Germans with better manners." Hassan took a bite of baklava and a sip of tea. "What did you study at university, Peter?"

"Business mostly."

"Ah yes, business. The business of America is business, is it not? Before I was trained to be a physician, I read Philosophy, Politics and Economics at Exeter College, where J.R.R. Tolkien, of Hobbit fame, attended."

That was close to interesting (Where did our love go was replaced by some indecipherable chatter). I read economics at the University of Southern California, where the famous OJ Simpson attended. Peter stifled a yawn. If Chubby here was coming on to him, he was doing one lousy job of it (unless he wanted to bore him to sleep before trying to meet Junior). He'd better keep alert, because there was definitely some plot or something going on here, otherwise Reham would not have insisted so strongly on this visit. And why was she still here (although he was grateful she was [and enjoyed her presence on his hip and thigh])? This was just ignorant: he should have turned and walked (weeks ago). He could still split, but he wanted that book, wanted that 411 about his father, about himself. And he wanted to avoid losing all those hours and bucks on what would be, if he left now, certainly a wild goose chase. It was like that time he went to Vegas (MGM) with Suarez, and he kept betting and betting (blackjack then roulette), unwilling to face the fact that he'd lost over six grand: he remembered sitting there at the wheel, betting a split (sixteen and twenty) over and over again (he had the ugly-ass canary yellow chips), thinking I'm going to make this up, I'm going to make this up, just one more hour, fifteen more minutes, one more spin. And the fucking thing is, he did it. It took him all night (and two sixteens in a row), but he broke even (exactly [he'd come out ahead if you counted the free Heinie's]). Same thing here: he'd wait this out, see what the shit was. And maybe he'd break even. He considered another bite of baklava but decided against it.

"Forgive me if my curiosity supersedes my manners, but I don't enjoy many opportunities to converse with Americans. I would like to learn from our meeting, profit from it, so to speak. May I ask you, what do you think of us?"

Peter shrugged. "I don't know. Like I said, we got here late last night."

Hassan removed his gray glasses, wiped them on his lab coat, and returned them to his face. "Forgive me for being obscure. What did you think of us before you arrived? While you were in the States? When you saw us on the news? What did you, or do you, think?"

Fuck, I don't know. To be honest, you were pretty much below my radar, if you get my drift, until I had to go to that art opening. "I don't know."

"I am very sorry, and don't mean to be insulting, but please, you must have possessed some impression of us, of Palestinians, of Palestine. Fiery young rock-throwing crazies? Prostrate mothers covered in black crying over coffins? You must have seen us on the television, at least our funerals. Yassar Arafat, with that Italian restaurant tablecloth on his head? Dreadful public relations, that. We need someone polished and photogenic like Netanyahu, someone who looks more

American. Surely you must have heard of the intifada? Shatilla? Deir Yassin? Or the American Zionist Baruch Goldstein, who opened fire with an automatic rifle in the Ibrahami mosque in Hebron, creating over forty martyrs for Allah, all shot in the back? Beirut? Erez Crossing? What do these names mean to you?"

Jesus, lighten up chief. Peter didn't know about any of that shit, although he was somewhat relieved to find that Hassan was more interested in dropping some poli sci smack rather than trying to open up his booty. Still, fatty was getting irritated, so if push came to shove, he'd try to outrun the lard-ass (he'd stay near the door), and even though this wasn't his barrio, he probably could lose Reham (smoker, workboots) as well (although he did have his computer and pack [he'd ditch the Mac before his Kitons and Banfis {although the Weil was with the Mac, fuck}]). He could always find a cab to the airport. He didn't say anything, and looked down at his tea.

"Hassan, remember yourself. Peter is your guest. He is my guest as well."

"Yes, of course, you are right, he is my guest. However, where does he think all of the weapons he saw this morning, Israeli weapons, came from? The sky? Yahweh? Did Moses go up and bring them down from the mountain? No. They came from his country, the United States. That is where they came from. What have we done to you that you arm our enemies?" Hassan removed his glasses and leaned forward toward Peter (the return of Blindness and Insight). "I ask you my friend, why does your country hate us so?"

"We don't hate you. I mean I don't hate you, and no one I know hates you" (we don't give much of a shit, pal, we got our own problems [like Mexicans, Crips and Bloods {and Y2K}]).

Hassan leaned back and smiled. "That is reassuring. I am very glad that you and your mates, at least, do not hate us. Please, please, take another piece of baklava."

Peter knew when he was being dissed. Fuck you very much. "No thanks." He turned to Reham for support. She smiled at him and gently patted his knee. Whoa. He thought about returning the gesture but didn't (she was his sister).

"When you were in university, did you ever study something called Business Ethics, or some such thing?"

"It was offered, but I didn't take it."

"Have you heard the joke that business ethics is an oxymoron, something like military intelligence or English cuisine?" Hassan paused but Peter clammed. "Why do you not treat us ethically? Why do you not treat us as your Jesus insisted?" He didn't wait for an answer. "Perhaps you do treat us according to your ethics: perhaps this is what is so disturbing. I will attempt to explain." Hassan reminded him of the large dude in that Bogie movie (Intro to Film as a freshman) about some statue.

"You have heard of Hegel, have you not? He was no friend to the Jews, certainly. Hegel developed this theory, this story really, about what happens when two men meet each other. Now according to Hegel, men are differentiated from animals, from dogs and sheep, by the fact that they desire something besides food and shelter, besides material comfort. Men want power. Now, when two men meet each other, they both naturally desire to have power over the other. They cannot help this, they have no choice. What can happen, then, when these two men meet each other, both desiring power over the other?"

Peter looked at Reham, who was looking at

Hassan. She had a sweet profile: a strong nose, high cheekbones, (not too) thick lips and beautiful olive skin (Wanda's could be a bit red at times [tanning was for trash], especially when high or aroused). He couldn't see anything of his father (himself) in her (Reham). Peter turned back to Hassan. He was waiting for an answer. "I don't know, what?" Like he gave two shits (speaking of which).

"There are three possibilities. One, they kill each other, end of story. Two, one man kills the other man. At first, this seems like a desirable solution, does it not, as one man has conquered and vanquished the other. But is this outcome truly desirable? One man alive, one man dead."

"Sure. One winner, one loser."

"Yes," Hassan was getting jazzed, "but if it is power that men truly desire, then what power can one have over the dead? The dead are dead. Do you see? If one man kills the other man, then the man who is alive cannot get what he desires, he is left standing over a corpse, as powerless as before. Therefore, the only possibility is a third, I will not say final, solution."

What was that knee squeeze all about? And that kiss? And the drawing? And the elbow touch? All those little gestures. In some ways, it was probably a good thing she was his half sister (if she was), because he wouldn't mind some of that right now. That what? You know. Bad thoughts bad thoughts bad thoughts.

"The third solution, and the only event that allows the story to continue, is for one man to enslave the other man. Here, at least one man is satisfied, for he now has power over the other: the master is master, and the slave is a slave. And the slave now does work for the master — that is the nature of slavery. But as I said, the story continues."

What if he put his hand on her knee? Just to show that he wasn't pissed. His guess was that she didn't let many men mack on her, so if she left it there (or covered it with her own), maybe she was interested. Interested in what? It would probably be this huge insult, especially in front of Hassan (who with his eagles and slaves wouldn't notice anyway). After all, she did tell the airport 5-o they were boyfriend and girlfriend. Me so horny, me so horny. This was crazy.

"The master is happy at first, for he now has someone over whom he has power. It is wonderful to have someone work for you; till your soil, plant and gather your crops, slaughter your animals and make your wine. But then he begins to think. The slave too begins to think, but we will talk about that later. The master begins to think that even though it is very comfortable being a master, that in some ways he has grown dependent on the slave. If not for the slave, he would not have wine to drink or food to eat. More importantly, for this is what makes a man, if not for the slave, the master would have no power over anyone. If the slave were to die, through overwork let us say, then the master would no longer be master. Do you understand? The master now depends on the slave, the master has, in some sense, become slave of the slave. And there is something else that bothers the master. It is not that wonderful to have power over someone who is a mere slave. The slaves are not really human, they are not masters by any means, so to have power over slaves is like having power over a donkey or a camel. And so, the satisfaction that they once felt begins to ebb. The slaves, however, have another story."

Four or five loud cracks filled the air. Peter jumped. Shouting followed, then three or four more cracks (gunshots?). (Singsong Euro) Sirens began to blare from further away.

"That was rather near, I believe. It would be wise to avoid the window and door for the time being."

"Were those shots?" Peter had heard gunfire before (he lived in LA after all [and had gone out with Wanda and father to the {Burro Canyon} gun club to squeeze off a few {Wanda was mad with her Glock 9 while he preferred the Walther PPK (borrowed from daddy [Kay wouldn't dig him owning a gun {besides all the fucking paperwork}])}]).

"Perhaps we are hearing those weapons you saw this morning: they sound to me like rubber bullets."

"What are rubber bullets?"

"The Israeli army and the IDF often use bullets made of rubber when they shoot at children. Irgun and Mossad have no such compunction. They always employ live ammunition. Lovely term that. Supposedly, these rubber bullets do not kill, unless they strike the head. Unfortunately, some of our children are young and not tall, and their heads are closer to the ground. The sound of rubber bullets is slightly different.

"Anyway, I was telling you a story, a story of mastery and slavery. After the beginning, after this encounter where the master has enslaved the slave, the slave is naturally very fearful of his master, and acts with this fear to serve his master. But as he works the land in service of his master, he begins to educate himself, to educate himself with work. He begins to see that the master is just another man, another man who is becoming dissatisfied. He begins to understand that while the master is dependent upon him, for without slaves there would be no masters, he is not dependent on the master, or he is dependent on the master only to the extent that he is, and remains, a slave. And he does not wish to do this. So the slave possesses, at first as desire, a freedom in regards to the master that the master does not possess in regards to the slave. The slave is, at least potentially, free, while the master is enslaved to his slaves for his mastery. You understand this, I am sure?"

Yada yada yada. What the fuck: here he was getting shot at (practically) in the middle of fucking Jerusalem, and this dude keeps droning on, laying down some incomprehensible bullshit. I think not. This is so bogus. "Yeah, I follow. The slaves are masters and the masters slaves."

"That is not quite correct, for while the slaves do possess potential freedom, it is not yet actualized. The slaves remain slaves, and the masters remain masters. It is only through a gradual process of work and education that the slaves finally realize they are free and that the masters are enslaved, and move to throw off their enslavement, to actualize their freedom and become truly free. This process, which was further developed by the Jew Karl Marx, is really the story of all oppressed peoples, of all slaves. Workers of the world unite! You have nothing to lose but your chains, and all that. I will bash on. Why am I telling you this? I want to offer a theory, a theory of why the West hates the Palestinians. Guilt plays a large role in my narrative, it is true. Put simply, the West feels tremendously guilty for trying to rid itself of its own Jews, and is so trying to exculpate that guilt by giving the Jews land and allowing them to do as they please within that land. I am not one of those revisionist historians who disbelieve what the West calls the Holocaust. The numbers were possibly exaggerated, but I do believe that Europe did actually make the attempt to purify itself. I personally find it telling that it was the pinnacle of Western civilization, Germany, with its philosophy, music, architecture and art, which actualized this process of purification.

"Have you ever thought about why the Holocaust is so terrible, why it is such a terrible mark upon the Western world? It is because for the first time in recent history, the killing happened within Europe's borders, right under your eyes and noses. There is no Holocaust when you come here to the Levant and murder, or to Africa, or Japan and drop atomic bombs on its cities. No, it is only when the killing happens in front of you that you begin to feel guilt."

Peter turned back to look at Reham.

"The West has attempted to appease its guilt with the creation of Israel. And we Palestinians are in the way of this self-absolution. This guilt is part, but not the only part. There is. . . "

There was more shouting, and then from the courtyard, "Somebody please help. I need your help. Hassan-bey please, help me. Hassan-bey."

Hassan looked at Peter, then at Reham. "Who could that be? Are you expecting someone?"

Peter shrugged and Reham answered no. Hassan went to the door and looked out, while Reham stood behind. Peter stayed put.

"It is that disc jockey, the fool with the baby squirrel monkey."

"Please Hassan! My mother's dog has been shot. Please help me." Twister.

"I will be down." He turned back into the room. "Reham, please go and calm him. Peter, please wait up here, I will require your assistance." Peter stood as Reham slipped out the door and Hassan quickly crossed the room and disappeared through another door in the far corner behind the desk and hotplate.

Peter could hear Señor Sonic through the window, "What am I going to do? What am I going to do? We were walking on Antonia near Simtat, and these youths, young hoodlums, not political, just hoodlums, came running up the street. A couple of policemen followed, and then some soldiers. Someone started firing, just a couple of shots, and I fell to the ground. When I looked to my side, I saw Twister covered with blood. Please, you have got to help me: she is still breathing. My mother will be so hurt, so hurt."

"Please, calm yourself. Hassan will be here to help."

"But where is he? Where is Hassan?"

Good question.

Hassan emerged from the back room and quickly moved to the glass case, where he proceeded to fill a black kit bag with instruments and assorted (doctor) paraphernalia. He turned and handed the bag to Peter, and Peter saw that Hassan had changed his clothes. He'd removed his Pink (along with the Fish tie), keeping some sort of white tee under his coat. He'd substituted army pants for Henry Poole's, and Reebok low cut Players for the John Lobb's. He'd evidently freshened the Blindness and Insight, as the wave of scent seemed much more forceful than before.

"Please, take this bag, while I look for a book. I am not skilled with canines." He turned toward the bookcase, and quickly removed a couple of books from the bottom shelf. He then moved back behind the desk, where he opened a drawer, took out a folded white square, which turned out to be some sort of butcher's apron, and handed it to Peter. "You had better wear this to protect your clothing." Peter put it on (it smelled not unpleasantly of bleach) as they made their way out the door and down the stairs.

Sonic was a mess. Half of his long hair had come undone, and was hanging over the right side of his face. His white leather pants were covered in blood, and he had a large red splotch above his left eye. He had wrapped the dog in his jacket and was holding her against his stomach. Her long, elegant neck was limp and smeared with blood. Peter couldn't tell if she was breathing or not, or if her eyes were open. He glanced at Reham, to see how she was reacting to all this: stiff, but cool as a fucking cuke.

"Please, set the dog on the table, and we will see how it is doing."

"She. It's a fucking she. Not an it. She."

"She. Of course. There. Now, please remove the necklace, or whatever you call it. Thank you. Now, please go upstairs with Reham, who will fix you a cup of tea."

"I'm staying."

"You will only be a distraction if you remain. Please, I will give you a diagnosis as soon as I can. Peter will stay and assist me. Please."

Sonic shrugged and sighed, and moved slowly toward the stairs, the empty collar useless in his hand. Reham started to follow, then looked at Peter, directly into his eyes. "I am sorry. Obviously, I could not know this would happen. Are you fine?"

"I'm okay, sure."

"Perhaps you are not a bad American." She kept her eyes (huge pupils and deep, almost black corneas) locked with his, then looked away (not down) and walked past him up the stairs.

Hassan had switched on the klieg lights, and directed them on the body of the dog, which he had positioned on the dirty table. He was rinsing off the table and the dog with a small garden hose, which ran, as Peter saw, up along the wall to the roof. Numerous small flies had begun to attack the bloodstains on the ground, and he heard a couple of cats mewing behind.

This was going to be quite a trip.

"There is a can of aerosol disinfectant in my bag, please remove it and coat both of your hands, and then mine as well. Be generous with the spray."

Peter did as instructed, and his hands were soon colored a surprisingly bright, deep neon blue. Hassan set the hose on the table and held out his hands. "What is this stuff?"

"It is disinfectant. For sheep. Now, please coat the dog as thoroughly as you can. Again be very generous. I will give it a shot for the pain." He took his bag and drew out some glass works with an ampule of something.

Peter had so far managed to avoid looking directly at the wounded animal, and hadn't prepared himself (how could he) for the sight of the small, skinny torso with the huge red wound, not quite golf ball size, in the middle of its flank, just below the ribs. Blood was oozing from one side, and dripping down the belly, where it mixed with a pool of blood and water on the table. The dog's eyes were closed, foam on the corner of its lips, and it was breathing heavily, jerkily. He looked closer into the wound (he couldn't help himself), but all he could see was reddened, bloody flesh. The dog began to shiver slightly as Peter coated the wet fur and the red wound with blue sheep disinfectant. Hassan gave a shot in the left buttock, and very soon, the shivering stopped and the breathing became less labored. Hassan had taken what looked like small salad tongs and a small blunt hook from his bag.

"Please spray these as well."

"What are you going to do?"

"I will need to see if the bullet is inside of the body, and if it is, remove it. I will then suture it, and hope for the best. As you see, the wound is quite large, which would indicate those rubber bullets I was speaking of, as they are often larger than regular bullets because they are not designed to penetrate, only to stun. As you see, our little friend here is more than stunned. I will need some assistance, as I am not completely familiar with the anatomy of canines."

"I don't know what I can do: I don't know much about dogs and their bodies and stuff. I never even took bio, biology."

Hassan smiled. "You will not require any biology to hold this book open." He handed Peter one of the books he had gathered in his room, his thumb inserted to hold the page. When Peter opened it, he noticed a bright blue smear on the white paper.

Hassan placed one of those fifties doctor's hats with the little round mirror in front, adjusted one of the klieg lights, then pulled out a stool from under the table, sat, and leaned forward. "I don't think I'll need to spread the ribs, but I will have to retract the rictus abdominis, and some of the greater omentum. Could you hold its leg up a bit, so that the hips swivel? Thank you."

He raised his eyes to look at the book Peter was holding, then back down at the wound. "That must be the liver, which looks undamaged. Would you mind holding this clamp, please. You can keep the leg raised with your elbow." Sure doc (George Clooney you ain't).

A few of the more emboldened flies, not content with the dwindling plasma supply on the ground, began to buzz around the table, a couple even alighting in the pool near the dog's wound. Peter, with one hand on the clamp and the other holding the book (not to mention his elbow positioning the leg), could do nothIng. The presence of the flies really pissed him off.

Hassan worked silently for a while, looking a

couple of times up at the book, and once adjusting the clamp. Peter could hear Little Red Corvette on the radio above his head, and the fucking flies increased in number. Apply a couple of ligatures a little distance apart around the colon where it is entering the pelvis, and also at the juncture of the duodenum and jejunum.

"We were just about to talk about how the master and slave story relates to our story, the story of the West, or more specifically the United States, and Palestine, before we were interrupted." What the fuck! Pay the fuck attention! "Now while it is true, as I said earlier, that guilt plays a large role in determining, one can even say overdetermining, your feelings toward Zionism, and therefore towards Palestine, I would like to argue that guilt is not the grounding reason you are so hostile towards us. Your guilt for slaughtering the Jews is great, and makes you wish we Palestinians, and Palestine itself, would disappear, simply vanish, poof, like who was it? Jimmy Hoffa. We disappear, the Jews are happy, your debt is forgiven. Voilà, Peace in the Middle East."

A muscle in Twister's neck twitched and then stopped. Peter caught a whiff of shit cutting through the meaty odor of the blood. Peter looked down at Twister: she was (is? [probably was {Peter didn't see how any animal could survive with that big a hole in its gut (although if Hassan could cut as well as he talked she'd be up in a week or two chasing balls or whatever)}]) beautiful (if one ignored the gaping puncture under her ribs on her left side). Even lying there bleeding, perhaps dying, she looked like grace incarnate. That wonderful spade shaped head, those long white legs (one tawny) and delicate white feet, that deep chest with arching, almost minimalist torso, that elegant whip-like tail: she would go with just about anything (a cas Levis, Banfis and Lars Nilsson urban look, a more outdoorsy A & F or LL Bean ensemble, and even a relaxed Armani and Kenneth Cole semi-formal [although Kay didn't dig pets and as far as he knew {they had never discussed it} neither did Wanda {maybe when he moved a sort of housewarming present for himself}]). It was more than that: she was striking, sweet and, except for the blood, immaculate (how did one go about acquiring such an animal [pet stores were bad news he knew that {he could ask Suarez (owned a couple of Dobes) but supposedly he got his dogs from a meth dealer}]), and Peter wished she wouldn't die (he had never seen anything die before). God, if you're here. He blew at a fly that had settled on Twister's nose. It flew off, then returned. The ventral extremity of the spleen lies immediately caudal to the liver on the left side of the abdomen. Not infrequently the visible part of the spleen is more caudal in position and extends farther in position towards the middle line.

   "It is partly guilt, and partly public relations. The Jews have done a wonderful job presenting their story. Many many American Christians come here, and after the Jesus tour, they all go to visit Masada. It is simply brilliant. I am not one of those Jewish conspiracy fanatics: I do not believe that there exists some sort of underground organization, although it is true that many Jews are prominent in newspaper publishing and other media corporations, and so are naturally predisposed to the Zionist cause. But this still is only a partial answer. Why are the Americans, and Westerners in general, so eager to believe the Jewish story? Why do they ignore reports of their own organizations, Amnesty International, for example? Why do they turn their heads when images are presented to them, images of children, rocks and funerals on one side, and soldiers, tanks and guns on the other?

Why do you Americans disbelieve your own eyes?"

Why don't you shut your own mouth? This was getting way old. He wished Reham was out here with them. He tried to concentrate on Little Red Corvette, but it was too faint to compete with Hassan's dissertation.

"Remember that I said that the slaves were freer than their masters, in the sense that they are not dependent on their masters, or dependent on their masters only so long as they wished to remain slaves. They are also tied, in a way the masters are not, to history. Slaves, because they can work in the world and therefore progress, therefore educate themselves out of slavery, possess history, possess progress, possess movement and momentum, while the masters, because they are, always already, as soon as they become masters, outside of progress, outside of movement, outside of history. Americans, and you must agree with me here, are the most ahistorical people the world has ever known. To paraphrase the brilliant Czech writer Milan Kundera, America is the land of laughter and forgetting. You forget that there already existed multiple civilizations when you began to colonize the Americas; you forget that your country's early economy was built of slave labor; you forget that most of your peoples, especially the people in power, are not native to the land, and it is these people who are attempting to keep immigrants from Mexico and Asia away. You are a state of squatters: you have no ties to land, no sense of the place or the past. And so you forget that there existed millions of Palestinians on the land you decided to give to the Jews. We do not forget."

The serous covering is complete except along those narrow areas following the curvatures by which vessels and nerves gain access to or egress from the wall of the organ.

"Palestine is nothing but history, pure history. We remember Mount Hira and the ascension as if they were yesterday, Tancred's lie and the First Crusade as if it were this morning, al makbah as if it were an hour ago, Qubiya, a single minute and Sabra and Shatila twenty seconds. Americans have difficulty remembering the winner of last year's Super Bowl."

Broncos. Before that, Packers.

"Jews too remember: we Semites are historical. The Jews remember what you did to them, and they remember what they are doing to us. The Jews are slaves in the process of overcoming their slavery, slaves in the process of becoming masters."

The duodenum should be opened by an incision along its greater curvature. The mucous membrane has a markedly velvet appearance due to the presence of innumerable delicate filiform villi, and is folded longitudinally.

"We, however, remain your slaves, your historic slaves. We are your history, reminders of what you try to forget. Eureka. I have found it! Near the stomach. You may dispense with the book and hold the clamp carefully with both hands. Up, up. There!"

Hassan slowly withdrew the tongs, flipped up his headlight, and then stood as he examined the dime-sized super ball he had removed from Twister's gut. The flap of his doctor jacket had opened, exposing an off white wife beater and a pale chest covered with dark black hair. "You may release the clamp now. I do not think this penetrated the stomach walls, although I cannot be certain. The ribs do not seemed damaged.

Hold out your hand." Hassan dropped the bloody ball into Peter's left hand. It was surprisingly heavy. "A souvenir from Jerusalem. If you look closely, perhaps you can see Made in USA etched on the side."

Fuck you. Peter turned to go fetch Reham and go, just go. For the first time, he felt bile rise in his throat. "Where are you going? Please, we are not finished: I will require assistance to close the wound. Please."

He couldn't just abandon the poor dog to the butcher and his slaves, but this anti-American crap was really beginning to torque him off. What about all the American movies and music (Little Red Corvette) and Levis and Walkmans (ok, Walkmans were Jap), what about those? He didn't want to argue; it would just set Hassan off on some other incoherent rant. "Alright." And just please please please shut the fuck up.

"Close the book and place it over there, carefully. Then spray the wound as generously as before. After I thread the suture needle, I will ask you to spray my hands as well." Hassan had brought his bag up to the table and had removed the blue can. Peter set the books to the side where Hassan indicated, then took the can and began to spray Twister's side again. The dog gave a little shudder, opened its eyes, and sighed. It did not continue breathing.

"Look. It stopped breathing. Hassan, it stopped breathing." Peter heard his voice become shrill and loud. Hassan looked up, then put his thumb on Twister's throat. He leaned over and looked into one of her eyes. He shrugged.

"It is difficult to survive such a wound."

"What?"

"There is nothing I can do. I am not an angel."

Peter grabbed Hassan's coat. "Do something you wordy motherfucker."

Hassan turned away and snapped his bag shut. "Do not be impolite. I can do nothing. I am not an angel." Peter leaned over and picked up Twister's Body, slippery with blood. "Do something." Hassan picked up his books and began to walk away. Peter wiped Twister's mouth on the front of his Terra Nova (no great loss), placed his mouth over her muzzle, and blew hard. Once, twice, three times, four times. He waited. The dog remained still, and very very heavy. He set it carefully down on the table, blew again, and waited. He wiped his mouth on his arm. Nothing. Nothing.

Peter removed his (butcher's) apron, placed it over Twister's corpse, turned and walked toward the gate. He could hear Señor Sonic wailing in the background. He heard Reham call his name. He continued walking.

CHAPTER SIXTEEN

His Terra Nova (dog blood, saliva, bright blue disinfectant) was ruined (although the Marks and Spencers [and his Vans] were okay [he didn't check the Bundeswehr]). He didn't give a fuck. He was sitting in an Al Zehra taxi, about twelve kilometers outside the Erez checkpoint into Gaza. He was tired, beaten, used up, played out: he just wanted to go home and get back to his real life (screwing Wanda, shopping, [hardly] working, making face and scoping a new crib). He was exhausted.

He'd made a mistake in coming (to Turkey, to Israel and now to Palestine), that was certain, and now he just wanted to survive the next day or so, climb aboard that large 747 and forget everything that had happened to him. He'd avoid Istanbul: he'd catch something direct from Tel Aviv to LA, first class, scrilla (and presents [unless he could find something {duty-free} at the airport]) be damned. He'd send Reham a few bucks (for all the shekels she'd dropped here) when he got home, and that would be it: taillights, shalom, sayonara, GTG, see ya, don't call us, adi-fucking-os. He'd been fine (even happy) without a family (except for Kay) before, he'd be just as fine now. The last thing he needed was this dark-eyed player-hater (half-sister or not [honest or not]) perpetually pissing on his parade.

No, he had to get back to the farm. He'd have Hector on his culo if he returned empty-handed, but he'd had Hector on his culo before (he could always write something up on Israeli fashion [uzis and Tevas] or the Grand Bazaar), but he sure wasn't going to access all this crap (the fruitless search in cousin Ali's apartment [under the darkly hostile eye of Ali {nice beard, bro'} himself], Twister, Hassan, Señor Sonic, Murat, Shamir, the whole fucking crew) just to avoid an ass-chewing from el jefe Fortunato. While he was without luggage (not counting his Eastpak full of clothes and his Zero Halliburton) or gifts, he did have a fine souvenir of his excellent adventure: the rubber coated bullet, about the size of one of his testicles, in the right front pocket of his khaks. Not too many peeps in his neighborhood had a rubber bullet to call their own. He yawned.

He had wandered (stunned, saddened, numbed [he'd never actually witnessed {live and in person} a death {one second you're breathing the next you're not} before]) a couple of blocks before Reham caught up with him. She didn't say anything, just walked beside him, carrying his Zero Halliburton and Eastpak. After a while he'd taken his things and looked at her (her brown eyes narrowed and brow slightly fur-rowed), and she'd looked at him, and silently wiped something (blood?) off of his chin with her thumb. They'd continued walking for a while, turning left here, right here, no real purpose or direction, moving only (as far as he could tell) away from that long-winded ham-fisted jumbotron (this was a poor country so how'd he get so hefty anyway [maybe that's was why those cats were around]) chicken hawk mother-fucker (if he ever took a slug he'd sooner lose a leg than visit Fat Frank [Burns] over there [what was with that Marcus Welby {odd childhood memory} mirror on his head?]). Any way away.

Reham stopped, removed her leather jacket, and tied it around her waist. She waited until catching his eye, and then spoke. "This is it. This is the house of my uncle, cousins and aunt. This is the house I was brought to after my mother died." They were standing in front of a narrow iron-fenced doorway, through which he could see a small but neat courtyard with a large fig tree in the center and a gray Alfa Romeo sedan crammed against the gate. Each window of the white washed three-story structure was covered by intricate wrought iron, and there was a satellite dish on the roof. Not too shabby.

"Do your cousins live here now? Is this where the book is?"

"As you remember, my uncle and aunt were removed, and my cousins as well. It is now occupied by a Zionist, a professor I was told. From the Ukraine. It is odd that we have walked here."

Yeah right. As if you couldn't have stopped in front of any house and dropped your bullshit. Was she still playing him, even now? God he was depressed.

She looked at him. "What would you like to do? Rest, sit, take a water or a coffee? My cousin lives not far from here, about ten minutes walking. We could go there and I will look for the book you desire."

"I thought you wanted to go alone."

"That is no longer important. I will explain to my cousin and there will be no trouble."

Whatever. He'd go along, but he'd bet his Saab that she wouldn't find the book at this cousins, or the next cousins, or in some auntie's fucking attic or best friend's fucking car trunk, cuz there was no book, there was never any book, and this entire episode was just some shitty movie that was not going to get better, but one that he was going to sit through because he'd paid his ten bucks and he'd wasted all this time already (fuzzy logic but screw it). "Sure, since we're so close."

So they'd walked for a while longer (a while longer than he'd expected), past ancient stone archways with posters in three or four languages, crumbling brick walls, an abandoned lot with rocks, garbage and the smell of animal shit, a train of braying donkeys led by young dark boys smoking cigarettes, a set of posters with photographs of three young girls against a black and red background with lots of that weird script (the sun was relentless [everything bleached white or beige {he needed some Ban de Soleil 50 block}]), to a relatively new (this century) building, through a solid iron front door (after buzzing), and up some cool, clean stairs. Reham knocked on a door (quickly answered). And then she had argued with her cousin. And her cousin had argued back. And then the cousin had let them in, after which Reham disappeared for a time while they (the cousin [Ali] and he) sat on a futon couch covered with a tremendously ugly orange, white and violet geometric print, and silently (although Ali offered and Peter declined tea [he did excuse himself to wash the dog blood off of his face and out of his goat {he even had a few splotches in his hair near the right temple}]) stared at the darkened thirteen inch Quasar in front of them for what seemed like hours (Peter yawning [too beat to give a shit] every five minutes) until Reham returned. "The book is not here. We will have to journey to Gaza." He almost laughed out loud.

And now (after a long late lunch [he wasn't that hungry], a crowded walk in the sun [from Bab as-Silsila to David Street to the Jaffa Gate] and difficult sherut search [I will not pay that you are a thief]), he sat slouched in this (thankfully musicless) Opel taxi, going five miles an hour behind some prehistoric Volvo van (was everything is this part of the world at least two hundred years old?), on his (bumpy) way (between Hebron and Erez Crossing) to Gaza. Wherever (or whatever) that was.

He was so tired he was nauseous (or maybe it

was the constipation), but he knew he had at least four or five hours (a couple of [pointless] hours in Gaza, another to the airport [at least] and then who knows how long until his plane [assuming he'd even be able to get a quick flight]) before he could sleep again (he'd check into a Marriott or something at the airport). Maybe he could beg a cot off of the Gaza cousins (would that be rude?). Maybe Reham was planning on spending the night there. He didn't want to spend the night there (he didn't want to spend the night any-where in this part of the world ever again) but if push came to shove he wasn't sure he had enough energy to resist. God he was tired.

He turned and looked at Reham, sitting bolt upright next to him. She felt him shift and turned to face him, smiling. What did she want from him? What did he want from her? He returned her smile, then turned back, closed his eyes, and rested his forehead in his hand.

He'd managed no sleep, not a wink, not a nod, not a second of unconscious (unthinking) bliss. In fact, the longer he closed his eyes, the more wired (and queasy) he felt. So he'd looked out the window, out at the dry barren hills, the desert scrub, the occasional olive grove, and it reminded him somewhat of California (a little like the 15 from Barstow to Vegas and a lot like Route 60 Riverside to Palm Springs), which of course reminded him of Kay (the Givinchy) and Wanda (Viva Los Vegas in her dad's Boxter [a small {she didn't want to nag} fight on the way back about his so-called exclusive interest in blackjack and roulette and resulting apathy toward his girlfriend {who want-ed to see Elvis Costello at the MGM but not alone and so flirted at the pool but wasn't yet (emphasis on the yet) into the revenge fuck mode and so decided to drink herself silly with champagne (Dom 75) instead and when deep in her cups had checked their still empty room at 4 am and had wandered (staggered) from the MGM first to the Tropicana (where she had been hit on by every Eric Roberts in the entire casino [one asshole even asking if she had ever heard of the Mustang Ranch]) and then to the Excalibur, where she finally located him at one of the roulette wheels, surrounded by (a small stack of red chips and) Suarez and a bunch of cholos she had never seen before, and where he had said, get this, I'll be up in a minute}, which of course reminded him of their slightly more bitter fight in the Saab {did they always fight in cars?} when she had called him boring and which had, more or less directly, led to his current predicament {and then there was the dog}]).

After a while, the Opel turned into a dusty parking lot half full of bedraggled buses, vans and taxis, with shacks and tents (some selling Coca-Cola, tea, cigarettes and food, some seemingly offering only shade, some abandoned and some shut tight) on three sides. There were six or seven sick looking palm trees flanking a rather wide paved road which led, Peter following with his eye as he exited the sherut, down a small hill to a fenced compound of three long, green fortified concrete buildings, set close together, with another, larger but similar building set further away, and four or five smaller, military hut things on the right of the path. A large Israeli flag flew from a pole on the top of one of the buildings. There were two tanks, one on either side of the road, and a whole bunch of soldiers. Two fences funneled people down the path into a thinner, more manageable crowd. This obviously was some sort of checkpoint, and from the looks of things, quite busy. He noticed a tall chain link fence with barbed (razor) wire on top running on both sides from the compound. The fence ran as far as he could see. Reham (after paying the driver) motioned for him to follow as she began walking quickly toward the checkpoint.

"Please hurry: I do not wish to queue for ever."

"What is this?"

"This is the Erez crossing. Into Gaza. It is crowded now because the Palestinians are attempting to return home from work."

"Why the tanks?"

She looked at him and smiled. "In case there is trouble. Please hurry, the queue is often quite long."

They stood in line for quite a while, not speaking. Peter's exhaustion, which had diffused slightly with the sight of the soldiers and tanks, quickly reformed, and his knees felt almost shaky. He wasn't sure how long he could last in the line in the heat.

"When we get closer, you can go to the right, across the road in front, to a small house with an Israeli flag on the door, and show your American passport there. It is called the VIP lounge. Ignore the taxi drivers, and wait for me at the teashop on the other side. It will be much better if we do not cross together. I do not know about your computer. I would not say that you are a journalist; say instead you are just a tourist. I do not know if they have information that we entered together, but I do not think they will trouble you. You can always say 'I do not know,' and they will likely believe that from you. If I do not meet you soon, return here and meet me in the parking lot where we first arrived. I am not a man so they will not place me in Siyah-Chal."

Peter was having a hard time concentrating on Reham's instructions, and so fastened on the last word. "Siyah-Chal? What's that?"

"The black pit. That is the building alone, far to the right. It is where they keep men who try to cross without proper permission. Do not worry, they would not let an American within kilometers of it: it shames them."

The line (composed of the same tired, smelly, dark brown hairy people [some with American clothing and accessories some in full native garb {tablecloths and robes}]) was not moving. The sun was beating down. Peter felt dizzy and sweaty. Reham stood stiff, motionless, staring straight ahead. He needed some water (and some sleep [in a first class seat over the Atlantic]). Perhaps Reham had some Evian in her North Face. He touched her lightly on the shoulder and waited for her to turn, "Do you have any water?"

"You do not look well. No, I have no water. Perhaps you should cross the border now, and take some water and tea at the place I spoke of. You will be alone for a time, but will be safe as long as you wait for me there and do not listen to anyone." She hesitated, looking at him. He felt his heart beat faster (in spite of his exhaustion [in spite of everything]). She smiled, "You look like you have been slaughtering sheep. Perhaps you should exchange your shirt."

He looked down at the white cotton, smudged with streaks of bright blue and various shades (from saucy tomato to vintage burgundy) of red (plus patches where Twister's saliva had thinned the blood, creating a sort of watercolor wash). He hadn't yet looked beneath the Terra Nova (at Ali's he somehow wanted to keep his battle clothes intact [to remind himself or Reham {or to stain that ugly couch}]) to see if his Bundeswehr was marked: it was (there were even faint streaks of red and blue on his skin [one light blue blotch near his right nipple and a sticky red spot over his left kidney]). He removed the Terra Nova (when he wasn't covered with dog plasma he thought he looked fairly good in a sleeveless tee) and, lifting up the Bundeswehr, scratched away some of the blood on his skin with it.

His Bundeswehr was only in slightly better shape than the Terra Nova, which meant that his Dolce and Gabana was his cleanest (least stained), although he had sweated in it for quite awhile (three days?) before cramming (somewhat folding) it into a back-pack and schlepping it around the Levant with the rest of his soiled laundry. So it was wrinkled and stinky, bloody and filthy or only slightly less bloody and filthy and without sleeves. If he were an Israeli soldier, what shirt would he find the least repulsive, the least likely to be the terrorist jersey of choice? He couldn't think. He stood there, stupefied, paralyzed in the dust, the sun hot on his bare shoulders.

He had to concentrate, focus. There was some-thing wrong with this picture (he wasn't going to wear the D&G because he might still have some dog blood on him [plus he'd have to remove his Bundeswehr and didn't want to strip nude in front of the crowd]). It was a question of what shirt would be the least con-spicuous, thereby allowing him inside the gate (and God knows what was inside, this was not The Viper [or even Rockenwagner or Chinois on Main] after all). But he didn't (really) want to go through the fence. What would they (he and Reham) do if he were to be stopped at the border? She'd probably continue (playing out the charade of the book [he realized the book of pho-tographs of his father had always been a mirage {not exactly a lie because he (so) wanted to believe}]) and promise to meet up with him later, and he'd wave and smile until she was out of sight and take the fastest taxi back to the airport. Or they'd both give up, head to the airport and say their goodbyes there. Either way, he'd be on his way outta this shithole much faster if he were to be denied access to whatever was on the other side. He put the Terra Nova back on. "I don't have anything else." Reham shrugged (that shrug).

"It will probably be best for you if you do not wait here with me, if they do not see us together. It is inappropriate and the soldiers might think something is suspicious. Besides, you are tired. Please, go across the road now and wait at the teashop. You can rest and take a drink there. Do you have money?"

He squinted. He was past tired, almost light-headed now, and the sun would not give him a break (he could use a [Starter] cap or something). Reham was right, he needed to get out of the sun and sit down in the shade, drink some water, relax, maybe rest his eyes. Besides, if he went in alone, maybe he could play it so they wouldn't let him through (although he didn't want to end up in the Black Hole or whatever the fuck it was). Okay okay.

"Yeah, I have money. So I just go to the right here?"

"Yes. Leave the queue to the right, cross the road to that small house and present your passport, as I have told you. When you are allowed across, wait for me at the teashop, and ignore everyone who is not a soldier. Tell them you are visiting Gaza because you are a tourist."

"What should I tell them about my clothes?"

"Tell them a dog was injured by an automobile. Do you have many credit cards?"

"A couple."

"If you can show them that you have money, they will not question you too strictly. Go, and rest. I will see you in an hour possibly."

He picked up his Zero Halliburton and his backpack of clothing, and without looking back, crossed through an unguarded gate into a street, where there was a small, olive guard building in the center with a couple of soldiers, rifles on backs, smoking outside. He nodded to the soldiers and walked quickly through the open door.

"Yes?" a lightly accented (not British), although not unpleasant male voice asked immediately. Peter looked behind the (almost collar) high counter that ran the entire length of the room: there were two or three large computer monitors, a bank of bright florescent lamps on the ceiling, as well as a number of imposing gray metal filing cabinets against the far wall, and he could see the tops of assorted desks and empty chairs, and a collection of black telephones to his right. He couldn't see anyone. He blinked and looked again. No one. He was too tired for these games.

He cleared his throat. "I'd like to cross the border."

"Yes, of course. You are American, yes?"
Peter looked around. As far as he could see, he was alone in the room.

"To whom am I speaking?"

"Major Mordachai Jacobi. Of the Israeli Defense Force. At your service." A face (shaved head and cheeks, a small goat [not unlike his own]) appeared on the side of one of the monitors, followed by the unfolding of Major Mordachai Jacobi from his seat. It was impossible to determine his age (anywhere from thirty to sixty), but it was easy to say that he possessed some serious height: not quite Mutombo tall, but certainly Pippen high. Peter noticed that his uniform was immaculate, pressed and crisp (Jacobi's khakis, almost the same color as his, sported a crease that could slice through shrink-wrap), almost in mockery of his own clothing. He also noticed that Jacobi's Glock, strapped to his belt, was exactly at Peter's eye level.

"You are American, yes?"

Peter looked up. "Yeah. How did you know? My accent?"

Jacobi blinked heavily before answering. "Yes. You speak English, but different from British English: more like the shows on the television. I am fond of Dallas and Jeopardy, and I like to watch Michael Jordan. We get far more British than Americans visiting Gaza. I believe you are my first American. Many French come, and of course the Scandinavians, but very few Americans." Jacobi leaned forward with his hands on the counter (looking directly down at the top of Peter's head), and Peter could see that there was some sort of raised platform on the other side of the counter. Still, the dude was at least six six. And thin (maybe one eighty). "Have you been in some sort of scrap?"

Peter looked down at his shirt. "No, the taxi I was in hit a dog. In Jerusalem."

"And you tried to assist?"

"Yeah."

"And was your assistance successful?"

He thought of Twister and how he had stopped breathing just like that. He was so fucking tired, but he did manage to raise his head and look up at Jacobi in the eye. "No."

"That is too bad. You do have a passport, yes?"

Peter removed his passport and his Coach from the front pocket of his khakis, walked forward and placed them both on the counter. Jacobi sat and (without glancing at the Coach) examined the documents. He looked at Peter, sighed, then typed something and stared at his terminal.

"You entered Tel Aviv yesterday, correct, from Istanbul? To visit friends in Jerusalem. You entered with a Reham Al-Safia. And where is Miss Al-Safia at present?"

"She's in the other line."

"She is accompanying you to Gaza?"

"Yeah."

Jacobi typed a few more lines, then looked across at Peter carefully. "You have no weapons I am assuming?"

Peter remembered his rubber bullet, but a used bullet wasn't really a weapon, was it? "No."

"And that is a portable computer, yes?"

"Yeah. An Apple Powerbook."

"Please open it."

Peter picked it up, placed it on the counter, and opened it. He switched it on and waited for it to boot up. Jacobi waited as well. "Thank you. You may switch it off now. And what is in the other bag?"

Peter turned back and picked up his laundry. "Clothes."

Jacobi motioned for him to set the pack on the table. His eyes locked on Peter's as he unzipped the main compartment and ran his right hand around inside the bag. He zipped it and slid it back. He then sighed again, entered a few more lines, then stamped Peter's passport and placed it on the near edge (to him) of the counter, so that Peter had to rise up on his toes and stretch across the counter to reach it. Jacobi blinked heavily. "Please, keep your eyes open, my young American friend. That computer is worth three years salary here to the jiffa tembels here. And your clothing probably two. Keep your eyes open."

Keeping his eyes open was the one thing he was going to have trouble doing. "Thanks. That it?"

Jacobi sighed again. "Out the door to your right, cross the road and through the wire gate. The PA may have a few questions for you, but I doubt it."

Peter gathered up his things and walked slowly out the door. He crossed the asphalt toward an unmarked and unmanned gate. To his left, separated by a high chain-link fence, was a long line of the same (if not identical, then the brothers and sisters of the) unwashed extras he'd seen (usually in the background [thankfully {he thought of that little fucker in the U of Miami tee that had chased him down}]) ever since he'd arrived in Turkey (who, if he thought about it, were cousins of the bit players who parked and washed his car and cooked his food etc. in Bel Air [he didn't want to think about it]). As he approached the entrance, a small, scruffy man with four days growth, a red beret over a brown uniform, and a huge rifle slung back over his shoulder scampered up to greet him. "Passport?" he grunted. Peter saw that his teeth were black.

Peter set his bags down on the pavement and handed him the passport from his pocket. The man flipped through it, looked at the picture then at Peter, then carefully and slowly removed an inkpad in a metallic case and stamp with a Kleenex stuck to the business end from his shirt, and just as carefully and slowly opened the inkpad, removed the tissue, moistened the stamp and pressed it firmly down on the page, bracing it with his other hand. He then brought the passport up to his mouth and blew (Peter caught a whiff of some nasty onion breath) the ink dry. He then smiled and handed the passport back. "Welcome to Gaza."

"Thanks chief." As Peter walked past him through the gate, the guard carefully and slowly returned the implements to his pocket.

As soon as he crossed the threshold into Gaza (he noticed that the razor wire was slanted inward, to keep fuckers in rather than out), he was set upon by five or six predatory bird-like men (vultures), all dressed in the ugliest clothes imaginable (plaid long sleeve cotton shirts with cut-offs and sandals, or too-short gym shorts [Celtics circa 1970] with old fleece Umro warm up jackets and black socks) offering taxi rides into Gaza city. He clutched his Eastpak and Zero Halliburton tightly (I am not in the mood for this) and looked around for the teashop. Across a paved loop full of taxis and minivans to his right he saw a cinder block shack with a red and white sign (in that weird, flowery script) that was attached to a decrepit concrete pavil-ion (thick exposed metal rods sticking straight up from the roof [like a bad haircut]) with a couple of white plastic tables and chairs underneath. Next to the pavil-ion, further to the right, a large bill-board of the king of the towel heads — that slob with the green skin, the three day growth, the fat lips and those jumbo suitcas-es under his eyes — rose above an empty plaza of dust. Without saying a word, he charged through the crowd (of five skinny men) crossed the loop into the pavilion and sat heavily down on one of the plastic chairs. Finally, he was out of the sun.

He jerked awake to Reham's hand on his shoulder — his head resting on his left hand with his elbow on the table, his right firmly clutching the Zero Halliburton and his Eastpak, a half full cup of tea and nearly empty bottle of water (no label) in front of him. He had been dozing. He hadn't slept that deeply or that long (he was still weary, exhausted). He blinked his eyes and looked around.

"You are good, yes? You have been sleeping long?"

"No, I just drifted off."

"Be careful of your possessions. Poor people

steal."

"So I've been told." He covered his mouth and yawned. He felt like shit: tired, cranky and without patience. He wondered how long this would take.

"Would you like to finish your tea?"

He shook his head. "Now what?"

"Now we go to Shati, the camp near the beach. If you are tired, you can sleep there. Or perhaps you would like to go swimming?"

He could use a swim; it might wake his ass up. He didn't have any trunks (he had one sweet pair of SquidInk boardshorts at home), but maybe that didn't matter. The nap sounded better. "Come. It is not far, but we will take a taxi."

He stood up awkwardly (his knees were weak) and saw the blood on his Terra Nova (poor fucking dog). "I need to get a new shirt."

"I know a place to buy goods, near Al-Shajaria Square, the entrance to the city. It will not be smart, but it will not be stained with blood either. Come."

He bought a short sleeve dark green Hanes v-neck (good heavy cotton) at a narrow, dank and ill-lit clothing and souvenir (featuring bearded guy blow up dolls) emporium (he bought Reham a bottle of water), and after he had discarded (he thought briefly of Twister as he stripped) the Terra Nova (Set it down near the building: someone will soon pick it up and bleach it) he felt a little better. Still exhausted, but not knee-shaking weak. They hopped back in the cab, and continued up the street (Al-Wahida).

The place was a mess. It looked like the city had been bombed (Peter did have some idea of what a bombed city might look like: he, along with Wanda, had toured [in her Z3] the destruction of south central LA soon [two days] after the Rodney King riots) many years, even decades, before, as the clumps of random bricks, the fallen tin roofs, the broken carts and piles of garbage had obtained a kind of permanence, had become naturalized into the landscape, as if the residents (or their ancestors) had long ago made some sort of conscious aesthetic, religious or political decision (for reasons now forgotten) to live in harmony with the chaos, decay and rot. It didn't have the post-apocalyptic, still smoldering aura of fresh violence (like in LA) of something once recognizable now destroyed (the broken plate glass and scattered cardboard of The Footlocker, the toppled drive through menu and charred adobe [above the windows, like thick eyebrows] of the Taco Bell) but rather the chronic ambiance of damage assimilated and endured (enduring).

Peter looked out the window of the taxi at the bustling and lively (much more animated than Jerusalem, with its permanently bowed heads and whispered prayers) crowd (the women either veiled or covered completely, the men in western clothing [pants and a shirt or suits] or in robes, all with that headgear [except the muzhiks, who could usually be spotted by their baseball caps], the children in scrappy streetwear [shorts and tees for the boys long skirts and blouses for the girls] or school uniforms [green and black vests, white shirts and shorts {boys} or skirts {girls}], and a lot of [colorfully wrapped] babies) walking (dodging rubble), chatting and laughing beneath the decrepit beige and white buildings (many with those weird iron rods sticking out the top).

He yawned and turned to look at Reham. She was in that stiff posture of hers, leaning forward, staring straight ahead: she seemed no more at home here than she did in Istanbul. Perhaps she wanted to find that book as much as he did; perhaps she needed to believe that she had a connection with another person in this world, a connection that wasn't subject to political, social or other temporary whims (like affection or sexual interest), a connection that was, at least theoretically, somewhat permanent. Maybe she had gotten her story confused (he remembered her tenuous relationship to narrative), mistaking an album of her mother's father, another uncle or distant cousin for their supposedly shared daddy (she had only seen the thing as a young child, and everyone knows how desire can play tricks on one's memory). Whether she did honestly expect to find it around the next corner, or whether she was just playing him for a fool (for dollars or something else), he knew that he would never see the book of photographs. He wondered who was the real dupe here.

He touched her on the shoulder. "Are you from around here?"

"No. My cousins lived in Jerusalem. I showed you the house."

"No, not your cousins. You, or your mother's family. Where are they from?"

She smiled sadly at him. "My mother was born in a village called Al-Tira, near Haifa. It no longer exists." She turned away and said something to the driver.

That was deep (although his own life hadn't been a family picnic). He was too tired to go there (not literally) with her: he felt sorry for her, yet slightly angry with her for making him (allowing him to) pity her. He was sick of thinking about all this shit, all this sadness and depression. Yeah, you're alone, I'm alone, so what, find some one to fuck and have babies, or do whatever it is you want to do, make those goofy pictures or whatever, but leave me out of it (her posture began to irritate him). We ain't kin, blood or otherwise, you just heard some weirdass story told to a poor young thing to give her some kind of hope or something, some reason or explanation. And you ran with it. And yeah, you had to drag me into it. No big deal, really, I should have been more careful, that's all. But it's over, time to pack it in. Say goodbye. Say goodbye.

"How long will this take?"

"I do not know. An hour, maybe two." He sighed heavily, certain she noticed. The cab pulled up into a large dirty archway between two buildings and stopped. Three young boys were kicking a soccer ball around in the dust, and five or six young men were hanging and smoking, leaning against one of the buildings. A thin stream of workers, male and female, shuffled in from the street. Reham sprung out, paid the driver, walked around the cab to the archway, and turned and waited for him to follow. He exited the cab slowly, hoping to signal his displeasure with every unhurried movement and sluggish gesture. He closed the cab door, stood and yawned, covering his mouth with his bicep. He was (justifiably) being a prick.

She waited for him, a tight smile on her face. After he caught up, she turned and lightly grasped his elbow. "Welcome to Shatila. It is a refugee camp. My cousin Zehra lives here, and if the book is still in existence, it will be here." She dropped his elbow and began to stride down the dirt street, some sort of foot wide concrete irrigation trough with a stream of dirty brown water on the right. He sighed again and followed.

Great, a fucking refugee camp. What next, a concentration camp, like Auschwitz or Nuremberg or something? His (half) sister (if she was his half sister and not a deluded loony) was certainly no laughs. And personally, he, Peter the Great, could do without all the (brown) people with their ugly clothes, facial hair, tobacco yellow teeth and crumbling buildings: if he wanted some poverty action he'd take a drive down to Suarez' former hood, Montbello (for a burrito or to pick up some leño or something [although they at least had cars in the barrio {not to mention some phat influencers and even edgers}]). No, if he wanted to see poor folk, there was really no need to travel halfway around the world when he could go down to Hollywood Blvd and view some old alkie with one shoe (or one foot) sleeping in the street. So what was the point? Why was he here?

He was so fucking tired. The street began to narrow and wind, and the people (and their accompanying odors) began to thicken and clot (he had never seen so many children [screwing must be free]: some eating ice cream, some running around, some carrying smaller children [while a few stopped at least they didn't beg]). The smells shifted, combined and recombined as he passed open windows, open doors and clumps of pedestrians — sour sweat and cigarette smoke mixed with frying lamb, mixed with olive oil and onions, mixed with donkey and old dust, mixed with seawater and fish, mixed with incense and sesame, mixed with gasoline and paint, mixed with rosewater and jasmine. And the shacks, which had been limited to mostly twelve by ten brick and mortar tin-roof jobs (through the windows he could see bedsheets on ropes dividing the space into [basically cooking and sleeping] rooms) near the archway, had now morphed into two and three story concrete block houses with stairways and shutters (the taller structures did provide shade, but also made him feel even more trapped and claustrophobic). And the people multiplied (they were seemingly a fruitful race [weren't they always]), and the buildings multiplied, and the road narrowed further, and he followed

Reham, stumbling, twisting and turning (gripping his bags tightly) toward some unknown destination (more of the same).

What the fuck had he ever done to deserve this? Exactly what past deed was this punishment for? Perhaps this was some future karmic deposit that he'd be able to bank on later, because he had never committed any crime that could possibly account for the third world hell he was in now. He'd have to treat himself big time when he got home: first class flight, that was for sure, and some sleep (two days at least with the phones off [after calling Wanda]), but maybe a new outfit (a Katherine Hamnett suit or a Kors jacket), a new crib (with or without Wanda) or a nice dog (like Twister [he'd talk to Tina first, see if she would watch it when crashed at W's {an extra fifty a week and it would be all good}]). He so needed to get the fuck outta here, and instead he was going further, deeper into this septic tank. Could this street get any more crowded (you people ever hear of condoms [he remembered a bumper sticker: If you can't feed 'em, don't breed 'em])?

What the hell was he thinking when he agreed to all this? Was it just little Pete, was that it (what kind of perv wants to do his [half] sister)? Was he so hard up for family that he'd follow some crazy bitch half way around the world for some ancient artifacts of dad? Artifacts that didn't even exist (never even existed)? Was he that bored with his California life? Did he have something to prove (what and to whom)? If she had flown all the way from Istanbul to see him, he wouldn't drag her around from Bel to Berdoo, hitting all the flops and soup kitchens. He'd treat her right; maybe put her up at the Bev, lunch at the Polo, dinner at Mr. Chow's. Although fuck it, he wouldn't spend another dime on her now (except maybe the double grand for the drawing): she had either lied to him or was significantly deluded, and if he gave her anything she might stalk his ass. He was getting thirsty again. He'd hang for a while, maybe lie down if he could (a catnap would be heaven with fries [get everyone out of his face for a while]), and in a couple of hours it would be goodbye for freaking ever. Sister.

Reham finally stopped at the doorway of one of the old-style brick huts (little more than a lean-to, fat chance any book of photographs would be in there). "The beach is straight. You may leave your things here if you wish to swim. If not, I will ask Zehra if you may borrow a cot."

He nodded, "Thanks. A cot would be great."

She smiled, and without knocking, walked through the door.

"Come. Gather your things, we must leave now. Immediately."

"What? What's going on? What time is it? How long have I been sleeping?"

"I do not know. It does not matter. Please, we must leave now. The Israelis will soon close the border, and I will be forced to remain here. Please hurry."

He sat up (with difficulty) and rubbed his eyes. He was even more exhausted than when he had first collapsed into the cot (which was when [fifteen minutes, half hour, hour ago]?). He remembered removing his C & G's to his Eastpak, then carefully placing both the pack and the Zero Halliburton underneath the cot, along with his Vans. He remembered laying his head on the pillow and turning toward the wall, away from the low voices (in that weird, guttural singsong) of Reham, her cousin, and her cousin's daughter (the owner of his makeshift crib), and he seemed to remember sporadic chanting, or wailing or maybe even singing drifting in and out from the opened window near his feet (but he wasn't sure about that). He was a bit queasy, and dizzy, and he closed his eyes again.

"Please. Your shoes and belongings are beneath you. If we do not hurry, I will remain here, and you will be alone. Come."

He opened his eyes and focused on her, standing expectantly near a small wooden table. He could feel her tension, her fear, but he was sick of following her orders. As he found his Vans and began to slowly put them on, he decided to be a prick. "Did you find the book?"

"No, but I did not have time to search carefully. Zehra is certain it is not here and at Ali's house. But come, I will tell you all about this as we walk."

"But you looked at Ali's house, right? I mean that's what we did in Jerusalem, look for the book at Ali's house. Is there someplace you missed, you forgot?"

He didn't see her stiffen, but felt he had hit something (good). "I am leaving now. You may follow or you may remain. As you wish."

The streets were not as congested as before, but still far from deserted. Night was falling, and the pace was much less frenetic. Men strolled leisurely along, smoking and talking (sometimes with women and children [with ice cream] four or five steps behind, sometimes alone) and groups of children easily kicked soccer balls up and down the alleys, or against the more sturdy concrete block walls. They passed a brightly lit tea shop, where a group of men were clustered around a fifteen inch color tv, the unlucky forced to stand on chairs in the street.

Peter concentrated on following a few steps

behind Reham, who was walking quickly, sometimes trotting, down the center of the road. Peter would break stride whenever she did: while he didn't want to walk with her (he had nothing to say and was tired of her bullshit) he didn't want to lose her either (adrift in a third world barrio with no language and absolutely no idea of where the fuck he was carrying a computer, an eight thousand dollar watch and a six hundred dollar pair of shoes just as night was falling was not his idea of big fun), and so he kept himself three or four paces behind her lit Marlboro, her scrunchy, her North Face and her lying Levis-encased ass.

This was the final leg: to the gate, to the airport and then home. He was so tired, but he'd be okay, he'd survive, no sweat. He'd just follow her quietly, conserving his strength, until they came to the taxi stand where he could get a ride to the airport. No worries, no problems, no troubles, in an hour or so he'd be good to go. Just follow that glowing cigarette, don't interrupt, just follow quietly. He stumbled a bit, but quickly righted himself and continued. Fuck her and fuck her lies, fuck her and fuck her lies, fuck her and fuck her lies: he wasn't being fair but he didn't give a shit, he just wanted to go home.

The walk and subsequent taxi ride were uneventful (although the sheer speed over bone jarring potholes and the vicious and seemingly self-canceling changes of direction made rest in the cab impossible, as the act of placing one's head against the window would have been tantamount to inviting concussion) and made in silence. They quickly pulled up to the dusty loop between the billboard and the gate, and were soon standing in the back of a crowd of fifteen or twenty peasants, huddled near the threshold. The area around the gate was floodlit, with bright (halogen) searchlights on raised platforms on both sides of the road, and the fence was illuminated by floods on both sides of the gate. Peter looked closer: the crowd was largely composed of old women in ancient robes, some producing (louder than he had ever heard) that odd old woman clucking noise of disapproval (Isabel). Reham asked one of the women something, and spat into the ground after hearing the response.

"Fucking Zionists. They have closed the border."

"What does that mean?"

She turned to him. "For you, it means nothing, you can get on an airplane and go home, or wherever you wish to go. For me, it means that I cannot leave."

His ears seemed stuffed with cotton. "What do you mean you can't leave? For how long?"

She slowly took her pack of Marlboros from her jacket pocket, removed one, and lit it with a match. She breathed deeply before answering. "I do not know. A day, two days, a week, a month, as long as they wish."

Fuck! He was NOT going to wait here a day, two days, a week, a month. No fucking way. He could leave her ass now, standing alone in the dirt, the table-cloth dude as background (she deserved as much), but he was way too tired to have to say goodbye, to go through all that emotional shit. He didn't want to have to think up a semi-convincing lie either, like I'll meet you in Tel Aviv, or Istanbul, or anything like that.

"What should I do?"

"Show your passport to the PA guard at the fence. He'll admit you, and then you go to the VIP house, just as you did when you entered. I am sorry I suggested this." She looked him in the eyes. "I am sorry I suggested any of this. You must think I am not truthful."

"What if I try to get you out?"

She shrugged. "I do not think you can. I have no passport, only a brown travel document, which is not very powerful. I do not think you can do much."

Why was he getting involved in this? Why did he care? Because it was easier than leaving her here in the dirt. "C'mon, I'm Peter the Great, American. I can at least try."

The first part was not terribly difficult. He bullied his way through the gaggle of scarves, skirts and toothless mouths, Reham close behind. He flashed his passport to the soldiers through the fence, and when they opened the gate, he simply grabbed Reham (who carried his Eastpak and Zero Halliburton) and pulled her through as well. The soldiers were surprised, but not upset, as they simply shrugged and focused on keeping everyone else (those old, clucking women) out.

As they crossed the paved road, Peter took his things from Reham. "That was easy."

"They are only the Palestinian Authority. It is the Jews who control passage, and the Jews will turn me back. You will see."

The VIP building was surrounded by Israeli soldiers, looking much more disciplined and alert than their Palestinian counterparts (Peter was beginning to be able to tell them apart: the IDF sported well-fitting and freshly pressed dark green or greenish gray paratrooper pants, matching jackets with and without recon vests, nice desert combat boots and either brown or red berets, while the Palestinians were limited to a more haphazard and often mismatched combination of khaki, beige and [light green and gray] camo pants and fatigues, with various footwear (sometimes Nikes or Reeboks) and black berets. The Israeli weapons looked more polished and dangerous [more adult] as well).

So it was obvious that seven or eight soldiers (rifles in hand, not slung across the back) assembled (all standing, in that half alert, half casual stance) around the VIP hut were Israeli. Peter and Reham approached, and Peter set his bags down and opened his passport.

One of the soldiers approached slowly, infinitely slowly (at NFL Films speed). He looked at Peter's passport slowly, and slowly, almost imperceptibly, he nodded his head toward the door of the hut. Peter slung his Eastpak over his shoulder, picked up his Zero Halliburton, took Reham's hand and proceeded into the hut. Or rather he tried: as soon as Reham twitched in the direction of the control booth, the guard who had examined Peter's passport deftly and gently inserted himself between them, blocking Reham's progress. One other soldier detached himself from the group and drew near.

"Passport" the first soldier said quietly.

Reham produced her travel document. The guard looked at it slowly, then handed it back. "No."

"What do you mean 'no'? She's with me. She's traveling with me. I'm an American citizen, and we're traveling together."

"She is not an American citizen. She cannot pass."

"But she's traveling with me." All the shit, all the long smelly plane rides, the lost baggage, the wandering around, the stupid conversations, the futile book pursuit, Twister, the various border crossings, searches and intrusive questions, the constipation, the lack of sleep and information came together at once and almost made his knees buckle. He had to close his eyes to regroup.

He breathed deeply, once, twice. As far as he could see in his exhausted state, there were two ways to play this, quiet or loud, and since he didn't have the energy for loud, it would have to be quiet. He opened his eyes, and in his calm (but firm), reasonable voice, he asked, "Would you please tell me where I may find the person in charge here? Your head officer or whatever?"

The guard answered him at a slightly lower volume than his question, "Major Jacobi is in passport control, sir. You may proceed. The Palestinian, however, must be returned."

Lower, just above a whisper. "Please. Let us both go to see Major Jacobi. I came through today and he'll remember me. If he says 'no,' then we'll both go back." He decided not to add another please: he wasn't going to beg.

The guard murmured back, so softly that Peter had to lean forward to catch his words. "It cannot be allowed. You may proceed, but the Palestinian must be returned."

Peter whispered back, even softer than the guard's response. "Please, let her come with me to see Major Jacobi. He will remember me. Or let her stay here and wait. Or maybe Major Jacobi could come out here. Could you send someone for him? We could wait here for him?"

The guard whispered back. "I cannot hear you sir. I cannot understand your words."

A voice from the porch of the hut barked. The soldiers snapped to attention, and the one Peter had been conversing with answered. Peter could see Jacobi's wiry frame silhouetted against the light from the hut's door.

"Ah, my young American friend, please come in. You may come as well, Miss Al-Safia. It is permitted, Mr. Simon, you may let them in. I see you are still in possession of your belongings. You must have taken my advice and kept your eyes open. Please, come in."

Peter picked up his Zero Halliburton and Eastpak, and, resisting the urge to give Mr. Simon a crusty, motioned for Reham to precede him into the building. As soon as he passed through the door, a soft electronic buzzer sounded somewhere. Major Jacobi turned: "Please place your computer and clothing on the desk, and walk back through." He did, and the buzzer sounded again. "Are you carrying anything metallic?" Peter remembered his rubber bullet. He nodded, and removed it from his pocket with his right hand, handing it to Jacobi. The Major's face darkened. "Where did you find this?"

"In Jerusalem. On the ground."

"Do you know what it is?"

"Yeah. It's a rubber bullet."

"Why were you carrying it? Why did you pick it up in the first place?"

"I don't know. I'd never seen one before. I just wanted a souvenir."

"An unusual keepsake, yes? I trust you will not be too upset if I confiscate your souvenir. There are many more appropriate objects to remind you of your journey to the Holy Land, are there not? Please, walk back and forth through the doorway." Jacobi held the bullet in his hand and looked at it carefully as Peter did as he was told. The alarm remained silent.

"Very good." Jacobi tossed the bullet in the air and caught it, then moved quickly around the counter and sat in his chair. He sighed, then tapped some information into his computer. He sighed again. Peter looked at Reham, who looked back at him and gave a little shrug. She looked even more unhappy than usual. He gave her what he hoped was a reassuring and intimate smile, but with his almost complete exhaustion, he wasn't sure how it came out.

He turned back toward Jacobi and waited. He needed to sit down, but there were no chairs on their side of the counter. Jacobi had a huge forehead, almost freakish. He wondered why he hadn't noticed it before. Jacobi tapped some more and then sat back and tossed and caught the bullet five or six times with his right hand. Finally, he turned toward Peter and spoke:

"You, naturally, are free to go. As an American citizen, you enjoy complete freedom of movement within Israel and between Israel and the Palestinian territories. As long as we are not at war, of course. The problem is Miss Al-Safia. I received orders to close the Erez checkpoint to all Palestinians at nineteen hundred hours today. It is now nineteen hundred hours forty five. And Miss Al-Safia is a Palestinian, yes?"

Reham placed her brown travel document on the counter. Without glancing at it, Jacobi turned his gaze to Reham and leaned forward. "You are living in Istanbul, yes? Are you an official citizen of Turkey? Are you the official citizen of any state, excepting Palestine?"

"No."

Jacobi leaned back in his chair. He turned his head to Peter. "I can do nothing. I cannot let her pass now."

Peter had difficulty finding the energy to speak. "What can we do?"

Jacobi shrugged. "As I see it, you have three options: you may go to on to Israel while she returns to Gaza; or you may both return to Gaza, or I will allow you to remain here in the building for a while, waiting. Perhaps the situation will change."

"There's nothing else you can do?" Peter's voice wasn't nearly as strong as he would have liked.

"No. I can not and will not allow a Palestinian loose in Israel proper when I have been expressly forbidden to do so."

"If we had to stay here, how long would we have to wait?"

"You do not have to stay here, either of you. You may go to Israel, Miss Al-Safia may return to Gaza. I am only offering you another option. As a friend. But it may mean nothing. I cannot tell how long you might have to wait. I have really no idea."

"And there's nothing I can do to speed things up?" Peter's glanced over at his Powerbook (nudge nudge) then back at Jacobi. Fuck, he'd even throw in the Banfis if he could get to the airport in an hour.

Jacobi kept his eyes locked on Peter's. "There is nothing you can do."

It was worth a shot. He needed rest. He turned to Reham. He couldn't just split and leave her here, he couldn't do it. No matter how much she had jerked his chain for the past month or so (especially the last couple of days), there was no way he'd leave her in this office, this city, this fucking country. Kay (and Julie and Paul) hadn't raised an asshole.

"So what do you want to do?"

"You should go. I cannot find the book, and I do not know how long they will keep me here. Perhaps you should return to America. I will search more, and contact you soon. Perhaps you should return."

"I'm not going to leave you here alone. Is there any possibility this will open soon? Has this happened before?"

"Yes, this happens many times." She glanced at Jacobi. "They open and close the border as they wish. They can open it at any time."

Peter yawned and rubbed the back of his neck. He wasn't sure if he could continue if he wanted to.

"Let's stay here for awhile, see what shakes." He turned away from the desk. There were no chairs; they'd have to sit on the floor. He turned back toward Jacobi. "Can we get a couple of chairs?"

"This is not a lounge." Jacobi threw up his hands. "I have a single chair." He stood, walked behind him, and returned with a single wooden chair in his hand, which he passed over the counter to Peter. He moved to another desk, sat and began to shuffle papers. The interview was over.

"You take the chair and I'll crash on the floor."

"You are tired and will require the chair."

"I'll be more comfortable on the floor. Sit."

He carried the chair over to a corner furthest away from the counter while Reham grabbed his bags and followed. He sat on the floor with his back against the wall and she on the chair next to him. He closed his eyes and barely heard Jacobi remark "Ah, Western style, woman in chair, man on floor. You will never make a good Arab if you keep this up."

He didn't want to make a good Arab, he didn't want to make a good anything, he just wanted to get some sleep. He opened his eyes and glanced at Reham. She was sitting slouched in the hard wooden chair, her legs crossed at her ankles, staring straight ahead. He had never seen her slouch like that before (she must really be bumming [he was way glad he didn't split]). Her thigh looked inviting (as a pillow), and they did have to convince Jacobi they were involved, and fuck it, what was she going to do and fuck it he didn't care and fuck it he just wanted to sleep so he leaned over and laid his head on her right thigh.

She tensed, but didn't move. And then after a while (he might have dozed), he felt her fingers gently caressing his temple. Maybe she was just playing for the major, and maybe not.

✧   ✧

He was sitting in an extremely uncomfortable plastic chair/bench (no way he could ever sleep on this fucking thing) in the Tel Aviv airport (Ben Gurion), waiting for Reham to return from the bathroom (he hadn't checked flights yet [although there probably wasn't a direct flight] and was trying not to get too impatient [after all, they didn't have much time left]). And then they'd have to say goodbye. Maybe he'd walk her to the ticket office (he should probably get his own ticket first, and check on his Samsonite), or even to the passport control, but that was it, see ya later sister, have a nice life. They'd exchange addresses and phone numbers, and he'd send her a check when he got back, a few hugs and kisses and that would be it, back to the first world, back to his own life and (easily managed) problems.

Jacobi had let them go, just like that. Peter was catching a few z's when something made him open his eyes and look up, and it was the major, towering over Reham, his Glock and belt even with the top of her head. It seemed like he had been talking for a while, although part of this could have been a dream. He couldn't see her face too well (from where he was camped), so he focused (sleepily) way up on that silver medal that Jacobi wore on his collar.

"You and I, our peoples, we will never live in peace. I will tell you why: our God is a faceless God, a God without body and without image. We have nothing to see or to touch, nothing to envision, and so we cling to what we can see and touch with every prayer, with every bullet, with every muscle of our being. We cling to the land because we have nothing else. We have nothing but rocks, dirt and a little water. We have so little imagination we can not possibly imagine a street, a neighborhood, a city, a country where we do not hate the other and wish the other would disappear forever. We cannot picture going to the store to buy bread and greeting one another with genuine affection or even respect. We cannot conceive of sharing a table together, watching a football match in the same parlor, enjoying an ice cream side by side. We have difficulty accepting that we even swim in the same sea.

"We might enjoy weeks or even months of temporary quiet, provisional calm, a hot or cold cease-fire, but for all that time we are always alert, always tensed, always ready at a moment's notice to resume our airplane attacks and suicide missions, our bulldozing of villages, our machine gunning of worshipers, our car bombs in the market. We can live with guns, bombs, planes and death, because it is what we have seen with our own eyes. We, each of us and all of us, have felt the warm sticky blood on our hands, have carried the heavy flag draped coffins, have felt the concussion of a mortar or missile, have heard the sharp crack of small arms fire followed inevitably by the louder and deeper answer of rifles, and we all have smelled the antiseptic and medicine as we visit the eyeless or limbless or lifeless, lying bandaged in their hospital beds. In this dryness that cracks our tongues and lips, in this heat that wrinkles our skin and bends our backs, in this withering sun that bleaches the bones of our fathers white, we have no capacity for creating new images, for visualizing new possibilities, for dreaming a new world. No, we do what we know and do best, what we have done for fifty years and for five thousand years, we hate and kill each other. Our imaginations are as dry and barren as the land we both are willing to die and murder for.

"You think I exaggerate. Our God — for we

share the same angry and cruel God, a God of laws and plagues, a God who enjoys watching his children war and murder — warned us of images, and we took that prohibition to heart. Look at our arts, you make carpets with abstract patterns and designs, and we make music, the most intangible and theoretical of all the arts, but when it comes to picturing the human form or foreseeing human possibilities, we are both sorely inadequate. You might protest that we both come from a tradition of storytellers, but only under duress are we capable of such creation: Sheherazade was threatened with beheading every night, and our prophets were often escaped slaves, impossibly old, wandering hungry in the desert, desperately avoiding the next subjugation. Our contemporary writers, Oz, Grossman and Appelfeld in Israel, Weisel, and Levi in Europe, Bellow, Roth and Singer in America, found their voice only with the murder of millions of their mothers, fathers, brothers, sisters, aunts, uncles, cousins and neighbors in the camps. Perhaps Kafka, our Tiresias, is the exception, but I have never been able to decide whether he was foreshadowing central Europe or the State of Israel. It is not that we are strangers to language, far from it; we are both adept at manipulating words. But there is a large difference between the barren exploitation of semantics and the construction of enchanting, viable worlds. No, you best return to your looms and kilns, and we to our pianos and yads and leave the storytelling to others.

"I am not optimistic that we will ever live together, side by side, in peace. We are too close — we are both Semites, after all, although our side has managed to erase your half from the word, and we are both called People of the Book — and because of this excessive similarity, I fear we will never escape this endless repetition. Look at you now, a woman without a passport, without a country, without a place in this world, wandering about the globe, subject to the whims of indifferent or often hostile governments and peoples. You are living the life we had led for thousands of years, a life that thankfully ended in 1948. We have simply switched places, you and I, like the prodigal son who has returned home, forcing his once favored brother out into the street. I do not need to ask you what you are feeling: I know, and this knowledge of your suffering brings me joy.

"So I will not keep you in Gaza. I will allow you to continue to drift, to stray, to wander. Perhaps you will return to Turkey, living among strangers who want nothing to do with you, who admire us as brothers and think of you, when they think of you at all, with shame, embarrassment and irritation. Or maybe you can go to Jordan, Egypt or one of your compatriot states, countries whose leaders moan and complain bitterly of the injustice of your fate, all the while preventing you from crossing their frontiers and entering their lands. With friends like this, you do not need us. Do you hear their plaintive cries on your behalf in the refugee camps, in Rafah and Khan Younis? Does the desert wind carry their promises of support down through the garbage and the rubble of Nuseirat and Deir el-Balah?

"Or perhaps you can go to America, the land of the free and the brave. You have been to America, and so you know of their great affection for you, the way they have taken you to their bosom and embraced you. They will never trust you: we have seen to that. And even if you go with your American friend, how long will it be before he tires of you, before he wearies of your anger and your fear? How many months before your accent begins to irritate his ears, before your food begins to gag in his throat, before your clothing offends his eyes and your clumsiness his sense of order? You are beautiful to him now, but your beauty will become inappropriate, and he will turn that beauty against you. You are not graceful: you will never be anything but awkward because you are never at home, because you have no home. You will always be a foreigner, a stranger, a little mistaken, slightly off kilter. You do not belong anywhere. This is the legacy we have passed on to you, Palestinian. This is our gift to you.

"I can do much more harm by releasing you. So please, take your rich American and leave my office. Go into Israel. I am certain I will see you again, my sister. Go."

And then he had turned his back and had disappeared behind the counter. Wow. Peter sat up, and Reham looked down at him for a moment: they quickly gathered their things and hurried out the door (while he rubbed the sleep from his eyes). And now he was sitting on a butt-numbing chair at the airport. And he was tired, exhausted really, but relieved. He was going home.

There she was. She had put her leather jacket back on, and looked pretty nice. He had to admit a dude could do a lot worse (familial pride?). He was pleased to be seen with her. But in a few minutes, that would be all over. He could live with that.

"Let's go get our tickets" (he wanted to check schedules and flights so he could get the hell out ASAP [she could sell his ticket back to Istanbul and use that to cover any penalty for changing flights {plus he'd buy her a nice meal (if he could stay awake [he was starving])}]). "And then if we have time I'll buy you dinner" (and kiss your pretty face goodbye). That sounded weak, like he was breaking up with her. Fuck it: he was tired and was being as nice as possible. He hadn't yet told her he wasn't going back to Istanbul with her, he assumed she had figured that out on her own. He probably should say something. "I'm going back to LA from here."

She turned. "Yes, I know." She turned away.

Okaaay. This wasn't going to be easy (what more did he owe her now?). They picked up their stuff and headed toward the ticket counters (they had better be open [as soon as he got on the plane he'd dig his Raymond Weil out of the Zero Halliburton and slap it back on]). There was a short line at United and a slightly longer line at El Al, so at least that was cool. Without hesitating or turning back to him she bee-lined it for the El Al. He yawned. He needed some shut bad (the little nap on Reham's thigh hadn't helped).

He managed to pick up the next flight out, to Frankfurt at ten that night, then a two hour layover and the five am to LA, getting him in at about nine in the morning. Not bad. He had to drop five grand plus the Istanbul tick for the biz class all the way, but he didn't care (there was no way he was going to go sardine for sixteen fucking hours). He had gotten a bit confused at the agent's (a pretty blonde with dark blue eyes) instructions and had to ask her to repeat them twice (she did and printed out an itinerary for him as well). He was really beat. No fucking Samsonite either (it had arrived at Heathrow but that was all she could tell him). Maybe some cappuccino with dinner (or before) would help him stay awake (maybe Rehams's flight would leave quickly [he wasn't sure he could be up for anything as involved as a long goodbye meal]) and he could crash on one of the hard benches (good luck). He'd just finished stuffing his ticket and passport into his Coach when he felt a tap on his shoulder. Reham was smoking a cigarette nervously. "What time's your flight?"

"I have no flight."

"What do you mean you have no flight? What's wrong?"

"They will not let me leave."

Jesus Christ, not again. "Who won't let you leave?"

"The airline, El Al. They say that Turkey has closed its borders to Palestinians, and I will not be allowed off the airplane. And so they will not allow me on the airplane."

"Who said this? Take me to him."

Once again they took their bags and hurried off to another line, another counter, another border, another hassle.

They stopped behind two families (one with a youngish couple, an old [at least eighty] frail woman, two small children and a baby; the other with a pissy looking middle age man [in one thin short sleeve cotton shirt] with a long beard, his much younger wife and four toddlers [the toddlers positioned in those twin SUV strollers with fat rubber tires]) with enough luggage to fill an entire 767 cargo plane, along with a couple of impatient looking business men (probably trying to upgrade) in gray Armanis (one with a black Coach bag and the other with nice red Vuitton computer case): if it were just the dudes it'd be okay but he was not going to wait for the goddam Clampetts and all their crap. He was sick of waiting in lines and sick of getting the major (by the major) jerk-off, so he excused himself to the head of the line in front of the rather pudgy guy (staring at his computer screen) Reham had indicated.

"Excuse me, but there seems to be some trouble with my girlfriend's" (the word just came out) "ticket."

"I have been to America," the man said, without

looking up from his screen, "and am quite certain that you also have what are known as 'lines.' So perhaps you and your Palestinian girlfriend would like to join one and wait your turn."

And perhaps you'd like to kiss my ass. He was too tired for this, too used up and played out. He was too tired to even raise his voice (it was his exhaustion, rather than inherent patience, recently learned caution or considered strategy, which prevented him from speaking above a fairly steady and controlled mezzo piano), "Is there someone else who can help us?"

"No sir, I am sorry, but there is not. Now if you'd just pop back to the end of the queue there, I will be with you shortly."

He could see why people carried guns and grenades and shit: if he had his Walther he might cap the motherfucker right now. He hated this place. "My girlfriend has already waited in line. She was told she cannot board her flight, a flight she has a ticket for. I would like to know why she cannot board a flight she has a ticket for. I don't think it's fair to have to wait in line twice." The evenness of his voice surprised him.

"It is not your turn and I have nothing to say to you. If you don't join the line now I should have to inform the police."

"Please. Call them right now; at least I can get some answers. Call them, hurry up. Call them. Goddam Nazis," he added, under his breath.

The dude finally looked from his computer screen. His face was the color of the surf half of a Marinetti's surf n turf. "What did you say?"

Probably never a good idea to call someone a Nazi (except in Orange County). "I said go ahead and call the cops. There seems to be one at every corner of this country: bring them on, since you can't handle it yourself. Pick up the phone."

"What seems to be the trouble here, sir?"

Peter turned to face two policemen (that was quick), both packing and tall, both swarthy and cut (navy pants, lighter blue shirts, navy combat vests and uzis). Both had those friendly, don't-screw-with-me looks that could turn medieval at any minute (the psycho rent-a-cop who took his job seriously look, or the expression on the faces of the two thick-legged and thicker-necked bouncers at Club Stick who, it was said, came directly from Quentin [dudes looked like they had done some serious prison rape {tops not bottoms}]). These 5-O didn't look quite that bad (they looked like refugees from Venice Beach or Gold's Gym, not Quentin): they were definitely not from the same hood as Jacobi (who would probably be one intense prick if you crossed him), although Peter did notice an identical medal on the collar of the less (this wasn't saying much) stupid looking one.

"They won't let my girlfriend on the airplane. She has a ticket for the airplane. I'm trying to find out why. And this guy," Peter turned to indicate lobster boy (who was in the middle of trying to pull the biggest of the Clampet suitcases onto the scale), "won't give me any information."

"May I see your documents?"

Reham (who looked scared, vulnerable but above all, angry) handed I'm with Stupid her papers. He examined them quickly, and then held out his hand to Peter. "And you?"

"We're not traveling together."

"Your passport sir. And your ticket."

Peter sighed, then dug his Coach out of his pocket, opened it, and extracted the necessary papers. I'm with Stupid examined them as well, then said something in another language to Stupid, who said something in the same language into the walkie-talkie he had attached to his shoulder. Stupid and I'm with Stupid waited, the walkie-talkie answered, and then I'm With Stupid said, "Please come with me."

Another office, another counter, another policeman (or soldier, or guard) with a computer. They had been waiting for a while, standing, and Peter felt he was about to collapse. He was almost asleep on his feet. He had tried to lean against the counter and had been told to please step back. He had asked Reham what was happening, and all she had said was she could not remain in Israel and that if she could not return to Turkey she didn't know what she would do. What a fucking mess. Peter slouched in a corner. They waited some more.

"Miss Al-Safia. Mr. Nicholas." They stepped forward. "There does seem to be a problem. Miss Al-Safia, the Turkish government has temporarily rescinded its agreement with the Palestinian Authority regarding the settlement of refugees. They will not let you return. I am told this is a temporary condition, but for now, you cannot go back."

"But my family left in 1948. I have a Turkish residency permit and twelve month visa. I renew it every year."

"I can see that, Miss Al-Safia. But there is noth- ing I, nor the Israeli government, can do. This is a Turkish decision, Miss Al-Safia. You may contact the Turkish Embassy tomorrow: perhaps they will be able to assist you. You will of course need to register with the Israeli police, but I can help you with that."

Peter saw the absolute despair on her face. "Is there anywhere else you can go? Your cousins?" She shook her head. "Any other country?" He turned back to I'm with Stupid. "Is there anyplace else she can go?"

"Her travel documents show a valid visa to the United States. She can legally go to the US. In fact, once she is there, she may be able to arrange her return to Turkey with much more speed than from here. This I say in confidence."

Peter cashed in his business class ticket (alas) for two coach class seats to Los Angeles. Whatever.

BEL AIR

BOOK VI

CHAPTER SEVENTEEN

The traffic on Sunset sucked big time.

Construction on the Bev Glen interchange plus an accident (ambo, cops, rescue truck, broken glass, bent Volvo S80 [$42,000]) on Roxbury snailed things down to a crawl (Traffic on the Tens, Stressed Out [Bjork's Say Dip Mix] from A Tribe Called Quest, Make Me Bad [Sickness In Salvation Mix] from Korn, On and On from Erykah Badu and Eve 6's Inside Out). Things finally cleared up on North Beverly (he caught a quick cappuccino venté [$3.69] at the Bev Starbucks), and he saw the signs for Bellini (not Benini) Baby and, a couple of doors down, Haute Baby right after Wilshire. This must be the place. He parked the Saab on Charleville, and carrying his venté, almost scampered toward the door of Haute Baby.

He was greeted by (the music box twinkling of Brahms Lullaby door chimes, the subtle scent of wax candles and) a gleaming seven foot high, round, (bird-) cage like object, stuffed with blankets, pillows and toys. My God! A tall, anorexic looking young (at first glance) brunette in a severe brown leather shirt dress from Ralph Lauren ($1995), a YSL Rive Gauche wide dark brownish green alligator belt ($375), fawn Roberto Cavalli calf-boots ($400), a large Agatha amethyst ring (right hand ring finger $700), a VC and A platinum wedding band with a modest (but nice) rock (Princess cut, Good E WS2 1.5 carat $6000), long Tracey Ross Dark Desire nails, Kiehl's moisturizing sunscreen ($35 per 8 oz) over Trish McEvoy Gel Blush Stick in Light Strawberry ($45), Brenda Christian Definer Eye pencil in Brown Sage ($15), a light touch of Tony and Tina Colour Frequency Shadow in California Tan ($20), Chanel's Lash Me Mascara in Midnight Brown ($25), Guerlain's Hydramythic Fresh Moisturizing Lipstick in San Tropez ($50) and the gentle perfume of Jo Malone's The Subjection of Women ($65 per 3.4 oz), with small and square LaFont glasses ($400) approached him from the back and informed him, "This is one of our most expensive cribs. It's made of pure brass, and it's from Posh Tots, the very best manufacturer of furniture for newborn to toddler. If you like, it is also available in 12-carat gold plate." Peter noticed a reggae version with children's voices and xylophones of I'm a Little Teapot in the background.

"How much does something like this cost?"

"The brass model is $4,400. The 12 carat gold plate is $7,000."

"That's a serious chunk." That was one more dif between he and his dad; he would not, would never, leave a child of his flat, with only the (ugliest) shirt on his back, a red Persian rug and some pasta bowls made in Italy. Good luck. See ya in the next life. No way José. His kid would have the wherewithal: good private schools, excellent college, maybe even grad school, whatever the fuck he (or she) wanted. Including a phat fucking crib.

"It is not appropriate for all families." She bent down to re-arrange one of the toys. She stood and faced him (met him eye-to-eye, was tall as he was). "My name is Melissa. How may I help you?"

"I'm going to be a father (she had said she was sure [one missed period, two EPT's {One Step Clear Blue Easy and Answer Quick and Simple (double stripes both times)}] and there was no reason to doubt her) and I'd like to pick out a few things for the kid, you know, just to get started."

"I see. And will the baby's mother be joining

us?"

"No. She's out of town." He smiled (recognizing and even enjoying her attempt at intimidation). "She has utmost faith in my taste."

She smiled back. "Of course. Please forgive me; it's just that we receive few unaccompanied male clients. Do you know the baby's sex?"

"No. It's too early."

"I see. The mother has just recently informed you of this blessed event, and you'd like to get a head start on things? Yes?" She removed her LaFonts and placed the earpiece in her mouth.

"Yeah. That's about it."

"Your name, please?"

"Nicholas. Peter Nicholas."

She put her LaFonts back on and frowned. "Congratulations Mr. Nicholas . . ."

"Call me Peter."

"Peter, it is sometimes advisable to delay a bit until we can ascertain the sex of the baby, and see if there might be other . . . special requirements or needs."

He hadn't thought about that. He hadn't even considered that something could possibly be wrong with his child. Shit.

Never let them see you sweat. He slowly took a small sip of his venté. "Look, Melissa, we're in the process of moving, and so I wouldn't even want the stuff delivered for a couple of months. But I'm guessing that if I spent some money here today, what I would consider a significant amount of money, and later found that, because of some special needs, I needed to change my order, perhaps even cancel it, that with a small restocking fee, I would be allowed to do so. I'm guessing that this is store policy, or if not, then would be, once I spoke to the owner." He kept his eyes locked with hers as he took another sip (now lukewarm and almost finished). They didn't call him Peter the Great for nothing.

She smiled back (but didn't look down). "Of course. I simply wish to save you inconvenience. And by the way, Peter, you are speaking to the owner. Now, where would you like to begin?"

"Let's start with cribs."

"Very good. The cribs you see here are all Posh Tot cribs: this wooden model is their Standard Cot. It is made of oak, and sells for $2,895." Peter placed his fingertips on the sideboard and tried to give it a little shake. It didn't move. "If you were to purchase linens, blankets and other accessories, I'd provide a ten percent discount on the crib. This is their hand painted sleigh crib, and sells for $2,600." He moved over to the next crib.

"What about this one?"

"That's the Posh Tots Cow Over the Moon. It sells for $1800."

"And these over here?"

"These are Bratt cribs, manufactured in Maryland. They are not quite as sturdy as the Posh Tots, and are somewhat less expensive."

A Bratt for the brat. "I like the one with the ostrich plumes."

"That is the Casablanca. The brass you see there is $1000; silver plate $1200 and gold plate $1500. It also comes in white enamel for $1000 as well."

"What's the difference between the Posh Tots and Bratt?"

"Besides price and a certain cachet — I recently sold a gold plated model of that round crib you were looking at near the door to Jodie Foster — they are sturdier and the iron tends to be slightly more finished."

"Jodie Foster huh? How much more sturdy? Three thousand dollars more sturdy?"

"No. If you plan to pass on your crib from generation to generation, or to someone else in your family, a sister or something, or if you plan more children, then perhaps the Posh Tots might be my recommendation. But truthfully, Mr. Nicholas, the Bratt will be there whenever you and your family, even your extended family, require it."

He was still annoyed (slightly insulted) by Melissa's suggestion that his baby might have special needs (or might not be born at all [they both were healthy as far as he could tell {he'd make absolutely sure they had a good doc}]), and didn't want to make things too easy on her (I'm a Little Teapot segued into The Lion Sleeps Tonight [for solo voice and thumb piano]), and so decided to make her work, even though he had decided on the Posh Tots Standard Oak Cot for $2800 (he liked the Casablanca but if it were a boy the ostrich plumes might be too faggy). "What about these?"

"That is the FAO Baby Crib and Trundle bed collection. As the infant grows into a toddler, the bed can be modified, enlarged. So, you only have to purchase the one piece of furniture. We have had some complaints regarding the construction of this particular model, the Sleigh bed. But as I've said, you only have to buy the one piece."

"What's the difference between an infant and, what was it you called the other one?"

"A toddler. A newborn is a baby up until three months. Then an infant is three months until he or she begins to walk, to toddle, anywhere from a year to two years, even longer."

"I'm leaning toward the Posh Tots Cot. What else do I need?"

"Without knowing the sex of the baby, you can think about a carriage. You can also think about bedding, although many parents prefer sex-specific linens. You can also look at receiving blankets, toys, jumpers and bibs that are appropriate for both boys and girls."

"The mother and I agree that we do not want the traditional pink and blue. What about linens?"

She moved effortlessly over to a cabinet near the wall, opened it, and brought down a large book of photos and fabric samples. "This is the Wendy Belissimo line. She makes everything by hand, and so usually we do not allow returns on her merchandise, not that we've ever had anyone who wasn't simply delighted by her work. However, in your case, Mr. Nicholas, perhaps we could, if necessary, work something out. I say this because I know that if you order something from Wendy and then your circumstances somehow change, I can easily sell what you've ordered: her work is that spectacular. Have you heard of her before?"

Peter shook his head no. Melissa removed her LaFonts again and leaned toward him.

"I will give you her card: she does custom decorating. Perhaps once you move into your new environment, you may find her useful. Anyway, this is the Indigo Star Crib Collection. It's all hand sewn and hand embroidered, and the sheets, pillowcases and bumpers are of the finest Egyptian cotton." She held out a swatch of the finest Egyptian cotton for Peter to feel: it was certainly fine. She turned the page. "This is the Wait for Me collection. The same material, although a bit more silk on the borders, and more embroidery. You see the detail on the edge of the pillowcase? Again, all hand sewn."

"How much?"

"The Indigo Star is $599. The Wait for Me is

$650."

"I like this little pillow here, the one with the dog."

"$80."

"I'll take two dog pillows and the Indigo Star."

"In what color? You said you and the mother wanted to avoid pink and blue. We have aqua, indigo, night red, Indian dusk, racing green, and morning violet."

"I like the indigo."

"I'm fond of it as well. Are you certain about this, Mr. Nicholas? Would you like to take some time to think it over? Perhaps bring in the baby's mother?"

"No."

"Would you like one set or more?"

"Just one. For now."

"You'll need some blankets. We just received some beautiful cashmere receiving blankets from France, from Tartine et Chocolat. Would you like to see them?" She was already moving to another cabinet.

"Sure. And then I'd like to see some carriages."

"Of course. I adore this cashmere: it is absolutely the softest material I have ever felt. Imagine your baby, snug as a bug under this material. We have four designs, in six sizes. Feel this, isn't this the softest?"

"It's quite soft. How much are these?" He pointed to a bright green with yellow stripes.

"Depending on size, from $175 to $300. Do you think this will go with the indigo?"

"No, you're right. How about this, this blue and white one?"

"Yes, I think this will match perfectly. What size would you like?"

"What sizes are there?"

"Let's see here: there's 12" x 18" for $225, 12" x 24" for $250, 18" x 24" for $300, 24" x 24" for $350, 32" x 32" for $400, and 36" x 36" for $500. This pattern is a bit more expensive than the green and yellow."

"Do you have any suggestions?"

"If you're not sure — babies come in different sizes you know — perhaps you could get a large one and a medium, say a 32" x 32" and an 18' x 24'."

"I'll get the big one, and think about another one."

"I have other blankets. I have some beautiful Italian wool from Pratesi. I also have some wool and silk blankets with animal patterns from Babylinens, an English company: they too are exquisite. As you know, I am the owner, but I am also a mother, and sell nothing I would not wrap my own children in."

"How many do you have?"

"I have two. A boy and a girl. Would you like to see more blankets? Or linens? Towels? Robes? I have the cutest hooded towel from Pratesi: it has tiny little bees on the hood. . . ."

"I'd like to look at carriages now."

"I carry only the finest prams. I have Maclaren, Silver Cross and Burberry. I have models that fold out, and models that do not. Will you be obtaining the services of a nanny, Mr. Nicholas?"

"Yes, probably."

"I only ask because some of these carriages are rather large and unwieldy, and require a certain amount of strength to operate, and sometimes smaller nannies or younger au pairs find them difficult to maneuver."

"We haven't picked a nanny out, if that's what you mean."

"If you do purchase a pram today, you might keep that in mind when you solicit for help. Of course, you can always exchange the pram for a smaller model before you take it home. This is our finest model, used by Fergie and Diana. You see the Royal Seal here, right under the bonnet. It's from Burberry, with leather and fine tartan merino plaid, and sells for $4250. It has an optional matching cashmere blanket for $375. It's very luxurious and comfortable, as you can see, and also very very sturdy: nearly indestructible." Peter rattled it around a little bit: it felt like a tank. "It makes a statement on more than one level, don't you think?"

"Yeah, it says 'kidnap me.' How about this one, with the big white tires?"

"This is a Silver Cross. Also British, also very sturdy. It comes in many different models and sizes, with different materials for the bed. This particular model is canvas and leather, and sells for $1000."

Jeffrey DeShell is the author of two previous novels, *S & M* and *In Heaven Everything is Fine,* and a critical book, *The Peculiarity of Literature: An Allegorical Approach to Poe's Fiction.* He has co-edited two collections of fiction by contemporary American women, *Chick-Lit I: Postfeminist Fiction* and *Chick-Lit II: No Chick Vics* (both published by FC2), and was a Fulbright Teaching Fellow in Budapest, Hungary, 1999-2000. He has taught in Northern Cyprus, the American Midwest, and was on the faculty of the Milton Avery Graduate School for the Arts at Bard College. He is currently an assistant professor and Director of the Creative Writing Program at the University of Colorado at Boulder.

Also from Starcherone Books

PP/FF: An Anthology, **Edited by Peter Conners.** ISBN 0-9703165-1-8. $20. Genre-defying writing by 61 contributors, including Lydia Davis, B.Evenson, Mazza, Ronk, Dybek, etc.

Endorsed by Jack Chapeau 2 an even greater extent, **Ted Pelton.** ISBN 0-9703165-0-x. $14. Expanded 2nd ed.

Hangings: Three Novellas, **Nina Shope.** ISBN 0-9703165-3-4. $16. Winner of the 2004-05 Starcherone Fiction Prize.

My Body in Nine Parts, **Raymond Federman.** ISBN 0-9703165-4-2. $16. Newly avail. in English, with 10 photos.

My Body in Nine Parts, **Kenneth Bernard.** ISBN 0-9703165-6-9. $18. 40 stories. "Gloriously antic" - David Markson.

Woman with Dark Horses, **Aimee Parkison.** ISBN 0-970-3165-5-0. $16. New Southern Gothic stories, by the winner of our 2003-04 Prize & numerous other awards.

Black Umbrella Stories, **Nicolette de Csipkay.** ISBN 0-970-3165-7-7. Original Chick-Lit, w/ 6 superb etchings. $15.

The Voice in the Closet/La Voix dans le Cabinet de Débarras, **Raymond Federman.** ISBN 0-9703165-8-5. $9.

Order by mail (with $4 s/h for the first book and $2 each additional) at Starcherone Books, PO Box 303, Buffalo, NY 14201; via the internet, at starcherone.com or spdbooks.org; or through your local bookseller.